IN COLD
CHOCOLATE

Previously published Worldwide Mystery titles by
DOROTHY ST. JAMES

PLAYING WITH BONBON FIRE

IN COLD CHOCOLATE

DOROTHY ST. JAMES

TORONTO • NEW YORK • LONDON
AMSTERDAM • PARIS • SYDNEY • HAMBURG
STOCKHOLM • ATHENS • TOKYO • MILAN
MADRID • WARSAW • BUDAPEST • AUCKLAND

W⊙RLDWIDE™

Recycling programs for this product may not exist in your area.

ISBN-13: 978-1-335-40550-0

In Cold Chocolate

First published in 2018 by Crooked Lane Books, an imprint of The Quick Brown Fox & Company LLC.
This edition published in 2021.

This edition published by arrangement with Harlequin Books S.A.

For questions and comments about the quality of this book, please contact us at CustomerService@Harlequin.com.

Harlequin Enterprises ULC
22 Adelaide St. West, 40th Floor
Toronto, Ontario M5H 4E3, Canada
www.ReaderService.com

Printed in U.S.A.

For Avery.
(Your kisses are sweeter than chocolate.)

ONE

I LOVE THE taste of the ocean. After an early morning swim, the salty flavor lingers on my lips for hours. And at night, especially after a steamy August day, that same salty flavor floats in the air on tiny droplets of water imprinting the memory of how the moon shined against the backdrop of a twinkling starry sky. Or how I'd ohhed and ahhed over the dinoflagellates, those single-celled, ocean-drifting plankton, caught up in the tide as they glowed fantastic colors with each crashing wave. Or the excitement of finding evidence that a sea turtle had laid her eggs on our humble coast.

Since moving to the small island town of Camellia Beach tucked away in the Lowcountry of South Carolina seven months ago, the taste of salt in my food (especially when paired with dark chocolate), has made me feel at one with the coast and all the teeming sea life that resides just beyond my adopted small town's shoreline.

On what seemed like an uneventful Tuesday night in the back kitchen of my boutique chocolate shop, the Chocolate Box, I set out to develop a sea salt chocolate turtle candy that captured the flavor and wonder of the ocean and its special creatures that live there.

Sometimes, though, *sometimes* that same flavor mimics the salt of tears, serving as a bitter memory of painful losses and heartfelt failures. And fear.

As midnight approached I hung my apron on its peg.

The pecans had burned. My turtles oozed out of their molds. And they tasted nothing like the majestic ocean. Hopefully tomorrow I'd have better success.

I exited the shop through the back door, locking it behind me as I stepped onto the building's back patio. A few feet away the land faded into the grassy marsh. The summer wind playing in the tall cordgrass made soft swish-swish sounds. The night hung like a bar of unsweetened chocolate over the river. In a few hours the moon would rise. But, for now, the darkness made the world seem wider, emptier.

Despite the disappointing mess I'd made in the kitchen (I was used to those) and despite the gloom outside, I smiled as I breathed in the salty air that made the island smell almost sugary sweet. This tiny piece of paradise was my home. I still couldn't believe my good luck in finding it.

That silly smile was still plastered on my face as I moved toward the exterior back stairs that led up to the building's two second-story apartments. I didn't see the movement in the shadows until it was too late.

A dark figure jumped out in front of me.

Startled, I swung my fist. The person ducked. I swung again. The shadowy person, who must have been some kind of master ninja, ducked again. Suddenly, fear beat like a drum in my throat. I screamed and clutched my chest as if I'd suffered a fatal heart attack and screamed again. You'd better believe I screamed.

My assailant started laughing. It wasn't a happy sound. But then again her laughs never sounded happy.

"Jody Dalton, what are you doing? You scared me half to death," I managed to say even though my heart was beating faster than a marathon runner's at the end of a race. "If you're here to see Harley, he's not home. He's attending some kind of lawyers' conference in Columbia."

Harley Dalton lived in the apartment next to mine. He also had once served as my grandmother's lawyer and now looked after my legal interests. I considered him a friend and felt rather protective of him, especially when it came to Jody, his ex-wife. She'd come by from time to time to cause him grief.

I fisted my hands on my hips and stood my ground. Jody was a tall woman, taller than most men. I was as well, which meant we glared at each other on an equal plane. She wore her hair in a no-nonsense pixie cut. I did too. Her hair was silky black while mine was blonde and awfully frizzy in all of this humidity. She looked me up and down, lingering on my frizz, before she also put her hands on her hips.

"You were just bursting to tell me that Harley's away, weren't you?" she snapped. Her snippy tone reminded me of my little papillon dog who nipped and snapped at pretty much anything that moved. "Were you hoping I'd be crushed to learn you knew something about that no-good ex of mine that I didn't know? Don't be. I know where he is."

I opened and closed my mouth while I continued to worry about what was going on in my chest. My heart still didn't feel as if it was working quite right. Until tonight, I only knew of one person who could elude my carefully honed self-defense moves. And that was my halfsister Tina. It startled me to realize my skills weren't quite as invincible as I'd once thought.

"If you knew he was away, what are you doing here? And why in the world are you jumping out at me in the middle of the night like some kind of madwoman?" I demanded.

"I didn't jump—" she started to say. But she abruptly stopped when my business partner and roommate, Bertie Bays, called down the stairs, "Are you okay down there, Penn? I heard screaming."

"Jody's here," I yelled back because I didn't know how else to answer the question. Was I okay?

"Tell her Harley's away at that conference," Bertie called down to me. She'd leaned so far over the porch's railing it looked as if the bright yellow scarf she'd used to tie back her hair might slip over her face.

"I know full well where he is!" Jody shouted. She then said to me, "I'm here because Gavin left his board shorts up there. He's got an early morning surf competition, and he thinks those pants of his lucky." Her voice suddenly sharpened as she bit out, "I don't need to explain myself to the likes of you. Get out of my way."

"Harley lets you go into his home when he's not there?" I moved to block the stairs. Just last month Jody had called the police simply because Harley had parked his car in front of her house while Gavin, their ten-year-old son, had run inside to pick up his laptop computer. She told the police that she'd felt her ex's presence outside her home had constituted a threat. She'd wanted them to arrest him. They didn't.

I knew this, not because Harley had told me. He hadn't told anybody about it. It was their son who'd come into the shop, tears flooding his eyes. Gavin had begged me to tell him why his mother hated his father so much. Unable to explain what even I didn't understand, I'd wound my arms around the skinny boy, hugged him, and told him that both his parents loved him and that was all that mattered.

"Harley has no say in this. My son's belongings are in his apartment. As Gavin's mother, I have every right to go in there and get them."

"That's not true," I said. "Where's Gavin?"

"He's spending the night with a friend. Get out of my way."

I stood my ground. "Call Harley. Get his permission. And then I'll move."

"Oh, I'll call him." She started to move away. But then she turned back to me and smiled viciously. "Be warned, Penn." She took a step toward me. "You think this town actually loves you? You think you can wave your chocolates around and charm Harley? You think you can take over as Gavin's mother?"

Did she really think I wanted to date Harley? He'd made it clear that he considered me his friend and only a friend. Did she think I wanted to take her place in Gavin's life? "I would never try to take your place."

"Watch yourself, Penn. I know you. I've also heard all about the lies you've been telling everyone."

"Lies?" I abhorred lies.

"Don't pretend to be innocent. Not to me. I know all about who you are...and more importantly who you *aren't*." With a look of triumph, she crowed loud enough for even Bertie (who was still standing at the top of the stairs in her quilted housecoat) to hear, "Mark my words. As soon as the truth comes out, *Charity* Penn, Sunset Development will own your chocolate shop. And you'll have nothing. You don't belong here. You've never belonged here."

"What are you talking about?" No one could take

my shop away from me. My maternal grandmother had left it to me in her will.

Jody didn't answer. Instead, with a sharp laugh, she said as she walked back toward the road, "I'm going to enjoy seeing everything you don't deserve stripped away from you. It's time people around here start realizing the emperor has no clothes." She was halfway down the road. Her voice seemed to echo in the darkness as she called over her shoulder, "In case you're too dense to get it—you're the emperor and those clothes of yours are sorely lacking."

TWO

"WOULD IT KILL you to move a little faster?" I asked the painter a little over a week later. He'd been repairing and repainting the Chocolate Box's stained and lumpy ceiling for the past eight days.

I stood next to his ladder, tilted my head back, and squinted as I looked up. His brush moved like a snail sliding across a leaf. However, the ceiling looked perfectly smooth.

"Can't rightly rush if you want me to do what needs to be done," he drawled. His Southern accent, unique to the natives of Camellia Beach, lacked the hard twang most people associated with the South. While the island accent was sometimes difficult to understand, the slow cadence of his words sounded melodious to my Midwestern ears. "The layers of paint up here tell the story of the hacks with a paintbrush who have done this ceiling wrong. Takes precious time to fix it."

I squinted up some more, admiring his work. The Chocolate Box had been selling the world's best chocolates for nearly a hundred years. When I'd inherited the building (which included this shop, the Drop In Surf Shop next door, and two upstairs apartments), the roof leaked, the stairs were rotting, and the water-stained ceiling looked as if it might fall. Johnny Pane's efforts with spackle and paint were impressive. But that didn't keep me from wishing he'd hurry up and finish already.

Since I couldn't afford to close the shop while we waited for him to finish, we had to block off half the shop with a curtain of plastic that surrounded his ladder. In doing so we had to remove the tables and chairs from the area where he was working, which meant we'd lost about a third of the seating area for our customers.

On this particularly sticky Thursday afternoon, the Chocolate Box was packed with residents and beachgoers in search of a cool break from the seemingly endless August heat. I needed that seating area.

Despite the ocean breezes, the beach in August felt like the inside of an oven. The unrelenting heat prickled the nerves of even the incurably happy. But inside the shop, which had survived hurricanes and murders, the newly renovated air conditioner provided a welcomed blast of cold air. Laughter filled the space as Bertie and I each carried trays of gourmet chocolate milkshakes to our eager customers.

I handed a tall, frosty glass to Bubba Crowley, the president of Camellia Beach's business association. I still couldn't believe my good fortune. And I don't mean the kind of fortune that could be spent in a store. That kind of fortune rarely made anyone smile. I meant the kind that came with finding a place where I was surrounded by friends, a place where I felt like I belonged. No matter what Jody had claimed, I wasn't going to let anyone take this place away from me.

"The shop looks fantastic," Bubba said in his jovial booming voice after he took a long sip of the wintry milkshake. Bubba was a big man around town, not just because of his positive influence on the business community. He resembled a small-sized giant. "Adding milkshakes to your menu was a stroke of genius."

He took another sip. "Plus, like everything else in here, these are remarkably delicious."

"That's high praise indeed. Thank you." After I'd inherited the shop, Bubba was one of the first and most vocal supporters of my efforts to keep it open. "I'm always drinking chocolate milkshakes in the summer. I figured since I was making it for myself, I might as well start making extras to share with everyone else."

He nodded as he sipped some more. "Makes sense. Good business sense." His gaze traveled around the busy shop. "They certainly are a hit with…" His voice trailed off.

His roaming eyes had come to an abrupt halt. His mouth tightened as if suddenly pained. "What is it?" I started to ask with concern. But then I saw what he'd seen: Bertie Bays.

Bertie had been my grandmother's best friend. For decades she lived with Mabel Maybank in one of the upstairs apartments and worked with her in the shop. Despite her seventy-plus years, Bertie had more energy than I did when I was in my twenties. She loved Camellia Beach and this shop nearly as much as Mabel had. After Mabel's death, Bertie had agreed to stay on (temporarily) as my partner. She'd told me more than once that she planned to retire and move to a retirement resort community in Florida after I mastered the recipes.

I *never* wanted her to leave. I'd be lost without her. Luckily, it didn't look as if I'd ever learn Mabel's recipes. I was a disaster in the kitchen.

Dressed in mom jeans and a faded blue "Chocolate Box" T-shirt, Bertie served a trio of milkshakes to a table of giddy teenage girls. Her dark skin glowed with a youthful luster she claimed was from good genes and not an antiaging serum. It had to be true. I'd searched our apartment more than once for her hidden stash of facial creams and found nothing.

Bubba lowered his voice and asked, "Has she said anything? I mean, about me?"

"Not a word," I whispered back. "Have you said anything to her?"

His head dropped to his chest. "Haven't had the nerve."

"She's not married anymore." Bertie had been a widow for nearly twenty years. A few months ago, Bubba had confessed that when he was young and foolish, he'd fallen for Bertie. She'd been older and married, and he'd been engaged to another woman, so he hadn't acted on his feelings. But now, forty years later, neither of them was married or dating. And he still cared for her.

I nudged his shoulder. "You should sit up. She's looking this way."

His head snapped to attention. His back straightened. An awkward, almost grotesque, grin took over his usually handsome features.

Bertie noticed and laughed before turning her attention back to serving the milkshakes on her tray.

I needed to do the same. "Call her. Ask her out for lunch. As friends, if it's too scary to call it a date," I suggested as I headed toward the next table.

"I'll do that," he said. "Next week. Or perhaps the week after that."

"My gracious, Penn, you've been busy," Ethel Crump, who was sitting with a couple of full-time residents from the Pink Pelican Inn, exclaimed when she looked up from her cross-stitch project and noticed me approaching their table. Her voice sounded hoarse, like the scraping of branches against a window. She cleared her throat. It didn't help. "I was a little girl the last time this place looked this good."

Her friends both agreed with great enthusiasm that the shop had never looked better.

"Thank you." I set down napkins and drinks for Ethel and her friends. I dearly wanted to ask Ethel how many years had passed since she'd been a little girl coming to this shop. In a town where nearly all of its residents qualified for senior discounts and the local hotel, the Pink Pelican Inn, doubled as an informal retirement home, Ethel Crump was considered as ancient as the island's weathered oaks with their twisted and gnarled branches. No one knew her age. And like a proper Southern lady, she wasn't telling.

Ethel set aside her needle and rubbed her knobby and stiff knuckles. The almost translucent skin on her face was loose and hung from her jowls like a pleated silk skirt. "Does the fact that you're fixing up the building mean your grandmother's children are no longer contesting her will?" she asked.

Her question shouldn't have surprised me. This was a small town. Of course everyone would know all about how Mabel's children wanted to get their hands on the building. They didn't want the shop, mind you. None of them seemed to care about keeping their family's legacy alive with the chocolates. They only wanted the land so they could sell it to Sunset Development, the local development company where Jody worked.

Why would Jody accuse me of lying? More than a week had passed since my late-night encounter with her, and I still had no idea why she'd said such a thing to me. Even if I had told a few lies (I hadn't), how could a lie or two make me lose what Mabel had given me? This was my shop.

"Mabel's children have dropped the lawsuit," I said more for my own benefit than for hers. While the funds Mabel had set aside for the building's upkeep were still tied up in probate court, the objections to the will were now gone. "Even if they hadn't dropped the lawsuit, it wouldn't have mattered. No one is getting their hands on my shop," I told the ladies.

Ethel nodded. "You're doing good work here. Mabel would be proud."

Again, her friends agreed.

"Thank—thank you," I stumbled over my words. I seemed to always stumble when it came to accepting compliments, especially when those compliments were in reference to my skills in the kitchen. They weren't… stellar. If not for Bertie staying on after Mabel's death and helping by making nearly all of the chocolate truffles and bonbons, I don't think I would have been able to keep the shop open.

But, as I'd already told Ethel and her friends, whether Mabel had made a good decision or not in naming me her heir, this was my shop now. No one was getting their hands on it.

I was about to move away to serve the next table when Ethel wrapped her crooked fingers around my wrist. The strength of her grip surprised me.

"How is your relationship with Florence these days?" she asked.

"I—uh—uh—I—" I stumbled again.

"I know you were hoping to discover proof that Mabel's oldest girl, Carolina, was your mother. Shame about that poor girl, God rest her soul. It was such a shock to learn she'd died way back in nineteen seventy-five." Which was five years before I was born. "You have to hand it to her sister Florence, though, for stepping up and finally doing the right thing when she admitted she'd birthed you."

That's about all Florence had done. Just thinking about my mother made my chest ache. My birth mother had abandoned me on my father's doorstep hours after my birth. My father, who'd been a college sophomore at the time and unprepared for fatherhood, had swiftly handed me over to his mother, Cristobel Penn. For my entire life, I'd been told that my mother had been a fortune teller and con artist who had taken advantage of my young, innocent father.

I now know that had been a lie.

This past winter, I'd come to Camellia Beach to investigate my friend's death. What I'd found was Mabel Maybank, the maternal grandmother I hadn't known existed. Both Mabel and I had suspected that her daughter, Carolina, was my mother. After all, Carolina would have been older than my father. She'd also run away from home at a young age, never to be seen again.

Running away seemed be a trait that perfectly fit the profile of a woman who'd abandon her child. So of course I had believed Carolina was my mother. Yet after investigating the circumstances surrounding her disappearing act, I'd learned that she hadn't run away as everyone had believed. She'd died.

At about the same time, Mabel's middle daughter Florence had come to my apartment to inform me that, while on summer break from college with her friends, she'd hooked up with my father and had gotten herself in a difficult situation. She'd also demanded that (for her sake) I keep our relationship secret. She'd wanted me to tell everyone that Mabel wasn't my grandmother and that I wasn't related to anyone in the Maybank clan.

If she'd taken any time at all to get to know me, she would have discovered that I seldom did what I was told and rarely kept my mouth shut about anything. For several months now the entire island had been buzzing about Florence's *indiscretion* some thirty-seven years ago.

"I haven't heard from her in a while," I said to Ethel as I served the next table. "I'm not sure either of us is ready to pursue any kind of a relationship." That tidbit of news should keep the gossipmongers happy for a week or so.

"Well, I heard from a friend who saw for herself that Florence has been visiting the island regularly. She's been meeting with a real estate agent, that cutthroat Cassidy Jones fellow. At his house, no less." She'd gagged a little when she said his name. "Do you think your mother is looking at buying a piece of property because she wants to move closer to you, her only child?"

Not likely.

She liked to openly display dislike for me and this town. If she'd been visiting a real estate agent in town, it was probably because she was trying to figure out how to make trouble for me.

Florence had wanted me to deny our relationship. I hadn't. Was she now planning a devious plot to accuse me of lying to the town in an attempt to get back at me for revealing her secret? I'd only told a few people. But gossip on this small town spreads like a wildfire in a windstorm.

Oh, I didn't want to think about Florence. I certainly didn't want to talk about her. So I asked Ethel, "How are you and that sweet kitty of yours faring these days?"

"Didn't you hear?" the white-haired woman on Ethel's left said, while clicking her tongue.

"That Cassidy Jones fellow hit Charlie with his behemoth of a car last Tuesday night," the other woman said in a stage whisper that was actually louder than her regular speaking voice.

"No!" I pressed my hand to my heart. "Is he going to be okay?"

"My boy broke his leg and banged up the rest of his old body pretty badly." Distress deepened the wrinkles on Ethel's brows. "He spent three days in the hospital."

"But he's home now and healing?" I hated the thought of Ethel going home to an empty house. Charlie may have only been a cat, but to Ethel he was her only living family member.

She nodded but still looked worried. "It's just… Honey, I don't want to bore you with my troubles. You're so busy today. The vet says Charlie should make a full recovery. But he's sixteen. I worry about him so."

The other women nodded in unison.

"Of course, you do." I moved to another table that was near theirs and quickly served the last of the milkshakes on my tray before heading back to their table. "If there's anything I can do to help, please let me know." I made a mental note to send her some colorful flowers and cat toys in hopes the small gifts would help ease her worries.

Ethel took a sip of her milkshake. The tension in her shoulders loosened a bit. "I hate to drink and run," she said both to me and her friends. She then looked directly at me. "I have a meeting with that handsome lawyer of yours about Tuesday's car accident."

"*Har-ley*," Ethel's friends sang in unison as they gave me goofy looks.

Harley Dalton wasn't *my* lawyer. Well, I had hired him to represent me and the shop. I liked to think we were friends. And for a while I had tried to move our relationship out of the "friends" category. But Harley either wasn't interested or hadn't noticed my coy advances. Bottom line: He wasn't *mine*, not in the romantic way that would make others sing his name while waggling their eyebrows at me. "He's just a good—" I started to tell them when the brass chime over the shop's door clanked.

The bell usually tinkled serenely. Sometimes it jingled excitedly. It never clanked. I looked up in time to see the door swing open as if blown in by a hurricane.

Jody stepped into the shop. A scowl hardened her already sharp features. I instantly tensed. Had she come to expose whatever lie she thought I'd been telling around town?

With her head held high, she made her way across the shop. My heart beat in time with each of her quick footfalls. I held my breath, preparing for the confrontation.

She walked by me as if I didn't exist and then stopped at the plastic draping that was serving as a barrier to the painter's work area. Her lightly tanned hands curled into fists. They landed on her trim hips.

I'd started to ask her to leave, but before I had a chance her voice boomed angrily throughout the room. "Johnny Pane"—since she originally hailed from the upstate, her clipped accent had the familiar twang I'd associated with a Southern accent—"what in blue blazes are you doing wasting your time in here? Putting lipstick on this pig, that's what you're doing. I told you I needed you to get to work on the new construction out on West Africa Street."

"I'll get to it when I can," he answered without altering his steady brushstroke. "It'll likely be sometime next week." He dipped his brush into the paint can. "Or the week after that."

I groaned. He needed to finish this week. I squinted up at the ceiling again. Certainly, he was nearly done with his job here. I started to tell Jody that she needed to leave my painter alone, and that she needed to leave my store...preferably forever.

But she wasn't paying attention. With an angry grunt, she tore down the plastic draping with one violent tug. "Johnny Pane, your obstinance is making me a crazy woman." Her voice was nearing a screeching pitch. "You git down here right now, you hear me?"

"I hear you. With all due respect, I reckon half the state hears you." His brushstrokes remained as steady as ever, which was amazing considering how loudly Jody was ranting at the base of his steps. "You need to listen to me, Miss Jody. If you want my services, you'll get them when I'm available. Otherwise, you'll need to hire someone else."

The patrons of the shop all seemed to hold their collective breaths, eager to witness Jody's reaction.

Surprisingly, she didn't shout. She didn't explode. She spoke so quietly that if I hadn't been standing as close to Johnny's work area as I had been, I wouldn't have heard her. "Do I need to ask Cassidy Jones to come and have a talk with you?"

I didn't know what kind of pull this Cassidy Jones

fellow could have over my painter. But it must have been something big because his brush stopped. For the first time since she'd arrived, he took his eyes off his work and looked down at her.

"What did she say?" someone behind me yelled out.

"If you hush now, perhaps we'd hear," someone else answered.

Jody turned to glare at them…and at me. The killing look lasted for just a brief moment, but it still made me shiver. She put her hand against the ladder and lifted her gaze back to Johnny Pane, who was now looking down at her with worry darkening his eyes.

"I'm dating him, you know," she said, her voice still pitched low.

That last bit of news surprised me. Jody had found a man willing to date her? *Her*? The woman was a thorn in the side of everyone who knew her. At least it seemed that way to me. When I'd first met Jody, she'd pretended to be my friend while trying to convince me to sell my chocolate shop to her employer, Sunset Development. When I didn't sell the shop, she turned on me faster than a sailfish in pursuit of its prey.

Jody had a man in her life? *And I didn't?*

That…stung.

"He promised just last night to do whatever I ask of him," she told Johnny. "He's that smitten."

Although I'd never met the man, I'd seen real estate signs around town with Cassidy Jones emblazoned in bold letters across the top and a picture of an older man with Fabio-styled long blond hair and wearing a flashy Hawaiian shirt. What kind of pull could a Fabio looka-like have over my painter?

Apparently the kind that had him climbing down off

his ladder. "Let me clean up here," he said, his voice unusually subdued.

"What did he say?" someone behind me shouted.

"He said he's leaving," someone else shouted.

"Even with these ear-cheaters, I can't hear a dang word of what anyone is saying," I heard Ethel Crump complain.

Several people chuckled. And, as if everyone had then taken a collective cleansing breath, the conversations in the shop started up again. While I was sure my customers were still keeping a keen eye on what was happening at the work area, things seemed to go back to normal in the shop as Johnny Pane wiped his hands on a clean rag.

"I expect to see you at the worksite in ten minutes," Jody said. Was she serious? Had she seen how fast Johnny Pane moved? It took him longer than ten minutes to fold up that ladder of his.

Before she left, Jody turned her killer glare in my direction one more time. "Enjoy this place while you can. As I already told you, your lies will be catching up to you. Any day now, it's going to happen."

"What lies?" I demanded. "I have no idea what you're talking about."

Instead of answering, she swept out of the building as if pushed by the same ill-wind that had brought her into it.

"Sorry about this, Penn," Johnny mumbled as he started to gather up his painting supplies. "If you don't mind, I could come back tonight and work on the ceiling then."

"Of course I don't mind." If he worked when the shop

was closed, it would allow me to move the tables and chairs back into place during operating hours.

While Jody's threat (*I don't lie!*) unsettled me, Johnny Pane and the tortured look on his face troubled me even more. "Are you okay?" I asked him.

He looked down at his hands as he wiped them on his rag again, this time with an odd sort of determination. "I will be."

THREE

"ARE YOU OKAY?" Althea Bays called to me.

"This adventure you promised, it doesn't involve magic, does it?" I yelled back as she stood on the ocean side of a wooden walkover while I hesitated near the road. We were headed toward the beach late at night. Or was it early the next morning? I never knew what to call the small hours after midnight.

Althea was Bertie's adult daughter and my closest friend in Camellia Beach. Heck, she was my closest friend in the *world*. I loved her like a sister. What I didn't love was *magic*. Not that I believed in magic. I didn't.

"It's not magic," Althea called back. Her voice sounded different in the darkness. Deeper. More mysterious.

"You know how I feel about magic." I detested it.

But because I trusted her, I'd agreed to meet her near Camellia Beach's centerpiece, the public pier and pavilion that stretched out from the middle of the island into the dark ocean. She had arranged for the two of us to go on a midnight adventure. Now that I was out here and standing at the base of the walkover that led down to the beach, doubts started to run circles in my mind.

Althea owned a crystal shop. She believed the crystals she sold contained magical powers. She also believed in ghosts, voodoo, and fortune tellers. I believed in none of that. Magic didn't exist. It was a tool swindlers and con artists used to trick those who were too innocent and too trusting.

"Don't fret so much, Penn." Barefoot, with her naturally kinky black hair secured with a yellow bandana and a shovel slung over her shoulder, she paced the sandy beach while waiting for me.

I stood my ground and stared at the Lights Out for Turtles sign that had been posted on the walkover instead of looking at her. If I looked at her, I knew I'd give in. I knew I'd follow her anywhere, and I didn't want to do that. Not tonight. Not when I was still reeling over Jody's empty threats. They had to be empty, didn't they? "I need to know where we're going and what we're doing."

She didn't answer right away. The necklace with twin brass mandala Althea wore tinkled like tiny wind chimes. I looked up and saw that she'd turned toward the ocean. The water sparkled in the bright moonlight. "I think the first part is obvious," she said. "We're going to the beach."

"And the second part?" It was silly that we were shouting at each other with a beach walkover between us. But despite Althea's assurances that magic wasn't involved, apprehension had wound around the muscles in my neck so tightly I could barely turn my head.

She huffed. "I was hoping to make it a surprise. Some babies are about to be born. Actually, they're several days overdue. We're out here to greet them and make sure they get a good start in life."

"Babies?" That intrigued me. And since I really should trust my friends, I walked (albeit slowly) over the wooden walkover that served as a bridge over the beach's fragile rolling dunes. Once my feet reached the sand, I kicked off my sandals.

The midnight air still held most of the heat and humidity from its mid-August day. But the damp sand beneath my toes felt cool. Refreshing.

"There are babies on the beach?" I asked.

"Not yet. But soon there will be loads of them." She handed me her shovel and started searching inside the large red and white striped beach bag that had been hanging from her shoulder. From its depths, she produced a neon yellow T-shirt. She pulled it on over one of her favorite silky batik-dyed sundresses (this one was pale yellow). A silhouette of a sea turtle took up much of the back of the T-shirt with the word "volunteer" in bold block print underneath it.

"Turtle babies?" I jumped up and down like an over-eager child. "You're taking me to see baby sea turtles?"

Althea answered with one of her wide smiles. After she took her shovel from me, she turned her face to the sky. The full moon illuminated her dark, elegant features.

After exhaling a long, satisfied sigh she said, "They'll be Leos, you know, which means they'll have a strong will to survive. They'll need it."

"Baby turtles? We're going to help baby turtles hatch? Where's the nest?" I started a mad dash down the sandy beach, my arms pumping, because I didn't want to miss the little ones' arrival.

"Penn, we don't need to run," Althea whispered as she jogged next to me.

"But it's so late already. I don't want to miss it." I don't know why we were whispering, especially considering how we'd just finished shouting across an expanse. Perhaps it was the night's stillness or the darkness that suddenly had us keeping our voices low.

"I'll get a call from one of the other volunteers if the babies start to emerge. You need to pace yourself. It could be a long night."

"I don't care," I said, but I heeded her advice and slowed down. "This is so exciting. We're going to play midwife to sea turtles. I've been reading the literature you gave me about them. You can count on me."

"Now remember what I told you," she warned. "You've not been formally trained. You're not an official volunteer, so you'll just be observing tonight."

Gentle waves lapped at the shore. The pale full moon appeared to float on the water. A few tourists were still out roaming the beach, the light from their flashlights swinging like beacons from a distant lighthouse.

"I now understand why you didn't bring flashlights for us to carry," I said. The excitement had me speaking too quickly and too much. "We don't want to be seen." There were signs, banners, and flyers posted all over the island celebrating the sea turtles and reminding us to keep the lights on the beach turned off. It was the bright light of the moon that guided the babies toward their vast home in the ocean. And freshly hatched sea turtles, not much more than a few minutes out of the egg when they set out in search of the Atlantic, wouldn't know how to discern the glow from the moon from the glow from any other source.

Althea shifted the shovel that balanced on her shoulder and hooked her arm with mine. "That's right. A flashlight or a streetlamp or porch light could lead the babies astray. Instead of ending up in the water, they could lose their way in the sand where they'd be easy prey for crabs and raccoons. They might even end up trekking toward the road, a fatal situation."

For the most part Camellia Beach's coastline was veiled in darkness. Nearby street lamps had been equipped with shields that blocked their light from reaching the beach. The homes we passed on our way to the sea turtle nest sat like silent, shadowy sentries, watching and waiting.

As we continued down the beach at a more sedate pace, the activity inside an old beach house caught my attention. The home, with its redwood shingle siding and low, shallow-sloping roof, looked as if it belonged in a 1950s surfing movie. A faint jazz beat carried on the wind from an open sliding glass door to our ears. With it, Ella Fitzgerald's soulful voice gently crooned about lovers. A soft yellow light spilled out from around the home's heavy curtains, which had been drawn across the partially open door that led out onto a wide deck.

"Sounds like Cassidy Jones is entertaining a lady tonight." Althea nodded toward the house.

"Cassidy Jones?" I asked, remembering how upset Johnny Pane had gotten when Jody had mentioned his name. "I know he sells houses, but who is he? Why does he have everyone in town afraid of him?"

And what kind of man would date a woman as prickly as Jody? And, if what Ethel had said was true, why was Florence visiting him so often? Was he selling my mother a house on the island?

"Cassidy?" She stopped to gaze up at the house. "Never thought to be afraid of him. Actually, I never really took him seriously. The picture he uses on his 'For Sale' signs looks as if it belongs on the cover of a romance novel from the nineteen-eighties. How can anyone take someone who uses those pictures serious?"

"I've seen those signs everywhere. It's as if he's trying to seduce me with his eyes. And under the picture, doesn't it say 'I know what you want'? It's creepy."

"Oddly enough, many women around here fall for that slogan and his bedroom eyes."

"Ewww...why?"

"Don't ask me," Althea said. "I think it's creepy too. And yet women flock to him like maggots to rotten fruit. Every time I see him, he always has a new and different lady to...um...entertain. Nothing fearsome about that."

"A modern-day Casanova?" That didn't mesh with what Jody had said about him.

"Casanova is the perfect description for him. But not in a sexy way. In this day and age, what he's doing is unhealthy and gross." Althea started walking again. "The older generation doesn't understand the health risks to such hazardous behavior, do they?"

My gaze remained locked on Cassidy's love shack. "Jody told my painter today that she's dating Cassidy. She said he's devoted to her and only her. She was quite emphatic about it too. Do you think that means he's done with his philandering ways?"

"Cassidy Jones?" Althea stopped so quickly she nearly tripped. "Are you sure that's the name you heard?"

"That's who she said."

"Well, Jody would have had to cast a mighty powerful spell on Cassidy in order to tame him," Althea joked. At least I hoped she was joking. In addition to all the other woo-woo nonsense Althea believe in, she also believed in witchcraft. "But it can't be Jody up there. Isn't she home watching Gavin?"

"Harley has custody this week," I said, "so Jody is free to spend her nights any way she wants. There's no reason why she wouldn't be up there singing along with Ella."

"Ewww…" Althea shook her hands as if trying to rid herself of the image of Jody with the village lothario. "I hope she has good health insurance."

We both laughed as we continued down the beach.

The house next door to Cassidy Jones' kitschy love shack was one of the new hulking beach mansions built by Sunset Development. The lights on the porch facing the ocean blazed like an airport landing strip.

"We can't have that." Althea shaded her eyes as she turned toward the blaring lights. "The babies need it to be dark." With the shovel still slung over her shoulder, she marched up the steps of the beach house and started pounding on the glass double doors.

No one answered.

"Whoever is renting the house must be out for the evening." I peeked through one of the large windows into an empty, darkened living room with an amazing kitchen complete with commercial appliances.

"I heard the house recently sold to some fancy-schmancy chef from the north," Althea said as she knocked again. "Someone needs to tell him about the lights-out policy on the beach."

We waited for several minutes. No one came to the door.

"I'll have to come back tomorrow and talk with the owner," she said with a sigh. "In the meantime, we'll need to set up something to block the light. Otherwise, the turtles won't go where they need to go."

Althea marched back down the steps and hurried down the beach. This time I was the one who had to jog to keep up with her quick, angry stride. A few houses down, she stopped at the base of a sand dune where a small area was marked off with stakes and orange warning tape. By the light of the full moon, I could read the writing on an orange diamond-shaped caution sign: Loggerhead Turtle Nesting Area.

"So this is it?" I whispered as I squinted at the small mound of sand that looked like any other mound of sand on the beach. I tried to picture baby turtles emerging from the sandy lump.

"This your first hatching, honey?" A silver-haired woman I recognized from the Pink Pelican Inn gave me a toothy smile. She was wearing the same yellow T-shirt Althea had donned. "It's a blooming miracle to watch the little ones crawl out of the sand and waddle toward the water."

"They don't waddle, Harriett, they skitter," Harriett's dark-haired friend—who was also wearing a yellow turtle volunteer T-shirt—corrected with a shout. "They skitter and slide on those tiny flippers they have for feet down to the water. The little darlings swim toward the moon."

"She gets my meaning," Harriett Daschle said.

"It's important to be precise in our language. Otherwise, society will collapse," her friend countered in that loud voice of hers. "You must be Penn, the chocolate shop owner. I've heard all about you. I'm Lidia. Lidia Vanderhorst." She thrust out her hand for me to shake. "I moved into the Pink Pelican two months ago, and only recently passed the test to volunteer with the turtles. This will be my second hatching."

"Nice to meet you." I shook her hand. "You just moved here, and you've already been accepted as a volunteer?"

Althea must have heard the hurt in my voice. I'd signed up to volunteer on the turtle team as soon as I'd heard it existed and had been told that there was a two-year waiting list. "Lidia has been on the waiting list for two and a half years now. She put her name on the list even before moving to Camellia."

"That's right," Lidia's voice boomed. "I'd been living on nearby James Island before finally making my big move to Camellia Beach. Have always wanted to help with the turtles. Was willing to drive over the bridge in the middle of the night to do it. But I'm glad I don't have to. My eyes aren't what they used to be."

"I see," I said. My gaze kept going back to the mound of sand. Was that a sand crab or a baby turtle digging its way to the surface?

It was a sand crab.

"We need to do something about the porch lights over there. The owner isn't home." Althea pointed to the brightly lit beach house. "The turtles will think that's the moon and go toward the house instead of the water. Who has the cardboard?"

Lidia looked at Harriett who looked at Althea.

"Don't look at me." I threw my hands in the air. "I don't even have the T-shirt."

Althea stuck her shovel into the sand. "I'll have to go get some cardboard." She headed for the closest beach walkover.

"What do we do if they start hatching?" I called

to her, afraid to be left unsupervised with a brood of babies, each one precious and important to the survival of an endangered species.

"Herd them toward the water," she called back over her shoulder.

FOUR

TEN MINUTES PASSED. And then twenty.

Althea hadn't returned. The sea turtles hadn't emerged. I was starting to worry.

"Where is Althea?" a sharp voice demanded from the direction of the beach walkover. "She's such a flake she can't even remember to show up? Is that what happened?"

I whirled around and saw Jody coming toward us with the determined gait of a charging bull.

"Jody?" I glanced down the beach toward the darkened love shack and back at Jody. "What are you doing here?" Did this mean she wasn't the woman being romanced by Cassidy Jones' smooth jazz?

She didn't look like a woman leaving a man's arms. She was wearing one of the turtle volunteers' yellow T-shirts, cut-off jeans, and a large fanny pack. But what did I know? Perhaps she dressed like that to go on a date.

"What am I doing here? I'm a volunteer. What are you doing here?" She thrust her finger in my direction.

"Althea invited me," I said and then quickly added, "just as an observer."

She didn't look impressed. "Well, I'm looking forward to standing by as an observer when you lose your shop. And then you'll get exactly what you deserve, which is nothing."

"Stop playing games and just tell me what you are talking about." A feeling of dread landed in the pit of my stomach. Was Jody getting her information from Cassidy? Was Florence working with Cassidy Jones in a new plot to steal the Chocolate Box away from me? "I haven't lied to anyone."

Instead of answering, she chuckled. "You don't even lie well about lying. Where is that precious friend of yours?"

"*Our* turtle lady," Lidia stepped forward and said loudly, "is getting the cardboard to block the light and to funnel the babies to the sea."

"She should be back soon," Harriett added. "And you shouldn't even be here. Chief Byrd had warned you—"

"They're breaking the law." Jody glared at the house with the offending lights and acted as if she hadn't even seen Harriett. "The ordinance clearly states that lights on the beach need to be turned off from May to October. I don't know why Althea didn't tell them that."

"She tried," I said. "The new owner wasn't home."

Jody muttered something under her breath and then announced, "I'll take care of it."

"Penn said"—Lidia spoke even louder and slower, as if addressing someone with an acute hearing problem—"the owners aren't home. There's no way to turn out the lights."

"Yes, there is." The confidence in Jody's statement made me wonder if her experience working in construction had taught her how to turn off the power to a house.

"Jody, no." Harriett lifted both her hands and stood in front of Jody. "Don't do it."

"Don't do what?" Lidia asked.

"It's what needs to be done." Jody nudged Harriett aside with her shoulder and kept walking.

"What are you going to do?" I demanded.

Jody paused just long enough to flash a wild grin in our direction. "I'm going to take care of the lights." As she headed toward the house, she pulled a gun from her fanny pack. A *freaking* big gun.

Lidia and Harriett both threw their hands in the air as they backed away from Jody and her firearm. Harriett shouted to Jody's retreating back, "The police chief warned—"

"I'm saving the turtles," Jody called over her shoulder as she started to run. She ran toward the brightly lit house with the loping gait of one of those predatory coyotes that had recently moved onto the island. "It's a community service. Y'all should be thanking me."

At that very moment, Althea came over the walkover, her arms weighed down with stacks of black painted cardboard.

"Jody's here," I said.

"*No.*" Althea dropped the stacked cardboard. "Please tell me she doesn't have her gun."

"She has her gun," both Harriett and Lidia cried.

Althea started to sprint down the beach. We all ran after her.

"That gun is why Jody isn't the turtle lady anymore," Harriett explained as she jogged next to me. "She waves it around like a crazy lady. Last year she shot up a house. According to the police, she's not even supposed to volunteer with us anymore."

"I hope Althea can stop her." I started to run faster. Too late. The sound of gunfire ripped through the humid air. One by one, the blaring lights on the mansion went dark. Even after it was dark, the gun kept firing. A woman on the beach started to scream.

Lidia and Harriett had both fallen behind by the time I reached the house. I found Jody standing at the base of the mansion's steps, a gun in each hand. Wait a blasted minute. She had *two* guns in her fanny pack? Was it even big enough for two guns?

Her breaths sounded loud and ragged. So did mine. So did Althea's. But Jody was no longer staring at the now darkened mansion. Her gaze had latched onto a shadowy lump on the beach about fifty yards away and the screaming lady standing beside it.

"What were you thinking, Jody?" I demanded.

"Chief Byrd had warned you more than once to stop acting like this is the Wild West," Althea said as Jody whirled around to face us. "I don't know how you handled things in the upstate, but here in Camellia Beach, we don't whip out our guns at every little provocation."

Jody's face looked pale in the ghostly moonlight. Paler than it had before she'd started shooting up that brightly lit beachfront mansion. She started to say something, but before she got the first word out, one of the guns in her hands fired.

I saw the flash of the blast. Heard Jody's shout. I even remember thinking I needed to duck. But my muscles couldn't move fast enough.

The bullet hit my shoulder with the speed of a freight train. It knocked me flat on my back.

She shot me?

Jody freaking shot me!

I was lying with the back of my head half buried in the dry sand while staring up at the moon. The top of my shoulder burned like it was on fire. Was I dying? I didn't feel like I was dying.

Jody shot me. I still couldn't believe it. She had actually shot me.

FIVE

THE WOMAN DOWN the beach only screamed louder.

Althea cursed as she pried both of the guns from Jody's grip. "What were you thinking? You shot Penn!"

I watched my friend toss the guns to the ground. The hand I was using to grip my burning shoulder felt sticky from blood. I still didn't know if I was going to die or not. I'd never been shot before. I suspected I might bleed to death unless someone got me some medical help. Like now. I was beginning to feel lightheaded. Was I losing consciousness?

Lidia dropped to her knees beside me and peeled my hand away from my shoulder. "It's just a little scrape," she called to the others. She then said to me, "Slather some antiseptic on it and slap a bandage over the whole thing and you'll be fine."

"Really?" I slowly sat up. "I'm not dying?"

"It'll leave a nasty bruise and hurt like the devil for a week or so, but I've seen this before. You'll be fine," she repeated.

I braved a look at my shoulder. She was right. The bullet must have simply grazed the top of my shoulder.

"It burns," I said, still not ready to believe that it was simply a scratch.

"I'm sure it does," Lidia offered me a hand to get to my feet. "Bullets tend to get seriously hot after they're fired."

Althea, I suddenly noticed, was kneeling down on the other side of me. When did she get there? She put her hand under my arm and helped me stand.

The world spun. My legs started to collapse beneath me.

"Breathe," Lidia barked the instruction.

I drew in a deep breath while the world continued to spin.

"You're fine, Penn," Lidia said. "You're simply hyperventilating."

Well, wasn't that embarrassing? And why was that woman down near the water still screaming? At least I wasn't screaming. That was something, right?

"Y'all need to get over here, now!" Harriett yelled. She was standing beside the screaming woman who was dressed in what looked like a turquoise flowered muumuu. Harriett had pulled her arm around the moon-faced woman's shoulder, hugging her tight. They were standing next to the dark lump in the sand that Jody had been staring at when we'd first run up to her.

Had Jody unwittingly shot an adult sea turtle laying her eggs on the beach? Was that what had so upset the screaming woman?

The urgency in Harriett's voice felt like a splash of cold water to my face. Suddenly revived from my dizzy spell, I ran with Lidia and Althea on either side of me.

"What's going on?" Althea called out as we ran toward Harriett.

Harriett tightened her arm around the screaming woman's shoulder. It looked as if she was using all her strength to keep the heavy-set woman standing. The woman's midlength hair was mussed and standing up on one side. She glanced at the three of us as we approached, dragged in a deep breath, and started scream-ing even louder.

When I got closer I saw right away why she was so upset. And why Harriett was upset too. It wasn't a sea turtle lying in the sand. Sea turtles didn't wear colorful Hawaiian shirts. Sea turtles didn't have long blond hair.

But Cassidy Jones did.

That was him on the beach with a bullet wound in his chest.

He was quite unmistakably dead.

"DON'T RIGHTLY KNOW why they called you," Police Chief Hank Byrd said as he scratched his thick belly. About a half hour had passed since we'd called the police.

Frank Gibbons, a homicide detective from the county Sheriff's department, had donned blue medical gloves. He held a flashlight in one hand as he crouched down and started sifting through a small pile of sand near where Jody had been standing with guns in hand.

Gibbons didn't answer Camellia Beach's police chief right away. He moved his hand through the sand like a child searching for shells. What he uncovered wasn't a seashell, though. It was a shell casing. A moment later he uncovered something else, something bright red. I leaned as far over the yellow crime scene tape as I dared, but was too far away to see what it was.

"Tag these," he said to one of the crime scene techs. A young man dressed in a white jumpsuit and a head-set that included a flashlight came running over with evidence bags.

Gibbons rose and dusted sand off his pants. Only then did he look over at Byrd. "The county attends all murder investigations on Camellia Beach. We provide the manpower and technical staff your department doesn't have," he said in that calm voice of his. "You know that."

"You attend at *my* request." The police chief didn't sound nearly as calm. "I didn't call you. She did." Byrd pointed an accusing finger in my direction.

Gibbons turned fully toward where Harriett, Althea, Lidia, and I had been watching from the edge of the crime scene tape. "I swear, Penn, I should start calling you a bad Penny," he said in a Southern accent that had been refined to the point that he nearly sounded British. It was an accent that reminded the locals he wasn't from Camellia Beach. He'd come over the bridge from Charleston's pricy historic district known as the South of Broad, or sometimes simply as SOB.

"The name's Penn, not Penny." He knew that. We'd first met after someone had killed my friend in a vat of chocolate.

"You turn up wherever there's trouble. In my book, that's a bad penny," he said.

Police Chief Byrd crossed his arms over his wide chest and grinned. "That's what I was saying. She had no right to call you. She's always causing trouble, not following the rules."

"We also called nine-one-one," Althea pointed out.

Hank and his men had arrived almost immediately. One of the officers had looked at my shoulder, rubbed it with some kind of stinging antiseptic and had slapped a bandage on the wound—just as Lidia had said needed to be done. While the police led Jody away in handcuffs and then turned the beach into a brightly lit crime scene, the turtle crew and I stood watch. It looked like something out of the movies.

"How's the arm?" Gibbons asked with a nod toward my shoulder.

"It still burns," I said.

He grimaced. "A little aspirin should help. Now I'm going to have to question each one of you separately," he warned. "Don't go anywhere."

"We're not leaving," Lidia said in that booming voice of hers. "We have a nest to attend."

"And these lights are going to have to go off as soon as the babies start to emerge," Althea added.

"What are you talking about?" Detective Gibbons sounded appalled at the idea anyone would interfere with his work. "We can't turn off these lights in the middle of an investigation."

"Federal law requires—" Lidia started to say.

"You don't need to fret about federal laws," Hank Byrd interrupted. "Don't you worry your pretty heads over there. I'll see that the sea turtles are protected. At the first sign of them, the lights will go off. I guarantee it."

"We can't turn off a murder investigation because a few turtles are popping out of a nest," Gibbons argued.

"It ain't as if we don't know who did it, now is it? A few hours delay in poking around won't change who shot Cassidy," Byrd argued right back.

Gibbons grunted and promised nothing.

In the end, it didn't matter. The baby turtles never did emerge from their nest. Althea continued to watch the mound of sand, her brows furrowed with concern. Didn't she say earlier that the turtles were already past their hatching date?

The sun was rising over the ocean by the time the police started wrapping up their work. Althea had decided to head home as well. I was helping her pack up her supplies when I spotted Hank Byrd plodding through the sand toward us. A shorter man wearing a stained chef's coat struggled to keep up with him. It wasn't that Byrd was moving that fast. A product of the South that had raised him, Camellia Beach's police chief's movements often looked as if he was working his way through a jar of molasses. It was the smaller man's oversized straw sunhat that slowed him down. Every few steps, the wind blew it off and he'd have to run after the floppy hat and then jog to catch up to Byrd whose purposeful stride never altered its pace.

"Ooh." Lidia leaned toward me. Her loud voice slammed against my ear. "Don't look now. But here comes that police chief we met last night."

"Don't let him bully you," I said. "Detective Frank Gibbons from the county Sheriff's office takes the lead on murder investigations in Camellia Beach. Byrd doesn't have the manpower or facilities to handle an investigation of this magnitude."

"Who are you kidding, Penn?" Harriett said. "Even Byrd can handle an open-and-shut case as easy as this one. We all saw Jody run down the beach waving that huge pistol around. We all heard the gunshots. We all saw her standing there with not one but *two* guns in her hands. Heck, she even shot you! And you told us yourself that you heard Jody say yesterday that she believed she was in an exclusive relationship with Cassidy." She snorted. "As if a chaser like Cassidy could ever be true to anyone. Sure as we're standing here, we know what happened. Jody saw Cassidy with another woman and shot him straight through his roaming heart."

"Chief Byrd." Althea stepped forward and greeted

the men as they approached. She'd plastered on a broad smile despite not having slept last night and her obvious frustration over the failed turtle nest. "Good morning, sir."

"Don't 'good morning' me, missy," he grumbled. "There's nothing good about the morning after a murder in my town."

He glanced in my direction. I held my breath expecting him to somehow blame me for Cassidy's death. According to him, Camellia Beach had been a peaceful town completely devoid of any crime...until I moved here. "Penn," was all he said.

His lack of accusations both last night and this morning surprised me a little. But, really, what could he say? Cassidy Jones had been a longtime resident. And Jody Dalton had moved to Camellia Beach a couple of years before I did. There was no possible way he could blame me for the trouble that had happened last night.

"Chief," I said with a head bob.

He gave a loud sniff in return then shifted his attention to Harriett. With a much more cordial tone, he shook her hand and asked after her health. Her husband had served as mayor of Camellia Beach. That had been decades ago, but as Althea had once explained, memories run long and deep in a small town like this one.

During the course of the night I learned that because Harriett was once Camellia Beach's First Lady, it afforded her an elevated status in town. Byrd, with a look that could almost be called a smile, introduced Harriett to the man in the chef's coat and floppy straw hat. He told the chef that Harriett was someone he needed to know on the island. He didn't say anything about the rest of us.

"And Harriett," he continued with his proper introductions, "you must meet our latest resident, Chef Bailey Grassi. We're real lucky to have him. He's from Baltimore, but we won't hold that against him. He opened up that new restaurant in Charleston's historic district this past winter. It's the one that has been getting all those awards. And out of all the places in the Lowcountry he could have settled, he decided to make Camellia Beach his home."

"Pleased to meet you, Bailey." Harriett yawned as she offered her hand to the restaurateur. "What's the name of your establishment?"

Instead of taking her hand, Bailey rubbed his own bandaged hand. "It's Grilled to Perfection. Perhaps you've heard of it?" He awkwardly offered her his left hand to shake. "Sorry, I had a little accident in the kitchen last night." He looked to be a few years older than my thirty-seven years. His brown hair was tied into a man bun, and he sported a shaggy beard that was peppered with gray.

Harriett introduced the rest of us, telling him that we were volunteers with the turtle team. His eyes lit up at the mention of my name.

"Penn?" His tired eyes widened. "As in Charity Penn?"

"It's just Penn," I corrected.

"Of course, Penn. I heard the gunwoman shot you as well. Are you…are you okay?"

"The bullet just grazed me." My hand instinctively reached for my shoulder, which was a mistake. It was still raw and tender. I quickly drew my hand away. "Other than a scrape and bruise, I'm fine."

"Oh, thank goodness." He nodded vigorously. "Despite these unfortunate conditions, I'm glad to finally meet you. I've been meaning to visit your shop," he said with a sudden burst of excitement. "The Chocolate Box's chocolates are legendary in the culinary world. You've inherited quite a legacy. If you're amenable, I'd like to talk about the possibility of having your shop provide some of its special chocolate to both my restaurant and online store. I'm building a clientele who appreciate the rare and finely crafted."

"Well, the Amar cacao beans we use to make our special dark chocolates are as rare as they come," I warned. "The beans only grow on one narrow slope deep within the Brazilian rainforest."

I'd heard from more than one chocolate expert that the surprisingly rich flavor comes from the harsh soils and the unique variety of cacao bean that produces a chocolate with the perfect combination of flavors. The Brazilian villagers who have grown the bean for generations claim the amazing flavors of their Amar chocolate beans comes straight from their Aztec gods. Those same villagers have cultivated and protected the cacao bean since the beginning of the ancient village's existence.

"We definitely need to talk," Bailey said, his eyes shining. "That is exactly the kind of high-quality foods I serve."

"The bean is rare," I warned again. For nearly a century, the Chocolate Box has held exclusive rights to buy the bean from the village of Cabruca where it's grown. "We barely have enough to sell in our own shop. I usually use only a little of the Amar chocolates in our recipes."

"Oh, so the idea of us collaborating is out of the question?" The sparkle suddenly left his eyes.

"I'm not saying that. I'm willing to talk." No harm could come from talking. "I'm simply saying I can't make any promises that we can work something out."

"Well then, I'm looking forward to convincing you to partner with me," he said.

"Don't waste your time with her," the police chief grumbled when he saw what I'm sure he assumed was rude behavior on my part. "From what I've been hearing around town, ownership of the Chocolate Box will soon go to the original owner's children."

"What?" Althea, Harriett, and I all cried.

"*What*?" Lidia cried a beat later. She'd cupped her hand to her ear.

"Who's been telling you that nonsense?" I demanded.

The police chief shrugged. The movement made his belly rise and fall like a surging wave. "As I've said, islanders all around town are saying you stole Mabel's shop from her family."

"She gave it to me." How could anyone believe otherwise? Mabel Maybank was my grandmother. Plus, I wanted the shop. None of Mabel's many children could say that. None of them wanted to keep the shop and continue the business their predecessors had built. I did.

Byrd shrugged again.

Bailey's thick brows dipped low as he watched the police chief. "I didn't mean to cause trouble. Not now and not last night. I didn't understand the importance of protecting the sea turtles. I didn't even realize they nested on Camellia Beach."

"We get over a hundred nests a year on our beach.

Many of the sea turtles that visit our shoreline are either threatened or endangered," Harriett explained gently.

"Unfortunately, the same beaches the turtles use for nesting are also prime vacation spots," Althea added. "That's why we give them all the help we can in hopes that the next generation of turtles will thrive."

"I am sorry about the deck lights." He put his hand on his chest and bowed his head. "I didn't know. I was at the restaurant until a few hours ago. The lights are on a timer because I get home so late. It's a security feature. I didn't know about the turtles. Honestly, I didn't. I grew up in the suburbs of D.C. The closest beach was about three hours away. I rarely ever got to the ocean and have never seen a sea turtle." He said it all in such a rush and with such angst, it was impossible not to forgive him. "And I never thought my deck lights could be the cause of a man's death," he nearly whimpered.

"Jody shot that poor man, not you, dear," Harriett said as she smothered another yawn. "The two of them were an item. At least she thought so."

"Is that true?" Bailey asked the police chief. "No one told me."

"I—um—um—I didn't know," Byrd stammered. He glanced at me as if I were the one who'd made him look ignorant. "I'd heard rumors, of course. But Cassidy Jones dated many women. All of them knew he couldn't stay true to one lady."

"Well, then." Bailey drew up his slumping shoulders, which gave him a few more inches. "I'll get the lights fixed and make sure they don't turn on during turtle nesting season."

Hank Byrd and the chef had started to walk back toward Bailey's house when Lidia, preening like a fluffed-up chick, waved her hand in the air and called, "Yoo-hoo, Chief Byrd." Her normally booming voice had suddenly turned all breathy and dripping with enough southern drawl to make Scarlet O'Hara cringe. "It's so nice to finally meet you, despite the horrible reason we'd had to call you. I've heard so much about how you keep our town safe. I didn't get a chance to introduce myself last night. I'm Lidia Vanderhorst." She held out her hand as if it were a limp rag. He stared at it for a moment before giving it a little squeeze.

Althea gave me a look of surprise. I'm sure my face mirrored back the same astonishment. Was Lidia actually *flirting* with the police chief?

Byrd, keen investigator that he wasn't, appeared oblivious. He curtly welcomed her to Camellia Beach and started to follow Bailey back to his house, but then he apparently had second thoughts. He abruptly turned back and wagged an accusing finger in Althea's direction.

"I thought I made it clear last year that under no circumstance could Jody continue her volunteer activities," he scolded. "I could have you up on charges for disobeying that order."

"This is a public beach, Chief. I can't exactly stop the public from coming out to witness a hatching. As soon as I knew she had a gun, I did try to stop her. But Jody has the longest legs and is as wily as a fox. Not even Penn could catch her. Not that I would have asked any of my volunteers to chase down an armed crazy woman."

"Has Jody said anything?" I asked as I rubbed my bruised shoulder. I bit back a whimper. Why did I keep touching it? "She and I may have had our disagreements"—a gross understatement—"but I find

it hard to believe she'd actually kill anyone." Well...
that wasn't quite true. For a while this past winter, I'd
suspected she'd drowned my friend from prepschool in
a large vat of chocolate.

But Jody was a *mother*. Although she often used
her young son as a way to hurt her ex, she appeared
to genuinely love the boy. She wouldn't do something
that would jeopardize her time with him, would she?

Apparently, she had. We all saw her with the gun.
We all saw her shoot *me*. And Cassidy had been shot
through the heart. What more evidence did a rational
person need? The police had arrested her. She was as
good as gone from Camellia Beach forever.

This should have been the end of the story, but the
back of my neck prickled a warning. I feared something deeper lurked behind Cassidy's murder. I feared
that "something" involved my mother and her desire to
steal the Chocolate Box away from me.

SIX

"CHOCOLATE MOON COOKIES," I said, more to myself than to anyone else, much later that same day. I was working alongside Bertie at the Chocolate Box. The idea for a new recipe had started to form as I spent the night standing under the full moon waiting for the turtles that had never arrived.

It was better to think about chocolate than about Cassidy Jones' murder. While I'd never met the man, that still didn't blunt the shock of finding his dead body in the sand or the horror of seeing Jody looming nearby with a smoking gun in each hand. Or the shock that she had shot me.

Chocolate was safer. Chocolate would never turn on me.

"What's that, dear?" Bertie asked.

"It's an idea I've been playing with this morning," I said. "Chocolate moon cookies."

"We sell chocolates, not cookies," she reminded me as she carefully placed several of her sea salt chocolate caramels into a gift box.

"I know that." The sign outside the shop simply said Chocolate. I loved that sign. It was direct and concise, with no question about what you'd find inside. "These will be chocolates. I'm picturing an ultrathin, perfectly round cookie coated with white chocolate on one side and dark chocolate on the other to represent the bright and dark sides of the moon. My main stumbling block is I don't know what kind of cookie would hold its own with the competing white and dark chocolate flavors."

"Benne wafers would work," she said without even looking up from her task.

I frowned. "Benne whats?"

"Not 'whats,' child." She closed the gift box she'd filled and looked up at me. "Wafers. They're thin, crisp sesame seed cookies. They should be able to hold up when sandwiched between your chocolate layers."

"Sesame seeds, huh?" The strong flavor of the sesame seeds might be just what I need to complement the white and dark chocolates. "Do you have a recipe?"

"Don't need a recipe. Like my mother and her mother before her, I've been making them my entire life."

"And—" This is where I hesitated. "Do you think you could teach me how to make them?"

It wasn't that I doubted her teaching abilities. No one topped Bertie when it came to patience in the kitchen. What I was really asking was if she thought I could learn how to make her cookies.

She patted my arm in a kind, motherly way. "Of course you can learn it." She knew me almost too well. "The trick to making the wafer is in how long you leave them in the oven. There's no one here right now. I could show you."

"That would be wonderful! If they're any good, we'll sell them along with our sea salted turtles and also donate a portion of the profits to the Camellia Beach Turtle Foundation."

Since it was nearing noon, a slow time for us because we didn't offer a lunch menu, I followed Bertie like a lamb down a long corridor and toward an oversized kitchen at the back of the building. My grandmother used to hold chocolate making classes back there. It was large enough to accommodate a dozen students.

An extra-long kitchen island spanned the center of the room. Burners lined two walls, and several sets of mismatched ovens covered the third wall. I flipped a switch. The overhead florescent lights flickered on. We didn't really need the artificial lights. A series of windows that looked out over a small patio and the tall green grasses in the marsh beyond let in plenty of natural light.

I retrieved the pen and notebook I kept in the kitchen, on one of the open shelves above a burner, to jot down what worked and what didn't when I was cooking. Bertie hummed happily as she started pulling out ingredients. She had a box of brown sugar in her hand when the brass bell above the shop's front door tinkled.

"Customers," Bertie sang out.

"I'll go take care of them," I said, hoping whoever had come into the shop wouldn't linger. Once I got a recipe idea in my head, it was difficult to stop thinking about it. Some might think that odd considering my dismal track record in the kitchen. But it wasn't the act of making the chocolate treats that drove my obsession for making them. It was the promise of eating them.

Since I'd inherited the shop last winter, I'd gone up a dress size. While a vain part of me was distressed by this, another much more relaxed part of me had been relieved. It'd been a relief to donate the clothes in my closet that no longer fit in more ways than one. Those stiff and rather uncomfortable dresses and suits represented my former life when I worked in advertising.

Today I wore a pale blue sundress with low-heeled

strappy sandals. The sundress represented the causal and comfortable lifestyle living on Camellia Beach demanded of its residents. It was a lifestyle I had come to embrace…most of the time.

Over the sundress I wore a crisp white apron with "Chocolate is cheaper than therapy" embroidered in scrolling burgundy Victorian letters across the front.

When I reached the front of the shop, I found Johnny Pane moving tables from the middle of the shop. His ladder was leaning against a wall. His paints, rags, and brushes were sitting next to it.

"What are you doing here?" I asked, but swiftly added, "Not that I'm complaining. But I thought you were only going to be able to work on my ceiling after business hours."

Johnny set down the chair he'd been moving over to the wall. He turned to me and smiled. "Good afternoon to you, Ms. Penn. It's already hot enough to make a pig sweat. I reckon everyone on the island will come begging for your milkshakes before the day is through."

I nodded and tried to hide my impatience. Many on the island—especially the older crowd—considered it rude to talk business before fully dissecting the weather. "I suppose you're right about the heat. The humidity has made the air so heavy, I felt as if I was swimming when I took Stella for her morning walk."

He made a sympathetic "uh-uh" noise in the back of his throat. "If it continues like this, I wouldn't be surprised to see some kind of tropical cyclone bearing down on us soon."

We went on like this for several more minutes with me fighting my urge to jump back into talking about what had changed his work schedule. Finally, he said, "I reckon I'd better get started on that ceiling."

"So you aren't working on the new house for Jody after all?" I asked as he worked to clear out his work area.

"Don't rightly need to rush over there anymore considering…"

I waited for him to finish his thought. But he'd gone back to moving the tables and chairs. "Because Jody is in jail?" I prompted.

Jody's incarceration had surely lifted a heavy weight from the shoulders of many in Camellia Beach, myself included. Her continued efforts to sabotage the shop's success had been draining. Watching her threaten to take Harley to family court every few months over their son was exhausting.

Johnny shook his head but didn't answer. Certainly, having Jody off his back is what had gotten rid of the worry that had clouded his pale brown eyes yesterday. He moved with his usual deliberate pace as he set up his ladder and the plastic curtain. He then turned to me with a look of a man who'd just won the lottery. "After last night, I'm beholden to no one but myself again. I work where I want. And I aim to finish this ceiling before moving on to my next job. Ain't no one around to tell me otherwise."

"Because Jody is in jail?" I asked again, feeling awfully pleased I wouldn't have to deal with her and her mercurial moods ever again.

"Perhaps we should be thanking her instead of locking her behind bars," he said as he slid his leg into his white painting coveralls. "Perhaps she'd done us all a favor."

I started to ask him what he meant by that when the brass bell on the door rang with sudden urgency. A small figure darted into the shop so quickly the movement looked like a blur. A shouted, "Miss Penn! Miss Penn!" accompanied it.

I recognized the voice and the blur's blue and tan board shorts. They belonged to Gavin, Harley's and Jody's ten-year-old son. He came to a screeching halt right next to me. Tears streamed down his ruddy cheeks. They'd dampened the collar of his white T-shirt. "Miss Penn!" he cried and latched onto my leg. The puddling tears soaked through my cotton sundress almost instantly. "Tell them they are wrong. Please, you've done it before. Tell them they are wrong. *Pleeease*."

I awkwardly patted his head. "Tell who?"

He was crying too hard for me to understand his answer.

By this time Harley, Gavin's father, had jogged into the shop. His hair was in disarray. His suit, an off-the-rack midpriced suit that didn't quite fit right, was wrinkled. His green eyes were wide and troubled.

Their obvious distress shamed me.

Here I'd been, overjoyed that Jody's arrest would put a halt to whatever mischief she'd been planning for me and the Chocolate Box. But for both Gavin and Harley, her troubles must have felt as if their world was coming apart at the seams.

"Gavin"—Harley's voice was gentle—"we've already discussed this. Penn can't convince the police to release your mother any more than I could."

With an apologetic look, he tried to pry his son from his death grip around my middle. Gavin only tightened his hold.

"Nooo!" he screamed. "She-she could find who k-k-k-killed Mr. Cassidy. She-she could if-if she-she wanted to. Mommy d-d-didn't do what they're saying s-s-she did! She didn't!"

His pain gripped my heart as if it were my own. I knew that pain. I grew up without a mother in my life. Worse, I heard from my family endless tales of how my mother was a conniving fortune teller and a criminal who cared more for herself than for the child she'd abandoned in my father's unprepared arms.

"I'm sorry," he said. I don't know if Harley was apologizing to his son or to me.

"She has to help us. She does. School will start next week. Mommy always takes me shopping. She always takes me to class on the first day."

"Please, Gavin." Harley tried again to pry his son from the death grip he had on my legs. "I'll take care of those things for you. I'll take you shopping. I'll be there on your first day. It'll be okay."

"I need Mommy." Gavin looked up at me. Tears still flowed like a river. "You understand. Please, Miss Penn. Help me. *Pleeease*."

"Gavin, I know you're hurting and scared, but we can't ask Penn to do something like this. She isn't an investigator. She isn't—"

"I'll do it." The words popped out of my mouth without my brain's consent. But it was true. I looked into Gavin's teary eyes—kind green eyes that looked so much like his father's—and I knew I'd move heaven and earth to heal his shattering heart even if it meant bringing his mother back to him...and her back into my life.

I hadn't the first clue how I was going to manage it. As everyone had already pointed out, the evidence against Jody was stacked so high it probably violated some kind of municipal height ordinance. We all saw her with the gun. We all saw her shoot me. There was no doubt in anyone's mind. She was guilty.

Heaven help me, had I just promised a heartbroken little boy I'd prove her innocence? How in the world was I going to manage that? And in less than a week? His school started next Thursday.

SEVEN

"HAVE YOU LOST your ever-blooming mind?" Althea asked a few hours later. She'd met me as I walked Stella down the narrow path that followed the marsh at the backside of the island. My five-pound brown, black, and white papillon, who delighted in challenging anything larger than her (which was nearly everything), charged toward Althea. Her enormous ears flapped like butterfly wings with each menacing bark.

"Apparently I've lost not only my mind, but also what little good sense I'd once possessed," I said in a flat voice. I tossed Stella a bacon treat in an effort to distract her long enough for her to forget about barking.

Tossing the treat made my shoulder ache. I stopped underneath a scrubby oak tree with branches that twisted and a trunk that leaned as if it was standing on a swimmer's block while preparing to take a graceful dive into the marsh. "I suppose most of Camellia Beach knows what I told Gavin by now."

When she heard my voice, Stella barked some more. But with the promise of more bacon in my pocket, she no longer sounded as fierce as she had a moment ago. "Hush now, you know Althea. She's always bringing you treats whenever she comes and visits."

"And despite that, Stella is always barking at me the entire time I'm at your apartment." Althea shook her head in dismay. But then she smiled down at my little silky pup. "She's such a pretty dog. I love her black and mahogany-brown markings on that pure white fur. I'd dearly like to pet her one day. Will you let me pet you, Stella?"

Stella with her adorable little puppy dog face and expressive chocolate eyes looked up at Althea. And growled.

"That's what I thought." Althea clasped her hands behind her back as if trying to protect them from Stella's nubby but snappy teeth. "You're as prickly as your owner. Although, you have to admit that Penn has come a long way. She now lets me give her hugs without acting as if my touch scalds. But Stella, you need to tell your owner she's going to break that little boy's heart. We all heard the gunshots. Jody shot your owner. And she shot that man in a fit of jealous rage. The best she can hope for now is that the jury will believe a plea of temporary insanity."

I tossed Stella another bacon treat. "What was I going to say to Gavin? What would you have said to him?"

"I wouldn't have promised to clear his mama of a murder we all saw her commit," Althea answered without a moment of hesitation.

"Well…" I drew out that one word for several seconds. "We didn't actually see her shoot anyone, other than me that is," I said more to convince myself than to convince Althea.

"She was holding two guns. The morning newspaper said Cassidy died from a gunshot wound to his heart. He was still warm when we found him, which means he had to have been shot at the same time Jody was shooting those guns of hers. She was there. She had reason to be angry with him. Means. Motive. And opportunity. What other evidence does anyone need?"

"But she—" What could I say? Althea was right. "Are you going to help me investigate or not?"

"Of course, I'll help you. You know I will. That's why I'm here. That's what friends do." And that was why I loved Althea so much. I could always count on her loyalty. "But where do we start?"

"If you could answer a few questions for me, that'd be great," I said.

"What do you need to know?" she asked as she walked alongside me.

"First off, I need you to tell me why Jody was the island's turtle lady last year. How in the world did she get herself in a position where she was in charge of all the volunteers for the turtle watch program on the island? She works for a company that is all about tearing apart the land and building bigger and bigger homes and businesses. It seems like a contradiction that she could be so eager to tear down the Chocolate Box to build a multistory resort complex that is completely out of scale for this island, and yet at the same time so trigger happy when it comes to a little light pollution that might harm a few baby turtles. What's that all about?"

Althea tapped her chin. "I'd never wondered after her motives before, at least not in that way. From the moment she moved to Camellia Beach, she's been interested in the sea turtles. Don't forget she's also a competitive surfer, and surfers are great advocates when it comes to protecting the shore and the sea life there. After she'd moved to town, barely a week had passed before she contacted Harriett—the turtle lady at the time—to offer her services. A year after she was accepted as a volunteer,

Harriett abruptly decided to step down from the role of turtle lady, and Jody took over."

"But why? What was it about the sea turtles that made her want to bring a gun out to the nest?"

"This may come as a shock to you," Althea whispered, "but Jody is a bit of a hothead."

"Really?" I reeled back in mock surprise. "After seeing how she'd interacted with Johnny Pane at my shop the other day, I would have never guessed."

We both laughed. Mine was a nervous laugh, tinged with worry that I was doomed to fail and that Gavin would lose his mother. On multiple occasions Jody had showed everyone on the island how she'd let her emotions rule her actions. Common sense told me to give up already. Jody was guilty of murder.

But I couldn't do that. For Gavin's sake, I needed to find a different truth. Jody might not be a perfect mother, but Gavin loved her and needed her in his life. That was something my own mother had denied to me. Foolish or not, I intended to do everything in my power to keep Gavin from feeling the tearing grief I'd felt as a child.

"Despite her faults, Jody is truly passionate about protecting the sea turtles," Althea said, no longer laughing.

"You're serious?" I found that hard to believe. "If she cares about the turtles, then how can she work for a place like Sunset Development?"

"I might not like the buildings they're constructing or their philosophy that Camellia Beach needs to be renovated into something completely different, but they've been a good corporate friend to the sea turtle team."

She must have read the look of horror on my face.

Sunset Development had been nothing but a pain for the shop ever since I'd told them I wasn't going to sell them my building.

"Don't get me wrong," Althea said quickly, "I agree with you that the company is pushing to change what we love most about the island. If they succeed, we'll lose our tight-knit community to a sea of corporate-owned vacation condos. But at the same time, without their sponsorship, the turtle program wouldn't have been able to accomplish even a tenth of what it has been able to accomplish in the past few years."

"Okay, so Jody sees herself as an environmentalist?" I asked, still not quite able to believe it.

"She once told me that tourists want to see the sea turtles and other wildlife and have healthy dunes just as much as they want big, shiny, new buildings to shop and stay in."

That part made sense. I might not agree with Jody that Camellia Beach needed to change into a mini-Miami Beach, but I could certainly understand her reasoning for wanting to protect the sea turtles if she thought it was good for business.

"I also think Jody honestly enjoys being around sea turtles," Althea added. "The turtle lady position demands a tremendous amount of time and commitment. That's a lot of ask from a volunteer."

"Don't forget how she likes being in charge," I said.

"That's the truth. I just wish she hadn't gotten into that stubborn head of hers that she needed to bring guns to the hatching."

"What was she doing toting guns around in the first place?" I asked. "She has a young son in her house for goodness sake. She shouldn't even own a gun, much less carry it around with her."

Althea gave me an odd look.

"What?" I asked.

"This is the South, Penn." She'd said it as if that pronouncement should explain everything. It didn't explain anything.

"So we're in the South. What does that mean?"

She huffed. "Everyone owns a gun."

"Everyone?" She had to be exaggerating. "No, not everyone. You don't have one."

"Yeah, I do. I have my daddy's old handgun in a gun safe under my bed."

"What?" She might have well told me that purple dragons lived underneath the island. The thought of Althea with a gun was simply too unbelievable. "Don't tell me your mother has a gun, too." I don't know how I felt about living in an apartment with a gun in it.

My father, despite all of his faults, abhorred firearms. He made it clear that there was no place in a home for weapons. He found hunting barbaric and believed handguns only exasperated the troubles facing the country today. I disagreed with my father about pretty much everything. But when it came to guns, we agreed. Then again, I did grow up in Chicago. Whenever someone talked about a gun, it was almost always in reference to a deadly shooting.

"Does Mama keep a gun?" Althea repeated while she thought about that question. "You know, I don't know. You'll have to ask her. She and Mabel lived alone in that apartment of yours for decades. I wouldn't be surprised if they had a gun tucked away somewhere."

"But your mother seems so, so level-headed. And I'm

still shocked to hear you have a gun in your house. You own a crystal shop. You believe in new age woo-woo stuff. You carry spiders outdoors instead of squishing them. I would have pegged you for a pacifist."

"I am a pacifist, Penn. I don't want to hurt anyone. The gun belonged to my daddy. It's a part of my heritage. I could no more give it away than I could stop being Southern."

"I suppose your keeping a gun in the house is akin to Jody wanting to develop this island while still caring about the sea turtles. It's not what you'd expect. So she has a gun. Or rather, two guns."

"Most people around here do have more than one," Althea was quick to point out. "Some have complete collections that could number in the hundreds."

I shivered. "That's more than I want to know." I turned around on the sandy trail and headed back toward the shop.

Stella refused to follow. She tugged at the end of her leash. She sniffed the ground as if searching for treasures. She scraped the rocky sand with her tiny paw. She then sniffed again. A moment later she started scraping the ground again.

"If it makes you rest any easier, most of the residents don't tote guns around on their hip like some gin-swigging, card-swindling outlaw. This isn't the Wild West."

"It doesn't make me feel better." I bit my lower lip. "What did you find there?" I asked Stella. She'd stopped digging. She was now chewing on something she held between her front paws. I reached down and got my hand on what she'd found. Stella snapped the air. But I knew my dog well enough and to move my hand away before her little teeth clamped down on me.

"What is that?" Althea asked.

"Isn't it one of those stress relieving spinners?" I asked as I brushed away the sand coating the red plastic item.

Althea took it and turned it over in her hand. "It does look like one of those."

"Do you remember seeing Gibbons pull something red and plastic that looked like this out of the sand at the crime scene?" Was it a clue? "He had a tech put it into an evidence bag." Did the killer carry these around with him?

"Sorry, I don't remember seeing anything the detective was doing. I was too busy worrying about the nest. The eggs still haven't hatched. They should have hatched by now."

I put my arm around Althea. "I'm sure the baby turtles are just waiting for the perfect time to make a dramatic entrance."

Althea pulled away from me and hugged herself as if she suddenly felt cold. Stella, sensing something was wrong, sniffed Althea's leg before tugging on her leash to head back home.

"I don't think they're late bloomers," Althea said, still hugging herself. "I'm going to dig up the nest first thing tomorrow morning to find out what happened. That's the protocol. Seventy days after the eggs are laid, the team opens the nest."

"Maybe they hatched when no one was looking?" I said, sounding hopeful.

Althea shook her head as if I'd just uttered the stupidest thing in the world, but when she looked at me she said, "Maybe."

"Let me come with you tomorrow." I put my hand on her shoulder. "Just to observe. And to be your friend."

She gave a tight nod. "You should to talk to Jody."

"What?" Why did I need to talk to Jody about the sea turtles?

"If you want to help Gavin, you need to get Jody's side of the story about what happened last night."

"I already tried," I said. "But when I called the jail, the nice lady who answered the phone told me I couldn't see her. She was emphatic about it."

"You'll have to talk to the next best thing, then."

"Who's that?" I asked, although I was pretty sure I knew who she wanted me to question.

Althea waggled her eyebrows. "Har-ley," she sang. "That boy is sweet on you."

"Now isn't a good time to think about *that,* not when he has his hands full working to protect his son from what's happened to his mother."

"He's been too busy to talk to you?" Althea guessed.

"Yeah, I've been trying to get him on the phone or talk with him in person all day. But he's not been around, and he's not returned my calls."

We'd reached the back of the shop. Althea nudged my side and nodded toward the second-story porch that ran along the length of the building's back elevation. The two upstairs apartments opened up onto that porch.

Bertie and I shared one apartment. Harley and his son lived in the other.

Harley, still dressed in his business suit, stood on the porch. With his elbows perched on the railing, he leaned toward the marsh. He didn't notice us. His gaze was trained on some point far beyond the horizon.

"You could talk with him now," she said as she gave me a gentle push. "I'll see you bright and early tomorrow morning."

"I'll try to talk your mama into making pancakes for breakfast for us."

"Chocolate chip?" she asked.

"Is there any other kind?" I replied.

We parted then. She took the trail that led toward her small but tidy cottage several blocks away. I walked around the back of the Chocolate Box's building. Stella yapped and growled as soon as we reached the back stairs landing. Obviously, she'd spotted her favorite nemesis: Harley Dalton.

"I thought you might be out walking your noisy fluff ball tonight," Harley said as he pushed away from the railing. He straightened to his full height. He was a bit taller than me, which given my height, was something that I noticed. I also took note of his strong jaw, tanned skin, and kind eyes. When he smiled in my direction, there was no real joy in his expression. Only exhaustion. He loosened his red tie.

"She fusses if I don't keep her schedule." When Stella and I reached the top of the stairs, I tossed her a handful of treats to get her to stop acting like a rabid alligator.

"How's your shoulder?" he asked. He took a step toward me as if he wanted to touch me, hold me, kiss me. My heart beat harder as I let my mind stray in that silly direction. Of course he didn't want to *kiss* me.

"It's fine as long as I don't move it." I glanced toward Harley's apartment's door. "How's Gavin?"

"It took him a while to settle down. But after I let him play a few video games, he was finally able to fall asleep. He's worried about what's happening with his mom."

"I can only imagine." I said.

"I wish I could give Gavin a better life. First there was the divorce, then the constant battles, and now this." He shook his head as if trying to chase the truth away. "As much as I want to, I haven't been able to shield him from any of it."

"You can't blame yourself. This is all Jody's doing. No one forced her into waving that gun around as if she was Annie Freaking Oakley."

"No, but she loves Gavin." He gazed out over the inky darkness in the marsh. "Despite the war she's waged between us and the damage that does to our son, I truly believe that overall she's a good mother. She loves my son." He started to say something else, but seemed to change his mind. Instead he quickly said, "I hired the best defense lawyer in the state for her this morning. The first thing she told him was that she's innocent. She won't even talk about taking a plea deal. She claims she didn't know who owned the gun you found her holding. The second one, that is. It's unregistered. She said she saw it on the ground and picked it up." He dredged his fingers through his hair.

He then said in one long burst of frustration, "Can you believe that? Despite all the evidence they have against her, she won't even admit to doing what she obviously did in a fit of anger. She also says she shot you by accident, that the gun must have had a hair trigger because it just went off in her hand. She told the lawyer I'd hired that she planned to fight for an acquittal on all charges. When he'd tried to talk her out of it, she fired him. That woman is so dang stubborn, it's maddening. She fired the best defense lawyer in the state."

"Jody is insisting that she's innocent?" I asked.

He grunted.

"But you think she's guilty?"

"Of course I don't want to believe it. For Gavin's safe, I don't want to believe anything they're saying about her. But we all know how quickly she flies into her rages. And we've all witnessed her temper when things don't go her way. Why are you asking these questions?" He leaned toward me. "Does this mean you plan to investigate?" He didn't sound pleased about it. I couldn't figure out why he'd be surprised.

"I told your son I would."

"You don't have to. I've explained to Gavin that you were being nice, that you were trying to comfort him. He understands."

"No." Gavin might understand, but I knew the pain that borrows into a child's bones when one's mother is accused of being a monster. (Heck, even I was guilty of accusing Jody of being a monster.) "When I give my word, I keep it. I aim to find out what really happened last night on the beach."

Harley's lips compressed as if he were swallowing an entire dictionary of bitter words. "You do what you need to do," he finally managed to say. "If you don't investigate, that boy of mine might try to do it himself. But, please Penn, stay safe. If you run into any kind of trouble, promise me that you'll stop."

"I won't run into trouble." Famous last words? I hoped not.

"If by some miracle you can prove that Jody is innocent, I'll be forever grateful." He drew a shuddering breath. "If anyone is overdue for a miracle or even simply a turn of good luck it's that sweet boy of mine."

"Just call me the miracle-maker." I tried out a smile. "The master of the impossible."

"For Gavin's sake, I hope you're right," Harley said, grimly.

EIGHT

IMPOSSIBLE. THAT'S WHAT everything felt like the next morning as I dragged myself out of bed. It was a dark and obscenely early Saturday morning—five days before Gavin's first day of school—and far too early for rational people to be stirring.

Stella snored softly on the froufrou pink-and-white paisley dog bed I'd set up next to my own. She didn't wake up, not even when I started opening and closing dresser drawers as I donned pale pink shorts and a pale yellow cotton blouse.

A little while later, I moved around in the kitchen like a clumsy zombie, accidentally clanging my coffee mug against the counter and then banging the coffee pot against the stovetop. Bertie came out of her room, moving with a slight limp. I frowned. It wasn't the first time I'd seen her limp. She usually did it whenever she was tired or whenever she thought no one was looking.

"Are you okay?" I asked her.

"Of course I am." She wrapped her housecoat tightly around her. The limp disappeared. "What's going on?"

Her hairless cat, Troubadour, followed her. His tail, held high in the air, twitched as he glanced in my direction with the level of disinterest only a cat can manage.

"Althea is opening the nest this morning," I explained. Seventy days had passed since the mother turtle had laid her eggs there. "I told her I'd be there for her.

I also told her you'd make her favorite chocolate chip pancakes. Do you mind?"

"You want me to make pancakes in the middle of the night?" Bertie yawned into her hand before filling Troubadour's kitty bowl with dry kibble.

"No, it's morning. I need to leave now to meet her on the beach." While slipping on my sandals, I managed to slosh half my coffee out of my cup and onto the linoleum floor. Troubadour dashed over and started lapping at the puddle.

"Sorry about that." I put the mug on the kitchen table and fetched a damp rag.

Bertie took the rag from my hands. "I'll get this." She gently moved Troubadour away from the coffee puddle. "You go and help my daughter. I'll have the pancakes ready by the time you return."

I thanked her before stumbling sleepily out the door, banging into nearly everything I encountered.

A dim gray glow on the horizon hinted that the sunrise was on its way. I walked sleepily toward the beach. A wave crashed loudly against the sand a moment before I spotted Althea waiting at the beach walkover. Harriett and Lidia had already arrived. They were standing next to Althea, sipping what smelled like coffee. My mouth watered. I'd only had a couple of hours sleep over the last couple of days. If I'd been more awake, I wouldn't have spilled mine. But if I'd been more awake, I wouldn't need coffee so desperately.

Harriett offered a hushed welcome as I approached. No one seemed awake enough to converse as we made our way toward the carefully cordoned off nest. The three of them—official sea turtle volunteers—were wearing their bright yellow shirts.

On the way to the nest we passed Cassidy Jones'
ruddy red beach cottage. It looked dark and forlorn.
The rising sun cast an eerie amber glow on the pair of
large sliding glass doors that opened to the ocean side
deck. The glow resembled red eyes glaring out at us.

Seeing it made me shiver.

Althea looked at the house and then at me and then
back at the house. Her brows dipped lower. "You feel it
too, don't you? That's why you're shivering. I wouldn't
be surprised if in the next couple of days his restless
spirit starts making all sorts of trouble for us."

"Restless spirits? Don't be ridiculous," I snapped,
and then immediately regretted it. I was there to lend
support, not argue with Althea. In an attempt to soften
my blunder, I said the first thing that came into my head
while still transfixed by the house's red eyes. "Ethel told
me she and several others in town had seen Florence
Corners visiting Cassidy there, in his house. Ethel had
assumed Florence was meeting with Cassidy so often
because my mother is…looking to buy property on the
island to…um…"—I coughed—"be closer to me."

Althea whirled toward me. Her dark eyes widened.
"We both know Florence would never do that. I mean,
no offense to you. It's just that Florence, wicked woman
that she is, has made it clear what she wants and doesn't
want."

"She wants my building, she wants her mother's
money, and she doesn't want anyone to know she has
a daughter," I said.

Both Lidia and Harriett seemed to hold their breaths
as they watched me.

"Don't look so worried," I told them. "I'm not pining away waiting for Florence to love me. I've done

just fine without a mother in my life for the past thirty-seven years. Ethel may have seen Florence going into Cassidy's house, but we all know it wasn't to look at real estate."

"You mean to suggest… You mean that Mabel's daughter—that Florence…" Harriett sputtered, apparently unable to say the words aloud.

I had no trouble saying it. I crossed my arms over my chest. "I think my mommy was one of Cassidy's many lovers."

Harriett gasped.

"That makes her a suspect," Lidia's voice boomed.

"So it seems." A wicked part of me smiled as I said it.

"But she's so, so, so proper," Harriett barely managed to get out. "She presents herself as the finest hostess in historic Charleston. She runs the cotillion with an iron fist. She controls the invitation list for nearly all Charleston society events. One slip in propriety can get a person banned from Charleston's high society for life."

"I heard from Mama what she did to you," Althea said softly. She patted Harriett's arm, causing the older woman's face to turn every shade of red possible.

"What did she do?" Lidia demanded.

Harriett looked at Lidia and then at me. "I heard you promised that sweet little boy to get his mother out of jail, Penn. Why would you do something foolish like that? You know you're only going to break his heart. There's no question about who killed Cassidy."

Her clumsy attempt to change the topic surprised me. What could Florence have done to Harriett? And why didn't Harriett want to talk about it? "That's not what we were talking about," I said.

"It's what we should be talking about. You don't have

children. You don't understand how fragile they can be, especially young boys. He needs to start accepting the mistakes his mother made instead of clinging to the fantasy you're creating for him."

I knew her maneuver. I'd used it more than once myself. She was trying to upset me. She probably hoped I'd vehemently start defending myself and we'd all forget about whatever trouble she'd had with Florence.

Since I had no interest in playing her game, I shook my head and simply said, "You're right."

"What?" Harriett's head snapped back with surprise.

"What?" Lidia echoed as she cupped her ears.

"I said you are right. I should have never made a promise to Gavin I wasn't one hundred percent sure I could keep." What I didn't say was, crazy or not, I believed in Jody's innocence. It didn't matter that we all found her holding the murder weapon. It didn't matter that she'd shot me. And yes, that did sound crazy.

I kind of felt like a football fan who always roots for the losing team. At the start of every game, that fan honestly believes that tonight would be the night. Despite what we all thought we saw that night, Jody was innocent. For Gavin's and Harley's sake, I *needed* Jody to be innocent.

"You're right," I conceded, though. "I know how crushed Gavin will be if I fail him."

"Well, then." Harriett chewed her bottom lip until she realized what she was doing. She quickly straightened her spine. "We're not here to gossip like a bunch of old hens. We're here because the sea turtles need us."

We all followed Harriett as she marched toward the nest. I shot a questioning glance in Althea's direction. How had Florence hurt Harriett?

"*Later,*" she mouthed.

Soon we were standing silently around the area that had been carefully marked off with bright orange tape. We stared at the nest as if our combined forces of will could get the babies to emerge. Down the darkened beach, a dim light turned on in Bailey's house. Several minutes later he walked up to greet us. He was still dressed in his chef's uniform. His eyes looked tired.

"I was just getting in from work when I spotted the four of you out here," he said. He released his hair from the tight bun he wore at the nape of his neck. "The baby sea turtles, have they..." his voice trailed off.

Althea shuddered as she shook her head. I went to put a comforting arm around her shoulders, but Bailey was there before me. He pulled Althea close.

"I'm so sorry. I suspect every nest is special to you," he said. "What do we do now?"

"We see why they haven't hatched," she said with a resigned sigh.

The morning sunrise had tinted the ocean a shimmering red by the time she pushed her shovel into the sand and started digging into the nest. With great care, she dug deeper and deeper.

With each shovelful of sand removed, her expression grew grimmer and grimmer. She finally looked up at the rest of us. "The eggs aren't here."

"Coyotes?" Harriett asked.

"Raccoons?" Lidia asked.

"Maybe." Althea's brows furrowed. "Must have lost the eggs to a predator during a windstorm, otherwise one of our early morning beach patrol volunteers would have noticed and reported a disturbed nest. Predators make terrible messes. They would leave evidence."

I peered into the hole. The eggs simply weren't there.

"Are you sure the eggs were there in the first place?" Bailey asked. "I'd been reading about sea turtles. Apparently they sometimes crawl up onto the beach and return to the ocean without laying any eggs."

"Those are called false crawls," Lidia said in her booming voice.

"As soon as we find a new nest, we check to make sure eggs are present," Althea said. "And if a nest was laid where it's in danger of being damaged by a high tide—like this nest was—we'll move it to a more appropriate spot. I assure you, the turtle eggs were here, all one hundred and eight of them."

"And now it's empty," I said as I continued to stare into the slightly damp sandy hole.

Bailey's frown mirrored Althea's. "Mother Nature can be so cruel."

"Yes," she agreed while chewing on her thumbnail, "Mother Nature is cruel."

She sounded sincere, but I knew my friend well enough by now to recognize the slight increase in her tone and choppier cadence in her speech. Althea was lying. And I suspected I knew why. And I hated it.

NINE

"Mother Nature my foot," I said as we sat down around the kitchen table. Bertie had cooked enough chocolate chip pancakes to feed half the island. I piled my plate with a stack so high my shorts were going to feel tight all day. I then slathered the tower with maple syrup. Althea, on the other hand, took only two and opted to eat them dry.

If she hadn't been upset about the turtle nest, I would have called her a freak of nature. I didn't know what the secret ingredient Bertie used for these pancakes, but the results were amazing. How anyone could take only two was beyond me. And syrup was an essential component to a proper pancake breakfast. Everyone knew that.

"How is your leg, Mama?" Althea asked her mother.

Back in June a car had hit Bertie, leaving her with a badly broken leg. She'd been laid up for several weeks, healing while I went through one disastrous temporary employee after another. The cast had only recently come off. And Bertie returned to work in the shop a week before the doctor told her she should.

"It's fine." Although Bertie never complained, I'd noticed how she'd rub her calf at the end of a long day while grimacing in pain. And she limped whenever she thought no one was watching.

I didn't dare say any of that aloud. Althea had enough worries on her mind. The sea turtles needed all the help we could give them. She didn't have the time or spare energy to worry about her mother too. Not when I could do that for her.

For one thing, Bertie needed to stop working so hard at the shop. She needed to take more time for herself, time to allow her leg to heal. As I thought about how I could make that happen without resorting to hopeless temporary workers again, I took a bite of the pancakes. The chocolate chips, warm and melty, exploded in my mouth with a symphony of flavors.

"You used the Amar chocolates in this batch," I said, my brows shooting up into my hairline with surprise. The special Amar chocolates that we made in the shop had a flavor unmatched anywhere in the world: fruity and bitter with an undertone that tasted like the tropical rainforest where the beans were grown. It was a taste sensation that still took me aback.

"The occasion seemed to call for something special. Food, you know, can be a great comfort in distressing times." Bertie looked at me as she said it as if she was talking only to me. But perhaps I'd only imagined that, since a moment later she quickly put her hand on her daughter's shoulder. "I'm sorry about your turtles, Pumpkin. You think predators took them?"

"No, she doesn't think that at all," I answered for my friend. "I don't know why you're telling everyone that, Althea. Coyotes would have eaten the eggs and left the shells, right? Raccoons wouldn't have taken all hundred of them."

"One hundred and eight," Althea corrected as she stuffed a dry piece of her pancake into her mouth and swallowed. Had she even tasted the fusion of rich chocolate flavors?

"Then why are you telling everyone that you think a predator took the eggs?" I demanded as Bertie watched her daughter with a growing look of concern.

"Because that's exactly what I believe." She took another bite of the pancake. Again, she chewed and swallowed without bothering to enjoy its amazing flavors. "A predator took the eggs."

"We don't usually call *man* a predator," I said. "We call him a thief."

She looked up at me, her dark eyes wide. After a moment, she shrugged. "Thief. Predator. It doesn't matter what we call him…*or her*. The result is the same. An entire nest of eggs are gone. Gone under my watch."

Bertie shook her head in disgust. "Who would do such an evil thing?"

"There's a market for turtle eggs, Mama. It's considered a delicacy in some parts of the world. And an aphrodisiac. Whoever did this needed money."

"That's disgusting," Both Bertie and I said at the same time. No longer hungry, not even for pancakes with my precious Amar chocolate, I pushed my plate away.

"What are you going to do about it?" I asked.

Althea looked up at me with her tired eyes. Her expression hardened. "I'm going to make sure it doesn't happen again. Not here. Not on my island."

"We'll help you," Bertie said.

"Of course we will," I agreed, suddenly wishing I could clone myself, because as much as I wanted to do it all—run a shop, find a killer, and help my best friend catch an egg thief—there simply weren't enough hours in a day. But I needed to do it all. And I was clearly running out of time on all fronts.

"SOMETIMES THERE ARE things I really don't want to know," I said suddenly to Bertie.

Bertie and I had been working side-by-side in the Chocolate Box's kitchen ever since we'd finished breakfast. I'd invited Althea to join us. Not that I wanted to put her to work. I simply thought she could use the company right now. I'd never seen her look so dejected. She'd begged off my invitation, saying she had something she needed to go do and she wanted to get some sleep first.

So Bertie and I worked, barely saying anything until about a half hour before the shop opened.

"I don't want to hear the truth about that either, child. Makes my bones shudder to think one of our neighbors could steal those eggs. I don't want to know whose heart could be black enough to do such a thing."

"I agree," I said, "but that's not what I'm talking about."

"Then it's the murder that's bothering you, dear? You're afraid to learn the truth, because it might mean that Jody is guilty?"

"Yes, I'm worried I'm going to fail Gavin." I sighed. Jody had been holding the guns. The only evidence I had of her innocence was her insistence that she didn't kill anyone. And I suspected anyone in her position, guilty or not, would profess their innocence. "But that's not what I'm talking about either."

"Then spit it out already," Bertie set down the spoon she was holding and looked at me.

"It's the gun situation."

Her brows furrowed. "The gun situation?"

I nodded.

"Jody's gun situation?" Bertie asked.

"No. Not that." I swallowed. This was something I needed to know. I mean, I lived in the house with her. But what if she said she had a gun? What would I do? Could I live in an apartment where a deadly weapon was tucked away somewhere? Ever since Althea had told me that everyone in the South owned a gun, the worry that Bertie had a gun kept eating at me. I should be thinking about ways to prove Jody's innocence, but instead I was standing there obsessing over whether or not Bertie had a gun. "Oh heck, Bertie. Please tell me you don't own a gun."

She smiled and shook her head.

I felt such a flood of relief, I laughed. "Thank goodness."

"Mabel was the one who'd bought the gun," Bertie said. "It's still in the pantry behind the flour tin."

"In the kitchen?" It'd been behind the flour? Not locked up, but on a shelf where anyone could get it?

"It's a real pretty thing with a pearl handgrip." Bertie didn't seem to notice that I was suddenly having trouble breathing. She picked up the spoon she'd been using and started to stir the pecans for the sea salted chocolate turtles. I'd gotten close to perfecting the recipe, but it had never tasted quite right.

Bertie had taken one look at the recipe I'd been developing and immediately knew what changes needed to be made, including increasing the amount of the special Amar chocolate used. The results were stunning. The salty essence of the ocean swirled with a nutty tropical flavor. Sweet and salt, crunchy and smooth played like a symphony in my mouth. But none of that mattered because all I could think about was that my talented roommate kept a gun in the kitchen pantry.

She looked up at me and frowned. "Are you okay?"

"No. I'm not okay." I took several deep breaths before continuing. "There's a gun upstairs? And it's not locked in a safe or anything?"

"Yes, Mabel was real proud of it." Bertie still didn't seem able to grasp why I was upset, which was evident by what she said next. "Honey, I think I understand what's gotten you so riled up about a little handgun. You've been spending all of your time thinking about Jody and whether or not she shot her lover. And if she didn't own a gun, none of this would be an issue. I get that. I also get that you're worried that maybe she did shoot that Cassidy Jones fellow. But you've got to put all of those nerves aside." She wiped her hand on a towel before placing it on my shoulder. "I don't think you're crazy for trying to help Gavin. Whether you succeed or not, what you're doing for that boy will help him in the long run. You're showing him that people in the community care. You're showing him that he's not alone."

"Thank you." Hearing her say that meant the world to me. Even if she didn't understand my distaste for guns in general, her belief that I was doing the right thing calmed me down as effectively as a prescription anti-anxiety drug. Ready to get back to work, I reached for the chocolate molds shaped like baby sea turtles. They were stacked on one of the top shelves. I set them on the counter beside Bertie.

"I appreciate your support. But I do want to know one thing. Do you think Jody is guilty?" I asked.

She shrugged. "It's not my place to judge. That task is reserved for someone who resides on a higher plane."

"Oh, come on." I shot her a look that said I knew her better than that. She had her opinions, strong opinions.

"'Tis easier for a camel to fit through the eye of a needle…" she sang before continuing. "I remember a time years ago when a rabid possum took up residence at the shop's front door. It was hissing and snapping its jaws while foaming at the mouth, not letting anyone in or out. Hank had to come out and put the possum out of its misery. Jody often reminds me of that poor, angry creature."

I had a feeling Bertie wasn't done, so I didn't say anything as I moved across the room to where a bank of ovens lined the wall. I'd already measured and poured cacao beans into a large metal bowl. In the ensuing silence, I fetched six baking sheets and started to spread the beans on the sheets until none of them were overlapping.

The Chocolate Box wasn't just an ordinary chocolate shop. For nearly the past one hundred years, this tiny overlooked shop crafted its own chocolate directly from the bean.

"You have to agree that having Jody safely tucked away in jail makes life easier for the rest of us," Bertie said.

"That's true." I set the temperature on three of the ovens. Creating a smooth, flavorful chocolate was a multistep process that spanned several days. The first step, roasting of the raw cacao beans, would soon cause the fragrant chocolate aromas to rise up. A scent very similar to brownies baking in the commercial ovens occasionally made the island air smell extra sweet.

On the other side of the kitchen Bertie moved with efficient grace, despite the limp she kept trying to hide from those who loved her. She reminded me of a master violinist as her weathered hands poured melted chocolate into the sea turtle molds. A few moments passed. Bertie huffed. She wiped her hands on a white dish cloth that had been tucked into the tie of her apron before saying, "She didn't do it."

"What?" I asked.

"You heard me. You wanted to know what I thought. Well, this is it. She didn't do it."

"Really?" I turned my back on the chocolate beans roasting in the ovens. "You really think she's innocent? Why?" I thought I was the only one crazy enough to think it.

"Harley," she said.

"Harley? Why? What did he tell you?" I inched my stool toward her.

"Don't get all excited now. He didn't tell me anything. It's how Jody treats Harley that's telling. Death is much too quick, too final, for someone like her. That Jody-girl likes to keep her enemies close at hand so she can torture them. Just look at how she keeps her claws on Harley. Their marriage dissolved over five years ago."

"But with Harley, she was the one who'd cheated on him," I pointed out. "She was the reason their marriage fell apart. She wasn't the woman scorned."

"You think that matters to her? In her warped mind, the divorce is Harley's fault. I've heard her say as much to him more than once. If he'd been a better husband, if he'd been a better man, if he'd paid more attention to her she wouldn't have strayed. Nothing is ever her fault. She's a woman who in her own mind never makes mistakes. Why, she's utter perfection. It's the rest of the world that has failed her."

Bertie had a point. Jody *was* the kind of person who would have shot Cassidy's lover before shooting him. Which meant I really needed to find out who was with Cassidy in those moments leading up to his death.

The woman dressed in a turquoise muumuu on the beach. The one standing over his body. Screaming. Was she Cassidy's lover? Was she the one being serenaded by his smooth Jazz music? Even after he'd died, the music had played on. It'd been at least an hour before one of the police officers had entered Cassidy's home and turned off the stereo.

In all the excitement after finding Cassidy's body and getting medical attention for my shoulder, I didn't catch the screaming woman's name. Actually, I didn't remember seeing her at all after we'd called the police.

I reached into my back pocket and, after drawing a steadying breath, dialed a number I had hoped to never have to call again. Well, I didn't mind calling him for a friendly reason, like to invite him to a community picnic or a fundraiser hosted by the shop. But because of murder? No. He didn't approve of me poking my nose into police business, especially not into the business of a homicide detective.

"Gibbons," he barked into his cell phone. Wherever he was, it was noisy. The roar of machinery made my ear ache.

"Detective," I said, "there was a woman at the crime scene two nights ago. She was awfully upset. Perhaps she was one of Cassidy's…um…special friends?"

"Yes?" He sounded suspicious. But then again, he often sounded suspicious when he talked to me. "Why are you asking about her?"

"Why do you think?" I said because I hated to lie.

I then added, "The woman was so upset by Cassidy's death maybe I could send her some chocolates to help soothe her nerves. But I don't know her name."

He was quiet for a long while. The background machinery seemed to get louder. "What are you *really* up to?" he shouted into the phone.

He was a good detective, and I was a horrible liar. Which meant I had to tell him the truth, "I've been asking a few questions about the murder. It was all such a mishmash of happenings that night. I'm trying to put together in my mind what really happened."

"There's nothing to put together. There's nothing to investigate. The evidence—"

"Jody swore to her lawyer that she's innocent," I interrupted before he could start telling me about the mountain of evidence I needed to dismantle in order to get Jody out of jail.

The deafening sound of machinery suddenly got quieter. A bird sang. A horn honked. He must have stepped outside. "They all say that, Penn. You and your friends saw her running toward Cassidy's house after brandishing her weapon."

"She was running toward his neighbor's house," I corrected.

He huffed. "Y'all heard the gunshots. Y'all saw her holding the murder weapon. She even shot you when you confronted her. What other evidence do you need?"

"But there's a little boy, her son." I lowered my voice. "I promised him I'd get his mother out of jail before his school starts up next week."

"Aw, Penn, you shouldn't have done that." His voice gentled. "I've been doing this for more years than I care to admit. The children of the perpetrators suffer ever as much as the children of the victims. And there's not a damn thing you can do about it."

"But what if she's telling the truth? What if she is innocent? For her son's sake, I have to at least try to—"

"This case is as open-and-shut as they get. We're ticking off all the right boxes when it comes to the investigation. But I can tell you right now, we're not going to find anything that'll change the outcome. As tragic as it is for her son, Jody Dalton killed a man."

"If that's true, then you have no reason to get upset with me for asking questions around town," I said.

He growled much like Stella had growled at Althea last night. "You don't know what trouble you'll stir up when you start asking questions about people's personal lives. The victim was having multiple affairs. Often with married women. And doing who knows what else."

"I simply want to talk with the lady who was with Cassidy the night he died. She must have seen something. Certainly she gave you important information to help you with your investigation."

"I know you mentioned another witness, a woman, that night. But she wasn't at the crime scene when we arrived. Chief Byrd says the same thing. He didn't see her either."

Muumuu Woman had run off? "Who was she?" I wondered aloud.

"At this time, Penn, I don't know."

"Well, I know who she *could* be." My heart started to beat a little faster. "She could be our killer. She could be the one who owned that second gun, the gun that your ballistic tests show killed Cassidy. Jody could be telling the truth, you know. She could have picked up the second gun without thinking it'd just been used to murder a man."

Now, even more than before, I knew I needed to find her. I needed to find the woman in the flowered muumuu.

TEN

"Did we sell all of the salted sea turtles this morning?" I asked Bertie after the morning crowd had left and before the mid-afternoon crowd descended for their milkshakes.

When we'd opened, the display tray had held over fifty of the little treats. And now it was empty. We rarely sold out of any of our stock in one day, much less in one morning. But this was the first day we were selling them. And I'd posted a sign on the door explaining how the shop was donating fifty percent of the profits from the sale of the salted sea turtles to the Camellia Beach Turtle Watch Program. So it was possible that they could have sold out.

Bertie came over to the display case and peered inside. "I don't remember selling but a few of them."

"I only remember selling a few as well," I said.

I checked the cash register and the credit card receipts. There wasn't enough cash in the drawer or credited by any of the credit card companies to suggest that we'd sold even half of the chocolate turtles.

"You don't think someone stole them?" I tried to remember who had been in the shop earlier. It'd been the regular crowd. Hadn't it been? I wasn't sure.

Bertie looked at the display case again. "I can't imagine how anyone would have gotten away with taking the entire tray of turtles without someone noticing."

We looked for them in the storage coolers in the back of the store just in case one of us had inadvertently carried the tray of turtles to the back. They weren't there.

"Johnny Pane," I called to the painter who had become such a fixture in the shop lately I'd nearly forgotten about him. He was at his usual position behind the curtain of clear plastic draping and on top of a ladder, his brush moving with great care over the ceiling.

"Ma'am?" he called back down without altering his brush stroke. "What do you need?"

"Did you see anything odd happening over at the counter earlier today?" I asked.

"Odd, like how?"

"Like someone stealing chocolates out of the case?" Bertie called up to him.

He didn't answer right away. When he did speak, he spoke as if carefully drawing out each word, "Well…nothing…slithered across the ceiling. That's all I've been looking at. Can't say I noticed much else. Did something go missing?"

"A whole tray of somethings," Bertie said.

"I suppose we need to call Chief Byrd and report this." I was tempted to bite my tongue for saying it. The last thing I wanted to do was involve someone who believed I was cause of all trouble on the island. But he was the law around here, and he'd be angrier than a badger if we didn't call him.

Bertie scratched her head and huffed. "Yes, I suppose we'll need to tell him."

Neither of us moved. We simply stood there staring at each other while Johnny Pane continued his work on the ceiling.

"Why would someone steal just the salted sea turtles?" I looked at the display case again. None of the other trays were empty. I was still hoping to find an explanation for the missing chocolates because if we solved it, we wouldn't have to call the police chief. "Do you think it's a prank? It's got to be a prank."

"Honey, I don't know what to think." Bertie sat down on the stool behind the counter and rubbed her leg. "But I do know that you raise old Hank's blood pressure every time he sees you. Why don't you go run an errand while I put in the call to dispatch?"

"Are you sure?" I hated to leave her with the hassle of dealing with Chief Byrd.

"I'm sure. Go on with you now. I know you've been itching all morning to go looking for that woman who'd run away from the crime scene anyhow. And you're running out of time if you're going to have any hope of keeping that promise you made to Gavin."

I stripped off my apron so quickly, a seam ripped. I only felt a slight twinge of guilt at letting Bertie handle the police chief alone. After all, she was right. I had a murder to solve.

THE FIRST STEP in solving Cassidy's murder was simple. I needed to find Muumuu Woman. I needed to talk with her. I needed to find out why she'd left the crime scene. If she wasn't Cassidy's killer, she must have seen the gunman.

After leaving Bertie to deal with the stolen chocolate sea turtles, I hurried upstairs, clipped a leash to Stella's collar, and headed over to the Pink Pelican Inn. Harriett had been standing right next to the Muumuu Woman while she'd screamed loud enough for people in Portugal to hear. And Harriett knew pretty much everyone on the island. Certainly she'd recognized my key eyewitness. While Harriett didn't live at the Pink Pelican Inn, she did tend to spend most of her days with her friends who did live there.

The Pink Pelican Inn was a bright pink concrete-block one-story beachfront motor lodge from the 1950s. It served as a shabby punctuation at the end of Main Street. When I first saw the place, I pegged it as one of the worst eyesores I had ever seen. Now that I've lived in Camellia Beach for several months and learned to love the quirky lost-in-time feel of the island—I still thought it was an eyesore. But it's an eyesore with a purpose. Because it wasn't a high-end hotel, the cost of the rooms was ridiculously low. Many of the older residents used the motel as a *de facto* retirement home.

The thought that the fascinating islanders were able to live out their golden years on the beach, in a tight-knit, walkable community, and alongside young cash-strapped surfers made the eyesore one of my favorite places.

I walked under an eight-foot tall wooden cutout of a faded pink pelican that hung over the lobby's front entrance. The bird had an equally faded green fish tail sticking out of its oversized beak. And the sign tilted precariously to one side as if it'd had too much to drink.

Inside the lobby, several of the long-term residents were heatedly dissecting the latest town gossip from their perches on wicker rocking chairs. A lively bunko game was taking place at one of the tables.

I scanned the room, but didn't see either Harriett or Lidia.

Stella yelped happily and wagged her tail as I made my way over to Deloris, the hotel's desk clerk.

"Good morning!" I shouted. Deloris was notoriously hard of hearing.

Deloris' entire face lit up when she spotted Stella. "My little *szczeniak*!" she exclaimed in a booming voice that rivaled Lidia's. "Are you as feisty as ever?"

Stella barked and jumped up and down. She knew what was coming and looked forward to our visits with Deloris. The desk clerk reached over the counter and handed my little pup a chew stick that was nearly twice the size of her tiny head. With a growl, Stella ripped the treat out of Deloris' hands.

Deloris laughed. "Yep, my little puppy, you're as feisty as the first time I met you."

"She's calming down a little," I said even as Stella grred while she tore at the chew stick with her nubby little teeth. "Is Harriett or Lidia around this morning?"

"Who?" Deloris shouted.

"Lidia's out at the pool," a man in one of the rocking chairs answered for her.

"What?" a woman sitting next to him shouted.

"That's the new chocolate shop owner," another woman answered.

"I know that," the first woman said. "Everyone knows Penn. She brings us those lovely chocolates every Friday."

"Is it Friday already?" the second woman said.

"That was yesterday."

"What?" she shouted.

"Yesterday!" the other woman shouted back.

"That's when that Cassidy fellow got himself killed," the second woman said with a huff. "Heard she's investigating."

"What's there to investigate? Jody shot 'im," the man said.

The first woman smacked her lips. "That Cassidy liked to wrap himself in trouble. Watched everyone in town with those hawk eyes of his." She started rocking her chair harder. "Wouldn't be surprised if it were one of his victims that killed him."

"Ain't you listening to me?" the man shouted to the first woman. "Jody shot 'im."

She waved her hand as if trying to push him away and then grumbled something about not believing anything one hears on the news anymore. "Wouldn't be surprised to hear Ethel Crump pulled the trigger after what he'd done to her."

The second woman nodded in agreement. "She'd had good cause to kill him after the grief he'd caused her. That man…" She smacked her lips and started rocking with agitated vigor.

Ethel Crump? The woman who was older than the island's trees? Those women believed her capable of murder? That was interesting.

I moved to go question the women in the rocking chairs about Ethel when Deloris grabbed my arm. "That detective from the county came looking to talk with Lidia too," she said. "He's been by the pool with her for close to an hour."

"Really?" I said surprised by that.

While I wanted to know more about Ethel's troubles with Cassidy and I still wanted to talk with Harriett, I also needed to hear what Lidia was saying to Detective Gibbons and (more importantly) what Detective Gibbons was saying to Lidia. If he was certain he had the killer in custody, what brought him out here?

Nearly jogging, I made my way out onto the oceanside patio and pool area. Stella followed, dragging the oversized chew stick along with her. The pool, though not much larger than the size of an oriental rug, was clean and crystal clear. The rusty metal lawn chairs that surrounded the small pool offered incredible sweeping views of the Atlantic Ocean.

No one was in the water. The few tenants who'd braved the stifling heat had retreated to a cluster of lawn chairs under a canvas awning. The narrow strip of shade felt almost bearable when combined with the stiff sea breezes coming off the ocean.

Lidia had her back to the ocean. She was nodding as she spoke. Detective Gibbons perched on the edge of one of the lawn chairs as if worried the chair's ancient plastic straps wouldn't hold his weight. Or perhaps he was worried the chair's rusty metal rails would stain his crisply pressed suit pants. His back was to the motel wall. He held a small notebook in his beefy hands. His head tilted to one side as he listened intently to Lidia.

Much like Chief Byrd, Gibbons carried quite a bit of extra weight around his middle. However, unlike Byrd, Gibbons wore his weight like a pro. His light gray suit had been carefully tailored to fit his shape. Since it was already nearly ninety degrees out with close to one hundred percent humidity, he'd shed his suit's coat. It was carefully folded and hanging over the back of one of the empty chairs. His neatly pressed white shirt gleamed.

He continued to listen to Lidia and jot notes into his casebook as I walked up. But I could tell by the way his expression changed—a slight lift to one corner of his mouth—that he'd seen me.

"My bad Penny," he said without looking in my direction. "Why am I not surprised?"

"The name's not Penny," I said. "And you shouldn't be surprised because I called and warned you what I planned to do," I answered and then quickly added, "Wicked hot out, isn't it, Detective?"

While the Camellia Beach custom to talk about the weather before launching into any important business drove me crazy, sometimes (like now) I used it to my advantage. "You should follow the example of the police in Bermuda and wear shorts in the summer months."

His sharp gaze flashed in my direction. A ghost of a smile appeared. "No one wants to see my knees."

"Ooh! I think you'd look smart in Bermuda shorts," Lidia said in that booming voice of hers. "And you wouldn't have to worry about getting overheated."

He shook his head as he stood. "If you think of anything else, Ms. Vanderhorst, give me a call."

Startled by his movement, Stella dropped what was left of her chew stick and started barking. The detective had seen her antics enough times to ignore her bad behavior. He retrieved his jacket from the back of the chair and then started walking toward me. I quickly scooped up my little pup and held her tight to my chest to keep her from nipping at the hem of his pants.

Gibbons paused just long enough to say, "Don't forget what happened the last two times you stuck your nose where it didn't belong," before heading toward the motel's lobby.

"That sounded like a threat," Lidia said once Gibbons was gone.

"It wasn't a threat," I assured her. While the Charleston County detective didn't approve of my propensity to investigate happenings on the island, his concern for my safety made my heart feel all warm and squishy—a rare experience for me. My heart tended to stay prickly most of the time. "He actually worries about me. He worries about everyone on the island."

"You shouldn't hold your dog like that." Since Lidia's back was to the pool, she had to turn in her chair to face me. She was dressed in jeans shorts and an old T-shirt with a smiling cartoon dog on the front. Her jet-black hair had a purple tinge, which I hadn't noticed before. Her hair had been cut into an easy-to-manage pageboy style.

"I suspect I'm here to talk about the same thing Gibbons wanted to talk to you about." I walked over and took the chair Gibbon's had vacated so Lidia and I could talk without her having to twist into an awkward position.

"Your little dog," Lidia said with a nod in Stella's direction, "she's nervous. You shouldn't hold her like that. It's only making her feel even more powerless."

"I pick her up when I'm worried she might bite someone," I explained as I put Stella back on the ground.

"She bites?" Lidia frowned at my little pup. Stella looked back at Lidia and started barking so hard her front paws came off the ground with each high-pitched yip.

"Unfortunately, she does." I handed what was left of Stella's chew stick back to my greedy pup. "She's getting better. It's been over a month since she's bitten me."

Lidia's frown deepened. "She bites you? You're her owner, right?"

"Someone gave me her as a gift last winter." Stella gnawed at the chew stick while barking at the stern look Lidia was giving her.

Lidia shook her head. "Gift or not, you need to get your dog under control."

My cheeks burned. I might complain about Stella, but it rankled whenever others disparaged her behavior. I didn't know anything about her history. I'd received the full-grown papillon as a present from my thoughtless boyfriend this past winter because he'd thought she'd look good in a Gucci purse. The first thing she did when she met me was bite my nose.

While I'd gotten rid of the boyfriend (he'd considered dogs accessories and didn't know I've never owned a Gucci purse), I kept Stella despite (or perhaps because of) her flaws.

"I've never had a dog before. We're still working out how to get along," I explained while Stella continued to bark. Since she'd finished off her chew stick, I tossed her a piece of bacon.

Lidia looked me hard in the eyes. "What your dog needs is training."

"No kidding." I tossed the still barking Stella yet another piece of bacon. "Hush, now."

Thankfully, this last treat seemed to satisfy her. And since Lidia still kept her eyes on me and not on my little hellion, my little dog suddenly decided the older woman was no longer a threat. After finishing her treat, she started sniffing around the chairs in search of fallen scraps of food.

I glanced around to make sure Stella wasn't going to bother the other people relaxing under the awning. An older man had his chin to his chest as he snored away. A white-haired woman had her nose buried in a romance novel. She was so engrossed in what she was reading I didn't think she noticed either me or Stella. **And a young surfer dressed in board shorts was tap-**

ping away on his smart phone, equally oblivious to everything going on around him.

"Do you have some time to talk about what happened the other night?" I asked Lidia.

"That's what the detective wanted to talk about. I suppose I don't mind rehashing things with you too. Maybe the more we talk about it the less I'll feel horrified by the thought of a man being murdered practically in front of us." She shook her head unhappily. "It was just…awful."

"It was." I shivered at the memory. "It must have even been worse for that other woman who must have seen it all happen. I can still hear her screams. Do you know who she is?"

"Gibbons wanted to know the same thing," Lidia said. I was glad to hear the detective had taken my phone call seriously. Gibbons was one of the good guys. He wouldn't rush an investigation just because all of the evidence made it appear as if Jody was the killer.

"Of course I saw the woman," Lidia said. "We all did. But I didn't recognize her. Perhaps Harriett knows her."

"Do you know where I can find Harriett today?"

Lidia didn't. She suggested I look for her over at the Dog-Eared Café. "Now that Cassidy is gone, she can lunch there again."

"Because of Cassidy she couldn't have lunch there?" I asked. "Why was that?"

"I don't know the details. But I heard it had something to do with a fallout she had with Cassidy. I think it was over something Harriett's husband had done… or not done. Anyhow, as I said, I don't know the details. All I know is that Cassidy liked to take his lunch at the Dog-Eared, so Harriett stayed clear of the place. I tended to keep away from anyplace Cassidy frequented as well."

"You knew Cassidy?" That surprised me. Lidia had moved into town after I had. And I thought I'd been doing a good job getting to know all of the residents.

She made a face as if she'd bitten into a piece of rotten fruit. "I wish I'd never met the man. Cassidy was supposed to find me an affordable rental. He'd promised he could do it too. He'd showed me a small cottage at the far end of the island, down near Bubba's place. It fit my budget. I was all ready to sign the papers and everything. But at the last minute, he called and told me he'd rented the cottage to someone else."

"That doesn't sound right. Do you think he found someone who was willing to pay a higher rent?"

"That was what I thought at first. But I drove by the cottage just last week and saw it sitting empty. Kind of steamed me up. Why lie to me like that? I needed a place to live. I can afford better than the Pink Pelican. Don't get me wrong, I've enjoyed the community here, but I want to set up a small animal rescue organization on the island. In order to do that, I need a home with land. I need a rental that allows pets, like that cottage did. It was perfect."

Her brows crinkled as she looked down and frowned at Stella. My little dog had started to growl at a large green beetle carrying a potato chip on its back. "You really need to get your dog trained. Her behavior shows she's not happy."

"I've been working with her. She's still getting used to her new surroundings," I said.

"Honey, you need a professional to help you. Look, before I retired, I trained dogs," Lidia's booming voice got Stella barking again. "One thing I learned in all the years I've worked with owners is that dogs are happier if they understand what's expected of them."

"Aren't we all?" I said.

"Tell your dog what you expect of her," Lidia commanded. "If you don't want her to bark, tell her that."

I obeyed. Stella didn't.

Lidia stood up and stared down at my barking little dog. Stella growled.

"I know you," Lidia said. "I've met plenty of dogs like you over the years."

"Do you think you can train her?" I asked. It seemed as if Stella's unfriendly behavior was ingrained in her DNA.

"She won't ever be as tame as Lassie. But, yes, I can train her." With a click of her tongue inside her cheek, she got Stella's attention.

"Sit," Lidia's loud barking voice had softened, but it sounded as commanding as ever.

Stella barked even louder.

"No, sit." Lidia said with even more authority. She then did something with her hand. Amazingly, Stella stopped barking and parked her fluffy tail on the ground.

"You trained her to respond to a command that quickly? Unbelievable."

"Not unbelievable. Your dog has had some training, which is good. It'll give us someplace to work from."

She then took the leash from me and worked with Stella, having my pup walk alongside her and sit at various intervals.

By the time we called it quits, Stella was still barking at anything that startled her. But her barks were less emphatic and stopped whenever Lidia gave her "The Look." It was a look that said "I mean business."

"She's trainable," Lidia concluded when she handed the leash back to me. She then looked me up and down before adding, "I wonder, however, if you are."

I laughed.

Lidia didn't.

After saying my goodbyes, I was taking my leave when the lounging surfer looked up from his phone as I walked past his chair. "If you're looking into Cassidy's murder, there is someone you should talk to." He glanced down at his phone before adding, "But perhaps you shouldn't."

"If you know of someone who can help shed light on what happened, you have to tell me." Stella yipped twice as if agreeing with me.

"Fletcher Grimbal. Me and my bros were all hanging out at the Low Tide about a week ago when Cassidy Jones comes strolling in as if he owned the world. He was flashing his unnaturally bleached smile and swishing his long hair around like he was an aging movie star. He didn't even notice that most of the bar had moved away from him."

The Low Tide was a gritty bar and grill on the marsh that turned downright rowdy after dark. The place also served some of the best seafood in the Lowcountry.

"We'd all gone back to our drinking when we heard a shout. That Cassidy creep had apparently flipped his long hair into Fletch's drink. Fletch went ballistic, shouting with the stutter he's had for as long as I can remember growing ever more pronounced. He wanted Cassidy to buy him a new drink. Cassidy refused. People started gathering around, expecting a nasty fight."

The surfer chuckled to himself. "Instead of throwing a punch, Cassidy slapped Fletcher. And darned if Fletch didn't then slap Cassidy back. This went on for a while until the entire bar was laughing. Two grown men in a slap fight. It was ridiculous. Fletcher tried to get away, but Cassidy kept following him, slapping him in the face."

"And everyone kept laughing," I guessed.

"It was funny." He chuckled some more. "And Fletch was slapping back. They looked like a couple of sea lions with their arms flailing around like that."

"And Fletcher didn't like the laughing?" Lidia asked.

"Oh no, ma'am, he didn't. His face had turned redder than a cherry. And his stutter grew so bad no one could understand him. That's when Cassidy started laughing, too."

"What did Fletcher do?" I couldn't imagine that it ended well.

"He ran out of there like a whipped dog," the surfer said. "You would have thought that would have been the end of it. But I heard a few days later that Cassidy had pressed assault charges against Fletcher. Landed the guy in jail for the day, which wasn't the worst thing. The worst thing was that Fletcher lost his job as manager at the Grilled to Perfection restaurant for missing work. And now he has no job and is having to pay legal fees to keep his butt out of lock up." He shook his head. "If anyone wanted Cassidy dead, Fletch did."

ELEVEN

ALTHOUGH WHAT I'D learned at the Pink Pelican Inn was all good information, I still needed to talk with Harriett. Hopefully, she could help me find Muumuu Woman. I was growing more and more convinced the woman who'd fled the crime scene held the key to finding what I needed to prove Jody innocent of Cassidy's murder. As Lidia had predicted, Harriett Daschle was sitting at a small metal table located on the patio of the dog-friendly Dog-Eared Café. Harley and the president of the business association, Bubba Crowley, were sitting on either side of her. None of them looked happy, which was surprising. The Dog-Eared Café served the most delicious breakfasts and lunches. How anyone could frown after a masterpiece of a meal had been placed in front of them was beyond me.

Remembering at the last minute to practice the training tips Lidia had given me, I walked confidently over to their table while constantly rewarding Stella with bacon treats *before* she could start barking. Amazingly, the technique seemed to be working. Stella trotted beside me with her tongue hanging out the side of her dainty mouth as she drooled over the anticipation of her next taste of bacon.

"Sit," I said with the commanding voice Lidia had insisted I use. Stella looked at me, yipped, and then started to lick up crumbs from under Harley's chair.

Alarmed, Harley lifted his feet from the ground.

"Good afternoon," I said. "Another scorcher today, isn't it?"

Both Bubba and Harriett seemed pleased I was adopting the island way of chatting about the weather before business. Bubba launched into a lecture on the long history of August heat waves in Camellia Beach. Harley, on the other hand, gave a worried look at Stella and then at me.

"Got off the phone with Gibbons not ten minutes ago." Harley rudely cut off Bubba's lecture. "He asked me to talk with you, Penn, and remind you how danger-ous murder investigations can be. He made it sound as if he thought I had any sway over your actions."

"I made a promise to your son," I reminded him. Stella looked up at me and barked. I tossed her a treat. "I'm going to do my best to keep that promise."

He didn't argue with me like I'd expected. Instead he turned to frown at the glorious plate of baked floun-der sitting untouched in front of him. "Gibbons made it sound as if you've already gotten yourself in over your head," he said. "He doesn't want to see you get hurt. I don't want to see that either."

"I'm fine. I'm talking with upstanding citizens like Harriett, here. You don't think Harriett is going to do me harm, do you?"

"Of course not," he said rather quickly. His shoulders relaxed a bit. But his voice still sounded gruff. "I appre-ciate what you're trying to do. Helping Gavin and me. But at the same time I don't want to give Gavin false hope. The evidence—"

"I'm simply asking a couple of friends a few ques-tions," I put my hand on his shoulder.

"Yes, but Cassidy seemed to attract unsavory people like flies to a dish of honey. The man was a ball of slime."

"I'm fine. I promise. Friends...like all of us." I smiled at Harriett and Bubba. "We're all friends." My heart started to pound. Harley and I were friends. That's right. We were still just friends. If only I could convince my heart of that. Whenever I got near him, that silly organ would start to perform all sorts of calisthenics like jumping and sprinting around as if the devil were chasing it. I cleared my throat, pretending I'd been struck by a sudden case of allergies.

"Harriett," I said and cleared my throat again, "do you have a minute to talk about last night?"

"I can't stay." Harley dropped some meat from his plate for Stella before putting his feet back on the ground. He pushed back his chair. "I've got a meeting in ten minutes." He looked at me and heaved a deep sigh. "Be careful, Penn. Please, be careful."

With that, he paid for his untouched food and left.

"Do you need to go after him?" Bubba asked.

"No," I said a little too quickly, which made my silly heart sigh like a lovelorn heroine in a gothic novel. "What would I say to him if I did?"

"You'd tell him how you feel," Bubba said.

"Just like how you've opened up with Bertie?" I didn't give him a chance to answer. "Oh, right. I've forgotten. You won't even talk to Bertie. And it's not the same between Harley and me. I haven't been pining for him for nearly half a century. I haven't been pining for even ten minutes. We're just friends."

Bubba and Harriett exchanged knowing glances.

Small towns, I grumbled to myself with a bit of a

sneer on my lips. *The locals around here are too concerned about other people's personal business.* But I
supposed I couldn't be too upset about it. I planned to
make that annoying island trait work for me in finding
Cassidy's killer.

"Please," Harriett said, "join us."

I thanked her and then slid into the chair Harley had
vacated. "I heard you never dined here because Cassidy
often ate here. What happened between the two of you?"

For a brief moment it looked as if she was silently
repeating my thoughts on how secrets had a way of becoming public knowledge in small towns. She quickly
regained her composure and smiled serenely first at
Bubba and then at me. "There's no possible way I could
be a suspect, dear. I was running alongside you down
the beach and then behind you when Cassidy was being
shot."

That was true. I probably didn't need to know the
painful details about what Cassidy had done to make
her feel uncomfortable around him. "He wasn't the kind
of person who blackmailed others, was he?" I asked.

"My heavens, no," she exclaimed as she started nervously twisting and untwisting her cloth napkin. She
quickly realized what she was doing and settled her
hands in her lap. "Certainly, you have some other lines
on inquiry you can follow."

"I do. I do." I was sorry I'd embarrassed her. I was
sorry she'd had troubles with Cassidy that had caused
her to change where she took lunch. I was sorry that
she'd had troubles with my mother that had caused her
to lose her position in Charleston society. And even
though the troubles she'd faced probably didn't have
anything to do with why Cassidy was murdered, I still

couldn't help but wonder about them. But I knew I needed to stay focused. Instead of asking her about any of that, I said, "I've been trying to find the lady who was standing next to Cassidy's body."

"The one who wouldn't stop screaming?" Bubba asked.

"You heard about her?" I knew I shouldn't have been surprised, but I was.

"Lidia was talking about her this morning," Bubba said.

I turned to Harriett. "You were comforting the poor distressed woman. Do you know who she is?"

Harriett looked down at her lunch, a large bowl heaped full with spinach greens, walnuts, dried cranberries, apple slices, and plump fresh shrimp. "I didn't get a good look at her." She viciously stabbed a pile of baby spinach with her fork. "Why don't you ask that detective friend of yours to share her name with you?"

"He doesn't know it. She left before any of the authorities had a chance to talk with her. Sounds kind of suspicious, don't you think?"

"Sure does to me," Bubba grabbed a sweet potato French fry from his plate and dragged it through a ketchup puddle. "Sounds mighty suspicious, especially considering how the man was shot in the heart and all. That's got to be the work of a woman."

Both Harriett's head and mine snapped to attention.

"You can't be serious." Harriett tapped the tip of her finger on the table. "He was shot in the heart, so it had to be a woman who shot him? That's what you want to sit here and tell us?"

Bubba threw his meaty hands in the air as if surrendering. But what he said next didn't sound as if he was backing down at all. "It's what happened, isn't it? He fooled around with the wrong woman, and she killed him."

"Bubba Crowley, I'll have you know that a woman scorned would want her man to suffer and to suffer badly," Harriett said, echoing what Bertie had said. She sat back and sipped her sweet tea. "Such a woman wouldn't let her man get away with something as quick a death as a gunshot to the heart. If we hadn't seen Jody there with the gun in her hand, I'd be betting all of my money that a man had his finger on the trigger."

"What would a man want to kill Cassidy for?" Bubba cried. He dredged another sweet potato fry through his ketchup. "He was a kind of folk hero for us hopeless bachelors."

"A non-bachelor then," Harriett said. "Everyone knew Cassidy preferred his lover *du jour* to already be entangled in a serious relationship. Took the pressure off him."

"Do you think a jealous husband shot Cassidy?" I asked. "Did the woman in the muumuu say something to you last night about seeing someone else with a gun?"

Harriett sipped some more of her sweet tea. "No, honey. We all saw Jody with the gun. I'm just saying the way he died makes me think a man could have shot him." She took another slow sip of her tea. "But then again, maybe Jody simply missed the vital organ she'd been aiming for and accidentally hit his heart."

"Oh." And *ewwww*! "I'd still like to talk with that woman, just to find out what she saw. Are you sure you can't tell me who she is?"

Harriett shook her head so hard her Teflon sprayed curls actually bounced. "Afraid I can't."

"I still don't understand why she didn't stick around and talk with the authorities," Bubba said. But even as he'd said it, a look of understanding dawned on his face. "She's married." In his excitement, he waved the ketchup soaked sweet potato fry he was holding. Ketchup leaped off the fry and landed on my shoulder. "It might be dangerous to go looking for her, Penn." He then waved the fry in Harriett's direction, flinging even more ketchup. "That's why you're not telling us about her, Harriett, isn't it?"

"Either put that fry in your mouth or set it down, Bubba." Harriett dipped her napkin in the glass of water the restaurant had provided and dabbed at the red ketchup stain on her chest. I grabbed the napkin Harley had left and wiped my bare shoulder clean.

"Sorry." Bubba stuffed the sweet potato fry into his mouth. "But that's why you're not telling us about her, isn't it?" he asked as he chewed.

Harriett shrugged. "Maybe the woman figured there were enough eyewitness accounts of the shooting that the police wouldn't need to hear what she saw. Maybe she didn't have the energy to face the police after seeing Jody murder Cassidy."

"Or maybe she's the owner of that second gun Jody was holding," I said. "That second gun wasn't registered to Jody. And Jody insists she's innocent."

Harriett snorted. It was an unladylike sound, and surprising coming the refined first lady of Camellia Beach. "We all saw Jody holding two guns. Jody lost her mind and shot Cassidy. It's just that simple. The woman you're looking for won't be able to tell you anything different."

I leaned closer to her. "Bubba's right, isn't he? You know who that woman is."

Harriett shrugged.

"And you're really not going to tell me her name?" I couldn't believe it. "You're really not going to help me do this for Gavin?"

"No, I'm not."

Bubba's jaw dropped open.

So did mine.

TWELVE

"IF YOU ASK ME," Johnny Pane said as he dragged his brush across the ceiling, "someone doesn't like that you're asking questions."

"What's that?" I asked somewhat distractedly. The store was about to close for the day. Since the weather continued to be hot and sticky, the Chocolate Box had another busy afternoon selling its milkshakes. As closing time approached, Bertie had given up trying to hide her limp. As soon as I'd noticed, I sent her up to the apartment to take some of her prescription pain pills and to put her leg up.

The work at the shop was too much for her. I needed to get us additional help. But how? And who? I needed to find someone with experience in food service. I needed someone who wasn't a complete disaster at the register or with the customers. I'd had so many bad experiences with temporary workers when Bertie's leg was still in the cast, I was feeling gun shy at the thought of trying again.

"The theft, Ms. Penn," Johnny said as his brush moved at a slow, measured pace. "Do you reckon it's meant to distract you from asking questions about Cassidy's murder?"

"Is that what Chief Byrd thinks?" I asked. The shop had been so busy all day that I hadn't had a chance to talk with Bertie about what happened when she'd reported the theft to the police chief. We'd been too focused on filling milkshake orders to think about anything else.

Johnny Pane chuckled. "Old Hank thinks it's a prank."

"I think so too," I said. "It has to be."

"Timing is suspicious, don't you think?" he said and then quickly added, "Not that I'm telling you your business or anything."

Johnny was right. The timing was suspicious. And I'd be a fool to think it was unrelated. But if the thief thought stealing a few chocolates from my display case would stop me from helping a little boy get his mother back, well, obviously the thief was someone who didn't know me very well.

"Whoever did this could steal all of the chocolates out of the case, and I will still continue to ask my questions." Nothing would get me to stop this investigation.

It felt too personal. Whether Jody was flawed or not. A child needs his mother.

Florence. I sighed. I needed to call my mother. I needed to ask her about what she was doing with Cassidy and if she knew anything about his death.

I stared at my cell phone. Her number was in the contact list. But I couldn't seem to get my finger to press on her name. She'd made it clear that she didn't want anything to do with me, that she didn't want a relationship or contact from me of any kind. But this was for Gavin.

I swallowed my discomfort and slammed my finger against the screen to dial her number. After a few rings, it clicked over to her voicemail. I left a brief message, telling her that I needed to talk with her right away.

I then looked back up at Johnny Pane as he stood

on his ladder while he finished painting one corner of the shop. He knew Cassidy. Perhaps he could help answer some of my unanswered questions about the murdered man.

"Who do you think killed Cassidy Jones?" I asked him.

His brush came to an abrupt halt. "I already told you, he was a cancer to this town. Jody did us a favor by killing him."

"I don't think Jody killed him," I said.

"I know that's what you think," he sounded disappointed by that. "We all know that."

"What did he have over you?" I abruptly asked him. Should I add my painter to the suspect list? It seemed like a stretch. I had a hard time imagining Johnny Pane moving fast enough to murder Cassidy and make his getaway before we'd arrived on the scene.

"I didn't kill him," he said, his voice turned sharp. "I was having dinner with my daughter's family at Grilled to Perfection that night. It was her husband's birthday. We were out so late, she had me sleep over in her guest room after dinner. You can call her and verify that if you need to. And that's all you need to know about me and Cassidy, isn't it?"

"I'm not trying to upset you, and I don't care about spreading gossip about anyone. I simply need to get Jody home to Gavin before Thursday morning. And if I'm going to do that, I need to get the police to start investigating the other people Cassidy hurt."

He gave a sharp nod and went back to his painting.

"Do you know anything about Ethel Crump and her dealings with Cassidy?" I asked him. "I heard someone at the Pink Pelican Inn suggesting that Ethel should be a prime suspect."

"Cassidy was suing Ethel," he said.

"He was?"

"He's sued practically everyone in the town." He dipped his brush into his paint can.

"But why was he suing Ethel?"

"Because he hit her cat with his car."

"Wait." Johnny Pane had to be confused about things. "Don't you mean *she* was suing *him*?"

He shook his head. "No, ma'am. Don't mean that at all. He claimed that Ethel's beloved cat shouldn't have been roaming loose on the street. He was suing for damages caused to his car."

"What?" I could barely believe what I was hearing.

"That Harley fellow of yours agreed to defend Ethel against the lawsuit pro bono." Harley wasn't mine, but I didn't bother to correct him. "Ethel was terribly worried about what would happen if she lost the case. Cassidy claimed that old clunker he drove was a priceless antique."

"And a judgment against her could bankrupt her?" I asked.

He nodded as he started to climb down the ladder. "She barely gets by on what little she receives each month from her husband's retirement account and from Social Security. Even a small judgment against her could leave her homeless."

"But she's nearly as old as the island," I said. "I can't imagine she's a suspect. She's so...so sweet."

"The people around here do love her," he said as he started to slowly clean his brushes. "They love her nearly as much as they loved your grandmother."

I doubted Ethel could even hold a gun with those weak hands of hers. So even if she had a good motive, I couldn't believe her guilty. And with Ethel and Johnny Pane cleared of the crime, that left me with no real suspects other than Jody and the mysterious muumuu woman Harriett was protecting.

And Fletcher Grimbal.

I'd nearly forgotten about him. Cassidy had cost Fletcher his livelihood and, if Fletcher loses his criminal court case, Cassidy's actions could cost Fletcher his freedom.

"Do you mind locking up behind you?" I asked as I hung up my apron. I knew from experience it would take Johnny Pane at least an hour to clean those brushes of his and to put away his paints.

He readily agreed. He'd locked up before, so asking him to do so tonight wasn't that unusual.

I knew what I needed to do. I needed to find both Fletcher Grimbal and my elusive woman in the muumuu. Which meant I needed to take a trip to the seedy Low Tide Bar and Grill—where islanders with the deepest, darkest secrets tended to congregate.

Before I could walk out the door, Johnny Pane called out to me, "If you keep doing what you're doing, Penn, if you keep asking questions about the secrets Cassidy had gathered I fear for you. Whoever stole your chocolates might feel forced to do something worse."

THIRTEEN

I HATED MOVIES where the heroine would do something incredibly stupid and dangerous like walk into a dark basement knowing there was a chainsaw-wielding killer on the loose. "Get a brain already, you stupid ninny!"

I didn't want anyone to think I was a stupid ninny. I wasn't! And while I felt confident in my own self-defense skills, I had enough good sense to know I shouldn't wander into the Low Tide Bar and Grill alone. I needed backup.

My heart had beat triple-time when I called Harley. That everyone in town apparently thought of him as *my* Harley must have been rubbing off on me because I found myself starting to think of him that way too. And truth be told, I sure wouldn't mind him becoming mine (at least temporarily.)

I had also talked with Bertie about my plans for the night. Harley would need someone to watch Gavin while he was out sleuthing with me.

Amazingly, both Bertie and Harley readily agreed to help. In a strange way, I felt disappointed when they'd agreed so quickly. Had I wanted them to talk me out of going to the seedy bar? That would be crazy, right?

I firmly told myself I wasn't stalling when I decided to take Stella for one more walk that night, just moments before leaving for the Low Tide. I was simply being a responsible dog owner. Stella wagged her fluffy tail as

I snapped her leash to her collar. Troubadour, watching from his perch on the back of the sofa, sniffed loudly.

I led Stella down the narrow trail that snaked behind the building and paralleled the grassy marsh. My little dog ran this way and that while she barked and had a grand time chasing the tiny black fiddler crabs.

I was about to turn back toward home when the wind abruptly changed directions and started rushing toward a line of thick dark clouds that were advancing on the horizon. Thunder rumbled low and long in the distance. It sounded like a passing train.

Stella's ears perked up.

"Get her attention," Lidia's voice boomed as the older woman emerged from the bushes.

I jumped. Stella spun around, the hair on her hackles raised with alarm.

"Toss her a treat," Lidia ordered.

Nodding furiously, I fumbled with the treats. By the time I'd managed to get the bacon out of the baggie, Stella had already started barking hysterically at Lidia's sudden appearance.

"Hush," I said and tossed my little dog the bacon. She gobbled it up. Bacon was, after all, her favorite food in the world. But she didn't let a little chewing stop her from barking at Lidia and the coming storm. She did a little dance, stomping her tiny feet on the sandy path while tugging at the leash.

I couldn't really blame her. Lidia had startled me as well. "What are you doing here?" I had to shout the question in order to be heard over the barking.

"Bertie had said I could find you here," Lidia said in her loud voice. "I came by to help you with those exercises I gave you."

"Stella, calm down," I said as I tossed her another piece of bacon. She gobbled it and started barking harder. Her tugging on the leach grew stronger.

"Come on, Stella." I tried to make my voice sound happy. Excitement and distraction, Lidia had told me sometimes works. "Let's go this other way."

My silky pup remained (dare I say it?) doggedly determined to stand her ground and bark until she went hoarse.

"If you want her to listen to you, you have to stop being so scared," Lidia demanded.

"Scared? I'm not scared of Stella." I wasn't scared of anything.

"Then tell her to sit," Lidia commanded.

I did.

Stella kept barking.

"She won't obey until you get over your fear." Lidia sounded as if she was barking too, which only made me more frazzled.

Was the woman daft? Was she not paying attention? "I'm not afraid of dogs," I said carefully enunciating each word to make sure she heard me.

Stella tugged on the leash. Her barks had grown even more frantic. She started tugging so hard, I was afraid she might hurt herself. The last thing I wanted was for her to get hurt.

"Stella!" I yelled. "Sit!"

"Don't shout at her," Lidia's voice still boomed, but she'd gentled her tone. "Stay calm. Stay brave. You don't have to be afraid."

"I'm not scared," I had to shout over my noisy dog.

"Yes, Penn, you are."

"You think I'm scared?" I gestured toward my barking beast. "You think I'm scared of a dog that isn't much larger than the palm of my hand?"

Lidia took the leash from me. With a smooth hand gesture and a competently given command, she had Stella sitting by her side. And she'd done it without pulling on the leash. My little dog still shivered with nervous energy as she kept her oversized brown eyes in constant motion. But she was obeying.

In that moment, I hated Lidia.

"Penn," Lidia said with a sigh. "I know you're frustrated. I know you might not be ready to hear what I'm going to tell you, but I'm going to say it anyhow. Just listen. Think about it. Wait until tomorrow to tell me I'm wrong and crazy. Okay?"

"I simply need more practice," I grumbled.

"I have thirty years of experience working with dog owners. Just hear me out."

I pressed my lips together and gave a sharp nod.

"You're scared." She held up her hands before I could tell her...*again*...that I wasn't afraid of anything. "Yes, you're brave when it comes to investigating murders. And you're brave when it comes to running a chocolate shop with very little experience in the kitchen. But you're terrified to let yourself bond with anyone, not even with a dog that weighs less than a sack of groceries. I've seen it before, Penn. You won't get results with Stella until you let her into your heart."

"She's just a dog," I said.

"True. But dogs feel more deeply than humans. And the sensitive ones can sense things humans can't." She smiled down at Stella. "Your Stella might act all tough, but she's just as nervous as you are. What she needs is for you to stop being scared. She needs for you to let her into your heart. She needs you to show her that you can and *will* care for her."

"I do care for her." How could Lidia think I didn't? "I wouldn't be trying so hard with her if I didn't care."

"Of course you care," Lidia softened her voice even further. "If I thought you didn't care for Stella, I'd be trying to convince you to give her up." She held up her hands. "I'm not telling you to give her to someone else. I'm telling you that you need to stop worrying that the people and animals in your life are going to abandon you. Look at your little dog."

Stella was still sitting next to Lidia, but her large brown eyes were now trained on me. Why wouldn't her eyes be trained on me? I was the one with the bacon.

"She's a spaniel. And all spaniels deep down, no matter the size, want to please their owners. Stop worrying that she's going to end up hating you. Stop worrying that you're not good enough. She's a dog. All she cares about is making you happy. Give her a soft word and feel confident in your ability to take care of her, and she'll feel confident too."

I stared at Lidia as if she'd just told me that Stella was an alien from Pluto, which totally should still be a planet. She believed Stella misbehaved because I was insecure? She thought my abandonment issues made my dog bark like a mad dog and bite anyone who tried to get close to me?

Good gracious, was Lidia right? I wanted to love and be loved. But was I so scared of being rejected that I self-sabotaged all of the relationships in my life? No, she was wrong. I'd grown. I'd changed.

I'd been so proud of myself that I'd finally let down my barriers when it came to letting Althea and Bertie close to me. But I hadn't done that at all, had I? They were the ones who were tough enough to laugh off my attempts to keep them at arms' length. They were the ones who had put up with my prickly moods while working their way past the barriers I'd spent a lifetime erecting.

Even now, I continued to find ways to make them prove that they aren't playing me for a fool. I continued to make them prove they truly loved me.

"Stella," I whispered. I crouched down and reached out my hand. It wasn't the smartest thing to do. Fingers, in Stella's mind, were the perfect size for chomping. She leaned forward, sniffed my fingers, and then as if sensing something important was happening looked up at me with those expressive brown eyes of hers. "I still think Lidia is crazy. I'm not scared, but... I... I do have some work to do when it comes to relationships. I'm going to try to do better."

She may not have understood the words, but she seemed to like the tone. Her fluffy tail started to wag. She licked my fingers...then chomped down. Hard.

"Son-of-a—!" I curled my hand into a fist to keep her from biting any other part of my hand.

She yip-yipped as she danced around me. Her white fluffy tail wagged a little faster. Her dark brown eyes seemed to sparkle with mischief. Was she...was she *laughing* at me?

That little imp.

My imp.

I looked up at Lidia, who was shaking her head. "I wouldn't trade her for the world," I said.

Bites and all, I loved my little dog.

Now I simply needed to learn how to let her…and everyone else in my life know that it was safe for them to love me.

FOURTEEN

"READY TO GO?" Harley asked a little while later when I answered the apartment door to find him leaning against the jamb. Dressed in a light gray T-shirt that pulled tight across his muscular shoulders, a pair of relaxed-fit khaki pants, and leather loafers with no socks, he looked nearly as delectable as a scrumptious piece of chocolate. Did that scare me? Yeah, I hated to admit, it did.

Gavin scooted under his father's arm as he hurried into the apartment. He mumbled a hello in my direction as he passed, making a beeline for the kitchen where Bertie was preparing to bake a batch of chocolate chip cookies. Troubadour made a happy sound that was a cross between a meow and a purr when he spotted his young friend.

Stella, who'd also noticed Harley and Gavin, had a completely different reaction. With a low growl in her throat, she darted across the room to confront the pair of intruders.

Troubadour jumped out at poor Stella and swatted my pup across the nose. Stella stopped and yelped. After a few stunned seconds, she started barking while running in several tight, frustrated circles before disappearing into my bedroom. I followed her and comforted her for several minutes my while she sulked in her bed.

Once she seemed happy again—her tail was wagging—I headed off to the Low Tide with Harley.

The Low Tide Bar and Grill was located at the end of a dark and rutted dirt road. Twisting scrubby oak trees and a thick growth of palmetto trees created a canopy over the road making the stormy night feel that much heavier. Thunder continued to rumble. The wind picked up even more speed, promising one doozy of a storm would hit before the night was over.

The Low Tide was a shack built on top of a rickety-looking dock down on the river. The rusty corrugated building was about as far outside the business district as one could get. Surrounded by wetlands on three sides, water lapped at the piers holding up the building. A dim, flickering light marked the entrance at the end of a steep gangplank.

The inside of the bar was about as "rustic" as the outside, with its dark wood-paneled walls, yellow glass and black metal medieval-style lanterns hanging from heavy chains, and a thick haze of cigarette and cigar smoke floating in the air. The only redeeming feature was the view of the marsh and the Camellia River beyond. The oversized garage doors that served as a wall of windows in the winter had been opened up to allow the damp summer breeze to flow through the building.

Despite the heat, I shivered as I entered the bar. The last time I'd eaten here, I'd unwittingly dined with a killer. And here I was again, on the hunt for another murderer. Despite the police chief's assertions that his island was free from serious crime, I knew better. Even in paradise, one could always find a snake.

Lidia Vanderhorst, I was surprised to see, was sitting at the bar next to the young surfer who'd told me all about the slap fight Fletcher Grimbal had had with Cassidy a few days before his death. The two of them were both drinking beers and laughing.

Johnny Pane was sitting by himself on the other end of the bar. His hand moved slowly and steadily as he lifted a glass of what looked like bourbon to his lips.

Harriett Daschle was in corner booth cozying up to a silver-haired man I'd never seen before. An easy smile formed on her lips as her hand moved up his arm to rest on his shoulder. Was that her husband, the ex-mayor?

Even Ethel Crump was there with the same friends who had accompanied her to the Chocolate Box the day before Cassidy's death. They were at a table in the middle of the room. A bottle of champagne sat open on their table. The three ladies had their glasses raised in a toast to what looked like some kind of victory. Ethel took a tiny sip before tilting her head back and laughed.

Harley leaned closer to me and asked, "Where should we start?"

I shook my head. "It's a busy place." I didn't see anyone dressed in a brightly colored muumuu. "Do you know Fletcher Grimbal? Is he here?"

"I don't see him." Harley put his hand on my shoulder as a small crowd hurried past. I winced. "Sorry," he said, pulling away. "I forgot about your no touching rule."

"It's not that," I said wishing I hadn't winced. "Your hand hit the bullet wound."

"Oh!" He looked even more distressed. "I'm sorry. Are you okay?"

"Yeah," I said rubbing away the pain. "It just smarts when I bump it." I drew a quick breath and said in a burst, "I don't have that rule anymore. The no touching rule." I closed my eyes before bravely adding, "Not for you."

I wished I hadn't closed my eyes. He didn't say anything. And everything got real awkward real quick. I peeled open one eye—just halfway—to peek.

Detective Gibbons was standing next to Harley with his arms crossed and a smirk on his face that told me he'd overheard me bearing my soul.

"You called him?" I asked Harley. Both of my eyes were wide open now and staring daggers at Harley. I don't know why everyone kept telling me I needed to work on my trust issues when those trust issues were serving me just fine, thank you very much. Whenever I let down my guard—like right now—something like *this* happened.

Harley put his hand on my shoulder, the shoulder that hadn't been injured by his ex's bullet. "I didn't call anybody."

Before I could apologize, Detective Gibbons leaned toward me and asked, "Why should he have called me?" he asked over the driving beat of the beach music.

I bit my lower lip. "Because…" I looked around. I hated to lie. Lying made my face get all red and splotchy. It wasn't a pretty sight. "I'm here to find out who killed Cassidy Jones."

Gibbons just stared at me.

I mirrored his stance and crossed my arms over my chest. "If no one called you, what are you doing here?"

"Cassidy's funeral was this afternoon," Gibbons said unhappily. "The pallbearers included me, a fellow officer, and Bailey Grassi. For someone who was purported to be popular with the ladies, I'd expected at least a few more people would turn up. But no one else was there.

Not even his coworkers from the real estate office bothered to pay their respects."

"But Bailey was there?" That was odd. I'd gotten the impression the chef barely knew Cassidy.

"He said he felt guilty since he'd left on his porch lights that night," Gibbons explained. "He told me that if he'd turned out those lights, Cassidy would still be alive."

That was probably true. And it was decent of Bailey to show up to the funeral for a stranger.

"So why are you here tonight?" I asked Gibbons.

He gestured to the bar. "Clearly the wake is being held here. There's Ethel Crump, Johnny Pane, Lidia Vanderhorst, and Paul and Harriett Daschle…" He continued for quite a while naming people I'd never even heard about. Mostly women. Mostly women with "Mrs." in front of their names.

I looked around the bar with a new understanding. The drinking. The laughing. The toasting. No wonder they hadn't attended the funeral. The people here tonight weren't celebrating Cassidy's life (which was generally the purpose of a funeral). They were celebrating his death.

"Fletcher Grimbal isn't here," I said.

Gibbons, who clearly knew the name and, I suspected, knew why I would mention him, squinted as he looked around. "He isn't."

"I wonder why." I tapped my chin. Fletcher made a perfect suspect. He was angry, and perhaps he wouldn't want to return to the Low Tide after the humiliation he'd endured at Cassidy's hands within these smoke-stained walls. "Florence Corners isn't here either."

"Should she be?" Had I surprised him with some new information?

"Florence had been seen visiting Cassidy at his home several times in the weeks leading up to his death." I knew I shouldn't take pleasure in telling him this, but perversely, I did.

"Florence, as in your...?" He let the question hang in the air.

I nodded.

Gibbons shook his head. "I think you're looking too hard for someone to take Jody's place."

"The screaming woman at the crime scene, the woman who was dressed in that colorful muumuu isn't here either," I said. While I suspected she was another one of the married women Cassidy had dallied with, I had no proof. I knew nothing about her other than that she'd been present at his death and she'd been traumatized by it. "Any luck finding her?" I asked Gibbons.

He tilted his head and looked at me as if I'd just asked him if he thought aliens had come down and shot Cassidy through the heart. "You know I can't discuss the case."

"I do appreciate that you are conducting a thorough investigation," I said. "And I do hope you can find her soon. I suspect she can shed new light on the events that happened that night. Harriett knows who she is. But she won't tell me her name. Now if you'll excuse us, we have quite a few people to talk to."

"We do have a busy night in front of us," Harley agreed. Like a true Southern gentleman, he hooked my arm through his. "And since Penn has to be up early to open her shop, we need to get started."

Gibbons grabbed my other arm to stop us from walking away. "None of these people mourned over his grave today. Why do you think that is?" He didn't give either Harley or me a chance to answer. "It's because he dated married women. It's because he poked his nose into everyone's business and caused trouble for everyone else. No one wants to connect themselves to Cassidy."

"I think we've got that," Harley said, his gaze had hardened as he glared at the detective's hand gripping my arm.

"I don't think you do understand the situation. A woman in such a position might run away from a crime scene, even though doing so is a crime. A woman or man in such a position might even steal an entire tray of chocolate turtles as a way to stop someone from asking too many reckless questions. That's not a person you want to keep pushing, Penn."

"You heard about the theft?" I wondered if I'd ever get used to living in a small town. In small towns everyone talked. Everyone knew everyone else's business.

"Byrd called me," Gibbons admitted. "Told me the theft smelled fishy, especially considering your reputation for causing trouble. I agree with him."

"You're not changing my mind. There's a little boy—Harley's boy—depending on me to find out what really happened the night Cassidy was killed."

"When it comes to this, we're a team," Harley said, which got my heart jumping around like a cheerleader after her team scored a goal.

"Mark my words, Detective. I'm going to get Gavin's mother back to him before school starts on Thursday."

Gibbons shook his head. "You're more stubborn than a rabid raccoon. And potentially more dangerous."

"You're probably right." While I didn't agree with

him and I had no intention of stopping my search for the real killer, I did appreciate his concern for my safety. He wasn't holding onto my arm so tightly because he was worried I might actually learn something that would make him look bad. It wasn't an ego thing with him. He was scolding me as if he was scolding his own daughter because he cared about me. I pulled out of his grasp and put my hand on his cheek, prickly from a five o'clock shadow. "And thank you," I said.

"For what?" He jerked away from my touch. "Nothing I've said is going to change your mind about what you plan to do. And I can't stop you. Not legally. I suspect I'd get a better result if I'd simply banged my head against that wall over there."

"I suspect that's true. Still, I hear what you're saying. And I"—It took me a moment to come up with the right word—"appreciate your concern."

"We both do," Harley said. "And you don't have to worry about Penn. She's not in this alone."

"That's right. I don't go down dark alleyways by myself at night. And I haven't been going around accusing anyone of murder. See? That's growth on my part. And don't forget I grew up on the mean streets of Chicago." That last point was an exaggeration. While I grew up in Chicago, my family lived in the exclusive Oak Park neighborhood. No one in my household ever saw a mean street.

"And I'm with her," Harley's deep voice rumbled.

"I won't get hurt," I repeated.

"See that you don't," Gibbons said. He wandered off to chat with someone sitting at a nearby table.

"He's doing his job," Harley said. "He could be home, celebrating Jody's arrest. But he's not."

"He's one of the good guys, one of the best," I agreed. "But he still needs to be convinced that your ex is innocent."

A pained look suddenly appeared on Harley's face. "Yeah, I fear we all need to be convinced."

"Gavin loves her," I said.

"She's his mother," was his quick reply.

"It has to be more than that. There has to be something good in her that makes him so devoted to her." My feelings toward Florence were complicated at best, and none of them involved love. "Despite her taking you to court all of the time, she is a good mother to him, isn't she?"

"She is," he admitted. "She puts Gavin first in nearly everything she does. Sometimes I fear she spends too much time doting on him. He's at an age where he's trying to find his own way, where he wants to spend time with his friends and not have a parent constantly by his side. As much as it kills me to do it, I try to let him go off when he's with me. And Jody, she's slowly coming around and giving him some freedom to do the same. While she sometimes is a little too overprotective of him, I do believe she wants the best for Gavin."

"If she cares about Gavin that much, don't you think that she'd think about what her actions might do to her son before she squeezed the trigger and killed a man?"

He shook his head with real distress. "I don't know what to believe anymore. One moment she seems stable, and then she goes off and rages like she has no self-control. She's so filled with anger. For as long as I've known her, she's always had that anger simmering just below the surface just looking for a reason to come out."

That worried me. "But she doesn't take out her anger on Gavin?"

"No, never, thank God."

"That's good to know because I believe in her innocence. And I aim to prove it." I patted his arm. Touching Harley felt so natural. And yet, at the back of my mind Lidia's admonition that I let fear rule my life reminded me that whenever I took one step forward in a relationship, I would find other ways to pull back. Perhaps Stella came into my life to teach me how to change that pattern. I sure hoped I could change things, because I was tired of running from my life.

But first, I needed to change things for Gavin so he wouldn't have to overcome many of the struggles I still battled thanks to my motherless childhood. With my arm still hooked through Harley's, we made our way to the bar. We started chatting with Lidia and her surfer friend. Harley, being a surfer himself, knew the young man and had surfed with him in several regional competitions.

As I had suspected, Fletcher hadn't shown his face at the Low Tide since the night of the slap fight.

"I think I know where we can find him," Lidia told me. "Meet me at the pier Monday afternoon. We can do a training session with Stella while we look for him."

I hoped I would have Jody free from jail before Monday, but since I still needed help with Stella's training I readily agreed.

After leaving Lidia laughing with her surfer friend at the bar, Harley led me through the place, introducing me to anyone I didn't know. By the end of the night, we'd talked with nearly everyone there about Cassidy. We heard stories about how he stole his neighbors' newspapers, how he never left tips at restaurants, and how he seemed to be constantly watching what everyone around him was doing. None of that helped me at all.

My feet ached. My head throbbed slightly. I sank down into a chair at the closest available table. Harley left me there. He returned a few minutes later with two frosty beers.

I looked up at him and suddenly got a crazy idea about how I could accomplish something that night. I smiled and gave him my best come-hither look.

He slid into the chair next to mine. With a look of intense interest that had my heart slamming against my chest, he leaned toward me. "Is there something wrong with your eyes?"

"No. No. There's nothing wrong," I grumbled, frustrated he couldn't recognize my valiant attempt at flirting. I straightened in my chair and then stood. "Let's go home."

Like the famous Scarlett O'Hara, whom islanders revered as if she were a real person, I declared that tomorrow was another day. Tomorrow, I would find Cassidy's killer. Tomorrow, I would work on acting more confident with Stella and with everyone else in my life. Tomorrow, I would tell Harley straight out how I felt about him.

Out of those three things I had planned for the tomorrow, chasing down a killer felt like the safest. And easiest.

FIFTEEN

KEEP YOUR POINTY NOSE TO YOURSELF. OR ELSE.

Someone had carefully written that on a yellow sticky note and had taped it to the Chocolate Box's glass door. I'd found it when preparing to open up the shop the next morning. Since Bertie attended church services on Sunday mornings, I was handling the shop's opening alone.

I was glad no one else had seen the note. Bertie would insist I call Detective Gibbons. And Harley or Althea might insist I make a public declaration stating I'd given up on the investigation.

Obviously, my questions last night had made someone uncomfortable. I stood a few steps outside the shop, looking for clues to who might have put the note on my door. The Drop In Surf Shop, the other store in the old building, was closed on Sundays. The porch area in front of their entrance looked dark and quiet.

The neighbor to the right of the building was a real estate office that wouldn't open until one o'clock that afternoon. Cassidy Jones had been one of the company's top brokers. On the other side of the building was a vacation rental house. The latest renters in the house wouldn't be up until at least noon. I knew this because the large group of friends who'd moved in the previous day had stayed up half the night drinking and talking loudly on the house's second-story deck.

Across the street from the shop was a heavily treed vacant lot. I stared into the shadows and immediately spotted movement.

Something weaved through the vine-tangled underbrush with impressive grace. With the note clutched in my hands, I took a step toward the road. Maybe I could get a better look at the figure stalking me.

The shadowy figure must have noticed that its cover had been blown. For as soon as I moved, it ran. It darted deeper into the woody lot. No matter how hard I looked, I could no longer see it. I crushed the note I held tightly in my fist and remained standing there in the middle of the road.

"Did you see that?" Gavin ran up as he pointed toward the vacant lot. "There's a coyote running around."

"A coyote?" I parroted back at him.

Gavin nodded. He nodded so hard I thought he might be trying to launch himself straight into the stratosphere. He was holding a surfboard under his arm and was dripping wet in his board shorts and bright blue rash guard shirt. "It was grayish black." His voice was quick and charged with excitement. "I keep hearing people talking about how the coyotes have moved onto the island. But I've never seen one before today. Never. Did you see it?"

"Maybe." Had I been watching a coyote moving through the brush and not a stalker?

"He was big," Gavin said in a rush. "Not wolf big. I've seen the wolves at Charlestowne Landing. Those things look like giant fluffy dogs. The coyote looked more like a half-starved stray. Did you see it?"

"I don't know. Maybe. I saw…something."

"What's going on?" Harley came up the road to join

his son. He also had a surfboard tucked under one arm
and was wearing a pair of board shorts and navy blue
rash guard. He gave a pointed look at my closed fist.
A bit of yellow from the sticky note was peeking out
at him.

I crumpled the paper even tighter in my haste to get
it completely out of sight. I then asked him the one thing
about that note that suddenly bugged me. "You don't
think I have a pointy nose, do you?"

"What?" Harley asked.

"Your nose is fine, Miss Penn," Gavin answered.
"It's not nearly as pointy as the coyote's. Now that was
a long face. You saw it, right?"

"Not well enough, apparently." Was it simply a coyote in the woods?

"You saw a coyote?" Harley asked.

"Uh-huh, right there, Dad." While Gavin pointed,
I stuffed the note in the pocket of my blue and white
striped sundress.

Harley noticed. "Go on up to our place, Gavin, and
get some dry clothes on. I'll be up in a minute."

Gavin hesitated. "Miss Penn, have you made any
progress? My classes start on Thursday. And I'm starting a new school this year."

"I can take you, son," Harley said before I could answer him. "I already have the day blocked off on my
calendar."

"But-but I want—" Gavin sputtered.

"Go on upstairs and get dried off. We can talk about
it later," Harley said as I said, "I have several interesting
lines of investigation going on right now. I can't make
any promises, but I'm feeling hopeful."

"Oh! Thank you! Thank you, Miss Penn! I knew you

could do it!" he said, punctuating every sentence with at least one exclamation point. "Yes, Dad, I'm going. I'm going."

Harley watched Gavin run around the building, heading toward the back stairs that led up to the second story apartments.

"I wish you hadn't told him that," Harley said, his voice low and tinged with anxiety. "You shouldn't make promises to a little boy that you don't know you can keep."

"But I think I can keep it. I simply need to find… Well, I need to find several people. But I'm pretty sure one of them is responsible for Cassidy's death."

"You weren't feeling nearly this hopeful last night," he warned. "What changed?"

"Ummm…" I didn't want to tell him about the note because I didn't know how he'd react.

Thankfully, he let it drop. "Pointy nose?" he asked instead.

My hand automatically went to my face. Did my nose extend out too far? Was it freakishly skinny? "You don't think it's too pointy, do you?"

"I think it's perfect for your face." He leaned his surfboard against the side of the white clapboard building.

"That's not exactly the answer a girl wants to hear."

He smiled at that. "Why are you asking about your nose?"

"Oh, you know, womanly insecurities. They tend to rear their ugly heads without warning." Not quite a lie—the pointy nose dig *had* gotten to me—but still I could feel my face getting all hot and blotchy.

"Womanly…insecurities?" Harley knew I wasn't a

wilting flower with womanly insecurities. My insecurities were full-blown giant-sized ones I carried around with me twenty-four-seven. "What's in your pocket, Penn?"

"A sticky note," I answered without hesitation because the truth always worked better than a lie.

"What's on the sticky note?" he had the nerve to ask.

"It's a sticky note. There's a note jotted on it. That's what they're for. Notes."

He started to put his hand on my shoulder but stopped himself. He closed his open hand and lowered it to his side. I hated that our relationship was like this now. When we'd first met—well, after I'd socked him in the nose—it seemed as if our relationship had been on the road to blossoming into something beautiful. But then my sister, Tina, had meddled. She'd tried to hook me up with an uber-famous, single, and devastatingly handsome rock star. Having a rock star hanging around the shop and making outrageous passes kind of put the brakes on anything that might have happened between Harley and me. And now his ex-wife was in jail.

While I wasn't the touchy-feely type, my foolish heart seemed to be all gaga about Harley. And I had promised myself that I would tell him today how I felt about him. But now? It didn't seem like the right time. Yet I had to do something to keep the moment from getting even more awkward. So I forced my hand to reach across the expanse between us and closed my fingers over his.

He glanced down at my hand touching his and the corners of his lips lifted a fraction. That was definitely a step in the right direction relationship-wise.

His gaze touched mine. He looked confused.

The silence between us felt uncomfortable.

Perhaps I'd moved too quickly. Perhaps I'd been too forward. Relationships were like puzzles that I never knew how to put together right. I was constantly forcing pieces in the wrong places. The more I cared about someone, the more I'd say or do stupid things.

I was about to throw my hands in the air and walk away embarrassed and defeated when he tightened his fingers around mine. His upturned lips turned into a real smile.

Sure, his grin was tinged with sadness. But it was the biggest smile I'd seen on his face since Jody's arrest.

"Pointy nose, huh?" he said.

"What?" I slapped my hand over my nose. Did he think it was pointy? Did *everyone* think it was pointy?

He gestured toward the corner of the crumpled sticky note that was still poking out of my pocket. "Let me guess. Someone taped a note to the Chocolate Box's door. There's an insult on it about your nose being pointy. And there's also a threat."

How would he know? "Did you put it there?"

"Penn, now why would I do something like that?" He walked over to the door. "The tape is still on the glass. And you wouldn't ask me to critique your looks unless someone put that idea in your head." He held out his hand. "Can I see the note?"

I squinted at the tiny piece of tape on the door. He saw that? He saw that tiny piece of tape *and then* figured the rest out? "Dang, you have some mad investigative skills. And I did like having you at my side last night. If you ask nicely, you can stay on as my sidekick."

He sighed. He still had his hand out like a beggar. "Can I see the note? Please?"

Since he pretty much already knew what it said, there was no reason to keep it from him. Perhaps some of those detective skills of his would help me suss out what was going on.

I smoothed out the worst of the wrinkles and handed it to him. "Do you happen to recognize the handwriting?"

He studied the short note for several long minutes before saying, "Penn, this is serious. I think you need to back off."

"I think you're missing the point," I argued, feeling more than a little defensive. "The person who wrote this believes I have a pointy nose."

"No, your nose is the least of your worries."

"Are you saying I need to start worrying about my nose?"

"Of course I'm not. I'm not a fool. What I'm saying is that you're asking questions about the secrets Cassidy Jones has been keeping. You're making people nervous, nervous enough for someone to tape this threat to your door. You could get hurt…or killed."

"No, no, no. You're reading too much into what the note is saying. It said, 'or else.' That could mean any number of things could happen that aren't at all violent or scary. The people in Camellia Beach are good people. They wouldn't hurt me. Just ask the police chief. He's constantly telling me how there's no crime on the island."

"You left out the part where he says that there's no crime on the island unless it involves you," Harley reminded me quite unhelpfully. "And we both know that Camellia Beach is like anywhere else. Circumstances can push people to do horrible things. Just look at what Jody did."

"She didn't do anything."

"She shot you."

"Other than that."

"You need to be careful," he said.

"It's fine. I'm fine." Those words hadn't fully emerged from my mouth when someone hidden in the darkened wooded lot across the street tossed a stuffed toy dog at the two of us.

It landed at our feet like an unexploded grenade.

I screamed.

Harley kicked the toy and then wrapped his arms around me as if he was ready to use his body as a shield from a bomb blast.

We both held our breaths as we waited for the brown-and-white plush puppy with a stitched oversized smile to go ka-boom. Someone (not necessarily saying it was me) held onto him for dear life. Harley's body felt damp and cool from spending hours surfing in the ocean.

My grip tightened around him as we stood there watching the inanimate stuffed toy. It didn't explode. It simply sat in the middle of the road grinning at us.

"I don't think it's going to do anything," Harley whispered after several breathless minutes.

"I think you're right," I whispered back.

"I should go check it out."

"But what if—" I started to object.

"We wouldn't want a passing car to drive over it." He tried to move toward the plush pup. But my strangling grip held him back.

"We can cuddle another time," he said as he detangled his strong, blunt fingers from mine. "Let me get a closer look at that toy."

I kept glued to his side as he edged cautiously closer to the stuffed dog. As if hooked at the hip, we simultaneously crouched down next to it. There was writing on a paper dog tag that was hanging around his neck. Someone using a very different style of handwriting from the yellow sticky note had hastily scrawled:

If you don't want to die horribly, keep out of Cassidy's business.

Well, fudge cakes. There was no ambiguity about *that* note.

SIXTEEN

"No." MY HAND closed over Harley's in an attempt to keep him from using his phone to report the notes to the police. "Handing these over to Detective Gibbons will only add confusion to his investigation."

He stared at my hand touching his. We'd spent months avoiding even accidentally brushing against each other and now all of the sudden I couldn't stop grabbing onto him.

"Penn…" Was it my imagination, or did his voice sound husky? "I need to report what just happened. As your lawyer, as your friend, as your *whatever*, I can't stand by and do nothing while your life is in danger."

I snorted. "My life isn't in danger."

"Did you read that last threat?"

"I read it, but—"

"Horribly. It said you'd die horribly."

My shoulders slumped, and I released his hand. "Let me call."

He tried to hand me his cell phone.

"You mean now? You want to call him now?" I squeaked. Sure, I was stalling. I really, really didn't want to face this. I didn't have time for another crisis. With the missing sea turtle eggs, the missing *chocolate* sea turtles, and the fact that I'd promised Gavin I'd get his mother cleared of the murder charge before his first day of school on Thursday, my plate was overflowing.

"What I really want is for you to promise to stop asking questions about Cassidy's murder," he said.

"You know I can't do that. I already promised your son that I'd help him."

He framed his hands around my face. The intimacy of his touch should have had me jumping out of my skin with fear. I cared too much about Harley. I was terrified that if we got involved, he'd become just another one of my bad decisions. But gracious, his hands felt warm and strong against my cheeks. I suddenly had trouble thinking straight.

"I care about you, Penn. What you're doing is dangerous and sweet and it makes me want to do this." His lips brushed tenderly against mine.

Time must have stopped because I couldn't tell you how long that kiss lasted. It tasted like forever. But when he pulled away, I wanted to cry out that it had ended too soon.

We stared at each other, each of us breathing a little too hard. It was a tingly moment I wanted to grab onto and not ever let go.

Did this mean we'd finally pushed through the awkwardness between us? Had we'd finally taken our relationship to where everyone in town believed it should go? And we'd done it without my having to make a grand (and terrifying) confession of my feelings for him? Was this the beginning of what could bloom into something exciting and crazy and everything I wanted from him? It sure felt like it could be. And yet…

"We probably should pretend that didn't happen," I said.

"But it did happen and—"

"And with a killer running around and Gavin needing all of your attention, we can't do this." Oh, I wanted to slap myself silly for saying it. But it was the truth, and it needed to be said. "We can't let ourselves get distracted. We have to put your son first."

Liar, a voice in the back of my mind said with a sneer. *You're terrified and are grasping for a reason to push this fine specimen of a man away.*

He turned away from me and watched an ant carry a leaf across the shop's front step before saying, "Okay, but we're still calling Hank. We're still handing these notes over to him."

"Fine," I snapped even though agreeing to pretend our kiss hadn't nearly set the sky on fire felt anything *but* fine. I was upset and embarrassed and ready to stomp my feet like a bratty child. But since it was my idea—my *stupid* idea—to forget about the kiss, I had no choice but to pretend I was happy he didn't argue with me about it.

And like that, everything was awkward again.

"Have you heard about what happened this morning?" Ethel Crump asked loudly as she held court at a table in the center of the shop later that morning.

I froze.

Had someone watched as Harley and I kissed this morning?

"Oh, I can hardly contain myself. I heard it from a friend who heard from a friend," Ethel continued.

My heart pounded in my throat. If she said what I was afraid she was going to say, I would die of embarrassment right here. Right next to the coffee urn.

"No one is supposed to know," Ethel said.

I breathed a mini-sigh of relief. She wouldn't say that

if she was about to out Harley and I for kissing while standing in the street, would she?

If she wasn't talking about my love life, did that mean she was talking about the other thing that had happened this morning? Chief Byrd and Harley had both (reluctantly) agreed that we should keep the two threatening letters to ourselves. And though it pained me to do so, I hadn't even told Bertie or Althea about them.

If Ethel knew about the notes, her source for her gossip would have to be someone who had either written that I had a pointy nose or had threatened to make sure I died a horrible death. (I still wasn't sure which bothered me more.)

Byrd and Harley had agreed that the handwriting looked too different to have been penned by the same hand, which meant I'd prickled the nerves of at least two of Cassidy's victims with my questions.

"You didn't hear it from me," Ethel warned.

"Just spit it out already," one of her friends shouted.

Tourists and locals alike had crowded into the shop to indulge in mocha coffees and the chocolate pastries we had shipped in from a Charleston bakery. According to Bertie, the Chocolate Box had long been a popular spot on Sundays after church. The islanders lived on gossip and Sundays seemed to be the best day for those who worked fulltime to catch up on the latest dirt.

About a dozen residents, men and women alike, had pulled chairs from neighboring tables so they could sit near Ethel and hear her talk. No one spoke. It seemed as if no one breathed as they waited to hear the news Ethel could barely contain.

I used my nervous energy to rub down one of the

tables by the door while pretending I wasn't listening. I felt as if I was trembling from the inside out.

The older woman was a natural born storyteller. In the thundering silence, Ethel drew a shaky breath. Her roaming gaze went from person to person. It felt as if her rheumy eyes lingered on mine for the longest.

"Get this. Luella Marie Banks is going to start filming a new movie next month. And this one is already getting Oscar buzz," Ethel announced finally to the delighted gasps of those in her audience.

"Who is doing what?" I asked a bit more brusquely than I'd intended. Everyone in the shop turned to gape at me. I tried not to squirm. "Who is Luella Marie Banks?" I'd gentled my voice and no longer sounded like Stella when she was barking at anyone who dared come into the apartment. "I've never heard of her."

"You haven't?" Johnny Pane cried from his perch on his ladder. His paint brush moved carefully over the ceiling, covering up the stains from what I hoped was a repaired water leak. "Haven't you ever been to the movies?"

"She's a local who is about to hit it big in showbiz," Ethel said.

"She has more talent than any of us put together," the woman sitting next to Ethel said.

"And she's quite a looker, too," one of the men said. All the other men nodded.

"How exciting," I said, sounding anything but excited. What I really wanted the gossip crew to talk about was Cassidy Jones. "Did she and Cassidy Jones know each other? It seemed like he had his own kind of star power."

"Child," Ethel drawled, "that man wasn't in the same

universe as our Luella Marie. Not by any measure. You're not still thinking you can convince the police that Jody didn't murder that no good bounder, are you?"

"Give the girl some credit. She's got more sense than to chase after rainbows and lost causes," Arthur Jenkins, an octogenarian resident from the Pink Pelican Inn and regular customer, said as he sauntered slowly over to the display counter. He looked sharp in his blue-and-white-striped seersucker suit, leather loafers with tassels, and natty straw hat.

"Sorry, Art. Our Penn was asking around about Cassidy yesterday at the Low Tide. Heard her myself," the woman next to Ethel said. "Wanted to know who else in town wanted him dead."

Ethel's thin gray brows rose as she turned her gaze back in my direction. "It would have been faster to ask who didn't want him dead."

"True. True," Arthur Jenkins agreed. "He liked to make life…painful…for the people around him. Don't know anyone who liked him."

"Jody liked him," I said as I returned to the counter to fill a golden box with chocolates for Arthur. Every Sunday, he bought a dozen chocolate covered cherries for his new wife.

"Look how well that turned out," Arthur Jenkins replied. Many in the shop nodded in agreement.

"Other women liked him," I forced from behind clenched teeth. *Florence had liked him.* I didn't say that aloud. But I did say, "A woman dressed in a flowered muumuu was there when he died. She was quite inconsolable with grief."

Since I figured pretty much everyone in the room believed I was crazy for trying to clear Jody of the murder charge, I decided it was high time these gossips started doing something other than talking about the degree of my crazy. I wasn't crazy. And there was no reason why the gossips shouldn't be using their power of gab for good.

"Ethel, you wouldn't happen to know how I can contact her, would you?" I asked as casually as I could manage as I tied a red ribbon around Arthur Jenkins' golden chocolate box. "She was dressed in a showy turquoise muumuu with giant flowers. I'd like to talk with her and find out what she saw that night. She might be the only one who actually saw Cassidy getting shot. But she ran off before anyone could talk to her. Not even the police know who she is."

Ethel appeared to be completely taken aback that there could be a missing eyewitness. She pushed back her chair and managed to get to her feet in record time. She followed me across the shop, peppering me with questions about what the woman looked like, her age, her height.

I shook my head. "I was hoping you and your friends could help ferret out her identity. It was dark that night, and I don't know much about her." I figured the less they knew about this mystery woman the more they'd be itching to find her.

"Well, someone must know something," Ethel exclaimed as she clapped her slightly crooked hands together. Determination brightened her eyes. "Don't waste your time asking around about Cassidy's victims, Penn. I'll find your mystery woman for you. Before the sun sets, you'll be talking with her."

I placed my hand on her frail shoulder and started to thank her. There wasn't a doubt in my mind she'd do as she said. But before I could utter much more than a quick thanks, Althea ran into the shop. Dark circles ringed her eyes, eyes that held a world of rage in them. Her dress, the same dress she'd been wearing the night before, was wrinkled and sandy. And she wasn't wearing any shoes.

"Go get Bertie. She's in the back," I told Ethel before I rushed to Althea's side and wrapped an arm around her shoulder. "What in the world happened to you?"

"Another nest," her words landed like lead weights. "It's empty. I've been checking them all. And I found another nest that is empty."

I tried to direct her toward the closest available chair, but she refused to sit down. "I'm going to kill whoever is doing this. I'm going to kill them," she kept repeating.

"Okay," I said and then hurried over to the coffee bar. I fixed Althea a large cappuccino with two healthy shots of dark chocolate. I pushed the drink into her sandy hands.

"Do you think it's the coyotes or the raccoons?" Ethel asked.

Holding the cup with both hands, Althea gingerly took a sip. "Does someone on the island think I'm an idiot? This never happened before I took charge of the turtle watch program this year. And I'm not going to let them get away with it."

"What does she mean?" Ethel asked me.

"I mean someone is stealing the eggs," Althea nearly shouted.

Everyone in the shop gasped.

"I heard it was wild animals," Ethel murmured.

Althea gave her head a hard shake. A bit of her coffee splashed onto the floor. "Wild animals would make a mess of a nest. No, whoever did this was careful and covered their tracks. Someone is poaching the sea turtle eggs right under my nose. And I'm going to kill whoever is doing it."

"What you need is a good night's sleep," Bertie said as she hurried over to her daughter. "You can't stay up all night monitoring turtle nests and expect to have a clear head in the morning. You need to take care of yourself."

"But the turtles—" Althea protested.

"There has to be a way to protect the nests." I was starting to understand why Jody had started carrying a gun with her to the turtle nests at night. As much as I abhorred guns and violence, firepower might be the only way to keep the sea turtle eggs safe.

"Nothing short of violence will stop those—" Althea started to say.

"That's because you're bone tired," Bertie cut her daughter's tirade short. She hugged Althea tightly. "You need to get some rest. You can take my bed upstairs, if you'd like. Troubadour would love the company. Once you've slept a few hours you'll be able to figure out how to go forward."

"I suppose you're right, Mama." Althea stifled a yawn. "I am mighty tired right now. So tired, I can barely hold a coherent thought in my head."

Bertie took the barely touched coffee from Althea's hands and set it on a nearby table. She then hooked her arm around her daughter's shoulders and led her out the back way. "I won't be but a minute. I'm going to take her up to my room."

"Take as long as you need," I said.

This wasn't the first time I had to handle the shop by

myself when it was crowded with hungry customers. But that didn't mean it was easy. Bertie couldn't have been gone more than twenty minutes. But by the time she returned, I would have sworn I'd been running from table to table for at least four hours. My feet hurt. My stomach rumbled with hunger. And I was starting to get a headache from having to constantly move from the register to the display case to the tables and to the coffee area. All of these places seemed to require constant attention that morning. We needed to hire more help.

"Thank goodness," I said with a huge sigh of relief when Bertie finally returned. Her crisp white apron was neatly tied. She headed straight to the cash register as if ready and eager to take charge. "How's Althea?"

"Sleeping." Her brows drew together as she stared into the display case where we kept all of the truffles and bonbons and dipped chocolates that were available for sale. "Where are the salted sea turtles?"

"On the tray," I said as I scrubbed a table while three customers with coffees in hand waited for me to finish. "I sold a handful of them while you were gone."

"The case isn't locked," she said. I could hear Bertie sliding the panel open. "I thought we were going to keep this locked."

"We are. I did," I called over my shoulder. I finished wiping off the table and straightened. "I know I locked it."

When I turned and peered into the display case, I saw something I couldn't believe I was seeing. The tray where we'd placed nearly two dozen salted sea turtles was empty. But how could that be? How could they go missing when I was working right there? How could they go missing when there was a room filled with customers who would notice someone stealing the entire batch of chocolates? How could they go missing from a locked case?

"Someone took them." I rubbed the back of my suddenly tense neck as I stared at the empty tray. I didn't know how. I didn't know why. All I knew was that the chocolate turtles were gone.

"Again," Bertie said.

SEVENTEEN

"LET ME GET this straight," Granny Mae, who wasn't actually my grandmother, said. I pressed the cell phone tighter to my ear. Her voice, the comforting voice you'd expect from a loving grandmother, came out of the receiver and seemed to wrap around me like a verbal hug. Oh, how I missed her. "Empty sea turtle nests, stolen chocolate turtles, a murdered man everyone wanted dead, and threatening letters against you?"

"Don't forget the bulletproof case against Jody I intend to disprove." I walked across my apartment's living room, wishing Granny Mae was here in Camellia Beach. Stella followed.

"How could I forget that? A noble cause if ever I've heard of one. If she went to prison for murder, you'd get her off your proverbial back. It'd make your life easier. Are you sure you want to do that?" she asked in that no-nonsense way she had about her.

"I have to," I said as I continued to pace. Stella continued to follow along. "I told Gavin I would."

"Hence the noble cause. I'm proud of you, Penn."

My cheeks warmed at her words of praise. Her opinion meant the world to me. But that wasn't why I'd called and told her all about the strange happenings on the island. I'd called because she had the sharpest mind of anyone I knew. She held doctoral degrees in biochemistry, astrophysics, and journalism, and taught at the University of Wisconsin, and loved chocolate nearly as much as I did.

I stood still as I gave her a detailed accounting of my long list of suspects. Periodically, her earrings clanked against the phone, a sign that she was nodding. Then after taking a long steady breath, I plunged ahead with the one question I really shouldn't have been worrying about, but was, "One of those two threatening notes I'd gotten today said I had a pointy nose. Do you think my nose is pointy?"

I don't know why the criticism had stung so badly. It wasn't as if I knew the note writer. And it wasn't as if his or her opinion should matter anyhow. The other note wrapped around the stuffed dog's neck had threatened my *freaking* life. And all I could do was obsess about the pointy nose jab in the first note. I'd let it distract me from wondering who'd sent the note. I'd let it distract me from thinking about why I received not one but two notes.

Heck, I was thinking about it even now. There had to be something wrong with me.

"Your nose is just right for your face," she said, echoing what Harley had told me.

"What's wrong with my face?" I demanded. Stella batted my leg with her tiny paw. Without thinking, I reached down and scratched her behind her ears. Surprisingly, she didn't try to nip at me. She rubbed her head against my hand, prodding me to keep petting her.

"Penn, you know you're asking the wrong questions."

"I know." I looked down at Stella. Why was she being so friendly? Was she sick? "I know, but—"

Granny Mae didn't let me even start to think about my body's imperfections. "You're a lovely woman with striking features. Don't let some anonymous nut with a pen and a pad of yellow sticky notes get under your skin. Focus, will you? The threats mean you've been asking questions whose answers could prove damaging for someone on the island. What you need to do, and do fast, is assure everyone that you're no gossip. You need to let everyone know that you're not out to dig up painful secrets. You're only looking to catch a killer."

"Yes, why didn't I think of that? My reassurances should keep future threats from being lobbed my way." I offered Stella a small piece of bacon as a reward for her good behavior. She took it politely from my hand without also chomping my fingers like she usually would do.

"Reassuring the people who Cassidy has hurt that you have no plans to expose them will also serve another purpose. If you receive more threatening notes you'll know that your questions are leading you to Cassidy's killer instead of one of his secret lovers."

"Do you agree with me when I say Jody didn't kill anyone?" I held my breath and waited for her to share her thoughts. Stella batted my leg again.

Granny Mae took her time before answering. While I waited, I scratched behind Stella's silky ears some more. Finally Granny Mae said, "I believe in you, Penn. That's all I need to know."

I spent the next half hour talking with Granny Mae, going over everything I'd heard and seen. Stella stayed by my side the entire time. She even sat on the sofa with me and put her head in my lap while Granny Mae and I discussed in great detailed who Muumuu Woman might be.

When we'd finished, Granny Mae suggested I stop looking for the mystery woman. "Let her come to you. Instead, focus on the others on your suspect list." She thought Fletcher Grimbal (AKA Mr. Slap Fight) sounded like the leading contender for Cassidy's murderer. "He already has a record of violent behavior."

"It was a silly slap fight," I reminded her. "It wasn't as if he'd pulled a gun on Cassidy."

"Even so, shortly after you start asking around town about him, you get a threatening note. In my mind, that moves him to the top of my list for potential murderer."

She had a point. "I have plans to talk with him tomorrow."

"Good. Good. Just be sure you're not meeting with him alone."

"It's going to be in a public space, and I'll have a friend with me," I assured her.

"That's my girl," she said, which made me smile.

"I'm glad I called you," I said and was about to say goodbye when she spoke.

"Penn?" Her earrings clanked against the phone again. "Are you sure there's nothing else going on that you want to tell me? Something that's upsetting you?"

Something like a heated kiss? Or a threat that I might lose the store? "I don't know what you could—"

"You're a smart girl. You didn't need me to talk you through any of what we just discussed. You would have come up with all of it on your own. So tell me what is really going on. What's happening that has upset you so much that you needed to touch base with me?"

"Being told my nose is pointy sure felt like a crisis," I joked. "Maybe that's why I called."

"Seriously, Penn, what's going on?"

"I love you. Do I really need a crisis to call?"

"No, of course you don't. I keep telling you that. But

you always wait until you're in the middle of a personal crisis before you call me. You have for years."

"That's not true. I called you on your birthday two weeks ago."

"No, Penn. I called you."

"I was going to call you. You simply beat me to it." Stella jumped off the sofa and ran to the door.

"Now don't panic, Penn. I'm not upset. But if there's something else that was bothering you, you can talk with me about it."

"Something bigger than murder?" Stella started barking. It sounded as if she was agreeing with me. I told her to hush and tossed her some more treats.

"No, honey," Granny Mae said, "something more personal."

"You're usually right, Granny Mae, but not this time. There's nothing else to say." Nothing. Nada. Zilch. Zero.

Just that ugly rumor going around about my losing the shop. Just that I kissed Harley while standing in the middle of the street this morning. And now I don't know what I'm going to do about him. "You don't think I have a pointy nose, right?"

Granny Mae chuckled. Her rumbly laughter rolled low and deep and sounded nearly identical to how Bertie laughed. "Your nose is fine. Now, get off the phone with me so I can call that capable police detective working on the case and tell him to watch out for you."

"I'm going to call you in a couple of days," I promised just as Stella started barking again. I had to nearly shout, "Just to chat."

"You do that, Penn." She didn't sound convinced.

"I swear I will. I'm going to…" What I was going to

say vanished. Stella had started digging at the door with both paws. And her barking had turned more intense.

I peeked out the window to see what had upset my little pup and spotted Detective Gibbons walking toward my apartment with his hands on his hips.

"I've got to go," I said. I hoped Gibbons had some good news for me. "And I will call you in a few days."

I hit end and thrust my phone into my pocket. A moment before the detective knocked on my door, I scooped Stella into my arms. The knocking only caused Stella to bark even more wildly. I swung the door open. "Detective, what can I do for you?" I shouted over the racket.

"Hank contacted me," he had to shout back. He crossed his arms over his broad chest. His brows were crinkled with concern.

"Chief Byrd?" My brows crinkled too. Not with concern, but with confusion. "Wait a minute."

Lidia had told me that holding Stella only made her more nervous. "Let me get her leash." I followed Lidia's instructions on how to handle Stella. I hooked the leash to her collar and instructed her to sit. More treats were given as soon as her cute little tail touched the ground. Since she was chewing, she was no longer barking, so I praised her and gave her a few more treats.

"Wow," the detective said. "That's quite an improvement."

"Lidia has been helping me train her." I told Stella to stay and quickly tossed her another couple of treats before she could stand up. Lidia was right. Timing was everything with the training.

"As I was saying, Hank called to tell me—"

"He told he wasn't going to tell anyone about the threats."

"Threats?" Gibbons dragged out the word. He tilted his head to one side. "What threats?"

I tossed Stella another piece of bacon since she was still sitting and not barking. It also helped buy me time to gather my thoughts.

"Oh. He didn't tell you." I waved my hand as if my mentioning it was a mistake. "Of course he didn't tell you. They were nothing. Jokes, really. What are you talking about?"

"Penn, I would have hoped that you'd learned by now that you can't ignore threats of any kind." He sounded like a stern father. Not like my father, who also sounded stern, but like a father who would stand against the world for his child, even if the child is behaving foolishly.

"I'm not ignoring them. I have a plan."

"A plan?" The look on the detective's face was a visual definition of the word skeptical—brows bunched together, corners of his lips drooping, forehead crinkled like a wrinkled cotton sheet.

"I mean it," I said. "Chief Byrd is even on board with this." Albeit reluctantly. "We're keeping the two threatening notes under wraps so that if someone in the community starts talking about them, we'll be able to track the gossip back to the culprit." I held up a finger because I could see he was going to cut me off. "And that person may also be the killer who so cleverly framed Jody."

Stella woof-woofed her agreement but amazingly didn't jump up from where I'd told her to sit and stay. Impressed, I tossed her another bacon treat.

"You're telling me you received two separate threats from two different people? When did this happened?"

"This morning," I admitted.

He drew a long, deep breath, but that didn't seem to calm him. "Penn. Penn. Penn." Each utterance of my name sounded like a new and more forceful curse. He started to pace. "You should have called me. You know you're getting threats because you're stirring the hornets' nest Cassidy Jones had created."

"I've got a plan for that too. The first chance I get, I'm going to reassure everyone that I'm not looking to expose anyone's secrets. I'm simply looking for the person who framed Jody."

"No one framed Jody," he sounded angry about it.

"Yes, someone did. And whoever did it is smart and had planned Cassidy's murder far in advance. This wasn't a crime of passion, not by a long shot. It was done by someone who is cold and calculating. It was done by someone who knew about Jody's crazy reaction to lights on the beach, who knew about her relationship with Cassidy, and who knew that the turtle team was going to be keeping vigil at that particular nest that night."

The frown on his lips deepened. "Are you trying to tell me how to do my job?"

"No, sir. Of course not. I'm trying to tell you something you might not know because you live in downtown Charleston and not out here on Camellia Beach."

"I swear, Penn—"

I never did get to hear what was going to come next. I liked to think he was about to swear that he'd never met a civilian sleuth with such sharp instincts. But at that very moment, Troubadour, Bertie's hairless cat, let out an ear-piercing yeow as he charged out of Bertie's bedroom. He looked like a blur as he darted across the room and made a beeline straight for the detective who was standing near the open door.

A shadow appeared on the floorboards of the porch beyond the door. I half expected to see either Harley or Gavin to walk by on his way to their apartment or to pause to say hello. Having one of them pass by would also explain Troubadour's sudden burst of energy.

I didn't have a chance to look outside. As soon as Troubadour appeared, Stella jumped up, breaking her stay command. Barking as if the world had just caught fire, she ran at the kitty, stopping only because she'd reached the end of her leash. No amount of treats was going to deter her from what she saw as her duty to keep her nemesis (the cat) from getting close to (well) anyone. She tugged and jumped and made a noisy menace of herself.

Troubadour, unimpressed by this display, growled low in his throat. He swatted Stella on the nose before continuing on his path toward the door. This only made Stella even angrier. With a growly bark, she tried again to chase after the platinum-colored kitty.

My attempts to rein in her bad behavior had absolutely no effect. I ended up doing exactly what Lidia had warned me not to do. I scooped Stella into my arms. My frustrated pup chomped down on my wrist as I carried her into my bedroom. I gently set her down, pried her mouth from my wrist, and provided her with a handful of treats before closing the bedroom door.

"Sorry about that," I said when I returned.

Troubadour was rubbing himself against the detective's leg and purring loudly.

"I see you're a cat person." I peeked out the door. The mysterious shadow was gone.

"Actually, I prefer dogs." Gibbons grimaced down at Troubadour, but didn't do anything to stop the kitty from rubbing all over his pants.

I was sure I'd seen the shadow of person approaching the open door. "Did you see anyone walk by?" I asked him.

"No." He suddenly looked suspicious. "Why?"

I peeked out the door again. "When Troubadour came running toward you, I thought I saw someone standing outside on the porch."

He peered outside. "There's no one out here."

"No, there isn't. But I'm sure I saw someone." Had someone been lurking outside the door listening? Was someone still out there waiting for me to be alone? I hugged myself and shivered.

Gibbons stepped fully outside and leaned over the railing and looked left and right. I didn't have to ask. I knew he didn't see anything. If someone had been there, he (or she) was long gone now.

I glanced at the clock. It was nearly six o'clock, a few minutes before the shop's closing time. I hadn't meant to stay in the apartment so long. "Can we talk while I walk back to the shop?" I asked. "I don't want Bertie to be alone at closing."

"I agree. If you've been receiving threats, neither of you should be alone anywhere," he warned.

I had to herd Troubadour back into the apartment before I could lock up and leave. The cat hissed at me, twice. But he finally relented. With his nose in the air and his tail held straight, he walked back into the apartment as if it that was what he'd planned to do along.

I locked up and walked down the steps with Gibbons. "You were saying that Chief Byrd had called you?" I said.

"He did." He huffed. "He called to tell me your shop has been robbed...again. That it'd happened this morning? Was that before or after the threatening notes appeared?"

"The theft happened after the incident with the notes," I said as we reached the bottom of the stairs.

"Was the theft like the other one?"

"Yes. Whoever is doing it only takes my salted sea turtles."

"The turtles are a new offering in your shop, isn't that right?"

"They are." My tone immediately lightened as I talked about my favorite subject: chocolate. "It's one of my original recipes. Bertie helped me develop it since I still haven't mastered all aspects of the candy-making process. They're caramel with—"

"I know what's in them." He patted his rounded belly. "I've eaten more than my fair share. Do you have any ideas why someone would want to steal them specifically?" he asked.

"Because they're delicious?" After I unlocked the back door, we entered the shop and headed down a long, dimly lit hallway that passed the kitchen, the office, the storage room, and opened up into the storefront.

"Everything in your shop is delicious." He patted his belly again. "It has to be something else."

Bertie was walking the last of the evening's customers to the door. She locked the front door behind them before turning to us. "Those milkshakes are too much work to make and serve. They're attracting too many people. My bones are tired from running around in a constant manic rush," she complained as she rubbed a hand up and down her leg. "We're a chocolate shop, not one of your northern malt shops."

"I'm from the Midwest," I reminded her even though she knew very well where I was from. I apologized for leaving her to handle the afternoon crowd by herself. I hated seeing her hurting. I should have never let her talk me into leaving to call Granny Mae. "Detective Gibbons is here because he heard about the stolen chocolates and wants to talk to us about them."

"Frank Gibbons." Bertie put her hands on her hips. "You've told me on more than one occasion that you're a homicide detective and that petty crimes like a little theft mean nothing to you. What are you really doing here?"

"I'm sure it's his fondness for our chocolates that has him alarmed that someone might be taking them before he can eat them." I fixed a small plate of chocolates and set it on the table closest to him.

He frowned at the plate. "No turtles?"

"The thief keeps taking them," I said.

"We're going to be up late again tonight making yet another batch," Bertie said. "Costing us a fortune to keep losing them."

"Have you considered not making them anymore?" Gibbons asked before biting into one of Bertie's sea salt chocolates.

I stifled a yawn. "I'm seriously considering it right now."

"We may have to stop making them. Although they're simply my sea salt chocolate caramels with some pecans tossed in," Bertie said, "they're made with more of our Amar chocolate than most of our chocolates. And as you already you know we only have a limited supply of the special Amar chocolate."

"We pour them into a cute baby sea turtle chocolate mold," I added. "They're adorable."

"And quite good," the detective said, patting his belly again.

"The special flavor Amar chocolate infuses into all of our chocolates is what keeps our customers coming back." I started wiping down tables. As I worked, I started to agree with Bertie. Adding milkshakes to the menu definitely made more work for us. Not only did we have to run around to mix the drinks and then serve them, we also had to contend with the sticky mess they made in the shop, and a sink filled with glasses that needed to be scrubbed.

"Bertie's special sea salt chocolate caramels still outsell anything else we offer," I explained. "And whenever we make any of our wine infused truffles using just our Amar chocolate, we sell out of that within the hour."

He nodded as he ate one of my special spicy bonbon fires.

"I'd like to kill whoever is taking them. They're a mess of work to make," Bertie complained.

"Speaking of homicide, did Harriett help you track down our mystery Muumuu Woman?" I asked him.

"You know I can't discuss an ongoing investigation." His hand moved toward the plate of chocolates again. "And I have no intention of encouraging you. The threatening notes should be incentive enough to keep you far, far away from anything that involves Cassidy Jones."

"Threatening notes?" Bertie howled. "What in Sam

Hill are you talking about Frank Gibbons? Someone has been threatening my Penn, and I don't know about it?"

"I don't know much about it either," Gibbons grumbled. "Hank didn't tell me anything about it, even though he *supposedly* knows all about them. He does know about them, doesn't he?" he asked me directly. His right eye twitched before the bushy brow above it rose up toward his hairline.

"Yes, he knows all about the notes. He has them in his office. I already told you why we decided to keep it quiet with everyone." I was sorry I hadn't told Bertie. Not telling her about the threats had eaten at me all day. "I should have told you, Bertie. It was wrong to keep you in the dark about them."

"You're darn right that you should have told her… and me," Gibbons said. "After I leave here, I'm going to go straight to Hank's office to take a look at them for myself."

"I just might come with you," Bertie said.

"I think you should." Gibbons nodded emphatically. "The way I read the situation, just by being in this shop you're in just as much danger as Penn."

He plucked one of the dark chocolate cherry cream truffles from the plate. "Look, you didn't hear this from me." He rolled the delicately decorated ball around between his beefy fingers. "I'm only telling you this because I hope it'll convince you leave the investigating to the police. Ballistics came back. The bullet that killed Cassidy came out of the gun Jody had in her hand when you and Althea found her."

"Which gun?" I asked.

"What?" he asked.

"Which gun did it come from? The registered gun or the one with the registration number scratched off?"

He leaned toward me. "Who told you that?"

"Harley. Did the bullet come from the gun that was registered to Jody or not?"

He ate the truffle he'd been playing with before answering. "It doesn't matter. Jody was holding both guns. She shot you with the same gun that killed Cassidy."

He refused to say more, but that was fine. What he'd told me was all I'd needed to hear.

Jody may have been holding both guns, but if she'd shot Cassidy with the gun registered to her, Gibbons would have told me. He would have crowed about it as if that fact alone would prove to me her guilt. And it probably would.

But he didn't tell me that. And Jody has maintained all along that she'd picked up the other gun from the ground, and that it wasn't hers.

The fact that nearly everyone on the island knew how she'd shot out porch lights in the past, the fact that Bailey Grassi had been leaving his lights on for days now, and the fact that everyone on the island knew Cassidy Jones didn't have it in him to be faithful to anyone in his life was pretty good evidence in my book that someone had set Jody up to take the blame for Cassidy's death. Leaving the gun in the sand only helped build the case against her. Even if she hadn't picked up the gun, the police would have found it and blamed her for tossing it away.

Whoever had planned Cassidy's death was smart. Scary smart. And that same scary smart killer now had me in his (or her) sights.

That realization hit me like a frying pan to the head.

Trying to save Jody from serving time for a murder she didn't commit might get me *killed*. I needed to be smart. I needed to think carefully before I did *anything*. But how did I go about being smarter than the killer when I didn't know anything about why someone had gone to such lengths to set up Cassidy's murder?

"You're right," I said to Gibbons. "I'm going to have to start doing things differently. I'm going to have to act with great care from now on." And I needed to act quickly because I was running out of time if I wanted to get Jody out of jail before Thursday.

EIGHTEEN

"I KNOW THIS has nothing to do with Cassidy's murder, but I'm dying to know," I said to Althea the next morning. I'd joined her at the pier to help with the early morning survey of the island's half-dozen remaining turtle nests.

"You're talking about Harriett?" Althea tied her wide-rimmed sweetgrass hat's silky ribbon her under her chin.

"Yes. Can you tell me what happened between her and my mother? And why did Harriett go out of her way to avoid any contact with Cassidy?"

Althea looked around before saying, "Not everyone knows about this. I think Mama knew because Florence went blabbing to Mabel who talked to Mama."

I nodded, even more eager to hear the scandal.

"Harriett cheated on her husband," Althea whispered.

"She cheated?"

Althea nodded. "From what I'd heard, it was a brief affair. A mistake."

"That's it?" It felt kind of like a letdown.

"Florence found out about it and had Harriett blacklisted from the social scene. I don't think Florence ever liked Harriett. I think she was jealous of the attention Harriett received because her husband was mayor of Camellia Beach. Florence's husband had run for mayor of the City of Charleston years before this all happened, and he was soundly beaten." We walked down the beach in silence.

"I suppose that's why Harriett is acting so protective of Muumuu Woman," I said. "She doesn't want to see anyone go through what happened to her."

"That's probably true," Althea answered.

"It's a nuisance, though. Harriett should know that I wouldn't do anything to hurt anyone."

"She should."

Although the sun hadn't yet risen above the horizon, the day already felt hot and sticky. "Isn't it supposed to cool off at night when the sun isn't shining?" I complained. "Gracious, it feels warmer this morning than it did yesterday afternoon."

"Welcome to August in the South." Althea was already fanning herself. "The temperature is probably cooler right now if you looked at a thermometer. The air just feels hotter and wetter because the wind isn't blowing like it was yesterday."

Althea took the red Wisconsin Badgers baseball cap off my head. She dipped it in the waves and handed the soggy thing back to me.

"What did you do that for?" I cried. Granny Mae, a professor at the university, had given me the cap for Christmas last year.

"Put it on," Althea said. She then chuckled when I sniffed my saltwater soaked hat. "The water will keep you from overheating. Let's go."

The soggy hat did help keep my head cool as we continued down the beach.

Althea seemed pleased with how the first two nests looked, but that didn't ease her worry. She continued on

down the beach at a quick pace. "In the history of our island's turtle watch efforts, which spans more than thirty
years, the team has never lost a nest to poaching. Astro-
nomically high tides and tropical storms can devastate
our nests. And I know some years in the past the island
has had a terrible time with predators. But we haven't
lost a nest due to theft. Our team has been vigilant…
at least they were before I took over as team leader."

"I'm sure it's nothing you've done wrong. Lidia and
Harriett both support you."

Althea didn't argue, but I could tell by the way she
kept her gaze locked on the dunes that she blamed herself.

By the time we'd walked at least two miles, sweat
had dampened my clothes. I'd worn a one-piece swim-
suit with an athletic skirt and had a towel slung over my
shoulders. After we'd finished, I planned to take a long
swim in the ocean to cool off. I also hoped to use the
time in the water to help get my thoughts in order. But
right now, I couldn't stop thinking about poor Harriett.

"Because Harriett cheated, Florence got her blacklisted from Charleston Society?" I asked as we walked
side-by-side through the shallow surf. "How did Florence even know Harriett had strayed?"

"I'm not sure. Maybe she found out from Cassidy?"
Althea said. "Now that we know that Florence visited
Cassidy's house on a regular basis, he might have told
her."

"And why did Cassidy know? Did he see her out with
her lover? Was she sloppy?"

Althea shook her head. Clearly, she was stalling.

"Just tell me," I said. "Who was Harriett's lover?"

"Cassidy," she croaked.

I nearly choked on my tongue. "Cassidy? Harriett and Cassidy? Ewww!"

"I know, right?" Althea said.

"Hello!" a man wearing a large straw hat called out from a few hundred yards away. He waved.

"But-but why?" I sputtered.

Althea nudged my shoulder with hers and then raised her hand. "Good morning, Bailey," she called to the man who was fast approaching us.

"Good morning," he said. I noticed again how Bailey Grassi was about the same height as Althea, which wasn't very tall. Today he was dressed in tan Bermuda shorts and a white linen shirt. Like us, his feet were bare. "Beautiful morning, isn't it? I still can't believe how lucky I am to be living on the beach. We get to enjoy all of this"—he made a broad gesture with his arms—"every day."

"It's a blessing," Althea agreed. Her smile grew wider.

I looked at Bailey. His grin looked about as goofy as Althea's as they continued to stare at each other. If they'd been cartoons, I believe their eyes would have turned into springing hearts by now.

I cleared my throat to remind them that I was standing there too.

"I heard you've been asking around about Cassidy Jones," Bailey said as he glanced over at me.

"Not anymore," I confessed.

"Oh," Bailey seemed disappointed. "I hated how he died. Shot like a dog. I attended his funeral Saturday."

"Detective Gibbons mentioned that he saw you there," I said. "Decent thing for you to do for him."

He nodded as his gaze traveled back to Althea. "I

haven't been in the house for very long," he said. "And with starting up the new restaurant, I haven't been home hardly at all. How are the sea turtles faring?"

"We've lost another nest," Althea whispered. The sparkly hearts disappeared from her eyes.

"I hope it wasn't because of my porch lights." He sounded alarmed. "Ever since that night, I've made a point to keep my lights turned off."

"We suspect someone stole the eggs out of the nest," I said since I knew it still pained Althea to talk about it. "Your lights had nothing to do with it."

His brows remained lowered with concern. He took Althea's hand in his. "I'd like to help. I could keep a late-night vigil on the beach. I could hold a banquet as a fundraiser for your organization. What do you think?"

Althea gave his hand a squeeze before releasing it. "A fundraiser would be nice," she said without much enthusiasm.

"Wonderful. Perhaps we could talk more about this over lunch some day this week?"

When she didn't answer right away, I gave her shoulder a little nudge and said, "Wow, that sounds like a great idea. Althea's favorite restaurant for lunch on the island is the Dog-Eared Café."

Althea gaped at me. But I didn't feel the least bit guilty about what I'd done. For the past several months, she'd been trying to set me up on a date. Why shouldn't I return the favor?

Althea sputtered. I smiled. So did Bailey.

"How about tomorrow?" he asked.

Althea sputtered some more.

I said, "You and I had plans to have lunch tomorrow, but we can have lunch anytime." I gently gave her shoulder another nudge. Although she appeared shocked now, I was sure she'd thank me later.

She looked at me. I could tell by the way the corners of her eyes crinkled that she finally realized I'd served her a little payback for her past machinations. "I'd love to meet you for lunch, Bailey," she said while still looking at me. "The Camellia Beach Turtle Watch Program is always on the lookout for new donors."

Once the two of them had finished making plans and exchanging phone numbers, I started to say goodbye so Althea and I could continue our beach walk. I was eager to hear more about how Harriett had fallen under Cassidy's spell. If I believed in magic, which I didn't, I would think Cassidy had been some kind of evil wizard.

Much to my chagrin, Bailey started to walk with us. "I still can't believe there was a murder right here on the beach. While I barely knew him, Cassidy seemed like a normal guy," he said as he scratched the back of his neck. "I would have never guessed he was bringing a different woman to his home every night. That's so nineteen-sixties." He wrinkled his nose as he said it. "But then again, I work nights. So I would have never seen any of that going on." He checked his watch. "When would be a good time for me to come by to visit your shop, Penn? I'm still very interested in selling your chocolates through my restaurant and in my online boutique."

It was now my turn to sputter. I don't know why, but I wasn't comfortable with the idea of letting anyone else sell my family's chocolates.

"I'll bring you by the Chocolate Box after our lunch tomorrow," Althea said as she nudged my shoulder. "That should fit your schedule, right?"

"It does," I had no choice but to admit.

"Two dates with two beautiful women in the same day. I'm a lucky guy. Until tomorrow, then." Bailey whistled a happy tune as he walked in one direction down the beach and we walked in the other.

"Do you think he could be the island's next Cassidy Jones?" I joked as soon as I was sure he couldn't hear us.

Althea playfully swatted my arm. "He's nothing like Cassidy."

"And you like him," I teased.

She acted as if she hadn't heard me. The waves lapping at shore were the only sound we heard for several minutes.

"Look," Althea said suddenly, "if your mysterious Muumuu Woman was married but fooling around with Cassidy—like Harriett—that means that when we found her at his side, she was in the wrong place. Someone who is cheating will use a lie that puts them far away from the scene of the crime. She'd tell her husband that she had a business meeting or was running errands off the island. The flaw in those lies is that being found on the beach would put her at the wrong place and expose her."

"Why wouldn't she just tell her husband she was taking a walk on the beach?" I had to hurry to catch up to her. "Taking a walk on the beach—like we're doing now—would be the easiest lie to defend if someone saw her."

"No, you're wrong. That lie carries too much of a risk. For one thing, her bored husband might invite himself along on the walk. Or he might try to catch up to her as she strolled along the beach, but she's not walking the beach is she? That would be a disaster."

"I suppose," I said. "Granny Mae says I should wait for her to come to me. But that's going to take too long. How do I get Harriett to tell me her name?"

"You don't. Harriett and this mystery woman are probably girlfriends. In the South, girlfriends keep each other's secrets. We keep them to the grave."

"Well then I'll simply have to hope Ethel and the town's gossips can come through for me and ferret out Muumuu Woman's name for me."

"I hope you're not putting yourself into a difficult situation by trying to find her," Althea said as she walked with a determined gait.

"You don't have to worry about me. I'm not asking questions about Cassidy's murder. At least not publicly anymore. It's too dangerous," I said.

We'd both stopped at a small mound of sand marked off with stakes and orange caution tape.

"This is the next nest scheduled to hatch. They could emerge sometime in the next three to five days." Althea placed her slender hands on her hips and frowned at the mound. "I checked yesterday. The eggs are still in there, thank goodness. It was such an honor to be named the island's turtle lady. But now I'm thinking the town should have picked someone else. Nothing like this ever happened to Harriett or even to Jody."

"You don't think—?" I started to ask. But the idea that had popped into my head was simply too crazy to voice.

"What?" Althea kept her eyes trained on the mound of sand. She sounded tired and irritated. My heart hurt for her.

"You don't think they'll hatch tonight, do you? I'm not sure I'll be able to make it tonight," I said even though what I was really wondering was whether Jody, angry that she'd been kicked off the turtle watch team, had decided to make Althea look bad by digging up the island's nests and stealing the eggs. I didn't say any of that because certainly it couldn't be true. No one, not even Jody, would sacrifice the next generation of sea turtles out of spite.

But if not Jody, who was stealing the island's eggs?

NINETEEN

For a small town with everyone watching everyone else's business, I was shocked at the lack of eyewitnesses for anything important lately. It seemed as if scores of islanders had seen Florence going in and out of Cassidy's home. It seemed as if scores of islanders had also seen Fletcher Grimbal slap fighting it out with Cassidy. But no one had witnessed Cassidy's murder? No one (save for Harriett) had seen Muumuu Woman or had a clue as to her identity? No one had seen the thief walking off with my salted sea turtles? And no had seen Althea's turtle egg thief?

It was maddening. I needed an eyewitness.

"I don't know why we didn't think of this right away," Althea said excitedly after we'd finished the turtle survey. She joined me as we walked down Main Street toward the marshy backside of the island. It was still quiet. Shops were dark. A few cars drove past as residents made their way into Charleston for an early start to the work week. Soon more cars would be on the road. But since it wasn't yet eight o'clock, the streets felt empty. Peaceful. Safe.

Althea and I parted ways at West America Street. She went toward the Chocolate Box to have breakfast with her mother while I headed in the opposite direction down East America Street toward the hardware store.

On the way, I passed a fish store. Water lapped at the

two shrimp boats that were tied up at the dock attached to the elevated shop that overlooked the Camellia River. The briny smell of seafood filled the air. Shrimpers shouted commands as they tossed baskets filled with their fresh catch to the dock. Men on the dock ran in and out of the metal building through a large set of double doors as they carried the baskets inside. On those trawlers, the day had started hours before the sunrise and wouldn't end until well after dark.

Across the street from the fish store sat the island's post office. While the main office hadn't yet opened, lights were on inside. The island was starting to wake up.

Next door to the post office was my destination. The small hardware store, owned by one of Sunset Development's smaller competitors, opened at seven every weekday morning to serve the needs of subcontractors who liked to get started on the endless stream of projects on the shabby island where it seemed impossible to keep up with the rust and rot that plagued even the newest structures.

I was reaching for the glass door when a prickling at the back of my neck made me pause. I looked around. Was someone out there watching me?

"I'm not asking anymore questions," I shouted just in case someone was lurking in the shadows of the thick maritime forest, someone who wanted to do me harm.

The blaring bright lights of the hardware store immediately made me feel safe. The young man manning the front counter cheerfully pointed the way to the aisle where they kept the security cameras. There were about a dozen contractors moving through the store. Many were heading toward the back where they kept the lumber. No one seemed the least bit interested in me or in what I was doing.

I had just started reading the specs of the different cameras the store offered for sale, when someone standing behind me cleared his throat. Thinking I was blocking the aisle, I moved closer to the display shelves. I had two camera boxes in my hand at the time, and was trying to decide between the smaller more expensive model and the cheaper, bigger one.

The man leaned his arm on the shelf above the security cameras right next to me. "You should have called me," he said.

My head jerked in his direction so quickly, I nearly dropped both boxes. "Harley, don't do that. You scared me half-to-death."

He threw held his hands out in front of him as if trying to protect his face. A heartbeat later he lowered his hands and smiled. "Hey, you didn't try to break my nose like you did the last time I startled you. I think we must be making progress with our relationship."

"Bust a guy's nose once you and never live it down."

"Look, we wouldn't be having this conversation if you'd taken me along with you this morning. I thought we all agreed yesterday that you wouldn't go out alone, not until this business with Cassidy Jones was resolved and done with."

"I didn't go out alone. I went with Althea on her turtle patrol, and then we parted ways a block before the hardware store, which is two blocks from the Chocolate Box. It's not as if I'm hiking across the island with a target painted on my back."

"Not a target, but it's still a risk. I saw Althea as she went to have breakfast with her mom. She's the one who told me where I could find you." His steady gaze warmed my cheeks. "I would have felt better if you'd called me. You know I would have joined you and Althea on the turtle patrol. And I would have walked you here as well."

"I'm not going to call you every time I step foot out my door."

"I wish you would." I found that hard to believe.

"You might think you want me to do that, Harley, but you really don't. You don't have the time to play babysitter. You have Gavin to take care of. You have a law office to run. You can't go running off with me just because I need to go somewhere."

"Gavin understands." He nodded toward the tool section where his son was playing with a bright orange power drill. "He wants to help."

"What happened to your concern that I was giving him false hope?"

"There's no way I can take away the hope you've already given him. I've talked and talked to him about it. I've told him again and again how you might not be able to prove Jody's innocence, but that boy must have inherited my stubbornness. He won't listen to a word I say."

I gulped. "I am sorry about that."

"Your heart was in the right place. I'll deal with the fallout from whatever happens when it happens. Right now, he's feeling hopeful, which might be a blessing."

I glanced down at the two cameras I was still holding and decided to go with the more expensive camera. I placed the other camera back on the shelf.

"I do have a plan." I held up the box for him to see. "Both Hank and Gibbons think my chocolate thief is stealing those turtles as a way to divert me from investigating Cassidy's murder. If that's the case, wouldn't it also mean that if I catch the thief in the act of taking my chocolates that I'll also catch the killer?"

Harley thought about it for a long minute, and then nodded. "It is a long shot, but that might be all we have right now. Plus, it couldn't hurt to beef up security around the shop. I always thought it was too vulnerable when Mabel was running it."

I headed toward the front counter to pay for the security camera. Harley followed.

"There's something else we do need to talk about," he said talking quickly, while he waved for Gavin to join us.

"I know." He wanted to talk about the kiss. It was sweet. My heart started up with its silly calisthenics. My stomach turned all fluttery. "We can't ignore it, can we? What happened the previous morning did mean something."

"It's your family," he said in a burst. He whispered the rest. "Your mother's family. I got word late last night from a friend of mine who works in your uncle's law office. Edward had his staff working through the weekend so he could file the paperwork with the courts first thing this morning. Your family is contesting the will. Again."

"What?" I stopped in the middle of the store and turned toward him. "Can they do that? On what basis? Florence has admitted that she's my mother." Saying it aloud still made me feel queasy. Florence Corners could barely stand to look at me without sneering. Clearly the woman was born without a heart, which explained how she could abandon her daughter and never try to make contact with her again. It also explained how she could coldly look me in the eye and tell me to keep our relationship secret. And it explained how she could come back into my life without an apology or teary explanation or hug. "Florence is my mother. And even if that weren't true, Mabel had named me in her will to inherit the shop."

"That's all true. I'm sorry, Penn. According to my friend, who couldn't divulge details, some new information has come to light, information that makes the Maybank family think they have legal footing to reinstate the suit. I'll let you know what it is as soon as I get my hands on the filing. But I wanted to give you a head's up that this is coming. Today." He twined his fingers with mine. "And yes, Penn, that kiss did mean something."

"The two of you kissed?" Gavin said as he wandered toward us. "Gross!"

Gavin refused to look at me as the three of us walked the two blocks back to the Chocolate Box. He talked about his mother and what she did every year to help make his first day of school special. "And ice cream," he was saying as we approached the back steps that led to our apartments. "She always takes me out for ice cream after picking me up from school. And she lets me get whatever topping I want, which she never lets me do any other time. I always get peanut butter cups."

While he went on and on about Jody and her skills as a mother, my mind kept swirling around how Jody had warned me that I was going to lose my shop. Had she known that Mabel's children were planning to contest the will?

When Gavin and Harley started to go up the steps, I

grabbed Harley's arm. "I need to talk to you for a moment. Alone."

"Eww! You're not going to kiss my dad again?" Gavin looked as if he might throw up.

"No! Of course not," I protested. "I just need to talk to him about…" About Jody. I couldn't tell Gavin that. And I didn't know what to say so I finally sputtered, "About…about the shop."

"Sure, let's talk," Harley said. He sent Gavin up to their apartment, promising to join him in a minute.

Once we were alone, Harley leaned toward me and whispered, "You want to talk more about that kiss, don't you?" The look he was giving me suggested he was interested in reenacting the heated moment.

"No!" I blurted, and immediately regretted it. I tucked my hands under my arms. "Well, yes, I do want to talk about it. But not right now. Not with everything else going on. Not when I can't stop thinking about Jody." I said his ex-wife's name as if were a curse.

"What about her?" he said with great caution. The way his brows crinkled just then was adorable. "If this is about Gavin going on and on about her, you don't have to worry. Yes, he cares for her, and that's a good thing. But I'm over her. I'm ready to move on. I'm ready to start dating again."

"You are?" My heart started leaping crazily around with joy.

He tilted his head to one side. "Do you really have to ask?"

"Yes, after the way you've been avoiding me I do have to ask."

"I'd been giving you space. Because"—he huffed—

"because you kept making goo-goo eyes at Bixby Lewis. I thought maybe the two of you might end up together."

"Bixby is a rock superstar. Everyone was making goo-goo eyes at him. Even you were."

"That's true," he admitted with a sheepish shrug. "I also thought I needed to give you space after how Jody treated you and after how"—he squeezed his eyes closed so tightly it looked as if he was in pain. His hands curled into tight fists—"after how my brother treated you, I thought perhaps you wouldn't want anything to do with me or my family."

"You've met my mother's side of the family. And my father's side isn't any better. You should know that I, of all people, wouldn't hold you responsible for the actions of your family members. That'd be just wrong."

His eyes popped open with surprise. "I hadn't thought of it that way. I was too busy worrying about my own baggage."

"Don't talk to me about baggage or else I'll start worrying about my own." I laughed. "Crud. Now I'm thinking about my baggage."

He grabbed both of my hands and pressed his lips to mine. The kiss, so unexpected and yet so welcomed, had my thoughts tumbling like the leaves blowing in the sudden gust of wind that swirled around us.

When we finally came up for air, I drew a deep breath and leaned into his chest. "If only we could stay like this forever."

"If only," he whispered. "But the island needs us, doesn't it?"

I forced myself to step out of his embrace. "Not to splash cold water all over whatever is happening here between us, I do really need talk to you about Jody. And it's not about her relationship with Gavin or about Cassidy's murder. Of course Gavin cares for her. She's his mother. I wouldn't be putting myself and those around me in danger for her sorry hide if I didn't think your son needed to keep his mother in his life. It's just that I'm worried she said something to the Maybanks that has caused them to contest Mabel's will again."

"Jody? What information could she possibly have against you?" he asked.

"She told me the other day that a lie I'd been telling everyone was about to go public. She said this lie would make me lose my shop."

"Have you been lying about anything?" His voice suddenly turned all serious and lawyerly.

"No, of course not," I cried. "But that doesn't mean she's not plotting a scheme to ruin me. After all she's still furious that I refused to sell my shop to Sunset Development so they could build their high-rise condos."

"I don't know…" he started to say.

"Oh, I know. I know this is her doing. She can't stand that I kept the shop, and she must have found out something through Cassidy, something she knew she could use to make trouble for me." *Ohhh…* I was so upset, I kicked a small wind-formed pile of sand at the base of the steps. That felt good, so I kicked it again.

That's when I saw it. It was sticking out of the sand like a tiny red finger pointing up at the sky.

I dropped to my knees and swiftly brushed away the rest of the sand that was covering it.

"What is it?" Harley asked as he peered over my shoulder.

I carefully placed it in the palm of my hand. "It's one of those stress spinner thingies."

Why did I keep finding these things? And who kept dropping them?

TWENTY

"I'M MAKING ANOTHER batch of salted sea turtles," Bertie announced when I returned to the Chocolate Box's back kitchen later that Monday morning. "I don't know why you asked me to do it. The thief will only take them again."

"I asked you to make them because I bought this from the hardware store this morning." I tapped the box tucked under my arm. "I'm hoping to catch our sticky-fingered friend in the act."

"A camera?" Bertie nodded her approval. "That's a good idea. Do you know how to hook it up?"

"The directions are in the box. After I get it set up, maybe you could give me some more lessons on making the benne wafer cookies. The last batch I tried on my own, the cookies all stuck to the baking sheets. I ended up throwing them all away."

"The baking sheets?" Bertie cried with alarm. "You threw away the baking sheets? Those were top of the line. Mabel invested in them a few years ago. Each sheet cost several hundred dollars."

"No. I tossed my cookies. Wow, that sounds gross. I mean, I put the cookies in the trash and washed the pans."

"You must have forgotten to put the liners on the pans for the wafers. You need to use liners or parchment paper. Otherwise, they'll stick. We can work through the recipe together after the morning rush."

I started opening the box for the security camera when I heard a loud knocking coming from the front of the shop. We still had about a half hour before we opened the doors for business.

The knocking came again. More urgent this time.

Bertie had her hands busy with the caramel for the turtles.

"I'll go get the door," I said and hurried to the front to find a woman dressed in a flowered sundress standing hunched at the door. Her gnarled hand with paper-thin skin rose to wrap against the glass.

I quickly unlocked the door and pulled it open. "Ethel Crump, what are you doing here so early in the morning? Don't tell me you're having a chocolate emergency."

"Chocolate emergency?" She coughed, trying to clear her raspy voice. It didn't help. "Do you get those?"

"Not in the morning. They mainly come in the middle of the night. And it's generally the men knocking on my door desperate for 'forgive me' presents." I took her arm. "Please, come in. Sit down. Let me brew some coffee while you tell me what's going on." I ushered her inside the shop, locking the door behind us.

By this time Bertie had come up front to see for herself who had been knocking. "I'll make the coffee," she offered.

"What's going on?" I asked Ethel as I led her to the nearest chair. I settled in the chair next to hers.

"I like you, Penn," she said instead of answering my question. Not a good sign. "You're doing good things with this shop. It's becoming popular again. Mabel would have loved that."

"Thank you, but you're not here to heap praises on my head. What's going on?"

Bertie carried over three mugs of coffee and joined us at the table. I noticed she was still limping. "What has put your knickers in a twist this morning, Ethel?"

The older woman opened her mouth and then closed it. She looked at me and then at Bertie. "I like you," she said again.

"Oh for Heaven's sake, Ethel, just spit it out," Bertie grumbled.

"The rumors against you are building, Penn. People all over town are talking about how you tricked Mabel into giving you her shop. They're saying you faked your DNA results and that you're no more of a Maybank than that feisty dog of yours."

Bertie slammed her mug down on the table. "Gracious sakes, Ethel, you'd have to have rocks for brains to believe that nonsense. As you've already pointed out, Penn is the best thing that's happened to this shop in ages."

"Florence is my mother," I said quietly. "She told me that herself."

"I know, I know, honey. I've heard you tell others about your encounter with Florence. And I like you. I want to be on your side. That's why I'm here. That's why I'm warning you."

I looked at Bertie. "This must have been what Jody was talking about a little over a week before Cassidy's death," I said. "She told me that my lies would cause me to lose this shop."

"That snake in the grass don't know nothing," Bertie grumbled, her Southern accent growing more pronounced, which only emphasized how much this upset her.

"Do you think she made up this rumor to make trouble for me and the shop?" I asked.

"Hard to believe that. If she was the source, it'd be mighty difficult for her to keep it going what with her being in jail and all," Bertie said shaking her head. "And who in their right mind would believe Jody when Florence has already confessed to having birthed you?"

"I heard from several people who seem to know what's what that what you've been saying around town about Florence ain't true," Ethel interjected. "They're saying that the Maybank clan is denying being related to you at all."

"That probably explains why Edward is filing a new petition to contest Mabel's will. Harley told me about it this morning. But if Edward or one of his sisters would agree to the DNA test I'd been requesting, all of this would be resolved. As much as it pains me to admit it, Florence is my mother."

"That's just the thing. Florence has never said anything about being your mother in public. So it's your word against hers," Ethel pointed out.

"Harley was in the room with me. He heard her say it."

"Child, that boy is sweet on you," Ethel sang in that half-scratchy, half-melodic island accent of hers, "which means he won't be a credible witness in the eyes of most in this town."

"Then the courts will simply have to order DNA tests. I'm ready to take one. Mabel was my grandmother. I only wished I had more time with her." I hadn't realized I'd jumped up from my chair and had started shouting until I saw the shocked looks on both Ethel's and Bertie's faces.

Ethel closed her gaping mouth. Her thin lips pulled into a broad smile. "That's all I need to hear, dear. I'd been telling everyone who would listen that you are who you say you are. I'll keep telling them that."

"Thank you. I can't tell you how much I appreciate your support."

"It's not just me, child. Half the town is behind you." Which also meant the other half of the town wasn't. And that worried me.

She must have noticed my frown. "Now don't you go worrying that pretty head of yours." She started to slowly rise from her chair. Her movements reminded me of an ageless oak creaking as it swayed in the ocean breeze. When I reached out to lend her a helping hand, she batted it away. "We'll help you stand up to your family. After all, this shop needs you. Heck, this town needs you."

I prayed their support would be enough, because I wasn't leaving this shop. At least, not willingly. It was my home now. It was where I belonged.

I thanked Ethel again for coming to us with what she knew. And while my family's determination to evict me from my shop was worrisome, finding Cassidy's killer was an even more pressing concern.

"Have you been able to find out anything about the identity of that woman who'd fled from the crime scene the night of Cassidy's murder?" I asked before she could leave.

My question seemed to bother Ethel. She gripped my hand, her nails dug into my skin. "You need to stop asking about that horrid man's murder," she whispered as if she was afraid someone might overhear us, which was silly since Bertie was the only other person in the shop. "You need to do it before you get hurt."

I pried my hand loose. "Why? What do you know?"

She shook her head. "Cassidy Jones was a bad man."

"Because of what he did to your cat?"

"Don't be daft," she rasped. "Running down cats with his car was just the tip of his wicked iceberg. In many ways, he was just like you."

"Like me? What do you mean?" How could she even think to compare me to a creep like Cassidy?

"He liked to poke his nose where it didn't belong. So do you. He liked to stir up hornet's nests. So do you. And honey, I'm worried. Look what happened to him." Her rheumy eyes seemed to clear for a moment as she leaned toward me. Her voice hardened. "Scores of people on Camellia Beach are thankful Cassidy Jones is dead. I'm sure there's been a line to spit on his grave ever since the mortician planted him in the ground. Your poking around in his affairs will only endanger yourself and your friends. It has to stop."

"It has stopped," I told her. "I'm not going to ask any more questions. I've decided everyone was right. Cassidy had too many secrets that too many people are desperate to keep."

Ethel's lips curled into a pleased smile, but at the same time she shook her head. "I feel so sorry for that innocent little boy. He's going to lose his mother, and she might not even be guilty."

"If you know anything, Ethel," I pleaded despite just vowing that I'd stopped the investigation cold, "please tell me. If you know where I can find the woman who'd run away from the crime scene, please tell me."

"Despite that pretty speech of yours, you can't give it up, can you? Your heart is in the right place, dear." Her scratchy voice sounded somber, almost as if she was delivering a eulogy. "Too bad it's going to get you killed."

TWENTY-ONE

"THAT'S HIM," Lidia said in that booming voice of hers. Everyone around us started looking around to try and see who she was talking about.

"Who?" I asked as I, like everyone else, looked around.

I'd met up with Lidia at the base of the oceanfront pier during the Chocolate Box's slow time. As I'd walked up, Stella tugged on the end of her leash while barking at seagulls. The birds seemed to be laughing at her, which only made her bark even more. She then started to jump in the air and snap her tiny jaws at the birds. I commanded her to stop. I begged her to behave. I tried bribing her with bacon. She would not calm down. The two of us made quite the circus until Stella spotted Lidia.

The older woman was standing with her hands on her hips. The stern look on her face was directed toward me, not my silky dog. Her fashion style reminded me of how Bertie liked to dress when working at the shop. The clothes—a pair of worn jeans and a baby blue T-shirt with a giant paw print on the front—screamed comfort and economy.

"Have your dog sit," she said in place of a greeting.

"Stella, sit." I copied the arm movement Lidia had taught me. Stella didn't seem to notice.

Lidia huffed and raised her hand. Stella woof-woofed twice before plunking her bottom down.

"She always has to have the last word, I see," Lidia had said with a laugh. "Did you practice the sit command last night when she was calm?"

"I practiced it with you yesterday afternoon."

"But did you have her do it over and over before bed when she was calm?"

My shoulders slumped. "Sorry, no."

"Repetition is key. It's important to practice this command and have her master it when she's calm. Being able to have her sit is a powerful tool. It lets her know what's expected of her even if she's in an unfamiliar situation. It also lets her know that you're in control."

While Stella continued to misbehave, Lidia reviewed the steps I needed to follow to get her attention and have her sit. I tried it. Stella ignored me. There was simply too much going on for her to look at and bark at. Or so I thought.

Lidia issued the exact same command, and Stella instantly plunked her silky bottom down and wagged her tail.

"It's all in the delivery," Lidia explained as she leaned down and gave Stella a friendly pat on the head. "Practice it at home every night. You'll get better at it."

As she'd straightened, she looked over my shoulder. That was when her loud voice had boomed, "That's him."

"Who?" I'd whirled around to look.

"Over there." She pointed to a short, round fellow dressed in hopelessly wrinkled khaki shorts and a stained white T-shirt. It looked as if he hadn't shaved in several days. The black stubble on his face had formed a beard in some areas, but was still just stubble in others. His scraggly reddish blond hair had been secured into a man bun at the top of his neck.

Stella growled low in her throat.

Lidia leaned in close to me and whispered in her not-so-quiet way, "It's Fletcher Grimbal. You wanted to talk to him about Cassidy, right?"

I'd forgotten that Lidia had promised to point him out to me. I'd also forgotten to tell her that I was no longer asking questions about Cassidy's murder. At least not in public.

I should have set her straight right away. But instead, I squinted at the man she'd pointed out to me and said, "That's him, huh?" I started to cross the pier to intercept him. I didn't get very far. The leash in my hand acted as an anchor.

Stella refused to move. Her growls grew deeper.

"She doesn't approve of him," Lidia said. "I'll hold onto her over here. You go catch up to him."

I hesitated. I was no longer openly questioning anyone about Cassidy's death. Besides the last time Stella acted all growly and frightened around someone, I'd later learned the guy was guilty of murder.

"You'd better hurry." Lidia gave me a little push. "It looks as if he's leaving."

Lidia's push got my feet moving. And since they were moving toward Fletcher, the rest of my body decided to go along with it.

I told myself that I was simply going to talk to Fletcher, not grill him like an angry police officer. I also told myself that I shouldn't ever let Stella's growls deter me. She'd done more than growl at Harley. She'd bitten him, and he was one of the good guys.

With a renewed sense of determination, I called out, "Fletcher!" and waved my hand in the air to catch his attention.

He stopped, turned, and scowled. "W-w-what do you w-w-want?"

"I'm Penn, the owner of the Chocolate Box. I heard you used to be manager at Bailey's new restaurant, Grilled to Perfection."

"I-I-I—" he stammered. He smacked his lips and then took a deep breath. "I was," he said with a slight lisp. He took another breath. "Excuse me." He started to walk around me.

"It's good to meet you." I stepped in front of him and thrust out my hand. He stared at it. When it became awkwardly obvious that he wasn't going to accept my handshake, I lowered my arm and clasped my fingers behind my back.

"Well, yes." This wasn't going anywhere. "I heard you knew Cassidy Jones."

He growled.

"You sounded just like my dog, Stella, just then." I forced a laugh. "Do you do any other imitations?"

He growled again and nudged me out of the way and hurried down the pier toward the street.

That was a bust. But I couldn't simply let him run off, not if I wanted to get Jody out of jail before Thursday.

"I want to offer you a job," I called to his retreating back.

He stopped. After a several long moments, he turned back toward me. His scowl suddenly loosened its grip on his face. "A job?"

A job? my inner voice screamed. *You're going to let a man who might have shot Cassidy Jones in the heart work in the shop with you? This isn't better than asking him questions about Cassidy directly. It's actually kind of worse. Far worse.*

"You're off-f-f-ering me a j-j-job?" he demanded, speaking slowly and carefully as if it took mountains of effort to form each word in his mouth. He jammed his hand in his pocket as if searching for something, but came up empty. "W-w-what kind of job?"

I cleared my throat several times before stumbling over my own words, "Well…um…yes…well, I heard you were a restaurant manager."

"So you already said," he answered in his slow, lumbering way. His eyes remained hard and unforgiving.

"I…um…also heard you're not working at Grilled to Perfection anymore. The Chocolate Box has been slammed with the summer crowds. What with managing the shop, working the front counter, and making the chocolates, my partner Bertie and I barely have time to sleep. We could use someone with your experience."

"Really?" He took a step toward me. He thrust his hand in his pants pocket again, searching.

I took a step back. "It wouldn't be a fulltime position, at least not at first."

He took another step toward me. "Y-you're that C-Charity Penn woman." He smacked his lips and drew another deep breath. "I've heard all about you."

I took another step back and bumped up against the pier's railing. "Good things, I hope."

"You're the one who'd inherited Mabel Maybank's shop under some q-q-questionable circumstances." His stutter was beginning to disappear as he turned from flight to fight, but the lisp remained as strong as ever.

"That pesky rumor? Oh, it's not true." I don't know why I let him make me feel intimidated. I had at least a foot on him in height. My self-defense skills were top-notch. Stella's growling must have spooked me. Or perhaps it was the way he kept flexing both his arm and jaw muscles that was making me nervous. Or perhaps I was simply a wimp.

Whatever the cause, my insides felt like jelly and my feet trembled with the desire to run away.

"I've heard some other things about you too. I've heard you're just like him." He spat those words in my face.

"Him? Who?"

"Cassidy Jones." He puckered his lips as if the name had a sour taste.

I wanted to scream, "No!" But I kept my cool. Instead I held up my hands in silent protest and asked as calmly as possible, "How am I like him? I didn't even know the guy, but from what I've heard he wasn't a nice guy. I'm—"

"Y-you're a meddler. You stick your nose where it don't belong. And I've got troubles aplenty thanks to Cassidy." He smacked his lips again. "I don't need no Nosey Nelly going and making more troubles for me."

"I'm not—" I protested.

"This is a small town." Both his stutter and lisp seemed to disappear for a moment as he continued to attack my character. "I know all about how you're trying to find someone else to pin the murder to so that l-l-little Dalton boy can g-g-get his mother back. Well, let me tell you something. I'm not the only person in town who had a beef with that man."

"I'm not saying—" I protested.

"I'm not the only one that man put in hot water in the last couple of weeks." Gracious, the man wouldn't let me talk. "Ask your painter Johnny Pane or your friend Harriett Daschle. O-o-or better yet, you should ask sweet old Ethel Crump. She stood to lose everything, her house, her independence because of evil m-man."

"Ethel? Because of that crazy lawsuit?" I still found it hard to believe Cassidy would sue a sweet old lady like Ethel after nearly killing her cat with his car.

"Not c-c-crazy. Evil. He knew s-she wouldn't be able to afford to pay a lawyer. He knew the l-lawsuit would ruin her."

"But Ethel? She's got to be pushing one hundred. You can't honestly believe she shot Cassidy."

"'Crack-shot Ethel' has won the annual Halloween turkey shoot for as l-long as anyone around here can remember." He stumbled over some of his words. "I-I should know. I've lived here my entire life."

"Camellia Beach hosts a contest for people to shoot turkeys at Halloween?" That was barbaric. But I suppose I should have expected some kind of blood sport like that from a town where everyone owned a gun.

"Where are you from, girly? The moon? We don't shoot turkeys. It's a target shooting contest," Fletcher explained. "A frozen turkey is the prize."

"Oh! And Ethel—?"

"Wins every year. So yeah, she could have shot Cassidy and no one would ever suspect sweet, frail Ethel."

"Ethel?" I still couldn't believe it. "Are you sure?"

Fletcher didn't answer. He was walking away. I supposed he'd said all he'd planned to say about Cassidy

Jones. For such a short man, he walked with a long stride.

"I'll s-s-see you tomorrow at eight," he called over his shoulder as he went. "I expect f-f-fifteen an hour."

TWENTY-TWO

"YOU DID *WHAT*?" Harley marched across the shop and then back to me.

"I think I hired him." I wrinkled my nose as I said it. I'm not even sure why I was telling Harley this. I hadn't even told Bertie about Fletcher. Perhaps the words came pouring out of my mouth as a way to keep Harley from saying why he'd come looking for me. I wasn't in a mood to talk about my family and their latest attempts to take my shop away from me.

He'd come to the Chocolate Box a few minutes before closing time. His brows were drawn. His lips were pulled into a deep frown. Clearly, he'd come to share some sort of unhappy news.

"You *think* you hired a man who might be a murderer to work with you in your shop?" He marched across the shop again. This time he was muttering to himself like a madman. That's what I did to those closest to me, apparently. I turned them into lunatics.

"Bertie won't complain," I explained. "She never complains. But she's been limping on that leg she broke. She's hurting and it's killing me to see her pretend she's not. The shop is busier than ever. And the milkshakes keep us running at full speed to serve them. We need the help."

Harley grunted.

"Fletcher said he's lived on the island his entire life.

Do you know him well? What do you think about his character?"

"He's about ten years younger than me." Harley stopped at the coffee bar and poured himself a cup. "I only know him in passing. Always thought of him as a nervous fellow with a mighty big chip on his shoulder. He's struggled with a speech impediment for as long as I can remember. And he's always been self-conscious about his height."

"He isn't very tall," I said. "And he did seem angry, but then again I did surprise him at the pier."

He took a sip of his coffee—no cream, no sugar. "Didn't you say you weren't going to ask questions about Cassidy's death and his secrets anymore?"

"I did. And I'm not asking questions anymore. That's why I ended up hiring Fletcher. I wanted to find out what he knew or if he was capable of premeditated murder, and I needed to do it without questioning him about Cassidy. Things came out of my mouth."

"I suppose I shouldn't worry too much. Every piece of evidence Detective Gibbons has uncovered so far points a finger of guilt toward Jody, not at Fletcher or anyone else," he said after finally returning to where I was working the front counter. "As horrible as it seems, I'm afraid Jody killed Cassidy." He dredged his fingers through his short hair. "I've been talking with the lawyer she hired to see if he can get the murder charge against her changed to manslaughter. But without a plea deal, which Jody is adamant against, her lawyer doesn't think he can get the solicitor's office to agree to anything."

That wasn't what I'd wanted to hear. I'd been hoping all day that Detective Gibbons would come through for me, locate Muumuu Woman, and get enough information from her to clear Jody's name. Obviously, the opposite had happened.

I closed my eyes and suddenly pictured Gavin's tearful face as clearly as if he were standing as close to me as his father was at that moment. I couldn't let that sweet boy lose his mother. I simply couldn't.

I no longer regretted hiring Fletcher. He might or might not be a killer. If he was a killer, I had him exactly where I needed him—close by so I could watch him and catch him if he slipped up.

"Thanks," I said to Harley.

He looked confused. "For what?"

"You've convinced me that I did the right thing after all. I was doubting myself left and right until you walked into the shop. And now there's no longer even a shred of doubt left. I need any piece of information I can get from Fletcher. And after what Cassidy did to him, Fletcher needs this job."

Harley moved closer to me. "You're crazy."

"And yet you still want to kiss me." I flashed him a smile. It felt good. We were becoming friends again. *More* than friends. All that awkwardness between us the other day after our first kiss was gone, hopefully for good.

Gone until you sabotage things again, a vicious voice in my head chided.

I'm working on that. So stop trying to scare me, I told myself rather firmly.

"I know you didn't come in here to lecture me. You're smart enough to know that would be a waste of everyone's time. So tell me. What was in those legal papers my loving family had filed against me this morning?"

"I'd rather kiss you and eat chocolate." He looked longingly at the shiny and colorful bonbons and truffles lined up like soldiers in the display case. "But unfortunately, I am here about the contested will. I read through the papers."

I held up my hand. "Don't tell me. The petition they filed today claims I'm not related to them."

His green eyes widened with surprise. "How did you know?"

"Half the town already knows, that's how."

Harley groaned. "Small towns can be a pain sometimes. No one ever minds their own business."

"Thanks to our town's intrepid gossips, though, I wasn't blindsided by this. The Maybanks don't think I'm related. They're telling everyone that because there weren't any witnesses when Florence confessed that she was my mother that it's my word against hers."

"Well, we already know that's absolutely ridiculous. I was there. And I've already filed a counter brief that includes the sworn and dated affidavit we'd written up right after the conversation with Florence detailing everything that was said."

"In light of that, can the court force a DNA test?" I asked.

"The judge won't have to. Mabel's children have already requested one."

"Finally." I breathed a long sigh of relief. "At least something is going my way."

"I wouldn't be so quick to celebrate. Something smells fishy about this whole thing. Edward, Florence, and Peach must think they're going to prove that you're not Mabel's kin. They'd been resisting our calls for DNA testing for months now. Why suddenly flip and demand *you* take one? I think you need to set up a meeting with Florence."

A face-to-face with Mommy Dearest? "How about I get a few teeth pulled without pain killers instead?"

"You need to talk to her. Find out what she's thinking." He put his hand on my arm. His touch felt like someone had flipped a switch and caused half my body to suddenly turn all tingly and happy. "I know it's difficult, but it's something you need to do."

"I know. I already had that same idea. I left a message for her to call me yesterday. I'll try her number again. We do need to talk." Not only did I need to talk with her about why she was going along with her brother and sister in contesting their mother's will, I also needed to find out what Florence had been doing with Cassidy and if she'd ever seen a woman wearing a muumuu hanging around his house.

Like before, my call went through to her voicemail. I started to leave another message for her to give me a call when a sharp pop, pop, pop had me throwing my phone aside and diving to the floor.

Sweet heaven, someone was shooting at us!

TWENTY-THREE

HARLEY LANDED ON top of me, sending a jolt of pain through my already sore shoulder. He used the full weight of his body to shield me from the bullets.

Pop. Pop. Pop. Three more shots.

We lay on the ground, not moving, as I strained to hear something, anything in the thrumming silence that had followed the brittle sound of gunshots. Harley's heart hammered against my back. His measured breath felt warm on my neck.

"Thank God no one was in the shop," I whispered.

"*We* were in the shop," Harley's rumbling voice corrected.

"Yes, we were." It felt like the last gunshot had happened hours ago even though I was sure only a few minutes had passed. I wiggled out from under him. "Are you okay?"

He rolled off me and started to brush glass cubes that had fallen from the shattered tempered glass window onto his clothes and hair. "Yeah, I'm okay. Are you?"

Was I okay? I climbed to my feet and propped my hands on my hips as I surveyed the damage. The front window had shattered. So had the glass in the display case. The chocolates were coated with slivers of tempered glass. My ruined delicacies sparkled as if they'd been sprinkled with stardust. A bullet had blasted through the heart of several of the chocolate covered cherries as it traveled through the case. Their bright red juices dripped as if the delicate treats were bleeding.

All of this destruction had happened in a matter of seconds. It'd happened because I'd promised Gavin to get his mother back to him. Was I okay?

"No, I'm not," I said. "This is not okay." Tears sprang to my eyes as I suddenly realized the mountain of cash I was going to need in order to repair the shop and replace nearly my entire inventory of chocolates. My jaw tightened as I blinked those stupid tears away. "It's not okay at all. But it could have been worse."

If the bullets had come tearing through the shop an hour earlier when the shop had been packed with the afternoon beach crowd, someone would have gotten hurt or even killed. I said a silent little prayer, giving thanks that this had happened on a Monday—one of our slowest days of the week—and everyone had cleared out before closing time. Even Johnny Pane had already packed up his painting supplies and had gone home.

I would have never forgiven myself if an innocent bystander had gotten hurt because I'd stuck my nose, *which wasn't at all pointy*, into Cassidy's dirty business. I cursed Cassidy Jones for being such a creep. He had no right to dig up everyone's secrets. And if he hadn't waved those secrets around like a red flag at a bullfight, he'd still be alive. Jody would still be free to harass me to her heart's content. And no one would be taking potshots at me or my chocolates.

I retrieved my phone from where I'd thrown it to the floor. The screen had cracked, but it was still working. The entire shooting had been recorded onto Florence's voicemail, which was still recording. I pressed the phone to my ear and said, "We need to talk," and hung up.

My first order of business was to call Detective Gibbons. He needed to know that someone was feeling all crazy and homicidal because of something I'd done or said today.

Harley already had his phone out. From what I could hear from his end of the conversation, he was reporting the shooting to Camellia Beach's police chief.

"What in the world has happened here?" Bailey Grassi, dressed in his white chef's uniform, ran into the shop and came to an abrupt stop right in front of the ruined display case. He whimpered. "Is the Amar chocolate"—he turned a pleading look in my direction—"Is it ruined? Is it all gone?"

"Not all of it," I said after I'd ended my brief conversation with Gibbons. After a couple of swearwords on his part, the detective had promised to drive right out to the shop. "Because the crop is so small, we use the Amar bean sparingly in our recipes," I explained to Bailey. Talking about creating luscious chocolates from the cacao bean helped calm my jumpy nerves. I drew a deep breath and actually felt the tension in my shoulders fall away. "I've been making a new batch of the chocolate from the beans this week. It should reach its peak of flavor and be ready for use in about ten days."

"I still want to distribute it," he said before I'd even finished describing the chocolate-making process. He spoke quickly, sounding a little too eager. "Connoisseurs from all over the world are searching for unique foods just like your Amar chocolates. It's exactly the kind of delicacy I aim to provide for the hand-selected clientele I serve in my carefully curated online business."

Harley pushed end on his phone and came to stand next to me. "Penn doesn't have time to talk business expansions," he said. Sirens blared in the not-too-far distance. It was, after all, a small sea island. "She has other things to worry about right now."

"Of course she has more pressing things on her mind," Bailey agreed. "I didn't mean to downplay what just happened." He grabbed both my hands. I struggled to keep myself from flinching. *He's not a stranger*, I reminded myself. *He's the guy who is going to start dating my best friend*.

"Are you okay?" he asked. "What happened? I was driving by on my way to the restaurant and saw the broken window."

"Someone took multiple shots at her," Harley said. "Did you see anyone or anything as you drove up?"

Bailey dropped my hands as he shook his head. "Just a few tourists walking toward the beach. Who are you?" he demanded as soon as he finished looking Harley up and down. It was actually more up than down since Harley had nearly a foot of height on Bailey.

While I introduced the two men, Bertie came limping in from the back door. "I heard a crash."

She came to an abrupt stop when she saw the smashed display case, shattered window, and bullet holes in the far wall. Her hands flew to her lips. "Oh no, child. This is exactly what Ethel had warned would happen. Is everyone okay?"

Before I had a chance to reassure her, Lidia came running in the front door, followed by Bubba and, a few moments later, Ethel.

On their heels was Chief Byrd. He drew his hands over his ample belly as his lips blew a low, slow whistle. "You sure made someone hoppin' mad with your meddling ways, sugar pie."

I was no one's sugar pie, but telling him that would only reinforce his impression that I was one of those uppity northern female troublemakers. So I gritted my teeth and nearly popped a vein in my temple as I forced myself to keep my mouth closed.

Harley sent a surprised look in my direction before stepping forward and shaking the police chief's hand. He took over, acting both as my personal lawyer and as the main eyewitness to the shooting (not that either of us saw anything since we'd spent the entire time huddled together on the floor.)

"Y'all are walking all over my crime scene," Byrd complained and instructed the two officers that had arrived with him to clear everyone out of the shop.

The seven of us left the building as a group and stood under the thick, sprawling branches of the ancient oak tree that reached toward the sky in front of the Chocolate Box. Bailey kept looking at his watch. He called his restaurant several times. And cursed under his breath a few times as well.

"I need to get downtown to my restaurant," he told the police chief. "Even if I leave right now, I'll still be late."

"You're going to have to resign yourself to being late, son. A shooting happened on the island. That's not something we take lightly around here. And as I already told you, we're waiting for the county folks to arrive before we begin processing the crime scene and questioning the witnesses," Byrd said.

"And I already told you I didn't see anything. None of us saw anything." Bailey's voice grew louder. "Save for Penn and her freakishly tall lawyer, we all got here after the shooting had stopped."

"Y'all are just going to have to wait," Chief Byrd drawled. "So you might as well simmer down. Sit tight. I'll get you out of here as soon as possible."

Bailey thrust his hands into his pockets and walked away. I thought he'd simply leave like the woman in the muumuu had done after Cassidy's murder. But he didn't leave. He stopped in the middle of the road.

What was he holding? It looked red…and familiar. I started to walk toward him. But Byrd grabbed my arm.

I froze.

"We need to talk," the police chief said as he started to lead me away from the rest of the group.

"Not without me," Harley said. He deftly removed the police chief's hand from my arm.

Byrd curled his lip, but kept his hands to himself as he led the two of us around the back of the shop where another one of his officers was standing with his fingers touching his sidearm.

"I didn't want to say anything in front of the others since we'd all agreed to keep the news about the threatening notes quiet," Byrd said, sounding terribly cross about it. "One of your letter writers has to be our shooter. So I need to know, what did you do over the past two days to cause this? I thought we all agreed you were going to give the investigating a rest."

"We did. I did," I said. "I haven't been asking questions. I've kept my mouth shut about Cassidy Jones." *Mostly.*

Harley started to back me up on this when Detective

Gibbons came walking around the side of the building. "Was told I could find the three of you back here." His brows dipped low on his forehead as he looked me over. "You weren't hurt, were you?"

"It hurts me all over that my shop is full of bullet holes, if that counts. Luckily Harley and I were the only people in the Chocolate Box at the time."

"Lucky, perhaps." He rubbed his chin. "Or the shooter planned it that way."

Byrd looked at Gibbons and started to rub his chin too. "Since you've been talking to nearly everyone who'd ever crossed paths with Cassidy, who do you think did this?" he asked me.

Names came flying at me too fast for me to categorize. There was Fletcher Grimbal who lost his job because of Cassidy, the woman in the turquoise muumuu who was found standing over Cassidy's dead body but felt her secrets too dear to stick around and talk to the police, Johnny Pane who'd been terrified by what Cassidy might say about him, and the island's oldest resident, Ethel Crump who could outshoot anyone. Even my own mother, Florence Corners, had been skulking around with Cassidy.

Anyone of them could have taken a gun and shot up the Chocolate Box. Considering how—according to Althea—everyone south of the Mason-Dixon Line owned a gun, with just a little more digging on my part, the list of suspects would surely grow longer. And that was what I told Byrd.

I don't think either man expected to hear any different. They both knew Cassidy Jones and the troubles he'd caused for everyone around him.

About an hour later, the police finished their work

and announced that the shop was no longer a crime scene. The technicians packed up their gear, pulled down the yellow caution tape, and left. On their way out, Byrd told me to keep my *pointy* nose out of his investigation. Gibbons asked me to stay safe.

Harley, Ethel, Lidia, Bubba, and Bertie followed me back into the shop, which was still a mess. The ruined chocolates were still sitting out in their shattered display case. Glass crunched underfoot wherever anyone walked. The front window had completely fallen out. And tables and chairs had been haphazardly moved.

The mood in the shop had a distinct funeral vibe. Everyone was speaking in hushed tones as they watched me take a hand broom and sweep the chocolates into a plastic trash bag.

"I'll be right back." I carried the bag through the shop, down the long corridor, and out the backdoor to drop it into the trash container. I didn't need to toss the bag immediately. It hadn't even been half-full. I could have used the plastic trash bag to hold the shattered glass that needed to be swept from…everywhere.

No, I'd taken out the trash simply because I couldn't handle looking at my shop in its broken state for one moment longer. I needed to step outside and catch my breath.

I leaned against the wall and took several deep breaths in a desperate attempt to get control over my emotions. It was simply a store. Those were simply things in a store that had been destroyed. It wasn't as if anyone had gotten killed.

The back door swung open. I steeled my spine as I waited to see who was coming out to join me. I really didn't think I could handle the company right now. Any encouraging words right then would probably feel like a jabbing knife to my chest.

Ethel stepped onto the back patio. She glanced at me, frowned, and then clasped her hands behind her back as she gazed out into the marsh.

"Is this the last nail in the shop's coffin?" I asked more to myself than to Ethel. All those repairs I'd made over the past several months, all those costly upgrades, had the money been wasted?

"Clamp your teeth, girl," Ethel rasped. "As sure as I'm standing here, you'll make this right and go back to business as usual. You're just like your grandmother— resilient as all get out. And as soon as you leave the sleuthing to the police, nothing like this will have to happen again."

I turned to study Ethel. Her simple gingham print dress cinched at the waist. Her large black orthopedic shoes seemed too big for her thin frame. Although she appeared frail as if a strong wind would sweep her away, there was strength in the way she held her chin. Fletcher had claimed that Ethel, even with fingers bent with age, was an expert shot. He made it sound as if she was the best shooter on the island. And she had a strong reason to want Cassidy dead. Plus, she was clever. I could easily imagine her planning the murder so Jody would be framed for the crime.

But why would she shoot at me?

"Other than that stupid lawsuit Cassidy had filed against you, did he do anything else to you? Did he"—I cleared my throat—"have embarrassing information about you?"

"Gracious, no. What are you trying to say?" Her faded blue rheumy eyes widened. "Oh my gracious sakes, you think I killed Cassidy and framed that little boy's mother for the crime. You actually think that, don't you? Only a monster would do something like that." She set her bony hands on her hips. "And what, pray tell, do you think Cassidy might know about me that would drive me to shoot at my friends?"

"Maybe he found out your age?"

Ethel swatted my arm. "Shut your mouth, child. Not even my dear late Stanley knew my age. A proper lady doesn't divulge—"

"Yes, yes, I know." I didn't have time to listen to a lecture about a lady's proper behavior. "But I also heard that no one around here rivals your abilities with a gun."

A sudden grin pulled Ethel's loose skin tight. "That's the truth!" She sounded proud of it. "Most folks around here couldn't hit the fat side of a barn. But not me. Ain't nothing wrong with my aim."

"So you could have done it," I said.

"Of course I could have done it." She squinted at me. "Are you back to asking questions about Cassidy Jones and his misdeeds again? Did getting shot at teach you nothing?"

"I'm not talking to the town about Cassidy's death. I'm talking to you."

"Sounds like you're accusing me of something."

"Should I be?"

This exchange led to a staring contest. Both of us had our lips pursed, waiting for the other to break. This went on for several minutes. It would have gone on even longer if I hadn't realized standing behind the shop silently staring at Ethel wasn't accomplishing anything.

"I think you're the one who shot up the Chocolate

Box just now." There, I said it. "And I'm starting to think you killed Cassidy."

Ethel blinked. "You think that I...?" She started to say before pressing her lips tightly together again. She blinked some more.

"I think you shot up the Chocolate Box," I prompted again, since I wasn't in the mood to start another staring contest.

"Well, doesn't that just beat all?" Ethel slapped her leg and hooted. "Penn, I knew I liked you, but now I really like you." She slapped her leg again and then did a little jig right there in the middle of the patio.

"Did you hear me correctly? I just accused you of shooting at me. And you're saying that makes you like me?"

"You'd better believe it." She held onto the hem of her gingham dress as her legs stomped to a musical beat only she could hear. "You're the first person in a long time who didn't treat my age like it was an infirmary. 'Oh, she's as old as the trees. Must mean she can barely feed herself' is what most people around here think when they talk to me. I can hear it in how their voices rise up an octave and how they slow their speech as if I wouldn't be able to follow their inane conversations otherwise. But you didn't do that. You took one look at me and thought, 'By Heavens, there's a woman who could be a mad murderess.' I love it, Penn. I absolutely love it."

"Um...thank you?"

She did a little twirl as the punctuation at the end of her victory dance before coming to stand directly in front of me. She sounded a little out of breath when she said, "Don't know anyone else on the island other than

Jody and me capable of shooting Cassidy through the heart at that distance. Take that to mean what you will because you won't hear me talk about it again."

She walked with a bounce still in her step down the marsh trail that led toward her cottage. And I was left standing there wondering if she'd confessed to killing Cassidy or had she just now accused Jody of doing the deed.

TWENTY-FOUR

BERTIE AND I had worked for hours that night melting down all of the chocolate we had left in our pantry so we'd have something to offer the buying public in the morning.

Early the next morning when the two of us came down to open up the shop, I was surprised to find Fletcher leaning against the back door with his arms crossed over his chest. For one thing, he'd said he'd show up at eight o'clock and it wasn't even seven yet. And for another, after how he'd acted yesterday I figured working for me was the last thing in the world he wanted to do. I'd assumed he simply wouldn't show up.

True, the sour look on his face as he greeted us suggested he'd rather be anywhere than here. But he was clean shaven. No wrinkles or stains marred his plain white and khaki clothes. He looked ready to work.

"Good morning," I said brightly. "You're early."

He shrugged. "G-got n-nowhere else to be."

"If you want to work with us"—Bertie frowned as she looked him over with that critical eye of hers—"you're going to have to keep out of trouble. No getting into late night fights. No more arrests. You show up for work on time. And if I smell alcohol on your breath, I will send you home."

"I-I thought"—He smacked his lips and then continued forming each word with great care—"I thought Penn owned the shop, not you."

"I do. But Bertie has much more experience running this shop than I do, which means you'll be working for the both of us. Do you have a problem with that?"

He held up his hands. "N-n-no, no problem. I'm here to work."

"Good." I unlocked the door. "There's plenty of work that needs to be done."

The front window had a board where the glass should have been. While the shattered glass in the display case had been swept away, there were two bullet holes in the metal frame. And the tables and chairs were still in a state of disarray.

Fletcher took one look and whistled. "You-you do need me," he said in his slow, carefully enunciated cadence. "This place is a mess."

"It'll look perfect by the time we open," Bertie said.

As much as I wished it, that wasn't exactly true. The shop wouldn't look perfect since there was nothing we could do about the half dozen or so bullet holes in the walls that had chipped off large sections of plaster. However we were paying the glaziers a ridiculous amount of money to replace the broken window and the glass in the display case before we opened to serve the public.

While I was busy directing the glaziers who'd arrived not long after we'd flipped on the lights, Bertie took over showing Fletcher around the shop. She then had him fill out the pile of necessary employment paperwork. He seemed to have left his attitude outside. Every time I glanced in their direction, Fletcher appeared to be listening intently. He even laughed a few times at something Bertie had said.

Satisfied that things were going well with them, I gave the store a thorough sweeping. Sure both Bertie and I had swept up the glass twice the previous night, but it didn't matter. My broom was still picking up those little glass shards. I had a feeling I'd be sweeping up those tiny buggers for days.

By the time we unlocked the door and welcomed our first customers, the Chocolate Box was nearly back to normal. The tables and chairs had been set back up. And while the display case looked half-bare, we did have five varieties of chocolates for sale. Plus, I was introducing for the first time my chocolate moon benne wafers. To be fair, Bertie had baked the benne wafers. They turned out thin and crispy instead of the dry puffy things I'd kept churning out all week. I dipped one side of the wafer in white chocolate and the other side in a thin layer of our special dark Amar chocolate. They looked beautiful.

All during the morning rush Fletcher moved through the store as if he'd always worked there. Anything that needed to be done, it seemed as if he'd already handled it. He kept the coffee urns filled and the tables cleared. Before I knew it the morning had flown by and we were preparing the blender and making sure we had enough milkshake ingredients for the afternoon rush.

"Holy moly, Ms. Penn, this is worse than I'd heard," Johnny Pane cried when he arrived shortly before noon. He dropped his tall ladder on the heart pine floor and hurried over to inspect the damaged walls. He tsked as he ran his hand over the plaster dislodging large chunks that fell to the floor with a puff of dust. "This is going to

take me at least a week and a half to repair and paint."
Given how Johnny Pane's estimates seemed to work,
it'd take three weeks. And plenty more money.

"Just do what needs to be done." I didn't have the
energy to worry about the paint job. I'd figure out how
to pay for it later.

Right now I needed to focus on my promise to Gavin.
I hadn't forgotten that today was Tuesday. Middle
school started early Thursday morning, which meant
I needed to get Jody cleared of all charges and out of
jail by tomorrow. And I needed to do it without putting
anyone in danger.

I looked around the crowded shop again. That's when
I spotted Bubba. As president of the downtown business association, he knew pretty much everything about
everybody.

"Have you talked to her?" I asked Bubba as I placed
a frothy double dark and white chocolate milkshake in
front of him. He'd been practically living at our shop
this past week. His choice of clothing was usually
shabby shorts paired with a bowling shirt worn over a
faded and threadbare graphic T-shirt. Today he'd up-
graded to khaki pants and a crisply pressed button up
shirt. Did that mean he finally planned to talk to Bertie?

He glanced over at her as she served milkshakes to a
group of tourists. His face lit up. "She's so dang beautiful, it makes my eyes ache to look at her."

Gracious, he had it bad. Bertie could look beautiful when she took the effort. On Sundays she wore her
best dress and styled her salt-and-pepper hair into an
elegant bob. But today she was dressed in her favorite
cheap mom jeans and one of the corny Camellia Beach
T-shirts she bought whenever they were on five for five

dollars clearance sale at the downtown tourist shops. A big-eyed lizard with a leering smile and a beer clutched in its claws spanned the length of her shirt. "Lounge lizard," was written in bold letters underneath the green reptile. She hadn't even bothered with makeup, not that her smooth dark complexion really needed any enhancements beyond a subtle shade of lipstick.

I nudged his shoulder. "Go talk to her."

"Tomorrow." He took a long sip of his milkshake. "I see you have a new employee."

Good old Bubba, he took the conversation where I wanted it to go without any prodding on my part. Fletcher was working the blender. He noticed us watching him and raised his brows as if asking a question.

I smiled. "He's a good worker. Have you known him a long time?"

Bubba had just started to tell me how Fletcher had grown up on the island when Bertie called my name and pointed to two trays filled with milkshakes that were waiting to be served.

I was glad someone had their mind focused on serving the public, because all I could think about as I walked through the shop—filled with our regular customers and gawkers who wanted to see the aftermath of the shooting—was that one of my customers sitting inside the shop right now had probably killed Cassidy Jones. That same person then also used the Chocolate Box for target practice.

When looking at the world through such a dim lens, every face looked like a mask. Every smile came across as cold and calculating. And every kind word spoken sounded like a lie. At least two of the islanders, lovely people I'd thought I could trust, had threatened me.

One of them had tried to kill me. How could I possibly trust anyone?

I needed to get back to Bubba and ask him more about my main suspects and what he knew about them. I was working my way back over to his table when a sudden chill shuddered through me.

"Lidia?" I nearly dropped the tray of milkshakes I was carrying when I spotted her following me across the room. The way she was standing too close and the way her eyes darted from side-to-side made me feel as nervous as Stella in a room filled with strangers. "What are you doing here? We didn't have a lesson set up for today, did we?"

"Our next training session is scheduled for tomorrow, not today," she said and then added sternly, "But be sure to work with Stella a few times today to make up for all that nervous energy last night's shooting has caused for you."

"I will. I will." I steadied the milkshake tray and started to hand the drinks to the waiting customers.

Lidia continued to follow too closely alongside me. "I do, however, need to talk with you," she hissed loudly in my ear.

"About what?"

She pressed a finger to her lips and glanced over at Fletcher who was watching us. "Not here."

I quickly served the drinks on my tray. "I'll be back in a few minutes," I called over to Bertie.

I could feel the press of Fletcher's hard gaze as I led Lidia through the long hallway and out toward the back patio.

The afternoon sun was high in the sky as it beat

down on the patio's stone pavers. I cupped my hand over my eyes to block the glare. Lidia did the same.

"What's up?" I asked her.

"Muumuu Woman," her booming voice seemed to echo across the open marsh.

She'd definitely caught my attention. "Yes?"

"I found her."

TWENTY-FIVE

"REMEMBER THAT COTTAGE I'd wanted to rent?" Lidia asked as she paced the patio. "I went by there yesterday after the shooting just to see if it was still empty. If it was, I'd planned to contact someone at the real estate office where Cassidy had worked to inquire about it. Well, it wasn't vacant anymore. A woman was living there. *Your* woman. Muumuu Woman."

"Really?" I could hardly believe it. Before I realized what I was doing, I'd untied the shop's apron and had lifted it off over my head. "Can you take me there? Now?"

As soon as I'd said those words a thought flashed through my head. I couldn't go with Lidia. Not alone. I'd promised, well, pretty much *everyone* I wouldn't go anywhere alone. And while I wasn't alone, I didn't trust Lidia. Not completely. Not yet.

Perhaps it went back to my trouble with trusting anyone, which showed that big flaw in my personality that made even my own dog so nervous she liked to bite me. Or perhaps it was that I wasn't a stupid heroine in a horror movie. I didn't want to end up dead.

I couldn't go with her. Not alone.

"Harley will want to be in on this," I told her as I fished my cell phone out of my pocket. The call went to his voicemail. I called his office and talked with Bunny, his secretary. Apparently, Harley was in court for the next hour. Well, drat.

I could call Detective Gibbons. But if I did that, he'd insist I let him handle questioning our missing witness. And since Gibbons was already convinced of Jody's guilt, I doubted he'd ask the questions I'd want to ask. And even if he did ask the questions that needed to be asked, he wouldn't share with me anything he learned from her. Instead he'd tell me he couldn't discuss an ongoing investigation, which is what he always said.

If I was going to have any hope of getting Jody cleared of the murder charge and out of jail by tomorrow, I needed to get over to the cottage and talk with this woman. Now.

Even though Althea was working at her crystal shop, I called her. Luckily for me, one of her part-time clerks was in the shop to help unload a shipment of new inventory. "Give me five minutes," Althea said. "I can meet you at the Chocolate Box."

"Can you just leave like this?" Lidia asked after I'd disconnected the call. "It looked awfully busy in there."

"It is, but that's why we hired Fletcher. He can fill in when one of us has to run a quick errand."

And that's what I told both Bertie and Fletcher when I went inside to hang up my apron: that I needed to go run an errand. Neither of them looked as if they believed me. But it didn't matter. I grabbed my purse and hurried out the door anyhow. Lidia hesitated for a moment before running after me.

"Where is this cottage?" I asked as we stood on the Chocolate Box's front porch. "Is it walking distance? Or do I need to drive?"

Lidia eyed my shoes. I was wearing flip-flops with

a braided leather thong. The sight of them made her frown. I glanced down at her feet. She'd worn sensible sneakers, the kind with the chunky soles. "It is a few blocks away." She sounded skeptical that I'd be able to handle it.

I could run a few blocks in high heels. I could walk the entire length of the beach in these flip flops. "I think we'll be fine walking," I said just as Althea walked up.

Althea, dressed in a long flowy skirt and white bohemian blouse, gave us both tight hugs. Her eyes were bright with excitement. "Today really is our lucky day. This morning we found a new turtle nest down on the west end of the beach. And now this. I can't believe you found her."

"It wasn't as if I was looking for her," Lidia explained as she led the way across the island. "It was dumb luck, really. I was looking at the cottage I want to rent."

Althea and I followed as Lidia walked briskly down the street. We ended up in the far west end of the island a few blocks from Bubba's house. Many of the homes on the street were newer, clad in varying shades of plastic siding, with attached garages that took up most of the front façade. All of them looked as if they belonged in a neighborhood in the Midwest instead of on a beach island.

The cottage that Lidia took me to looked much different from those homes. For one thing, it was a cottage with a generous wraparound porch. Unlike the houses around it, the cottage was set back from the road and at the top of the rise of one of the tall ancient sand dunes that still remained on the otherwise flat island.

The cottage was too far from the ocean and too far from the river to offer any kind of water view. But at the same time, the large treed lot provided plenty of shade. Silvery Spanish moss hung like lace from the ancient oaks' thick limbs.

The whitewashed cottage, set up on concrete blocks, couldn't have had many more than a few rooms inside. A white picket fence enclosed the entire yard. It'd be the perfect place for Lidia and any dogs she'd want to keep here. I wondered again why Cassidy had refused to rent it to her.

"Do you think she's in there?" I whispered as I swung open the front gate.

Lidia shrugged. "When I saw her, she was carrying in a bag of groceries from her car." Her voice, as always, boomed.

A shiny red Mercedes convertible sat in the driveway. "That car?" I asked, still whispering.

"That's the one," she shouted.

So much for trying to surprise her. Not that I really knew why I thought I wanted to surprise the muumuu woman. What was I going to do? Ring the doorbell, hide, and jump out at her when she opened the door? Of course not.

I simply wanted to have a civil conversation.

Althea gave my hand a squeeze as we made our way to the front entrance. All of the window shades that opened to the porch had been pulled tightly closed. Lidia looked at me and smiled before she wrapped her knuckle on the pretty yellow door. My heart hammered in my throat while we waited. We all stared at the door. It didn't open.

This time I knocked. Banged on it, actually.

The door creaked as it slowly opened no more than a

sliver. I leaned forward. The inside was dark, too dark to see if there was anyone peering out at us.

"Hello?" I said. "I was looking for the woman I helped on the beach the other night. The night Cassidy was killed. Is she home?"

The door slammed shut.

I banged on the yellow door again. I raised my voice. "I want to make sure she's okay. I want to talk to her about what she saw."

"I know she's staying here," Lidia yelled. "I saw her."

"Maybe we should tell the police that you saw her instead of wasting our time trying to talk to her," Althea said loudly.

The door swung violently open. A slender pale arm appeared. One long finger gestured that we should come inside.

Should we waltz inside the darkened home of someone who may be a killer? That seemed...stupid.

I had no intention of doing anything dangerously stupid. At least not today, not so soon after being shot at.

But Lidia had already hitched her purse higher on her shoulder and was walking into the house. I tried to grab her shirt to stop her but before I could, Althea waltzed inside too.

Although my mind kept screaming at me to stay outside, I had to step inside to try and pull my two friends back out of the house and onto the relative safety of the porch. As soon as both my feet were on the cottage's matted old carpeting, the door closed behind me with a bang that shook the walls.

I whirled around to find a woman standing in the shadows. She had a flowered scarf tied over her hair. The first thing I noticed was that she was shorter than me. But then again, most women were. She was wearing another muumuu. This one was black with gold piping. It completely hid her shape. Although the shadows hid her features, I knew I'd finally found our mystery woman.

"His death had nothing to do with me." Her weak voice seemed to crack with age. And she spoke with an odd Eastern European accent. The night of Cassidy's murder, she'd sounded young and vibrant. My ears had hurt for hours after hearing her scream and scream.

I leaned forward. "You're not the woman I found on the beach with his body."

"No, of course I'm not. You have the wrong person." She started to open the door.

I started to make my break for freedom. I didn't know who this woman was, but the peculiar situation was making my skin crawl.

Lidia stuck out her arm and blocked my exit. "This is the woman. She's hunching her back and using a fake accent."

I looked at the strange woman and then back at Lidia. "How can you tell?"

"I've trained dogs my entire life," she said as if that answered my question.

I waited for her to elaborate. She didn't.

"She's not a dog," I finally pointed out.

"Yes, but after a lifetime of dog training, I've learned that reading human body language isn't that much different from reading dog body language." She pointed to the woman who was now snarling at us. "She's hunching because she doesn't want us to see her. And her voice is wrong. Only actors on bad sitcoms use accents like that."

"Or actresses," I said, mentally slapping myself on the forehead for being so dense. "Luella Marie Banks? Is that you?"

Ethel had gone on and on about that new role Luella Marie Banks had landed. The local actress had gotten the part despite the fact that some in Hollywood thought she was too old to land a leading lady spot. Arthur had said he'd heard she was planning on visiting Camellia Beach before filming started. And I'd been learning how Cassidy liked to torment the people in his life by dangling his knowledge of their secrets over them.

"Lidia was supposed to rent this cottage," I said. "But Cassidy rented it to you. He knew you needed a small, tucked away place where no one would think to look for you. I have a feeling that's why he kept Lidia from taking the place, because he knew you'd need it."

"I have no idea what you are talking about," the woman said. She'd dropped the fake accent.

"You needed a place where you could heal from plastic surgery without anyone knowing," I said. "And Cassidy knew the perfect place for you to stay."

She stood a little taller. "Did *he* tell you that?"

"He didn't need to," I said.

"Honey, you just told us everything we need to know," Lidia said.

I held up my hands. "We're not here to cause trouble. No one needs to know your secret."

I nudged Althea's side with my elbow. "That's right," she chimed in to say. "We aren't ones to blab."

"We're not gossips," Lidia said. "No, ma'am, we're not."

"We simply want to know what you saw the night of Cassidy's death," I said.

Luella Marie huffed. "That terrible little man. He tried to act all helpful, but his help came at a price. Didn't learn that until it was too late."

"What did he do?" Althea whispered.

Luella Marie gestured toward a lumpy sofa. "Might as well sit. This might take a while."

So Lidia, Althea, and I sat in a tight row on the small, grimy sofa. A broken spring jammed into my upper thigh.

Luella Marie moved with grace as she moved toward a wicker rocking chair while keeping to the room's deepest shadows.

Now that she was closer to us, I could see the features she was trying to keep hidden. What I'd thought was a round face the night of the murder, I now saw was puffiness. What I'd thought was dark bags under her eyes, I now recognized as bruising from the surgery.

"What were you doing with Cassidy that night?" I asked. "Were you two...?" I couldn't make my lips finish that question.

"He wished," she said with a barking laugh. "I had stopped by to pay my rent—in cash—for my stay here. But he wasn't alone."

"Jody was with him," I guessed.

She shook her head. "That hothead who shot him? No. The voice I heard was definitely male."

"He was with a man that night?" Althea gasped as she said it. "Cassidy? With a man?"

"They were arguing," Luella Marie said with an elegant shrug. "I did hear someone get slapped. What else they were doing together?" She waved her arm in a dramatic gesture. "I don't care to speculate."

"But we found you outside with Cassidy. How did that happen?" I asked.

She waved her arm again. "I'd started to leave when the man who'd been arguing with Cassidy stormed out of one of the sliding glass doors, the ones that opened up to the beach. Cassidy stood at the door and watched him go. He was laughing."

"Did you see the man who'd stormed out?" Lidia demanded. "Can you describe him?"

Luella Marie shook her head. "It was too dark. But he did speak with a stuttering lisp."

"Fletcher Grimbal," both Lidia and Althea said at the same time.

"Savannah's boy?" Luella Marie sounded surprised.

"Savannah's boy," Althea said with a slow nod.

"Last time I saw him, he was a little thing, always getting underfoot. Don't remember him having a speech impediment."

"He developed it during puberty," Althea said.

"It grows stronger whenever he's stressed," I added.

Luella Marie stood up with a spectacular flourish and sashayed over to the small corner of the room that was being used as a kitchen. "Well, t-t-that's troubling to know." She'd started talking with a stuttering lisp. "N-n-nervous ticks hint at all m-m-manner of inner turmoil. Guilty minds. S-s-secrets. Lies."

That wasn't true. Speech impediments were often simply just that, impediments. I started to tell that to Luella Marie, but Lidia voice was louder and commanded more attention. "The boy might be guilty, especially if you saw him arguing with Cassidy moments before his death."

"But we need proof," I jumped in to say. "You need

to talk with the police. You need to tell them what you saw. Immediately."

"I c-c-can't escape this p-p-prison for another t-t-two weeks," she said, her stuttering lisp even more pronounced.

I was offended for Fletcher. "Do you mind not talking like that?"

"L-like w-w-what...? Oh, sorry. I sometimes don't realize what I'm doing when I think deeply about another person." She cleared her throat. When she spoke again, she seemed to be using Lidia's booming voice. "The press is vicious. They can't accept that a woman ages. No one in La-La Land accepts that a woman ages. It's even harder now with high definition 4K cameras. Those darn things highlight even the faintest facial lines. If I want to work, I have to have this work done. But Heaven forbid anyone discovers I actually went and got plastic surgery. That's unforgivable. That's admitting that you're too old."

"I'm sorry about that, but your silence may cause an innocent person to go to jail for a murder she didn't commit," I said. "You need to talk to the police."

"Ah, but the bobby's 'ave their culprit, now don't they?" she said, with a terrible Cockney accent.

"Did you see Jody shoot Cassidy? Did you actually see her pull the trigger?" I demanded.

"I saw 'er shootin' all manner of things until all the lights on that mansion went dark." She pulled a bottle of water from the rusty fridge, twisted off the top, and took a long sip. "But even after the lights went out, the shooting continued. Two more shots." Her voice was now as flat as the Midwestern plains. "Then I saw him. Flat on his back. Staring at the stars, but not seeing them. He was dead. I loved him. I loved him like I'd loved no other. But he died." She drew a long, deep breath. "And you can't get warm at night by loving a dead man."

Luella Marie had loved Cassidy? My jaw dropped from shock.

At the same time Lidia jumped to her feet and started clapping wildly. "Brava! Brava!"

Althea laughed and clapped as well.

My mouth still hanging open, I stared at my two friends. Had they lost their minds?

Luella Marie smiled broadly. She flung her arm out as she dipped into a low bow.

"*A Rocky Love Story* is one of my all-time favorite movies," Lidia boomed. I'd never seen her so animated.

"It is a classic," Althea agreed.

"I don't know why the critics were so hard on it," Lidia continued. "I cried my eyes out when I first heard those words. Look." She touched her cheeks. "Tears. They're here in my eyes even now."

"The best movies are always scorned." Luella Marie now sounded like a professor in a lecture hall. She drew out her words, putting emphasis on the vowels. "Jealousy. Pure and simple. They are afraid of the powerful, the brilliant. They applaud the mundane because it's safe."

"So...wait," I said. "Were you in love with Cassidy or not?"

She laughed a long, fluid chortle. "I thought I'd already made that obvious. He was an odious little man, a nobody from nowhere. How could I love him? He'd do nothing for my career."

"Then why were you so upset? Why were you

screaming as if you'd just lost your best friend…or your lover?" I demanded.

"Because," she said still using her professor voice. "Because," she said in her English accent. "Because," she said in what I assumed was her natural voice. It sounded lyrical and Southern. "He was shot a few feet from where I was standing. The killer could have easily missed and killed *me*! I'm a star about to embark on the role of a lifetime. And some nobody who was angry at another nobody had nearly killed *me*! Honey, if that wasn't something to scream about, I don't know what is."

This conversation wasn't getting me anywhere. I had too much to do to waste my time here. "You didn't see who shot Cassidy. But you heard Fletcher arguing with him. You saw Jody shoot the lights on his neighbor's house. But you didn't see her shoot Cassidy. Did you see or hear anything or anyone else?"

I got up from the sofa and started to move toward the door even before she answered. Lidia and Althea remained planted on that horrible sofa.

"*Did* you have a reason to kill Cassidy?" Althea asked.

"Of course I did. He wanted me to…er…entertain him. The jerk said that if I kept his bed warm he wouldn't call TMZ and tell them what I was doing here in Camellia Beach. But I didn't kill him, see," she said, sounding like a female Carry Grant. "Someone wacked him before I could."

TWENTY-SIX

"Do you believe her?" Althea whispered. The three of us had left Luella Marie's cottage soon after the actress had confessed to wanting Cassidy dead. Lidia had started to hurry away toward the Pink Pelican Inn.

"You're not going to tell anyone, are you?" I'd called after her.

"I told Luella Marie I wouldn't," Lidia had actually whispered. "But I need to talk with someone about this. I figured since Harriett already knows about Luella Marie, I could gab with her about...*you know.*"

While Lidia had vigorously and loudly promised Luella Marie not to tell anyone what we'd seen or heard today, both Althea and I had only promised not to cause trouble for her. I'd also crossed my fingers behind my back for good measure. For one thing, Detective Gibbons would arrest me for obstruction of justice if I didn't tell him all about this meeting with Luella Marie. As soon as Lidia was out of sight, I sent him a quick text, telling him that I'd found Muumuu Woman and included her address.

I then followed Althea to her crystal shop. Her part-time helper could only stay through lunch, which meant Althea needed to get back right away. As soon as we got to the shop, Althea took over unpacking a crate that her helper had been working on. One by one she carefully unwrapped what looked like (to me) the kind of rocks you could find in any gravel parking lot. After she removed each stone, she applied a price sticker.

"Do you believe her?" Althea asked again.

I leaned against her checkout counter and rubbed my chin. Did I believe an accomplished actress' protestations of innocence? "I think I do believe her. Why would she admit to wanting to kill him if she actually killed him? That'd be stupid. And she didn't strike me as a stupid woman."

"If not her or Jody, that just leaves Fletcher. He had motive and was at the scene of the crime," Althea said.

"That doesn't mean he's guilty," I was quick to say. "He's only been working at the Chocolate Box for less than a day, and I already can't imagine not having him around. He could easily become an asset wherever he worked. Why would someone like that get so upset over losing a relatively new job that he'd commit murder? He could get work anywhere and in any town."

"Why would someone like that kill? Pride? Ego? Money?" Althea ticked those points off far too quickly.

"He's not a killer." I refused to believe anything different.

"I'm not so sure. Luella Marie heard him arguing with Cassidy right before his death. She—" Althea dropped the rock she'd been holding. It landed with a crash on the floor. "Wait a blasted minute. What did you just say? Fletch is working at the Chocolate Box? At the Chocolate Box? As in right now? You left him working alone with Mama in the shop *right now*? You left Mama alone with a killer?" She ran toward her shop's front door, pausing only to flip the "open/closed" sign over to the "closed" side. "Don't just stand there and gape at my agates. Come on."

As I jogged down the street alongside her a text message came in from Detective Gibbons. Call me, he'd written. When I didn't call him right away he texted again, We need to talk. When I didn't respond to that text he wrote, I'm coming over.

Great, just great. I didn't have time to calm Althea down *and* deal with Gibbons. I'd given him the information he needed. All he had to do was drive over to the cottage and talk with Luella Marie. He didn't need to talk with me about it first.

"I swear, Althea, if you scare off the best employee I've ever had, save for Bertie not that I consider her an employee, I'm never going to forgive you. He's a wizard with the blender. And he does things before I even have to ask," I shouted as I struggled to keep up with her.

Althea glared at me before picking up her pace. For someone with short legs, she could sure move fast when she wanted to. We rounded the corner onto East America Street. The shop, less than a half-block away, came into view. Customers were wandering in and out of the front door. A small crowd had gathered on the wide front porch. They were talking, laughing, and enjoying themselves. Standing as far away from any of that without actually stepping foot into the road was a sour-faced woman with her arms crossed over her chest.

At the sight of her my feet stumble over themselves. Before I could catch myself, I ended up face down on the pavement.

"What happened?" Althea reached down to help me back to my feet. "What made you trip?"

"Stupid. Clumsy. Graceless," I muttered under my breath, unconsciously repeating the litany of descriptions Grandmother Cristobel used to call me. As soon as I realized what I was doing, I bit my tongue. Hard.

With Althea's hand under my arm, I started to crawl to my feet. The woman had marched over, not out of concern for my safety, but to stand with her hands on her hips and glare down at me as I rose. First I saw her shiny teal leather pumps. Then her perfect knees, knees that looked as if they'd never scraped against the pavement. Her neatly pressed teal and white flowered flare dress looked as if it'd been stolen from the nineteen fifties. Her blood red painted lips pursed with a look of distaste. And finally her hairspray had glued every piece of her artificially blonde hair into place.

"Mother," I said.

She visibly shuddered at the word.

"What are you doing here?" I asked. Althea hugged my arm in a show of support.

"You called. You told me that you wanted to talk. And I agree. We do need to talk." She turned and curled her lip at Althea before adding, "In private."

"No," I said. "Not in private."

"That's right. I'm not leaving," Althea agreed.

We then did the one thing I knew someone like Florence Corners, AKA Mommy Dearest, would hate the most, we walked past her and headed toward the Chocolate Box.

The clap, clap, clap of her heels followed us.

Inside the shop, we found Bertie and Fletcher standing nearly toe to toe, their hands on their hips. They were singing at the top of their lungs a peppy show tune. *A peppy show tune?* Bertie and Fletcher were two of the least peppy people I knew on Camellia Beach.

They were singing a show tune?

I shook my head.

"Mother!" Althea cried in horror.

The song abruptly stopped.

The handful of customers cried, "Hey!" and "Don't stop!"

"Althea Truman Bays," Bertie snapped the name out with an angry slap of her hands. "You interrupted us mid-verse. Is that how I've taught you to act?"

"But-but-but," she stuttered as she waved her hands at both Bertie and Fletcher. "You-you-you-you are singing a show tune about love. With him. Where anyone can hear you."

Bertie slapped her hands together again. "There ain't nothing wrong with what I was doing and don't you pretend otherwise."

The customers in the shop seemed to agree. All of them clapped and whistled except Bubba. Bubba was sitting slumped on the sofa near the coffee station. His arms were crossed over his broad chest. His lips were pulled down as if they were trying to reach the ground.

Gracious, that man needed to swallow his fear and ask Bertie out on a date already. Getting jealous over her singing with a man who was younger than her own daughter was ridiculous. Heck, if he wanted to sing with her, he should have simply gotten up and joined in.

Althea continued to sputter until I nudged her arm with my elbow. "You shouldn't be embarrassed. Everyone loves your mother's singing."

"I'm not embarrassed. I'm just…" Althea looked at me, at Fletcher, at the smiling customers, and finally at her mother. With a shrug, she walked over to Bertie and gave her a big hug and a heartfelt apology for interrupting the song.

Bertie hugged her daughter back, but still scolded her a bit more for her rude behavior. After that, things in the Chocolate Box seemed to go back to business as usual. Fletcher returned to work the milkshake blender. Bertie checked the coffee urns. And I slipped a crisp white apron on over my head. This one read, "A day without chocolate is like...just kidding. I don't know what a day without chocolate would be like."

"See?" I whispered so only Althea could hear as she followed me behind the counter. "There was nothing for you to worry about. Fletcher isn't a killer. Killers don't sing show tunes."

She didn't argue, but she did keep a cautious eye on Fletcher as she nudged my arm. "Are you going to just let her stand there?"

I glanced over at the entrance where Florence Corners glowered.

"Sometimes I envy those baby sea turtles you work with," I said.

"Why's that?" Althea asked.

"It took me close to thirty-seven years before I got to meet my mother. And your lucky sea turtles never get to know if the turtle swimming next to them is related or not." It was such a sad thought. Every living thing deserved to know the power of a mother's love. A mother's love was supposed to be like a healing balm. It was supposed to make life better. "I kind of wish I was a sea turtle," I said while keeping my distance from Florence.

"She's going to scare off customers," Althea warned. "You need to do something."

"I was hoping that if I pretended she wasn't there she'd go away." Clearly, my ploy wasn't working. "I suppose I can't just ignore her. I did call her. And she did come." I had to force myself to lift my head and look directly at Florence. "Would you like to try some of our new chocolates?" I asked her. "We have a new spicy bonbon that's wildly popular. And our new salted sea turtles are so popular someone has been stealing them."

"I wouldn't touch anything you made," she called from the doorway. "You don't even belong here. You stole this place from my family."

"Oh, come now. You shouldn't say that. You're my mother."

Florence's eyes grew wild as they darted around the room. She sucked in several sharp breaths. "Don't say that."

"It's not a secret," Bertie said. "You should come into town more often. If you did, you'd already know that everyone on Camellia Beach has heard all about what you told our Penn."

Like a banshee set on vengeance, Florence crossed the room to stand directly in front of me. With her hands on her hips, she glowered. I wondered if she practiced that angry look in a mirror. It was flawless.

"We had an understanding," she growled. "You weren't supposed to tell anyone what I'd told you."

"Didn't seem like information I should keep quiet about. You're my mother. People would talk if you showed up for Thanksgiving dinner with Bertie and me with no explanation why you'd be invited."

"I would never have Thanksgiving with you," she spat.

I shrugged. "Maybe we can bond over Christmas, then. Your place or mine, Mother?"

Without warning her hand shot out and slapped me

so hard across the face I stumbled backwards several steps.

"Don't call me that." Her voice sounded like the low warning of a cornered animal. "Don't *ever* call me that."

I rubbed my sore jaw. "But it's what you are. By blood, at least." It wasn't as if she'd ever been a real mother to me. Real mothers didn't leave infant daughters on doorsteps. Real mothers didn't try to steal their daughters' chocolate shops.

"You lying, scheming witch." She may not have used the word "witch," but that's the word I chose to hear as her low, raspy voice grew a decibel louder. "Carolina died before she had any children, which means you're not my sister's daughter."

"No, I'm not." The truth of it still hurt in my chest. "I'm—"

She swung at me again. This time I was prepared. I grabbed her wrist before her open palm could strike flesh for a second time.

"Don't," I said. "Don't you ever raise your hand to me again."

With a violent twist, she pried her arm from my grip. "You and I both know you're not *my* daughter. I only told you that I'd birthed you when I thought you might be Carolina's kin. You'd already conned my mother out of her shop. I didn't want you getting your filthy hands on the big, fat pile of money my mother had set aside in case Carolina or one of her heirs ever returned to Camilla Beach. But now we all know the truth. You're not Carolina's daughter. And you're certainly not my daughter. You are nothing but a lying, scheming witch."

"I haven't lied about anything." Why in the world was she saying this to me? Was she so embarrassed about the circumstances of my birth that she felt she needed to publicly deny our connection? Since Carolina couldn't possibly be my mother, it had to be Florence. My father couldn't (or wouldn't) tell me anything about the woman who had dropped me off on his doorstep. He claimed he couldn't remember anything about the one-night-stand that had produced me. But the DNA test that the now deceased Skinny McGee had arranged for me had concluded I was Mabel's granddaughter. This meant my mother was one of Mabel's daughters. Simple genetics. They were Mabel's daughters, and I was her grandchild.

"Don't act shocked," Florence snapped. "You and I both know you don't have a drop of Maybank blood in those ugly veins of yours. I'm going to do everything in my power to make sure you lose this shop and the land it stands on. You have no right to it. No right at all."

Well if that's the game she wanted to play, I no longer needed to pretend to be civil. "Get. Out." My voice sounded airy, as if I'd just finished running halfway across the island. "You may pretend that I'm not yours, but know this: You. Will. Not. Get. My. Shop."

"Mabel wanted Penn to have the Chocolate Box, and by gum, she's going to keep it," Bertie said as came to stand shoulder-to-shoulder with me. She crossed her arms over her full chest. Bubba had crossed the room to stand next to her. And Althea stood next to him. My personal wall of support—what a blessing. Ethel cheered, "hear, hear!" from her chair. Others joined in.

Fletcher watched with great interest from behind the counter, his expression blank as a sheet of paper.

Florence refused to leave.

"You've been visiting Cassidy Jones," I said quietly. "That's why I called you. That's what I wanted to talk about."

Florence snapped her head back. "Don't spout more lies."

"I saw you," Ethel said and coughed. "We all saw you going into his house."

"Were you having an affair with him?" I asked, and then suddenly remembered how dangerous those kinds of questions were. So I said before she had a chance to answer, "Never mind. I don't need to know why you were there. All I need to know is if you were at his house the day he died, and if you noticed anything off about him. Did you see anyone hanging around the house?"

"You're insane!" Florence screeched. "Certifiable. I'm going to have you locked up before this is finished!" She lifted her hand as if to strike me again.

Bertie cleared her throat. She took a step toward Florence. "I think you'd better leave before we call Chief Byrd and have him arrest you on assault charges."

"Oh, I'll go. But this isn't the last you'll hear about this. You won't get away with stealing this shop away from its rightful heirs. The game is over, Charity, and it's time for you to go crawling back to your loser life."

TWENTY-SEVEN

"THAT-THAT WOMAN, she couldn't answer one simple question?" I sputtered as soon as my mother had flounced out the door with her head held high looking as if she'd won whatever battle she'd come to fight. I stamped my foot on the wood floor. "If I believed in magic and curses, I'd hex her. I'd hex her so hard she'd turn into the toad her shriveled heart resembles."

"I could do it," Althea was quick to volunteer her woo-woo services. Her mother sent her a sharp look. "But it'd be wrong," she added hastily.

"Penn, we shouldn't be cursing her. It's the ones with the most hatred in their hearts that we need be praying the hardest for," Bertie said quietly. "They're the ones who need the most redemption."

I heard her words and recognized the wisdom in them. But I wasn't ready. I wasn't ready to forgive. I wasn't ready to let go of the anger that burned in my chest. Florence had plucked at my emotions as a means to control me.

Someone else in my life liked to do that. I carried the scars from a lifetime of listening to my grandmother Cristobel Penn tell me how I wasn't good enough, pretty enough, smart enough.

Florence wanted to deny that she was my mother? Fine. The DNA test *they* were now requesting would settle this madness once and for all. And then the truth would come out. I was just as much part of their family as any of them, and I had just as much claim to the shop as any of them—more so, since Mabel had picked me to carry on her legacy.

"What was that about?" Detective Gibbons asked.

I jumped. How long had he been standing there a step inside the door? How much of my family drama had he heard? My face must have turned all sorts of shades of red from embarrassment. My skin burned as if it'd been scalded.

"A family dispute," I said with a wave of my hand as if Florence's rejection meant nothing. (Oh, how I wished her words had meant nothing.) My heart was still pounding wildly in my chest and a stinging pain started to throb in my temples. What game was that woman trying to play? Did she really think she could take away her earlier confession of being my mother? Did she really think denying our relationship would work? I closed my eyes and drew a long breath. This was a legal problem I needed to let Harley handle. I had other matters that couldn't be ignored.

I opened my eyes, grabbed a damp cloth from a plastic bin, and started wiping off tables. Whether they needed to be cleaned or not, it didn't matter. "I sent you the information you needed. I don't see why you came here instead of visiting the address in the text."

"Penn," he said.

"I didn't do anything wrong. I simply talked with the woman who was so upset the night Cassidy died. I asked her why she was so upset."

"You found Muumuu Woman?" Ethel jumped out of her chair when she heard that. "Who is she?"

"Penn," Gibbons said, his voice a notch tighter.

"I didn't do anything wrong," I repeated. "And I told you about it." I turned to Ethel. "Sorry, I can't tell you about her." If news got out about Luella Marie's plastic surgery meant she'd lose important movie roles, I'd take the silly actress' secret to the grave. I hoped Althea, Lidia, and Detective Gibbons planned to do the same.

"I'm sorry, Detective. I don't have time to answer your questions or listen to lectures. Let me summarize what happened today." I held up my index finger. "Lidia, Althea, and I went as a group to call on the woman who was with Cassidy on the night of his murder." I added another finger to my tally. "She told us what she saw and who she saw." I held up a third finger. "And I reported all of this to you immediately after leaving her house. Now, if you'd excuse me." I had a killer to catch. If what Luella Marie had told us was true, Fletcher looked like our most likely suspect. Luella Marie saw him at the scene of the crime arguing with Cassidy. Did I need more proof than that?

Apparently I did, because I was having a devil of a time believing him guilty of murder. The murderer couldn't be Fletcher, the best worker I'd ever hired. As soon as I finished up with Detective Gibbons, I was going to ask him about what he was doing with Cassidy. Hopefully then I'd get the information I needed to get Jody out of jail.

"Deal with your family crisis," Gibbons said as he headed toward the door. "But we're going to talk. We're going to talk soon, and you're going to listen to me," he warned before he marched out the door like a man on a mission.

I hoped the mission driving him would take him to Luella Marie's house. If he talked with her, and really listened to what she was saying, he'd be back at the Chocolate Box within the hour to question Fletcher. I needed to move fast.

TWENTY-EIGHT

BEFORE I HAD a chance to say anything to Fletcher the copper bell over the door tinkled. Bailey Grassi, looking cool and relaxed in his tan khaki shorts and white lawn cotton shirt, stepped into the shop. He took a long look around before closing the door behind him. His face was cleanly shaven. His shaggy brown hair was secured in a neat topknot on the crown of his head. His cotton button-up shirt, although worn with the shirttails hanging out, looked as if it'd been pressed. His khaki Bermuda shorts had knifepoint creases.

He completed his survey of the shop before smiling in our direction. With a wave, he started across the room toward us. At the sight of him, Althea hissed a breath. She latched onto my arm and ducked behind me.

"Oh no! I forgot I was supposed to meet him for lunch at the Dog-Eared Café. This is your fault," Althea whispered.

Fletcher, who was on the other side of me, hissed a breath as well when he looked up from the blender and spotted his former employer.

Sympathetic to their discomfort, I hurried forward to greet Bailey. With hand extended, I said, "I bet you came to talk chocolate."

He met me halfway. Our hands clasped. "I can't tell you how much I'm looking forward to taking a tour of your shop. You did an amazing job getting it cleaned up after yesterday's incident." He continued to hold onto my hands tightly as he peered intently into my eyes. "You are okay, aren't you? I mean…mentally. After what happened with the shooting and all." He released my hands and pointed to his temple.

"Oh, yes, yes. I'm fine with all that. It's not the first time someone has taken potshots at me."

Bailey's brows shot up into his hairline. "Really?"

"It's a story for another time," I said. "Should we start the tour?"

"In a minute." He glanced over my shoulder to where Althea had been trying to duck behind the display case and frowned. "I also came here to find…" His frown matched hers. After a moment he shook his head. "It doesn't matter."

I hooked my arm with his as a reward for him for giving Althea time to come to him. "Do you know much about the chocolate making process?" I asked him. "I don't want to be telling you something you already know, especially since I imagine that as a chef and restaurant owner you already know all of this much better than I do."

"I am quite the chocolate lover," he admitted with a smile. "While in culinary school, I had to pick between a study focus on the art of chocolate and candy making or on the business-end of running a restaurant. And since I'd always known I wanted my own restaurant one day, I decided to focus on the business-end of the degree. But let me tell you, some days I wish I'd taken that other route."

"Not knowing anything about chocolates hasn't slowed me down," I said with a laugh. "Not one bit."

"Not everyone is as brave as you."

"Me? Brave? No. My ignorance probably keeps me from knowing how big a task it is that I've undertaken. Let's get started with the tour." The sooner I got this over with, the sooner I could get back to questioning Fletcher about what he was doing at Cassidy's house that night.

Before answering me, Bailey glanced beyond my shoulder at Althea again. "Yes…um…yes. I'd love to get a tour and hear more about the process you use to make your Amar chocolates. I'm most anxious to sell some of your stock in my restaurant and online. I carry only the best and rarest items."

With my hand still in charge of his, I directed him over toward Bertie and away from Althea. I usually flinched at the touch of anyone other than close friends, but here I was hugging onto this stranger's arm for an extended period of time. It was terribly uncomfortable. Althea would owe me for this one.

Yet Althea was in no state to talk with the man she'd just stood up for lunch. When I'd glanced in her direction, she'd stuffed two sea salt chocolate caramels into her mouth…at the same time! Clearly she was still struggling to compose herself. With two caramels in her mouth, it would be quite a while before she'd be able to talk to anyone. I knew that—*embarrassingly*—from firsthand experience.

"You want to wholesale our chocolates?" Bertie asked after I'd introduced her to Bailey. She sounded suspicious. "Why?"

"Why? Are you serious? It's because the Chocolate Box produces the finest chocolate in the world. I like to bring my handpicked clients the finest products. My website is accessible by invitation only. It's very exclusive."

"Sounds like a terrific opportunity to get your chocolates into the hands of influencers, Penn," Bubba said. He'd been hanging around Bertie like a nervous teen ever since Florence had left the shop. But at the mention of marketing, the president of Camellia Beach's business association regained his confidence. He talked up several of the island's other businesses, including Althea's crystal shop.

"That does sound impressive," Bailey said without much enthusiasm.

"I hear a 'but' in that sentence." Bubba must have noticed Bailey's lack of excitement too.

"It's the murder." The chef looked honestly worried. "How safe am I on this island?"

"It was just one murder," Bubba said jovially. "A freak occurrence for Camellia Beach."

"Is it? Penn was just telling me how she'd been shot at more than once since moving here. To be honest, it's kind of freaking me out."

Bubba gave the younger man's arm a friendly pound. "It's not like that, not at all. Talk with our police chief. Hank will tell you how Camellia Beach is one of the safest places to be in the state."

"The night of Cassidy's murder, I was working at the restaurant," Bailey said. "I still can't stop thinking that if I'd been home or if I hadn't left on the porch lights that none of this would have happened."

"Jody didn't kill Cassidy." I was emphatic about it. He didn't need to beat himself up over Cassidy's murder. He had no reason to feel guilty. He couldn't have controlled Jody's crazy antics or stopped the second shooter from using the cover of Jody's gunfire to shoot a bullet through the local lothario's heart. "Jody shot out your lights, but someone else shot Cassidy."

Bailey looked confused. "I heard that the gun—"

"I don't care what you heard. Jody didn't kill that man." I slammed my hand against my leg to provide the extra emphasis he clearly wasn't hearing in my tone.

"Penn promised Jody's young son that she would get her mother out of jail before school starts on Thursday," Bertie explained gently. "Did I hear Althea correctly when you came in? You had made a lunch date with my daughter?"

Bailey looked at me. He then looked at Althea. And then back at Bertie. His eyes widened. "Althea is your daughter? I don't know why I didn't see the resemblance before. Yes, we were supposed to have lunch today. As you know, I'm new to the area. I was really looking forward to getting to know some of its residents better."

Smoothly done, I thought to myself.

Bertie seemed pleased by his answer. "My Althea is passionate about her crystals. I've known her to miss all sorts of important appointments whenever she gets a new shipment of those shiny rocks of hers. And she did get a new shipment in just this morning. So don't take it personally."

"I didn't," he said with a wink in Althea's direction. "Well, I did at first. No man wants to be left sitting alone at a restaurant like that. It's hard on the ego."

"We can't have that," Bubba said with a laugh that sounded a touch nervous. "Bertie, in order to make it up to the poor guy you'll simply have to invite us all over to dinner tonight."

"Is that what you think, Bubba?" Bertie propped

her hands on her hips. "And you expect me to single-handedly cook a feast for half the island? With no advanced notice?"

"I...um... I could help," he stumbled over his words. "I have a recipe for a pork rub that you'd love."

"You think I'll love it, huh?" Bertie said, her hands still on her hips.

He nodded. "It has chocolate in it."

"Chocolate?" She didn't sound convinced. "And you make this dish all by yourself?"

"I do! And you're going to love it. So it's a date?" Bubba's smile froze on his lips as the word "date" came out of his mouth. He cleared his throat and started to backtrack right away. "I mean, for Althea and Bailey here. It's a makeup date for them. For them."

While Bertie laughed, Bailey shifted uncomfortably from one foot to the other. "I'd really like to taste that pork rub and spend more time with you, Althea, but I can't make it tonight. The restaurant still needs me there every moment of every evening. It'll be a while before I can start taking nights off."

Bubba looked crestfallen.

"You can still make your pork rub, Bubba," Bertie said kindly. "Penn has kept me so busy these last couple of days, I'm bone tired. Don't have much energy when it's time to think about cooking dinner."

"Really?" Bubba grinned so big his mouth nearly engulfed the entire shop.

"Maybe we could plan another lunch date," Althea offered Bailey as she finally came over to stand with the rest of us. "Call me later, and we can compare our calendars."

"I'll do that. Now, about this tour, Penn," he said. "I'm eager to see everything."

Althea accompanied me as I showed Bailey around the shop. I took him through the steps we used to roast and grind the cacao beans and craft our unique chocolate bars. In the kitchen, Bailey happily tasted one of our one hundred percent Amar chocolate squares. His eyes turned dark and smoky as he held onto the edge of the counter. I wasn't surprised. That was the standard reaction by anyone who tasted the chocolate for the first time.

"This chocolate's reputation doesn't do it justice," he said once he got over the shock of how deep and rich the flavors actually were. "This is better than anything I've ever tasted. And I've tasted delicacies from around the globe."

Before he left I told him I'd think about his offer to sell the chocolates through his online shop, but I couldn't make any promises.

"Thank you," Althea said as the two of us stood at the door and watched Bailey walk happily toward his car.

"No thanks necessary. You stood him up in order to come with me."

"No, I stood him up because I'd forgotten about him." Her cheeks darkened as she admitted it. "I don't think I'm cut out for dating. Not anymore."

I was about to ask her what had happened to make her think that when someone came up from behind and tapped me on the shoulder. Startled, I whirled around like a dervish, but I didn't swing at the unfortunate soul who'd sneaked up on me. See, that was growth. I was getting better at controlling my jumpy nerves.

"S-sorry. I didn't mean to scare you." Fletcher didn't sound sorry. He sounded determined and more in control of his speech impediment that ever. But he had thrown his hands in the air in a protective move. Apparently, he'd heard about how I had a tendency to go on the offensive whenever someone on the island was trying to kill me. Something red and plastic flew out of his hand. It skittered across the hardwood floor and came to stop at Bubba's feet.

"What is that?" I demanded.

"It's one of them spinner doodads," Bubba said as he bent to pick up the small plastic device. It had a round disc in the center with three rounded spokes that rotated around the center. He held the disc with his beefy thumb and forefinger and started to spin the rounded spokes. "They're mighty popular right now. Gives people something to do with their restless fingers other than tapping on relentlessly on their phones."

Fletcher snatched it out of Bubba's hand. "It's nothing. J-j-just a w-w-way to"—he took a deep breath and spun the plastic wheel before jamming it into his pocket—"calm myself." He turned back to me. "I'm going to have to leave for a little while."

"Where are you going?" I asked as he skirted around Althea and me to get to the door. "Now isn't a good time for you to leave. Our afternoon rush will be starting soon. I need you here."

He shook his head. "I h-have to go."

"Wait. I have something I need to talk with you about. It's urgent," I said.

He opened the door and paused. He turned and looked me over from head-to-toe before saying, "Sorry. I have s-s-something I n-need to do."

With no other explanation, he was gone.

"Jumpy little fellow," Bubba said as we all watched the younger man leave.

"No wonder he can't hold a job." Bertie clucked her tongue. "The boy has no work ethic."

"Murderers rarely do," Althea whispered in my ear. "You need to fire him."

TWENTY-NINE

"He's too good a worker to be a killer," I muttered. After the job he'd done that morning, I didn't want to lose him. It didn't matter if he did have one of those red anxiety spinners I kept finding whenever I felt like someone was following me. It didn't matter if he felt the need to take breaks in the middle of the day. If he continued to do good work when he was at the Chocolate Box, none of the other stuff mattered. He wasn't a killer.

"Don't forget what Muumuu Woman told us." Althea tapped her nose. "She saw him arguing with Cassidy. What more do you need to know?"

I shook my head. While Luella Marie had all but pointed her finger at Fletcher and dramatically pronounced his guilt, something bothered me about her version of events. But I couldn't say exactly what it was about her story that bothered me. It was a queasy feeling in my stomach, the same feeling I'd get after I ate too much fried food.

Althea grabbed my arm and pulled me away from the others and over to the relative privacy next to the cash register. "What's wrong?" she whispered in my ear. "I should be the one looking green after humiliating myself in front of Bailey."

"You didn't humiliate yourself. He's a good looking guy, and I think he finds you charming even though you left him to eat lunch all by himself. Who knows? Maybe he found that charming too."

She shook her head. "Don't try to make this about me. What did you see that has made you react like you've finally seen a ghost? *Have* you seen a ghost?" She glanced over to the wall where the chocolate boxes were displayed and shivered. "I've always felt this place was haunted."

"Oh, stop being ridiculous. There are no such things as ghosts."

She was used to that knee-jerk reaction from me whenever she mentioned the paranormal. She smiled that sly smile she'd get when she thought she knew more than I did. "We'll have to agree to disagree on that one." She crossed her arms over her chest. "If not a ghost, what did you see?"

"I didn't see anything." That anxiety spinner Fletcher had dropped didn't mean anything. I'd seen loads of people with them. I should have been surprised I hadn't found more of them on the ground.

"I won't feel comfortable until you fire him," she said. "Mama can't fight off attackers like you can, and you can't stop people from shooting at you. It's not a safe work environment. I worry about Mama and about you."

"I worry, too," I was forced to admit. "But there's something about Muumuu Woman's story that is bugging me."

"What?"

I held a finger to my lips. "In a minute."

The line at the counter had gotten long again. I needed to get back to work. Althea jumped into the fray, working the blender even though she really needed to get back to her crystal shop.

One-by-one the customers finished their milk-shakes and polished off their chocolates. The crowd in the shop thinned. Actually, after Fletcher had left, the shop seemed to clear out faster than usual. I suspected many of my customers were running out to tell their friends about the string of dramas they'd just witnessed. I overheard Ethel telling the woman sitting next to her how the show at the Chocolate Box had become more exciting than any of her daytime soaps.

Bubba was one of the first ones to leave. He went home to start working on his pork rub for the supper he planned to serve Bertie. About a half hour later, Bertie had grabbed her purse and left to buy vegetables and ingredients for a cake, since she was sure all he planned to bring was the meat. And she wasn't going to pretend someone could make a full meal out of nothing but grilled pork.

Over the next hour and a half, a few customers, mainly tourists, came into the shop buying milkshakes and chocolates. Soon, there were only a few customers left sipping on their milkshakes.

"Let's take a break," Althea suggested as she plucked a salted sea turtle from the case. "We need to figure out what's bothering you about Cassidy's murder."

When I hesitated, Althea tapped her foot on the hard-wood floor. "What?" she demanded.

"Maybe I'm afraid I won't like what a review of the facts will show me." Many of the suspects for Cassidy's murder were friends. Did I really want to know that someone I liked, someone I was trying to learn to trust had killed a man? Talk about putting a monkey wrench into my efforts to improve myself. How could I possibly become the confident, loving person I needed to be to calm Stella's nerves and to pursue a relationship with Harley if whenever I trusted someone they turned out to be a murderer? Don't get me wrong. I knew we needed to do it. I simply needed time to work up my nerve.

But I didn't have time for nerves. "You're right. I'm being silly. Let's sit over there and talk."

We were heading over to the sofa when the bell on the door rang. Harley entered dressed in his second best court day suit. It was an off-the-rack gray wool suit that was a touch too long in the arms and not wide enough in the shoulders. Still, my heart stuttered at the sight of him. My tongue wet my lips as if expecting they might get some action in any moment.

Althea must have noticed. Her eyes widened. "Oh my goodness," she breathed as her gaze bounced from me to Harley and back to me again. "You two hooked up."

"Not really," I murmured out the side of my mouth. "But we did kiss."

Althea slapped her hands together. "I knew it!"

"Hey, Thea. Penn just told you the news, I see," he said while his expressive green eyes were locked onto mine. Oh, that man was going to give me a heart attack. "I am sorry I wasn't here for you earlier, Penn. Miss Bunny told me what happened." He brushed a kiss on my cheek, the same cheek Florence had slapped. "Are you okay?"

"She's never been anything but ugly to me, so today's performance didn't surprise me. Not really. However she refused to tell me why she was seen visiting Cassidy at his house or if she saw anything suspicious the night of Cassidy's murder," I said. For some reason Luella Marie's story didn't feel right. But why? Was she covering for someone?

"Did you really think she'd help you?" Harley asked.

"Of course Penn didn't think that," Althea said. She continued to grin at the two of us as if we were the sweetest treats in the shop.

Harley nodded. "Hopefully, you won't have to deal with any of them for much longer. We'll move forward with the DNA test right away. Once it's done, none of Mabel's kids will be able to say you don't deserve the Chocolate Box. You're Mabel's kin, and you're the one she wanted to take over after she'd passed."

"You're doing another DNA test?" Althea asked. The grin dropped clean off her face. She clutched her stomach. "Do you have to take the DNA test? Can't you refuse?"

"Why would she refuse? Mabel's children have requested that we take a new test using one of them for their DNA," Harley said. "It's what we've been asking them to do all along."

"I can't wait to do it," I said. Finally, I was going to get my wish and find out exactly which of Mabel's daughters was my biological mother. "It has to be Florence," I hated to admit. "I don't know why she thinks she can get away with denying it."

Althea bit her knuckle and gave a strangled cry.

"What's wrong?" Harley asked.

"Are you sick?" I asked.

"Not sick," Althea managed to squeak. "But in a minute I'm afraid you're going to be."

THIRTY

ALTHEA LOOKED ASHEN as she started pacing the length of the Chocolate Box. "I can't talk about it here," she said. "Where can we go? It has to be private."

"What is it?" I demanded. She was starting to scare me.

"You look like you need some fresh air," Harley said. I agreed.

"Could you watch out for customers for me?" I asked Johnny Pane who had nearly finished painting the ceiling. "We're going to walk down to the park. We'll be back in a few minutes."

"No problem, Miss Penn. I'll give a holler on my mobile if someone stops by," Johnny called down from his perch on his ladder.

"Just don't let anyone walk off with our chocolate turtles again." I checked the display case. It was locked.

We headed down the block to one of the island's public parks. This one was located on the marsh. A long fishing pier jutted out over the marsh and kept going over the grassy salt flats until it reached the Camellia River. A man stood on the railing as he tossed a plate-shaped cast net out into the water. A moment later he pulled up the net now filled with shrimp and small wiggling fish.

At the base of the pier, under the canopy of oaks and palmetto trees, three porch swings hung under a tin roofed pergola. Althea dropped down on one of the swings and cradled her face in her hands. "You're going to hate me."

"I'd never hate you." It was Harley who'd said that.

I, on the other hand, had been down this path before. It was the Cheese King all over again. Whenever I trusted someone—*anyone*—I ended up hurt.

"Just spit it out," I said more than prepared to hate her and already hating myself for feeling that way.

"We faked it," she said to the ground. "Mabel and I. It wasn't very clever of us. But did you really think your friend had taken a sample of your DNA before he came down here? Mabel had gathered it all up. I don't know how she got your friend to go along with the ruse. Maybe she was communicating with Skinny without anyone knowing about it. Or maybe she tricked him into stealing the samples from her. I was shocked when he was the one who had the report. I swear I thought Mabel was going to send those samples to the lab. But she always had plans I knew nothing about."

"You faked it?" My tone had taken on a razor-sharp edge.

Althea nodded. "The DNA test, we faked it." Her confession felt like a slap in the face. I'd trusted her. I'd loved her like a sister. And she'd done nothing but lie to me since the day we'd met?

"It's not real?" Harley demanded. "I've built Penn's case almost entirely around a DNA test that isn't real?"

"It's a real DNA report," Althea offered. "It just doesn't use Penn's DNA. We got a spit sample from Edward's daughter. Mabel had told her that she was sending her spit to one of those ancestry places as a present."

Harley's face turned a molted shade of red. "And you didn't tell us about this sooner because why?"

"I hoped it would never come up. And then when it looked like it might become an issue, Florence confessed out of the blue that she was your biological mother, so I thought maybe Mabel had been right all along. Maybe you are a Maybank."

"I'm not related." My legs collapsed under me and my bottom hit the seat of one of the porch swings with a thud. "I should have known. It's all been a grand con, one that I'd bought into wholeheartedly. I really should have known better than to believe any of this could be real."

"You might be related," Althea said. "Mabel had hoped you were Carolina's daughter. But she had no way of getting her hands on your DNA. She'd said the fake DNA test would convince you to stay." Althea looked up at me. Tears were swimming in her eyes. "Don't you see? She needed you to stay long enough to fall in love with the chocolate and with Camellia Beach. And it worked. The DNA report did convince you to stay."

"You should have told me." Harley dragged his fingers through his hair. "This changes…everything. It changes how I should have been arguing Penn's case all along. If she's not related, she still can inherit. But that's not how we've framed the case. And because of that, we've just given the Maybank family a big advantage with contesting the will."

"I'm sorry," Althea wailed. "I thought I was doing the right thing. You have to believe me, Penn. Mabel saw that article of you in the magazine and something clicked in her mind. She felt a strong connection to you. She truly believed you were her granddaughter.

And then when she finally met you in person, she saw in you the future of the Chocolate Box and her Amar chocolate."

I pinched my eyes tightly closed and wished I could put my fingers in my ears and block out Althea's voice. But adults couldn't go around covering their ears and singing "la-la-la," not without having their sanity questioned. So instead I sat there and listened to her while wishing with all my heart and soul that I could go back to yesterday, that I could go back to when someone was shooting at me at the Chocolate Box.

Ducking bullets had been much less frightening than listening to a friend confess her betrayal. I suspected Althea would simply go on and on digging deeper the pit of lies she and my grandmother—*scratch that*—the pit of lies she and the lady who had owned the Chocolate Box had created. And I really couldn't stand to hear anymore lies.

I forced myself to open my eyes. I forced myself to stand on the pair of noodles that had once been my legs. I forced myself to look at Althea while punching down my anger.

"*Enough*," I whispered.

She kept talking.

"Althea," Harley warned.

She kept talking.

"Enough!" I held up both of my hands and shouted the word so loud the fisherman at the end of the pier nearly fell off the railing and into the water. "Enough," I repeated in a calmer voice. "I have one day to catch a murderer. I don't have time to deal with this. Not. Today."

I kept my hands up as a warning that she really

needed to stop talking. We were supposed to be spending the afternoon talking about Cassidy's murder and trying to figure out why Luella Marie's story had hit all of the wrong notes with me. We weren't supposed to be ruining my life.

My hands stayed up like twin stop signs as I backed away from her and Harley. I needed to be alone. I needed time to think.

The beach was usually the best place to think. There was something about the feeling of wet sand squishing between the toes that sharpened my thoughts. But I'd left the Chocolate Box unattended. It'd be irresponsible to not return.

Although my father and Grandmother Cristobel believed me to be the most irresponsible creature on the planet, they were wrong. Besides I truly loved and respected Bertie and could never walk away from the shop without making arrangements with her first.

Did she know about the fake DNA test?

No, I couldn't think about that right now. I couldn't think about any of that.

I stole into the Chocolate Box like a thief through the back door and went straight to the kitchen. After everything that had already happened today I was glad to get into the kitchen. The tension in my shoulders eased as I started to gather ingredients for the recipe. My mind quieted, and I was finally able to start to focus on sorting what I knew about the events surrounding Cassidy's murder.

Luella Marie had been at Cassidy's house that night, as I'd suspected. She claimed she didn't see Jody pull the trigger. She does, however, claim to have heard Fletcher arguing with Cassidy.

Had Fletcher, in a fit of anger, killed Cassidy? I didn't want to believe the wiz on the blender could be a killer. I'd rather think I'd hired a great new employee. But why should that matter anymore if I was going to lose the shop to Mabel's greedy children?

I pulled out the double boiler I liked to use to melt chocolate. But I was getting ahead of myself. I needed to make the filling for the kiwi bonbons before I melted the chocolate. Bertie had told me more than once that I needed to execute the recipe in the proper sequence. Otherwise I'd end up with…

The proper sequence. That was it!

I pushed aside the baking tins and bowls and pulled out my notebook. That was what was bothering me about Luella Marie's performance. She'd sounded so very convincing, but she was a professional actress. Of course she'd sounded convincing. But the sequence of events she'd described didn't match what Althea and I had seen that night.

I started to write it all down. In one column I wrote what I saw. In the other column I wrote what Luella Marie had claimed she'd seen. It was so obvious. I should have done this right away.

When we'd passed Cassidy's house his sliding doors had been open to the beach. Jazz music had been playing loud enough for us to hear.

But Luella Marie had described a different scene. She said Cassidy had been arguing with Fletcher. She didn't mention anything about hearing the music. She didn't mention anything about Cassidy being there with another woman.

All she said was that she'd listened through the door,

which she'd claimed had been shut. She'd listened as Fletcher threatened Cassidy's life.

There was my first inconsistency in Luella Marie's story. Cassidy's sliding doors hadn't been closed.

My fingers felt a nervous need to create something. I crossed the room to the refrigerator and found the bag of kiwis. I pulled one out and set it on the cutting board. The small round fruit had turned bad. Its bright green flesh had turned mushy and black. And it was extremely stinky.

Just as stinky as the story Luella Marie had expected us to believe?

I dropped the bag of rotted fruit into the trash and gave up on making the bonbons. I needed to have a frank discussion with Fletcher. I needed to hear his version of that night. I needed to know what he was doing at Cassidy's house? Had he argued with Cassidy? Did he kill him?

I texted Fletcher, telling him I needed him back at the shop ASAP. I then texted Detective Gibbons, telling him the same thing—that I needed to talk with him ASAP. I was hitting send on that second message when the bell in the front of the shop rang twice.

"Customers!" Johnny Pane shouted so loudly I was sure he'd startled whoever came in the door.

I wiped my hands on a towel and hurried to the front. "So sorry to keep you waiting," I started to say when my gaze hit landed on *them*.

The last three people on Earth I wanted to see in my shop.

THIRTY-ONE

EDWARD STOOD IN front of his two sisters. He was dressed in a gray three-piece suit that had been tailored to perfectly fit his rounded contours. His bright red bow tie added a bit of whimsy to the monochrome suit. That whimsy didn't extend to his face. The scowl he'd donned made it look as if he'd taken a bite from one of the rotten kiwis I'd put into the trash.

Florence flounced around the shop as if she already owned the place. Her teal-colored high heeled shoes with the pointy toes clapped against the antique heart pine floor as she walked over to the display case and peered at the shiny chocolates inside. Her lips, painted a bright red that matched her brother's tie, were curled into a self-satisfied grin.

Mabel's youngest daughter, Peach, stayed near the door. She wore an aqua blue strappy athletic dress that was sensible in the August heat. She'd paired it with leather flip-flops. Her blonde hair was styled into an elegant twisting updo. Although her clothing choices were much more casual than her older sister's, the way she carried herself with her back straight and her chin slightly raised made her look as if she was walking the red carpet for a movie premier.

"What can I do to help you?" I asked, pretending they were simply customers and not my ne'er do well aunts and uncle. "We have a new item you might want to try.

It's my own recipe. Salted sea turtles. As I already told Florence earlier today, they're so good people are stealing them. They're twenty dollars for a dozen."

Edward acted as if he hadn't heard me. His gaze traveled over the nearly repainted ceiling and down the newly plastered wall. His head jerked when he saw the bullet holes. His lips tightened.

"We're not here to eat your chocolates," Florence bit off the words. She was so thin I doubted she ever ate sweets of any kind.

Peach glided across the room to stand next to her sister at the display case. Her gaze lingered on the salted sea turtles. She didn't say anything. But I think I saw pleasure in her carefully guarded expression. She nodded ever so slightly before looking up from the gooey turtle-shaped treats.

"I can get you one to try," I offered. Although none of Mabel's children had ever been friendly to me, Peach had never been hostile. Once, she'd even apologized for how her siblings had behaved. So even though her name was on the lawsuit, I didn't feel like I needed to be rude.

She tilted her head to one side as she looked to Edward for guidance. He shook his head. "Thank you, but no." Her voice was soft with a gentle but refined accent. "They do all look delicious. There are quite a few new flavors here. Many of these aren't Mother's recipes, are they?"

"They're not. I've been trying to come up with recipes of my own," I said. "The bonbon fires have been especially popular lately. Bertie's sea salt caramels are still best sellers, though."

"What are you doing? We're not here to praise her,"

Florence said at the same time. "She played us all for a fool. We're here to get what's rightfully ours."

"Rightfully yours?" I demanded. "Is that why you've been telling everyone in town that I've been lying to them?"

She didn't seem at all embarrassed to be called out on her bad behavior. She straightened and glared down her pointy nose at me. (A nose just as pointy as mine?) "I've only been telling people the truth. You should have never gotten your hands on Mother's shop. And now that you have, you're digging your claws even deeper into this building by doing all this construction. Did you think that if you fixed it up no judge would take it away from you?"

"No. I was thinking that I had better repair the building since someone drove a car through the front window. And why should you care? I'm not spending your money on the shop," I explained, even though I was sure they already knew that.

"Where are you getting the money to pay for all of this work?" Edward demanded. "Are you selling Mother's assets?"

"I haven't sold anything that belonged to your mother. The furniture she left you in her will is waiting for you in the upstairs apartment. You're welcome to take it at any time." Actually, I was disappointed that her children had turned their noses up at the family heirlooms Mabel had treasured.

"Edward means assets that actually have value," Florence said.

Peach, to her credit, winced.

"Many of the residents have donated materials and services," I said while fondly remembering how the residents of the Pink Pelican Inn had rallied around the store when it'd been damaged to the point where it could no longer stay open. "I've also taken out a business loan to pay for upgrades to the building's heating and cooling, electrical systems, and to repair and repaint the plaster."

"I don't think I've ever seen it look so good," Peach said in that quiet voice of hers.

"What did you use as collateral for this business loan?" Edward asked at the same time. "The building?"

"Yes, the building. The building your mother entrusted with me to keep and care for. I couldn't very well use any of the funds she'd set aside for its upkeep since your legal wrangling has kept them locked up in probate."

"That's why we are here today. We're here to protect our interests. You need to stop taking out loans where you use the building as collateral. You need to stop putting money into fixing up the building. While it's in probate, none of this is yours."

"But it will be," I said. "Mabel listed me as her heir. She wanted me to keep the shop going. She wanted me to take care of the building."

"Not for long," Florence said.

Edward cleared his throat. "We have reason to believe that the DNA test you claim proves your relationship with our family was faked," he said. "A fake DNA test will give us legal footing to overturn Mabel's will. We filed the paperwork this morning. We've reinstated our suit against you and we're asking the court to overturn our mother's will. We're also insisting on a new DNA test."

"Yes, I am well aware of that." I'd been so excited

about taking that new DNA test, so eager to get that dispute behind me once and for all. And now, after what Althea had told me, my heart ached. I put my hand on my chest. It really ached. Was I having a heart attack?

"I'm not your mother," Florence said, needlessly. "Carolina isn't your mother. Clearly, Peach isn't old enough to be your mother. You're not a Maybank. You have no claim on any of this." She gestured to the interior of the shop.

I stood there in the face of their assault, denying it all. This shop was mine. This was where I belonged. No one could take that away. It wasn't until Peach's softly spoken, "I'm sorry," that something inside me shattered.

I'm not Mabel's granddaughter.

My gaze shifted from Edward to Florence to Peach. I drew a slow, steady breath. "I see," I said, an unusually subdued reaction for me.

"You came to town and persuaded our mother that you were Carolina's daughter." Edward's cold voice sounded like an executioner reading the charges against the condemned. "You preyed on her sentimentality. You preyed on her desire to see this shop survive beyond her death. You did it so you could get your hands on something that you didn't rightly deserve."

I shook my head. I didn't. I didn't do anything of the sort. But my tongue felt paralyzed. *I wasn't Mabel's granddaughter.*

"*Why?*" my voice cracked as I asked them.

"Why did you conspire to steal the shop away from our mother's legal heirs? How should we know? We're the victims here. Not you." Edward tucked his hand into his vest as if he was a reincarnated Napoleon.

I turned toward Florence. She glared back at me.

"*Why*?" I whispered. "Why did you tell me that you were my mother?"

"Why? Did you not listen to me earlier?" Florence lifted a corner of her thin mouth. "I was afraid you were actually Carolina's daughter."

"It was something she shouldn't have done," Edward snapped. "She should have come to me before telling such a wild-haired tale to you, the defendant. Florence's 'so-called' confession has nearly destroyed our chances to overturn what you, Penn, have done to our family."

"What I did?" I suddenly found my voice. Apparently, it now sounded like a harpy screech. "I didn't ask for this. I didn't try and trick anyone. It was Mabel who had tricked me."

"Come now." Edward's voice had turned chilly again. "Don't try to make us feel sorry for you. You brought all of this on yourself by faking who you are. I spoke with your father and with your grandmother this morning. I heard all about how your mother was an older itinerant con-woman. Clearly, conning innocent people is part of your DNA. As much as you might wish it to be true, as much as you might want others to believe it, your DNA does not come from the illustrious Maybank family DNA. Not even close."

"You're calling me a con-artist, a swindler, a fraud?" I'd spent a lifetime making sure I was nothing like the mother who'd birthed me and abandoned me. I'd turned myself into a human version of a prickly pear cactus so I'd never let anyone like that ever hurt me again. "Are you serious?" I laughed like a mad woman.

"Stop screeching and, for Heaven's sake, take responsibility for your actions," Edward barked.

"How about your sister?" I shouted back. I whirled

toward Florence. The older woman smiled serenely as if she was enjoying every moment of my breakdown. That smile—that I-hope-you-suffer-terribly grin of hers made me feel even more out of control. I flapped my hands at her. "Why did you lie to me? Why didn't you want me to think I was Carolina's daughter? It was such a lovely thought. Why would you do something like that to a girl desperate to find her mother? What kind of heartless monster are you?"

Her smile didn't waver. She glanced down at her perfectly manicured nails. They were painted an ultra pale pink. "Dare-to-bare Pink" the polish was called. I knew that because it was one of my favorites. In that angry moment, I swore I'd toss out the bottle and never wear that shade or anything similar again.

"Aren't you paying attention? I already told you," she said, not at all rattled by my crazy-woman ranting and raving. She didn't seem at all fazed by what damage those lies of hers had done to my already battered sanity. "I was worried you were Carolina's daughter."

"I know! I heard you say that. What I want to know is why would that have mattered?" I shouted.

"Florence," Edward warned.

Her smile grew as she shook her head. "Eddie, it doesn't matter anymore. She's not Carolina's daughter. She's not anyone's daughter. I told you that little lie, because of our mother's crazy will. I'm sure you remember it well, Charity, since you helped write parts of it. Had you planned all along to masquerade as Carolina's long-lost daughter? Were you that money-hungry that you wanted not only what Mother had but also the considerable fortune that had been set aside in the off chance that Carolina or one of her heirs returned to Camellia Beach?"

"I would never—!"

"Tut-tut. Are those tears in your eyes? Have I struck a nerve? Well, I'm not sorry for it. You know how I feel right now? I feel vindicated. Now that we know Carolina is no longer alive and that she didn't leave any heirs, that money can finally come to Edward, Peach, and me. We're the ones who stayed and listened to Mother complain about her ungrateful children…save for her beloved lost Carolina. We *earned* that money."

"You can have it!" Though I really, really wanted to get control over my emotions, I couldn't seem to stop shouting every word that came out of my mouth. "Just let me keep this shop. You don't want it. I do. I want the shop. Your mother wanted me to have the shop. She wanted someone who loved the chocolate and who loved the shop to run it. That's me." I beat my hand against my chest. "I'm the one she picked."

"That's not the point." Edward said as he turned and headed toward the door. "You tricked our mother into writing that will. You don't deserve it. You don't deserve anything."

THIRTY-TWO

No, YOU DON'T deserve anything, you ungrateful wretches.
Of course those words didn't come to me until after the
Maybank children had waltzed out of the shop like a
parade of over-fluffed peacocks.

When I looked up I saw Detective Gibbons standing
just a step inside the door. His arms were crossed over
his wide chest. How much of that humiliating exchange
had he heard? "I got your text," he said.

His brows were creased as he watched me carefully.
It was the same way someone would watch a toddler
wobble around a room filled with fine china.

"They think I faked the DNA report," I said as I
lifted the apron off from over my head. I took extra
care in folding it and laying it across the display case.
"They think I lied to their mother in order to steal this
shop away from them."

He nodded while still watching me with concern.
"Is that what you urgently needed to talk to me about?"

"No." I dug my purse out from under the counter
and hitched its strap over my shoulder. "It's about Cassidy's murder."

"That's what I thought." He glanced up at Johnny
Pane, who had stopped painting. He stood on the ladder with his brush hanging loosely from his hand as he
watched me. His lips pursed in a severe frown.

"I'm going to close up for the day," I told Johnny. "And lock the front door."

"But it's not even four o'clock yet," Johnny said, shaking his head. "Shutting down early, that's not good for business."

Instead of explaining to him that I had to leave, that staying in the shop I was accused of stealing made my hands tremble, I said, "The back door is locked. You can go out that way when you're done here. Just make sure the door is pulled all the way closed behind you. It'll stay locked."

Johnny muttered something under his breath. I took it to mean he would do as I asked, so I left. I left without packing the detective a chocolate box to take back to the sheriff's department to share with his fellow officers. I left without emptying the chocolates from the display case for the day. I simply walked out the front door and locked it behind me.

A piece of me felt as if I might never return.

Detective Gibbons walked beside me like a silent sentry. His fitted suit still looked fresh and neatly pressed even though I knew he'd been working hard all day. I planned to ask him one day how he managed it. I'd only stepped out into the heat for a short time, and already my face felt slick from sweat and the back of my loose-fitting sundress was damp from the stifling August heat and humidity.

I headed toward the ancient oak tree that shaded the store and pressed my hand to its trunk. The silvery brown bark felt rough. Touching it was like shaking hands with a hardworking laborer, which made me think of Johnny Pane's hands.

"You know I'd thought I'd found a paradise here

in Camellia Beach," I said even though I really didn't want to talk about my family or how Althea had lied to me. "I'm starting to think it's all been an illusion. The quaint cottages, the welcoming islanders with their quirky way of thinking, and the soothing rhythm of the ocean waves drumming against the shore"—I sighed—"it's all been a pretty trap."

Gibbons remained silent.

"This wasn't why I texted you," I said, even though I'd already told him that.

"No, it's not," his low voice rumbled. "But if you need to talk about it, I'll listen. Just know ahead of time I'm not a priest. If you broke any laws and you tell me about it, I've sworn an oath. I cannot look the other way."

"I've not broken the law. I've not even lied about anything. I hate lies." Lies were what had gotten me into this mess, a mess I really didn't want to think about since thinking about it meant I had to think about Althea and the lies she'd been telling me. Althea's lies hurt even worse than finding out I wasn't actually related to those greedy Maybanks. I could live with not being a Maybank. But could I live with knowing my best friend in the world hadn't thought there was anything wrong with lying to me? Lies were like a cancer, eating away at everything that was good and beautiful in life.

"It wasn't lies, though, that got Cassidy killed. It was the truth," I said.

"He lied to Jody about staying true to her," Gibbons pointed out. "Lies about an intimate relationship—those are some of the deadliest lies we see in law enforcement."

I pressed my hand against the tree until the rough

bark actually bit into my skin. "Jody didn't kill Cassidy."

"So you keep saying. But I need proof," he said. "I have proof that Jody was at the crime scene. She had both guns in her hands. She'd fired both guns. She even had a pretty strong motive to shoot Cassidy."

"Did you talk with Luella Marie?" I asked.

He nodded. "Nothing she said changes any part of our case against Jody Dalton."

"Did Luella Marie tell you how she overheard Cassidy arguing with Fletcher?"

"She did tell me that. And I'll talk with Fletcher about it." He paused as if trying to choose his words carefully. "Still, that doesn't change the evidence we have against Jody."

"She's lying," I said. "She lied to me and she lied to you about what she saw that night. It makes me wonder why."

"She lied?" He leaned toward me, suddenly interested. "How?"

I explained to him how the sliding doors to Cassidy's house had been open and how the music had been playing. Someone was there with Cassidy, someone he was wooing. Was Luella Marie the object of his affection that night? Had he threatened to tell the world about her cosmetic surgery if she didn't sleep with him? Had those threats worked? Did she kill him to stop him from talking?

Had Fletcher even been there? These were all important questions that needed to be answered. These were all questions that put Jody's guilt into doubt.

"Jody was set up," I said.

"Nothing you've told me suggests that," he pointed

out. "All it tells me is that Luella Marie is embarrassed about what had happened that night, so she changed the facts around."

"Did she tell you that she went there to kill him? And that someone did the deed before she could?" I asked.

"She told you that? In those words?"

"Yes."

He groaned before saying, "That still doesn't change the evidence I have against Jody. I have evidence, Penn, not conjecture."

I wanted to stamp my feet and scream in frustration. While I appreciated that Gibbons was doing the legwork and actually interviewing witnesses and potential suspects, I couldn't understand why he was so stubbornly set on keeping Jody in jail. Clearly the facts he believed in so fervently, when looked at another way told a different story altogether. What I needed to do was to figure out who owned that second gun and which islander thought their secret was big enough to kill over.

But instead of actually stomping my feet and making a big scene, which would accomplish nothing, I lifted my hand from the ancient tree and rubbed my sore palm against the skirt of my sundress. "I'm worried about Gavin," I said.

"I know you are." His voice gentled.

While it looked as if I might never find my mother, there was still hope for him. He could still grow up with a mother who was present for him in his life.

He needed his mother. Jody might be a thorn in *my* side, but even Harley insisted she was a loving mother to her son. Yes, she'd made scores of bad decisions. Yes, she was always on the offensive. And yes, she distrusted nearly everyone. Good gracious, she was just like me.

I had no idea what had made her the way she was, no idea what had broken her. And her past really didn't matter. Whether she wanted it or not, I was going to save her and, in turn, save Gavin. After that, I had no idea what I was going to do.

"You found something plastic and red in the sand at the crime scene," I said. "Can you tell me what that was?"

"You know I can't discuss those kinds of details of the case. I've probably already told you too much."

I knew he was going to say that. But I didn't let it deter me. I pulled out the red anxiety-relieving spinner from my pocket. "Is this what you found?"

The way his jaw tightened told me all I needed to know. "Where did you get that?" he asked.

"They're all over the beach, aren't they?" I said.

He snatched it from my hand and slipped on his glasses so he could read the words printed in white on one side: Grilled to Perfection. "Not these," he forced through his teeth.

"Fletcher has one just like this," I said, feeling my heart rate start to speed up. "I watched him drop it today. And I found this one near the steps leading up to my apartment yesterday morning. Has Fletcher been following me?"

"Anyone could have dropped this outside your shop or on the beach," he said, but he frowned as he said it. Was the little toy a piece of evidence that didn't fit in with the rest? Was this the chink in their unbreakable case against Jody? "Fletcher could have dropped it after he and Cassidy fought."

"If they fought," I interjected.

"It's a toy, Penn, not a murder weapon. It doesn't point a finger of guilt at anyone."

"No, but it places Fletcher at the scene of the crime."

"So did Luella Marie. But that doesn't mean he pulled the trigger. He doesn't even have a gun registered to his name."

That gave me pause. "He doesn't?" I asked. "Althea told me that everyone on the island owned a gun."

"Fletcher doesn't," Gibbons said.

"He doesn't own a registered gun. Didn't you say the murder weapon wasn't registered to anyone?"

He held up his hands in surrender. "I understand what you're trying to do, and I respect it. But this"—he waved his hands around as if our conversation were a tangible thing—"this isn't going to work. You're grasping at straws and hoping one of them will look like a piece of evidence that proves Jody didn't do what every other piece of evidence says she did."

"There's Johnny Pane," I said desperately. "Cassidy had a powerful hold on him, and it clearly worried my painter. He told me the day before Cassidy's murder that he had a plan to free himself from Cassidy's clutches."

Gibbons rolled his eyes, but said, "He said that, exactly like that?"

"Not exactly."

Gibbons mumbled something under his breath and started to walk away. He didn't make it too far when he paused and turned back to me. "Are you coming with me?" he asked.

"Coming where?"

"To grab a few straws."

IT APPEARED THAT Johnny Pane was dragging his brush over the same spot on the ceiling as he had been when

I'd left with Gibbons. The detective put his hands on his wide hips and looked up at the painter.

"Could you come down here for a moment?" Gibbons said in an overly friendly tone. "I have a few questions."

"About the night of the murder?" Johnny's brush stilled. "I was wondering when you'd get around to talking to me about it."

Step after step, Johnny slowly made his way to the ground. He then carefully cleaned his brush before looking over at Gibbons who had silently watched with a funny look on his face. It almost looked like amusement.

"Yes," Johnny said as he came out from behind the plastic screening and settled into one of the café chairs. "I'm ready to talk."

Gibbons smiled at the older man. "How well did you know Cassidy?"

"He would hire me from time to time. He was a real estate agent, you know?"

Gibbons nodded encouragingly. But he wasn't writing any of this down. He hadn't even taken his little notebook out of his suit jacket's pocket.

"I'd work jobs for Cassidy from time to time," Johnny said.

"And what did you think about him?" Gibbons prodded.

Johnny shrugged. "He paid upfront and in cash."

"But he knew something about you, just like he knew things about many other people on the island?"

Johnny looked at the floor. "He's dead. What he knew or didn't know, doesn't matter much anymore, now does it?"

"Not really," Gibbons agreed. "But his death was a blessing to some around here."

"To some," he agreed. And that got me to wondering about Johnny's secret. It had to be something pretty damaging that just the mention of Cassidy's name had him agreeing to Jody's demands.

From what I could tell, Johnny lived and breathed for his painting business. He worked for Cassidy. And Cassidy noticed things.

"Were you at Cassidy's house the night he died?" Gibbons asked, apparently content to let Johnny's secret remain a secret.

"I may have stopped by his house before meeting up with my daughter's family for dinner," Johnny admitted.

"And did you talk to him?" Gibbons asked.

"I did."

Gibbons sighed. "What time was this?"

What secret might a painter keep that would jeopardize his business? The only hold I could think of that Cassidy might have over a man like Johnny was one that threatened his painting business. And what could a painter do when left in a home, alone, working? Oh my goodness, of course, my missing salted sea turtles.

"Cassidy caught you stealing from the houses you paint!" I blurted.

Both Gibbons and Johnny's heads snapped in my direction.

"You'd take things from the houses you painted. I imagine just little things," I said in a calmer voice. "Cassidy noticed and threatened to get you arrested." And I suddenly realized I was accusing him in front of a police detective. I held up a hand. "Don't answer that."

"Wasn't planning on it. Don't have rocks for brains, now do I?" Johnny said, which made Gibbons sigh.

"Did you confront Cassidy?" the detective asked.

"I planned to confront him, but when I got there he didn't have time for me. Some woman arrived not more than a minute after me, now didn't she? She was dressed in a large flowered dress, the kind you'd described, Penn. And she had a scarf over her head and was wearing dark sunglasses even though it was already dark out. Cassidy handed me a hundred dollar bill and told me to go away."

"So the woman wearing the muumuu was the woman Cassidy was romancing that night," I said, feeling a little triumphant. Luella Marie *had* lied to us.

Gibbons nodded, still focused on what Johnny had to say. "And Cassidy was alive when you left?"

"Very much so, sir."

"And this woman you saw. If we talked with her, do you think she could confirm your story?" Gibbons asked.

The old painter shrugged. "She was so covered up, I couldn't even begin to tell you how to find her."

"Don't worry about that. We already know her identity," Gibbons said. "I'm sure you can understand why we're not releasing her name."

"A gentleman never names names," Johnny said approvingly.

The two men smiled at each other. And that was it. Gibbons thanked Johnny for his time and handed him his card, telling him to call if he thought of anything else. And then the detective started to leave. Since I was still in no mood to stay in the shop, I followed him.

"Miss Penn," Johnny called to me before I made it

out the door. "I understand if you think you now know who's been stealing your chocolate turtles, but I'm telling you as earnestly as I'm able that you're wrong." He glanced over at the collection of vintage teacups displayed on a shelf that lined the length of one wall. Were some of them missing? "Ask anyone on the island, I can't eat chocolate. Gives me the worst kind of headache if I do."

"Okay," I said as I left the shop and locked the door behind me.

Gibbons was waiting for me. He gave me a sad smile. "Are you beginning to understand the trouble with grasping at straws when investigating a murder? It's a Pandora's box."

"I suppose it might be." Questioning Johnny didn't help get Jody out of jail, and now I knew something about him that I really didn't want to know.

"Look," Gibbons said, "sometimes it's not about the little details. Sometimes things are actually as they appear. For that matter, sometimes when I'm reading a crime scene what isn't there leads me to the biggest clues."

I nodded somewhat absently. I was still thinking about those missing salted sea turtles. If Johnny wasn't taking them, who was? The thefts had stopped after I'd installed the security camera. Only a handful of people knew about the tiny camera I'd installed near the display case. Was that a clue, or was it coincidence? "So are you saying I should be looking for something that wasn't at the crime scene but should have been?"

"No, I'm saying you should stop obsessing over tiny details that really don't have much, if any, bearing on this case. Jody was holding both of the guns. She fired both of them."

"She shot me with the murder weapon. But I don't think she meant to. Don't you see? It wasn't her gun. She didn't know it had a touchy trigger."

"How do you know about its trigger?" he demanded.

"I don't. Well, I didn't. But I'm right, aren't I? My goodness, I'm glad she shot me—*by accident*. This bullet wound might be the one thing that keeps her from spending a long time in prison."

Gibbons growled at me. He told me he didn't like the sudden gleam I'd gotten in my eyes. He told me not to go and do anything stupid. But I didn't listen. Why would I? While I didn't know who killed Cassidy Jones, I suddenly knew exactly how to catch him. Or *her*.

And after my dealings with the Maybanks, I was feeling more than a little reckless.

THIRTY-THREE

BERTIE WAS UPSTAIRS in the apartment, humming a happy tune as okra sizzled in a big pot of oil. I was glad she was happy. She deserved to be happy with Bubba.

"I'm going to walk Stella," I told her.

My little dog must have sensed my agitation. She growled and nipped at my hand when I reached down to clip the leash onto her collar. "I'm not upset with you," I told her, hoping my tone would calm her. She backed away and barked. It sounded like a warning, but I'm sure she was only reacting to my nervous energy.

My emotions felt like that sizzling pot of oil on the stove. I was still reeling from Althea's betrayal and the thought of losing the Chocolate Box. If I lost the shop I'd also lose this apartment, which felt more like home than pretty much anywhere else I'd ever lived. Not to mention I was determined to catch a killer tonight. Not the safest of undertakings.

"Dinner will start at seven," Bertie said as I headed out the door with Stella growling at me every step of the way. "Be sure to be back by then. Althea, Harley, and Gavin will be here as well as Bubba with his pork. It's going to be like a party." She must not have heard what had happened.

"Are you sure you don't want it to be like a date?" I asked her. "Just you and Bubba and soft candles and his pork?"

Bertie laughed. "That Bubba is going to have to work a good sight harder before I'm going to give him any kind of break. That lame excuse he gave that he wanted to do something for Althea and Bailey...did he really think I wouldn't realize that what he really wanted was an excuse to have dinner over here? If that boy wants to have a bona fide date with me, he's going to have to come to me with that grubby Camellia Beach ball cap in his hands and ask me proper."

"Good for you. You shouldn't demand any less," I said as I led Stella outside. I could learn a thing or two from Bertie about dating. She certainly knew how to stay in the driver's seat.

I took Stella down the marsh trail that wound through some of the undeveloped areas on the island. While Stella sniffed around in the underbrush near the grassy marsh, I sent Harley a text. The more I thought about what I planned to do tonight, the more I realized how dangerous it would be to try and handle things alone. I needed help.

My first choice would have been to bring Althea along as backup. But I wasn't talking to her anymore.

A hunky surfer with the ability to take care of himself (not to mention his awesome kissing skills)? I couldn't have asked for a much better second-choice to bring along with me tonight. I hoped he'd agree. He'd already proven how he'd make a perfect sidekick.

Really? Love to, he'd texted back almost immediately. I'll have Bertie watch Gavin.

That was an odd response to my asking him to risk his neck to catch a murderer red-handed. I looked back at the short text I'd sent him. "Oh, no," I said as I read what I'd hastily written. I hadn't wanted to give a lengthy explanation of the trap I planned to set for Cassidy's killer. For one thing, I didn't want him to try and talk me out of it. For another, I was still working on the plan. But I should have written more than, Could you join me on the beach all night tonight?

He must have thought I meant… "Oh, no." I mean, I wouldn't mind…maybe…in the future…when I wasn't still stinging from Althea's betrayal.

I started to write back to explain that he'd misunderstood. I'd started to type, I need backup, when Stella jerked her head up from where she was sniffing. A low growl rumbled in her throat as she watched the bushes.

A shiver traveled down my back.

"Hello?" I called out.

No one answered.

I looked around. We'd wandered far enough down the marsh trail that I couldn't see any other buildings through the jungle-like growth of bushes, vines, and small trees. I suddenly felt isolated and vulnerable.

"Let's get back to the Chocolate Box," I said to Stella. She seemed to understand my words. With a quick "yip, yip" she led the way down the dirt trail. I had to jog to keep up with the quick pace my tiny dog had set. Something out there had spooked her. We both paused in the courtyard behind the Chocolate Box. She sat down and started to scratch one of her oversized ears. I stared at the marsh trail for several minutes, half expecting a madman to coming running out at us. When no one appeared, I started to finish composing my text to Harley.

I was about to hit "send" when someone behind me cleared his throat.

My nerves still on edge, I jumped.

"Is s-something wrong?" Fletcher asked. He was standing right behind me. Was he peeking over my shoulder in an attempt to read my text messages?

I whirled toward him as I shut off my phone's screen and quickly stuffed it into my sundress' pocket.

"What are you doing here?" I asked him.

"Y-you texted me," he said.

"That was hours ago."

"T-took a while to f-f-finish what I started," he said as he smacked his lips nervously.

"Didn't you see? I closed up early."

"I-I saw that. I-I also n-noticed the ch-ch-chocolates aren't put away. Th-the t-t-tables need cleaning."

"Just a sec," I said to him. I tossed Stella some bacon to try and calm her. She gobbled it, but kept barking at Fletcher so vigorously her front legs lifted off the ground. "Shush, shush." I crouched down to try and calm her by petting her tiny chest.

She bit me.

Hearing Lidia's stern voice in my head telling me that I needed to take control of the situation and my dog, I quickly stood back up. In a firm voice that I hoped sounded like Lidia's, I said, "Stella, sit."

Amazingly, she sat.

I praised her and tossed her a handful of treats while Fletcher looked on. He'd twisted his face into an extreme expression of distaste.

"Don't you like dogs?" I asked him.

"Love them," came out of his mouth without so much of a stutter. "B-best thing that h-happened to m-man."

"Not sure it's the *best* thing." At least my little beast had stopped barking. "Good dog," I said and tossed her a few more treats. "I can put her in the shop's office while we properly close up."

"Th-this isn't charity. I-I'm on the cl-clock," he warned.

"Of course you are. But I'm not paying you for the time you spent running your errand. Being shorthanded was one of the reasons I had to close up early."

"Uh, uh, Penn, I heard you closed up because the Maybanks came by to harass you," he whispered in a singsong voice. "And it upset you. You had to run away."

"You seem pretty knowledgeable for someone who wasn't around this afternoon." I tilted my head to one side. "What were you doing?"

He shrugged. "C-c-can't stop the g-g-gossips from t-talking." He drew a deep breath and then sang, "Cursed nuisance, ain't it?"

"Gotta love small towns." I quickly sent a text to Harley, Fletcher here. Alone with him. at Chocolate Box. Can you join me?

After hitting "send" for that message, I unlocked the back door, settled Stella into the office, and got to work.

Fletcher, as usual, worked diligently. He seemed to always know what to do even before I asked him. And if he didn't, he asked. I couldn't believe such a conscientious employee could be a cold-blooded killer. How could such a thing be possible?

While he was emptying the coffee urn, I worked up my courage to question him. Forget what Gibbons had said. Someone on the island was a killer and while I thought I knew the why, I still hadn't worked out exactly who so had cleverly set up Jody. "I've heard some things about you around town too," I said as I watched him closely. "I heard you were seen at Cassidy's house the night of the murder. That you were arguing with him."

"Th-that's small towns for y-you, huh?" he said as he started to scrub the inside of the urn. He hadn't even bothered to look up at me. He kept his head down and kept working.

Frustrated with his reluctance to share what he knew about the murder with me, I blurted out in a rush, "Someone saw you with Cassidy. The police found one of your anxiety-relieving spinners next to the murder weapon. Cassidy made you lose your job. He'd pressed charges against you for the slap fight he'd started. You were going to lose everything financially fighting that charge. His death solved all that."

"Th-the ch-charges are st-still p-pending," he ground out.

"Oh." I chewed my bottom lip. "His death didn't solve your troubles, did it?"

"Hardly."

"But he knew something else about you. Something that would cause you even more trouble," I guessed.

Fletcher wrinkled his nose. "S-s-someone's been l-lying to you."

"Were you there that night?" I asked and then quickly added, "The version of the events I heard from...*someone*...doesn't fit what *I* saw that night. I'm hoping you can help fill in some of the details because I don't think Jody killed Cassidy."

He slammed the urn down onto the counter and turned toward me. Red-hot rage had colored his entire face. "You're walking dangerous ground with questions like that." He sang the angry words. His Southern accent grew as thick as the weeds that grew along the marsh trail. "I'm a-warning you. You gonna get those around you killed dead."

He charged toward me. I raised my hands, prepared to defend myself, certain I could defend myself against a man with his short height.

He didn't attack me. Instead he looked straight through me as if I were already dead as he hurried past. He went straight to the display case and took the tray of salted sea turtles. "I-I'm going t-to p-put these away now."

He marched down the hallway that led to the cooler in the back. I remained in the front of the store. I stood there like a useless statue, wondering how I could coax him to open up to me. He returned a few moments later, glared in my direction, as if daring me to say something stupid.

I held up my hands in surrender. "I'm sorry," I said. "I didn't mean to upset you."

That seemed to surprise him. "I'm s-s-sorry I y-yelled."

Encouraged by that minor victory, I pulled out a chair and then sat down in the one next to it. "I am glad you're working here. Bertie and I were going to hurt ourselves trying to keep up with the crowd. Please,"—I patted the chair—"sit down for a moment."

"Why?" he demanded.

"Because I want to tell you what I know about that night. You don't have to tell me anything. But if you know or saw something different from what I saw or heard happened, you can tell me if what I know is wrong. I'm trying to get the facts of Cassidy's murder straight. I don't think Jody killed Cassidy. Please, I need your help."

He flicked a glance at the chair. "You don't get it." He pulled out another tray of chocolates. This one was filled with my perfectly rounded chocolate moon benne wafers. Without saying a word, he walked back down the long hallway.

A few minutes later I heard a crash.

A muffled Stella started barking like crazy and scratching on the office door.

I jumped up from my chair and ran as fast as I could down the hallway. I tripped to a stop when I saw the tray and chocolate cookies scattered and broken as if they'd been violently thrown to the ground.

"Fletcher?" I called. Stella kept barking.

The back door was open and swinging in the afternoon breeze. Fletcher was gone.

THIRTY-FOUR

I WAS STILL standing with my hands on my hips dumb-founded by why my benne wafers were scattered all over the floor when Harley came in through the open backdoor. He looked at the ruined cookies and then at the confusion I knew must have been written all over my face, and froze.

"What happened here?" he asked, slowly. "Are you okay?"

I nodded.

Stella kept barking and scratching at the office door. I opened the door, but caught her before she could grab any of the chocolate-covered cookies. While chocolate was the food of the gods and heaven on earth for some of us mortals, it was poison to dogs.

"What happened here?" Harley asked again.

"Fletcher," I said as I gave Stella a piece of bacon as a consolation prize. "He was putting the chocolates into the coolers. I heard a crash. And when I came here, he was gone."

"Gone?" Althea poked her head through the open backdoor. "He smashed your chocolates and ran off?"

My jaw clamped shut at the sight of her. Childish or not, I wasn't ready to talk to her. I wasn't ready to pretend she hadn't hurt me.

"He was putting away the chocolates while Penn worked out front to close up the shop," Harley said when

I kept my mouth clamped shut. "She heard a crash and found this." He pointed to the wrecked benne wafers.

Althea frowned.

"Was that the first tray he'd taken back here?" Harley asked.

I shook my head. Talking in general seemed to break the no-talking-to-Althea rule. But that was crazy. "He brought the salted sea turtles back to the cooler first."

"How was he acting?" Harley asked while Althea edged around him to poke her nose into the storage room where the coolers were.

My eyes stayed on her. I watched her with the intensity that someone would watch a thief. "He seemed agitated. I asked him what he was doing the night of Cassidy's murder."

"You mean you asked him what he was doing at Cassidy's house?" Althea asked as she opened one of the coolers' doors.

Since I still wasn't talking to Althea, I said to Harley, "My talking about that night made his face turn bright red. But he kept working. He carried the turtles back here. He returned for the benne wafers."

"Are you sure that's what happened? Your turtles aren't here," Althea said as she opened all of the coolers' doors.

"What?" Harley and I both demanded.

Althea pointed to the cooler in front of her. "Your turtles, Penn. They're not in here."

"What?" I ran over to see for myself. "They're gone? Again?"

"Well, if that doesn't beat all." I looked up to find Bertie standing in the back doorway with her hands on her hips. She'd changed out of her work clothes. She'd donned a flowered dress she usually only pulled out of her closet for Sunday services. "Why would Fletcher want to steal those chocolates so fiercely? They're good and all, but they're not worth-going-to-prison-over good."

"I don't know that he stole them," I said. Why would he take the turtles but throw the benne wafers all over the hallway floor? And what about that crash I heard?

"Do you think any of this was caught on your security camera?" Althea asked.

"I only bought one camera," I answered, momentarily forgetting that I wasn't talking to her. "It takes video of the front of the shop. I don't have coverage back here."

We all headed to the front where I'd installed the camera. It was still there recording everything. Not that the footage would be any help to me right now.

Harley's frown deepened as he looked at the camera. He then went back down the back hallway that led to the back door, storage rooms, office, and kitchen.

"Did Fletcher say anything to you, Mama?" Althea asked. "Did he give you any indication that he was your chocolate thief?"

Bertie shook her head. "Other than running off and leaving us in the lurch—unprofessional, if you ask me—that boy worked hard and had an excellent singing voice. I was going to ask if he wanted to join the church choir."

"He had no way of knowing I would hire him," I pointed out.

"You had no way of knowing you were hiring your thief," Althea said, her voice growing even more excited.

"I'm not talking to you." I crossed my arms and turned away from her. "Where did Harley go?"

No one knew.

"Harley?" I called. Stella squirmed in my arms as I walked down the hallway. Had he disappeared the same way Fletcher had? "Harley?"

"I'm right here," he came out of the kitchen. "I was looking around to see if I could find Fletcher."

"And?" Althea demanded. "Did you find him?"

He shook his head. "He's gone. Looks like he ran out the back door with your chocolate turtles, Penn."

"I knew it!" Althea slapped her hands together. "You asked him about the night of the murder, and he ran like a cockroach running away from the light. I told you and told you. You hired a killer."

THIRTY-FIVE

As NIGHT FELL, the sea breeze stopped. The air stood still, as if the world was holding its breath, waiting. I stood in the wet sand waiting too. The waves rose and fell with gentle, rolling swells. Silver shimmered on the dark surface. The water was so calm I felt like I was gazing out over a lake in the Northwoods of the Midwest instead of a vast ocean.

I stood shoulder to shoulder with Harley. His fingers twined with mine. I looked down at our hands and smiled. There'd been a time when I pulled away from his touch. Right now I was grateful for it.

"You know I don't think this is a good idea," he said.

"Tomorrow is Wednesday," I pointed out even though I was sure he knew the clock was ticking ever louder on our deadline to get Jody out of jail in time for Gavin's first day of school Thursday morning. "Gavin needs Jody to be out of jail by tomorrow."

"There's a good chance she'll be out on bail by then."

"Gavin is a smart boy. He'll know the difference. It might even be worse, because he'll be constantly worried that someone will come and take her away."

He squeezed my hand. I took that as his way of agreeing.

"You do know you misunderstood my first text? We are spending the night on the beach to catch the killer and not do anything else." He'd come equipped for a romantic night on the beach with a heavy blue-and-green-plaid beach blanket neatly folded over his arm. At his feet was a picnic basket packed with cheese and crackers, wine, and even a thermos of coffee.

"There's no better cover for a stakeout on the beach than romance," he said. He had a point. Only perverts paid any attention to couples enjoying a little kissing under the stars. Beach blanket romances were nearly as common as the creamy white ghost crabs that darted here and there on the sand.

"It's a good cover," I had to admit. But the way his eyes had crinkled with pleasure and the way his voice had deepened just a notch as he explained the purpose for his romantic setup, made me wonder just how much kissing we would be doing while lying side-by-side on that soft beach blanket of his in order to maintain our cover. It also surprised me how eager I was to find out.

"Let's go. The new turtle nest is this way," I said and kicked off my leather flip flops. I dropped them into my own beach bag, which included essentials such as a beach towel, camera, cell phone, and the unloaded gun Bertie stored behind the flour tin in the kitchen. I then bent down and picked up the heavy picnic basket.

Harley silently lifted the burden from my hands and followed as we headed down the beach toward its undeveloped southern end where the beach was narrow, the currents dangerous to swimmers. In this area of the beach every sea turtle nest had to be moved to higher ground.

"Althea told me—that is when we were still talking—that the turtle crew found the nest this morning and moved it up into the dune above the high tide mark,"

I explained. "If the thief follows his pattern, he'll take the eggs tonight."

"And what makes you think the turtle thief has anything to do with Cassidy's murder?" Harley asked as we walked along the edge of the surf.

"Detective Gibbons told me today that I was wasting my time focusing on small details when the big details of the case against Jody painted such a clear picture. He then said something interesting. He told me that what they don't find at a crime scene is sometimes more important than what they do find. He'd meant it as a way to discourage me from investigating Cassidy's murder. I'm sure he'd hate to know how it made me think about the stolen sea turtle eggs in a new way. That nest was close to Cassidy's house. When he stood on his deck he had a direct line of vision to the nest."

"And he was someone who noticed things," Harley added.

I nodded. "He noticed everything that happened around him. And I'm betting he noticed someone digging up the turtle nest the night after the turtle team had moved it to higher ground."

"So you think he confronted the egg thief?" Harley asked.

"I do. I think he taunted the thief. I think he told our egg poacher more than once that he had the power to destroy him. Stealing sea turtle eggs is a federal crime."

"Not only that, taking those eggs would also be an unforgivable sin in this town," Harley added. "I've never been to a town that put more pride and value in its sea turtles than Camellia Beach."

"I agree. Even Sunset Development financially supports the turtle team. At first this confused me. But now

I understand. The turtle nests are a big deal to the town. No one in Camellia Beach is going to stand by and let someone sabotage it."

We walked a little farther on down the beach. "Chief Byrd has an officer watching Fletcher's house. They will catch him," Harley said.

"It's not him," I said.

"Really? You don't suspect him even a little?" Harley cried. "You accused me of being a murderer simply because I didn't say nice things about your friend after he was killed."

"I'm trying not to repeat past mistakes," I confessed. "Plus, I hate to lose Fletcher. When he was working at the shop, he was great. Sure, he ran off in the middle of the day to run some mysterious errand. Sure, he stole the chocolate turtles and ruined my benne wafers. But do you know how hard it is to get good people to work in food service?"

After Fletcher's rather stupidly planned theft of the chocolate turtles, Police Chief Hank Byrd showed up and filled out a report. He seemed to take the attitude that Fletcher would eventually show up at his house. There was no need to launch an island-wide manhunt for a chocolate thief.

Detective Gibbons didn't even bother to show up. He said he was busy with a new case. But he did listen to my concerns and suggested that Fletcher had sent one of the two threatening notes. But he still firmly believed they already had Cassidy's killer safely locked away behind bars.

"It does seem odd that all the other times the chocolate turtles were stolen, no one saw it happen," Harley admitted. "The thief seemed to be the invisible man. So why would Fletcher take them right in front of you this time? Did he want you to know he was the one taking them? Did he want to get caught?"

"See?" I said. "Nothing about him or his actions make any sense. There has to be an explanation that we're not seeing."

"Or perhaps he got sloppy…or desperate," Harley said slowly. We had almost reached the turtle nest. The beach along this stretch of island was dark. The land was too narrow to be developed. The dunes here had formed steep sandy cliffs from the constant erosion that ate at the island.

I'm not sure who spotted it first. We both stopped walking at the same time. Several hundred yards away in the line where the ocean caressed the sand was a creature bathed in shadows. It wasn't moving.

"What do you think that is?" I asked.

Harley squinted. "A sea turtle?"

"If it is, she didn't make it," I said. Occasionally a sea turtle would wash up onto the beach. Collisions with fishing boats and even larger ships often proved fatal for those gentle giants. "Maybe it's a log," I said. In the dark, logs often mimicked all kinds of dire shapes. Like dead bodies.

"Yes," Harley whispered. "That must be what we're looking at."

"I think we should go take a closer look."

He squeezed my hand before releasing it. "I'll do it."

"No way. We'll go together."

We walked over to the shadowy not-quite-log-like figure being washed by the gentle waves as they brushed against the beach. I sighed.

"Not a log," Harley said.

"Never thought it was," I said.
"I didn't either."
It was Fletcher.

THIRTY-SIX

HARLEY REACHED DOWN, hooked his hands under the man's armpits, and pulled Fletcher higher on the beach where the waves couldn't reach him. Even in the darkness, I could see his neck had turned several shades of blue. Someone had strangled him.

My phone was already out. I punched in the number for Detective Gibbons, wondering why I hadn't added him to my speed dial list.

Detective Gibbons answered the phone with a long yawn. "Penn, why are you calling me at this hour of the night?" I could hear his wife, Connie, talking in the background.

"He's dead," I said. "Murdered."

"What? Who?" Gibbons barked.

"He's breathing," Harley called over to me. "Barely."

I nearly dropped the phone as I ran over to where Harley was kneeling next to Fletcher. I fell to my knees beside him.

"He's alive?" I couldn't believe it. He didn't look alive.

"Barely," Harley answered.

"Who!" Gibbons screamed.

"Fletcher!" I shouted back.

My star employee reacted as if he thought I was calling out to him. He moaned. His eyelids fluttered. He looked at me and moaned again. I dropped the phone.

"Who did this to you?" I leaned over Fletcher and demanded. "Why?"

"Let's stick with who?" Harley said. "Who did this to you?"

"T-tried to chase after him," I think he said. I could barely make out his whispery, raspy voice. "Then s-searched for h-h-hours for him."

"Who?" both Harley and I shouted.

"Melty," Fletcher rasped, then coughed. His eyelids fluttered closed again.

"Did he say 'melty'?" I asked. "Like melty chocolate?"

Harley didn't answer right away. He was busy working to save Fletcher's life. He seemed to know exactly what to do with a drowning victim. He'd already turned his head to the side and had worked on getting all the water out of his mouth and throat. He was now doing it again.

"I'm a surfer and certified lifeguard," he said as his hands worked quickly and surely. "This isn't the first near-drowning I've seen."

"Is he going to live?" If he'd seen these before, surely he'd know.

Harley shook his head. "I don't know. Hope so. We need EMS out here now."

I found where I'd dropped the phone. I picked it up. Gibbons was still on the line. "Help is already on its way," he told me. Sirens blared in the distance.

Soon help did arrive. An ambulance came first, followed closely by one of Camellia Beach's police officers. The two EMTs took charge of the situation. Only a few minutes had passed before they had Fletcher on a stretcher and was rushing him back to their ambulance.

"Did he say 'melty'?" I asked Harley again after the EMTs had driven away.

He shook his head. "I don't know. That's kind of what it sounded like."

"But that doesn't make sense," I said.

The police officer busily wrote everything we said down in a notebook.

"He's been oxygen deprived for who knows how long," Harley said. "He might not know what he's saying ever again."

That was a depressing thought. "Gibbons will find out what he said. He'll find out who attacked Fletcher. He told me he's going straight to the hospital to be there when Fletcher wakes up," I said.

Harley nodded toward the round figure plodding through the sand toward us. "And we'll be giving our statement to Hank."

I groaned. "This is going to ruin our chances to catch our killer tonight, isn't it?"

"Your thief would have to be awfully stupid to show up to steal turtle eggs tonight," Harley said.

"Or awfully desperate," I added. "And for all we know *he* very well might be a *she*."

WE ARRIVED AT the nest much later than I'd planned. My heart beat in my throat as we approached the orange warning tape surrounding the turtle nest. I worried we were too late and that the nest would be empty.

Using our phones as flashlights, we walked around the cordoned off nest several times. There wasn't any sign of disturbance. The sand was smooth. The only footprints were ours.

Harley spread the beach blanket several hundred feet

away from the nest and as far away from the approaching tide as the narrow beach allowed. That's where we sat in the shadow of the dune's sharp cliff, side by side, not saying a word. Not touching the wine and cheese. Not touching each other. After finding Fletcher half dead, my thoughts of romance had dried up. I suspected Harley felt the same way.

With each hour that passed, my hopes that I'd be able to keep my promise to Gavin dimmed. I was about to give up and call the night a waste of our time when someone approached from the east. The figure wasn't very tall. Dressed in clothes that were solid black and loose, I couldn't tell if our villain was a man or a woman. But I could make out the metal tool cradled in the person's arms. It was a shovel.

The shoulder Harley had pressed to mine tensed as we watched the thief go straight to the turtle nest and pause. The thief's head swung from side-to-side, as if searching for witnesses. For a moment the villain seemed to be staring straight at me. I held my breath, waiting. But then the person's gaze moved on. After a few moments the digging started.

This was it! I reached into my beach bag and, after a little fumbling around, pulled out my camera. I double-checked that the flash was turned off before taking several shots. I also snapped several pictures with my phone and texted them to Detective Gibbons. Harley was doing the same, only he was texting his pictures to Hank.

These pictures were no good though. It was too dark for the photos to show the thief's face. *I* needed to see the thief's face. While sitting in the dark for hours waiting for something to happen, I'd spent the time thinking about Cassidy's killer. I'd managed to eliminate Ethel from my suspect list. With her arthritis, there was no way she could have strangled Fletcher nor could she handle digging up a turtle nest. I still considered Luella Marie and even Florence suspects. If I had to be honest, spite had me adding Florence to my list of suspects. But there were others in that list too. One person who hadn't landed on my suspect list before tonight was Bailey Grassi. He was a newcomer to town. And he was the only one who'd appeared genuinely distressed by Cassidy's death.

Ethel had told me that only two people on the island had the necessary skills to shoot Cassidy from across the beach: herself and Jody. But if Ethel wasn't strong enough to strangle Fletcher and Jody was in jail that would mean someone else on the island was also skilled when it came to handguns. It would have to be someone Ethel didn't know very well.

Ethel barely knew Bailey. She'd never seen him at a turkey shoot. After all, he was new to town. And Bailey had acted so very interested in the rare Amar chocolates. He wanted to visit the shop. He wanted to see all of my equipment. He wanted to taste the chocolate. He wanted to sell the chocolate to his elite clientele. He's said it himself—His elite clientele wanted to buy only the rarest delicacies. Besides chocolate sweets, rare delicacies could also include illegal sea turtle eggs that were highly sought after in the black market.

I had to refrain from shouting "Oh my goodness!" I did, however, jump. Harley, brows raised, looked at me in alarm. But really, all of my excited energy had to go somewhere, because the pieces had finally snapped into place.

Bailey had told me himself that he sold only the rarest delicacies to a select online clientele. Sea turtle eggs are considered rare delicacies in some parts of the world. This was the first year that turtle eggs had been stolen. And it had only happened at the end of the season. It had only happened since Bailey had moved to the island.

Bailey's biggest mistake had been to steal sea turtle eggs from a nest so close to Cassidy's house. Cassidy must have seen Bailey take the eggs. When Cassidy threatened to expose the newcomer's crime, Bailey probably panicked. And that was why he started planning Cassidy's murder.

It seemed so clear now. Bailey was the one who'd left his porch lights on. With an island this gossipy, he could have easily learned of Jody's past habit of shooting out porch lights to keep the lights from disorienting baby sea turtles. He would have also easily heard about Jody's delusional affair with a man who didn't know how to be true to any woman.

Bailey was obviously the turtle thief. And he was the one who'd framed Jody for Cassidy's murder. He'd even returned to the scene of the crime, acting all upset about what had happened while feigning complete stupidity over the nesting habits of sea turtles.

I wanted to tell Harley all of this. But I couldn't say a word without alerting Bailey that we were there watching him. And then I remembered I had my phone in my hand. I texted Harley, Not melty. Bailey.

Harley read the text and turned to me with a look of confusion. I nodded to the dark figure digging carefully deeper and deeper into the nest. If we didn't act soon, he'd reach the eggs.

I dug around in my beach bag until my hand touched the cold steel of Mabel's old handgun. Without much of a plan beyond: point gun at Bailey until the cops arrived, I jumped up from the beach blanket. Harley jumped to his feet too. But instead of rushing toward our thief like I was trying to do, he lurched at me.

"What are you going to do with that?" he whispered.

"Stop him," I hissed.

Harley grabbed my arm. "Swinging a gun around is a good way to go and get yourself killed."

"What do you suggest we do? Wait for the police to get here while he destroys the nest? I can't do that."

"Who's there?" Bailey turned toward us. It was definitely Bailey. I easily recognized that east-coast accent of his.

"Bailey Grassi," I called out to him as I stepped forward with Bertie's gun held level with his chest. "You're not going to get away with this. We've already called the police. I have a gun. So you'd better drop that shovel and put your hands in the air."

"Penn, no," Harley whispered. "You put him in a corner. His only escape now is violence."

"Harley is here with me," I shouted. I then broke my personal rule and told a whopper of a lie. "He also has a gun. So do as I say and drop that shovel."

Bailey snorted and kept digging. "If Harley had a gun, he'd be the one standing out front. He'd be the one shouting the orders. He wouldn't be the one tugging at you, trying to get you to stop whatever mad scheme you've hatched to stop me."

"You sexist pig," I shouted and batted Harley's insistent hands away. "That's not true."

"Isn't it?" Bailey laughed.

"Hey, mister, I'm the one with the gun." I shook it at him. "You'd better start doing what I'm telling you to do. Or I'll start shooting."

"You'd shoot an unarmed man?" Bailey shouted across the expanse. He sounded a little worried that I might be crazy enough to do it.

"We're passionate about our sea turtles around here," I pointed out, hoping I did sound a little crazy. Harley had let go of my arm. I heard him moving things around in the picnic basket. I wondered what he was doing. "The banners and signs hanging all over town celebrating the sea turtles not to mention the long waiting list to join the sea turtle team should have told you that."

"Okay. Okay." He tossed down the shovel. "You win."

"That's better. Now keep those hands where I can see them. Harley, do we have some rope?"

I don't know how I could have forgotten to bring rope. And I never realized how heavy handguns were. My arm was starting to dip.

Before Harley could answer, before I could shift the gun from one hand to the other, Bailey had pulled a gun out from somewhere in his pants.

"It's like an old Western standoff, Penn. Just you and me. But my gun is loaded," Bailey said with a laugh.

"Don't forget about Harley," I said. "He's got my back."

"He's run off like a whipped dog. I already have the perfect story too. I came across you digging up the eggs. You pulled a gun on me. In self-defense, I was forced to shoot you."

I glanced around. Bailey was right. Harley was gone. But I didn't think he'd run away, not for even a second.

And yet I was glad he was out of shooting range. This was how things needed to be. While he had a son to raise, no one needed me to return home alive.

"Another clever ploy to get away with murder?" I said. "I know how you set up Jody. I know you killed Cassidy."

"You think you know, but you don't have proof. If you did, you wouldn't be here right now. Heck, I wouldn't be here right now. Now do you want to pull the trigger, or should I just shoot you and get it all over with."

"You're crazy," I said. "No one will believe that I attacked you."

"It was so upsetting. There was so much blood. But what was I to do?" He made weeping noises. "She said no one could know that she was stealing the turtle eggs, just like no one could know about how she'd lied to Mabel, no one could know how she'd told Mabel she was her granddaughter."

Oh, fudge. He was right. Half of the island would probably believe that. "Why did you attack Fletcher? Was he working with you? Or did he know something that proved your guilt?" I asked because I wanted to buy myself time, time for Harley to do whatever he planned to do, time for the police to arrive.

I didn't expect my ploy to work. I expected him to shoot me.

He surprised me by answering, "Fletcher was there the night Cassidy died. I don't know what he saw. I actually don't think the sneaky jerk saw anything. I was careful. But ever since that night, he's been following me around, watching me. It's creepy."

"Why kill Cassidy anyhow?" I asked. "Was it because he threatened to tell everyone that you've been stealing the island's turtle eggs?"

Bailey grunted. "I didn't realize Cassidy would sit out on that porch of his and watch. If I'd known…"

"Cassidy would still be alive." I finished for him. "And Jody wouldn't be in jail. How did you know she'd pick up your gun?"

"I didn't. It was simply a stroke of good luck that she did. I waited until she came to shoot out my porch lights. And then I made my move. I figured just finding the gun in her vicinity would be enough to implicate her for his murder. She had the motive, the opportunity, and gun residue all over her hands from firing her own gun." He sounded proud of his accomplishment.

"You would have gotten away with it if I hadn't meddled," I said speaking quickly in an attempt to keep him talking for as long as possible. Harley must have called the police by now. "Is that why you started to steal my chocolate turtles, to try and distract me from asking too many questions about Cassidy's murder? Or were you stealing them to sell on that gourmet website of yours?"

"You'd think I'd sell a diluted version of the Amar chocolates? I should shoot you right now for even thinking that. I have a reputation to maintain. I stole them hoping I could keep you busy. I had to keep you from spending too much time helping that weird friend of yours figure out what happened to the sea turtle eggs."

"Weird friend?" Sure, I thought she was weird, but it rankled to hear him say it. "She's the best thing that could have happened to your life. She's a treasure. But you didn't take the time to see that, did you? You didn't want to date her. You were only interested in keeping tabs on what she was doing." And I'd stupidly helped him. "Am I right?"

"A treasure? That weirdo?" He snorted. "She's so not my type."

A terrifying sound ripped through the air. I nearly dropped Bertie's gun as a woman dressed all in black, yelling like an Amazon warrior, jumped off the sandy cliff, sailed over my head, and sent a spray of sand in the air as her feet hit the ground a few feet to my left. She'd landed in a crouched position, which made her look like a comic book heroine. She had a gun in one hand and her phone in the other. And she looked angry enough to rip Bailey's head off his shoulders with her bare hands.

"Althea?" My eyes must have been playing tricks on me. Because my *former* best friend wore long silky skirts, she invited ghosts to tea, she didn't leap around like she was freaking Avenging Althea.

"Drop your gun or I *will* shoot!" she shouted not more than a heartbeat after she'd landed in the sand.

Harley used Althea's distraction to grab Bailey from behind. He grabbed the killer's gun arm and pushed it into the air just as it fired. With a shout—I don't know which man shouted—Harley tossed Bailey to the ground. Bailey might have been small, but he was by no means a weakling. The two men wrestled in the sand. The gun went off. Twice.

I screamed. Twice.

And then silence.

THIRTY-SEVEN

"I MIGHT JUST shoot you anyhow," Althea said as she glared down at Bailey with a look of such raw hate, I barely recognized her. "Those weren't just eggs you stole. They were the future of a species." She moved to kick the man in the side as he lay in the sand hugging his knees to his chest. Harley scrambled to his feet in time to stop her.

"Is he hurt?" I asked surprised at how calm and detached I sounded. I felt like an astronomer who witnesses the most dramatic celestial events from light years away while squinting through a telescope. I turned to Harley. "Are you hurt?"

"No, no one got shot," Harley said, his voice a low grumble. He tied Bailey's hands with some rope he must have found in his picnic basket. "Why are the police taking so long to get out here?" He wasn't really expecting an answer. He pulled out his phone and started tapping the screen.

"What are you doing here?" I demanded of Althea who still didn't look at all like the Althea I was used to seeing. Her dark, usually springy hair had been flattened and was contained in a tight bun. "How did you know how to find us?"

"I followed you and Harley." She nodded toward Harley who was shouting into his phone.

"You followed us? You know we could have been coming here to"—I kicked a pile of sand—"you know."

"No, you weren't. I know you, Penn. And that's not how you work. I reckon you'll need to stress about whether or not you're making the biggest mistake of your life for at least another month before you let anything happen with this relationship."

"Oh, you know me now?" I crossed my arms over my chest. "I'm still not talking to you." But I was grateful for her flying leap rescue.

Harley came over. He glanced down at Bailey, who was still playing dead on the ground.

"Are you sure he's okay?" I used my phone as a flashlight and shined it on our captive.

"He's fine. I checked him over when I tied up his hands. I'm sure he's playing turtle while trying to figure out a way to escape."

"I'm planning on suing the three of you for assault and kidnapping," Bailey grumbled.

Harley nodded, but pretty much ignored him. "I just got off the phone with Hank. There's a house fire down on the other side of the island. Hank and his two officers have been busy working with the fire department. I stressed to him how we needed an officer here. Now. He said he'll personally come."

"And where's Detective Gibbons?" I gestured at Bailey who was still curled up in the sand. "He tried to kill us."

"Hello? You pulled the gun on me!" Bailey shouted.

"And I'll pull a gun on you again if you keep interrupting us. We're having a private conversation here," Althea said. "Penn, I don't know why you thought I should date this creep. Not only is he a killer, his manners are atrocious."

"Perpetual bad judgment when it comes to men," I said.

"Hey!" Harley cried. "Standing right here."

"Umm…" I frantically searched for something to say that wouldn't sound fake or hokey.

"Run, man," Bailey said. "She's going to be nothing but a headache."

"I should have let Althea kick you," Harley said and then took my hand. "You don't have to explain yourself. I think I hear a siren. How's that for a convenient out?"

I heard it too. A police siren. Hank could take over. But what had I accomplished? We proved Bailey was stealing the sea turtle eggs. But I had no proof that he killed Cassidy other than what he told us just now. But that would be his word against ours. That wasn't the solid evidence I needed to completely exonerate Jody.

"I'm sorry, Harley." My shoulders seemed to drop all the way to the ocean floor. "We still don't have hard evidence tying Bailey to Cassidy's murder. Gibbons won't release Jody in time for Gavin's first day."

"There's always the bail hearing," Harley said, as if that would make me feel better. It didn't.

"Hey! Wait, we do have evidence," Althea said.

I whirled toward her.

"What evidence?" both Harley and Bailey demanded.

Althea held up her phone and smiled. "I recorded everything you said, Bailey."

"Proves nothing. You pulled a gun on me and forced a confession."

That's when I noticed a few small puddles of blood on the sand. "I thought you said no one was hurt."

"No one was hurt," Harley said. "Bruised, perhaps, but that's all."

"Then who's bleeding?" I shined my phone's light on the blood.

Harley pulled Bailey to his feet. "Shine your light on him."

I held up my phone while Harley looked Bailey over with more care. "Looks like his gun's slide bit into him." He pointed to a bloody cut between his thumb and forefinger.

"That happens when someone holds a gun wrong. Even some of the best marksmen make that mistake," Chief Byrd said as he and one of his officers slid down the sandy cliff. "Someone care to tell me what's going on?"

"They attacked me!" Bailey shouted. "I tried to stop them from stealing the sea turtle eggs and they attacked me and tied me up!"

"And then they called the police? That's sounds like a lie." Chief Byrd, who wasn't known for his deductive skills, shook his head with disbelief.

"I recorded what happened." Althea handed her phone to the police chief. "He confessed to killing Cassidy Jones."

"Coerced!" Bailey shouted. "I want my lawyer."

"He also tried to kill Penn," Harley said.

"She pulled a gun on me!" Since Harley had tied Bailey's feet together, Bailey hopped around like a rabbit. "They held me against my will. It's kidnapping! I want them arrested!"

"He does need medical care," I said. "His hand is bleeding."

"Had such high hopes for you fitting into our fine

community, son." Chief Byrd waved for his officer to take charge of the situation. "Can't say I'm not disappointed, 'cause I am. The food at your restaurant was top rate. Top rate." While his officer untied Bailey and then snapped a pair of handcuffs on over his wrists while Bailey continued to protest, threatening to sue everyone south of the Mason-Dixon Line, Byrd walked over to me. "Thank you," he said, his voice somber.

"For what?" I asked.

"I appreciate your proving my point that it's the people 'from off' who bring troubles into my town. If we could keep all of you outsiders from moving onto the island, there'd be no crime on Camellia Beach."

That wasn't exactly correct. If I'd wanted to, I could have named several incidences where local residents had committed quite serious crimes. But since he was trying to be friendly by thanking me and all, I just smiled and said, "You're welcome."

"Perhaps I'll have to start calling you my lucky Penny," Detective Gibbons called as he slid down the sandy cliff in much the same way the police chief had. A small army of officers followed him.

"My name's not Penny." He didn't need me to tell him that, but I said it anyhow.

"Perhaps not, but you are certainly lucky you're not dead right now." He'd peppered this with a few curse words, which let me know how much I'd upset him. He rarely swore.

"I had backup." I glanced over at Althea who was keeping her distance. "Even more than I realized." While it'd be a while before I could forgive Althea for tricking me, I still loved her. I had faith we'd be friends again…eventually.

Gibbon continued to scowl as he scoured the crime scene. He pulled on a pair of gloves as he walked over to Bailey's gun and called to one of his own men to come over with a large flashlight.

"Same model of handgun, a glock, and the registration number has been scratched off in the same way as the gun used to kill Cassidy," Detective Gibbons said as tucked the gun into a plastic evidence bag. He looked up at Chief Byrd. "Did I hear you say that the suspect cut his hand when he fired this gun?"

"He got a nasty cut on his hand from the slide's kickback," the police chief said.

"And didn't Bailey have a bandage on that same hand the morning after Cassidy's murder," I said, surprised I'd forgotten about it. Bailey had told us that he'd cut his hand in the kitchen.

Gibbons sucked in his cheeks. It looked as if he'd just bitten into a lemon. "Forensics had found a small smear of blood on the murder weapon," he admitted. "It's still out at the lab for testing to see if it matches Jody's DNA."

"It won't," I said.

"I'll have them send Mr. Bailey Grassi's DNA to the lab to see if it matches," he said.

"Does that mean you're going to release Jody?" I asked.

"Don't get ahead of yourself. I'm going to have to review all of the evidence," he said.

"But then you'll release Jody?" I asked.

"No. I'll have to talk with Fletcher, who by the way, looks as if he's going to make a full recovery thanks to the two of you."

That was good news. "And then you'll release Jody?"

"No. I'll have to meet with the solicitor's office and the prosecuting attorney."

"And *then* you'll release Jody? Tomorrow?" I pressed.

"I can't guarantee that it'll happen by tomorrow. But if everything checks out, and the prosecuting attorney agrees, the charges against Jody will be dropped."

"But not in time for the first day of school." Which would mean I'd failed Gavin.

"Don't forget the bail hearing tomorrow," Harley pointed out. "With this new information, it'll be a breeze. She'll be out of jail by lunchtime. And cleared of charges before she picks Gavin up from school on Thursday."

Gibbons held up a hand. "She will still have an illegal discharge of a weapon charge to answer to."

"I'm sure the lawyers working her case will be able to handle it," Harley said as he pulled an arm around my shoulder. "You did it, Penn."

And then he kissed me. After sitting with me in the sand for hours, he tasted fresh and salty like the ocean. If only I could melt into his kiss and live happily-ever-after forever.

But I couldn't. Because of Althea and Mabel's deceptions and lies, I still had to face the fallout from their fake DNA test and the very real possibly that I'd lose the Chocolate Box forever.

THIRTY-EIGHT

"WHAT IF IT'S TRUE?" I asked Harley on Thursday morning, two days after Bailey's dramatic arrest. I was working the front counter at the Chocolate Box while Bertie sat on the sofa with her leg propped up on a pillow. "What if I'm not related to Mabel? What if she gave me the shop out of some misplaced belief that I was Carolina's daughter?" After finding Cassidy's killer, life should have gone back to normal.

To an outsider, life appeared normal as the locals indulged their sweet tooth at the shop. But normal looked very different to me. Was I a fraud? Was time running out for me? Was I about to lose everything I had come to love?

Harley and I had spent the previous day at the county courthouse. First, I'd provided a DNA sample while a county court clerk watched. Afterwards, Harley and I spent several hours explaining to the judge assigned to preside over the hearing for Mabel's contested will how I'd been tricked into believing the validity of the original DNA test. The judge had growled his displeasure when he'd heard this.

Harley wasn't deterred by the judge's reaction. He jumped into the fray, talking quickly as he defended me. He assured the judge that I had nothing to do with the fake DNA results. He then offered a new argument as to why Mabel's latest last will and testament should be allowed to remain in full force despite the outcome of the court-ordered DNA test. He argued that the case should be ruled on as soon as possible and in my favor. While his passionate speech had brought tears to my eyes, the judge remained unmoved. The court hearing would not be schedule until after we received the results of the new DNA test.

It was going to take three weeks for the lab where the county had sent the DNA samples to process and reviewed the results. Three weeks of limbo.

"We've got this, Penn." Harley set his café mocha on the counter so he could cradle both of my hands in his. "You're the best thing that has happened to the Chocolate Box in a long time. If not for you, this shop wouldn't even exist right now. More than anything else, that was what Mabel wanted. She didn't care if you were family or not. All she cared about is that you'd love and care for the Chocolate Box. Don't worry what the court might say. We'll work something out."

He was right, of course. Still, that didn't make the waiting any easier.

"How did Gavin do with going to his first day of middle school this morning?" I asked, anxious to change the subject.

Harley shrugged. "Jody was in charge of all of that. She's not one for sharing details. I'll get to hear about school when he stays with me this weekend."

The bell above the door rang. Jody, dressed in jeans and a flowered tunic, marched in. Her arms pumping, she marched over to Johnny Pane. My painter had finally finished with the ceiling. He was now patching and painting the bullet-riddled wall.

"Johnny Pane, you were supposed to be working on

the new construction out on West Africa Street," she said as if she hadn't just spent the past several days in jail accused of murder. "And here I find you still wasting your time in this dump."

"Find someone else." Johnny didn't even bother to turn his head in her direction. His brush crawled across the wall. "Got my hands full here."

"What?" Jody screeched.

"Good morning, Jody. He said he's working here," I said as I came around the counter to greet her. "Would you like some coffee?"

She whirled around and glared at me. "I'm not here to buy coffee. And what business do you have to look so happy? You know the court is going to give the shop back to Mabel's rightful heirs after hearing all about the fraud you perpetuated."

"We'll just have to wait and see." I put my hands on my hips and made my superwoman pose. I could conquer whatever the world sent at me. "In the meantime, I'm going to run this shop as I always have because that's what Mabel would have wanted."

The patrons in the shop cheered.

Jody snarled.

"I am glad you were able to take your son to school this morning," I said. "He really wanted you there."

"What is that supposed to mean? What do you want? A medal or something? You meddled. You always meddle in business that has nothing to do with you." She stepped toward me. Because she matched my height, we stood chin to chin. Her skinny finger poked me in the chest. "I know you fancy yourself in love with my ex." She poked my chest again. "And I know the only reason you investigated Cassidy's death was to try and win Gavin's affection."

She tried to poke my chest again, but I weaved away from her. "I didn't—"

"But let me tell you something. I'm not going to let you steal him from me. He's my son, *my* son. Not yours. If you don't like being a dried up old maid, you should have had a baby when you still could because you're not getting mine."

"I would never—" I started to say, but abruptly changed gears. Whatever emotional wounds and demons that were chasing Jody, they were too ingrained in her personality. She'd never accept anyone's attempt to comfort, not when she'd made it her personal mission to rail against the rest of the world. So instead of trying to explain myself and instead of trying to have that woman-to-woman moment where we shared our mutual hatred for the cheating jerks who'd lied and sneaked around behind our backs and toyed with our hearts, I simply said, "You're welcome."

I then wrapped my arms tightly around this woman who had wrapped herself so tightly in anger that she didn't have any friends. I answered her anger with kindness, because I knew what it was like to be Jody. I used to be Jody. But I no longer felt angry. Not all of the time. Not anymore. It felt good.

"Oh, look!" Lidia said in what I supposed she thought was a whisper. Her voice didn't quite boom, but it wasn't by any means quiet. She pointed toward the small mound of sand. A few grains had shifted.

It was five o'clock on the Saturday after Bailey's arrest. I should have been at the shop, but Althea had texted to tell me that one of the sea turtle nests was hatching. While I wasn't yet ready to pick up our friendship as if nothing had happened—there was still a good chance I was going to lose the Chocolate Box thanks to her deception—I couldn't pass up an opportunity to finally witness a brood of baby sea turtles as they waddled toward their new lives in the wide-open ocean.

Excited to get to the nest, Bertie and I had closed up the shop early and hurried down to the beach. Several of our customers followed, including Bubba, Ethel, and Detective Gibbons. Actually, Gibbons had barely had a chance to place his order before I'd chased him out of the shop.

Once we'd all arrived at the nest, located at the end of the island near the old red and white striped lighthouse, the spectators formed a large horseshoe a respectful distance from the nest. Althea paced. She looked worried.

"They're coming," Harriett assured as she patted Althea's shoulder.

Gibbons eased into the space between me and Lidia. He'd shed his suit's jacket but was still too warmly dressed for the heat and humidity of an August afternoon. He dabbed his brow with a linen handkerchief. "Fletcher was released from the hospital today," he said. "He's home with his parents."

"That's good to know. I brought him a box of chocolates yesterday. He looked well. I told him that he could return to his job at the Chocolate Box whenever he felt up to it. He didn't seem excited. I'm sure I'll only be able to keep him for a short time before he finds somewhere else to work, somewhere that pays more money. He'll be an asset for any establishment."

"He might surprise you," Gibbons said. "You do realize the young man nearly died trying to stop Bailey from stealing from you, don't you?"

I glanced away from the nest's shifting sands to look over at Gibbons. "What do you mean? I assumed Fletcher walked in on Bailey as he was stealing the chocolate sea turtles, and Bailey had no choice but to kidnap him. And then Bailey tried to kill him."

"According to Fletcher, that's not what happened," Gibbons said. "Not at all."

A turtle's tiny flipper popped out of the sand. I held my breath. A second flipper appeared. And then a head. My heart beat a little faster. The first sea turtle was emerging.

As I watched, Gibbons kept talking. "Fletcher had suspected Bailey had something to do with Cassidy's murder, but he wasn't sure what or why. The night of the murder, he'd spotted Bailey's car parked on the road several blocks from Cassidy's house, which seemed odd since Bailey lived next door and should have parked in his own garage."

"Why was Fletcher there that night?" I asked.

"The boy had gotten himself drunk and had gone to Cassidy's house to punch him. When he got to the open sliding glass doors—the one's you'd noticed—he shouted for Cassidy to come out and face him like a man. Well, Cassidy did come out. He had a lady on his arm. She looked so unhappy, Fletcher said he lost his nerve and ran away."

"Muumuu Woman?" I asked.

"The description matches. When Fletcher ran away, he passed a man standing in front of Bailey's brightly lit house. He also ran past Jody. He remembered seeing her flinging her gun around as she came up to Bailey's house."

A second tiny sea turtle had worked its way to the surface, followed closely by a third.

"Why didn't Fletcher come forward and report any of this?" I asked.

"I asked him the same thing. He claims he didn't think what he saw was important."

"I'm not sure that's true," I said. "Bailey told me that Fletcher had been following him around town. Perhaps Fletcher pictures himself an amateur sleuth. That would explain why he ran out of the shop to 'run an errand' so abruptly after Bailey had visited the shop. Perhaps he left to see where Bailey was going."

"You think there's another pretend sleuth on the island? Heaven help me, I don't think I could survive it."

The first baby sea turtle had reached the water. A wave crashed over its tiny back and pushed it back onto the shore. The mighty ocean didn't deter the tiny creature. It kept moving forward, swimming when it could, fighting to get past the waves. For some reason, tears sprang to my eyes as I watched it try and accomplish the impossible. I quickly blinked them away.

"I'm not a pretend sleuth. I'm simply a concerned citizen doing her civic duty. Besides, you shouldn't groan at me. I get results," I argued.

"You get yourself in dangerous situations," Gibbons argued back. "So does Fletcher, apparently. He told me he was putting away the chocolate benne wafers when he noticed the chocolate sea turtles he'd just put in the cooler were gone. He suspected that Bailey had been stealing them. And he went in pursuit. The problem with that was that when he caught up to Bailey, he didn't have a plan. He's lucky you and Harley found him when you did. Otherwise, Fletcher would be dead right now."

"Bailey had been telling the truth about that. Fletcher had been following him."

"He apparently followed Bailey all over the place. He saw that Bailey kept coming to your shop. He saw Bailey leave a threatening note on the Chocolate Box's door. He saw Bailey hanging out near your apartment. He saw Bailey follow you to the hardware store to buy the security camera."

"He saw all of that? My goodness, that explains why I kept finding those anxiety spinners all over the place. He was the one dropping them, not Bailey." And then a thought struck me. "Bailey was the one who posted the threatening note on the door? Fletcher was sure about that?" The yellow note on the door hadn't been that threatening. It seemed tame when compared to the second one. "I'd assumed Bailey was the one that had tossed the stuffed dog at me with the note that said that if I didn't stop asking questions I die a horrible death."

"I'm having forensics work on matching the handwriting, but it looks like Fletcher is telling the truth about seeing Bailey post the threatening note," Gibbons said.

I tapped my chin as I wondered about the second note. It'd clearly been written by a different person, which meant someone else in town had been prepared to kill me, and not just kill me but make sure I died horribly. Luella Marie Banks was the first name that came to mind. She definitely had a flare for dramatics, and she did have a strong motive for guarding her secret.

As more baby sea turtles struggled to get past the waves and into the deeper part of the ocean, I glanced around at the crowd that had gathered on the beach. Standing apart from everyone else was a lady wearing a large floppy hat, oversized sunglasses, and a flowered muumuu. This one was a pale shade of pink.

I thanked Gibbons for telling me what he knew and then slowly approached the woman.

"Thank you," she whispered when I got close. She touched a finger to her nose, which was still slightly swollen from her plastic surgery. "You guarded my identity despite pressure to tell others on the island that I was in town. You could have blabbed how I'd let that nasty Cassidy Jones fellow coerce me into his bed." She coughed delicately. "Not many would do that for a stranger."

"Perhaps that's true for the world you live in," I said, "but here in Camellia Beach, nearly anyone would have done the same."

She sniffed. "I've been gone from this town for too long. I've forgotten how people here are different. Kinder. I hate to leave it."

"It is a special place," I agreed. "When do you have to go back to California?"

"In a few days. I've already lingered here too long, I'm afraid." Her accent, I suddenly noticed, had remained flat and unremarkable. Forgettable, even. She sounded completely different from the dramatic actress I'd met only a few days earlier. "Harriett told me how your friend Lidia wants to use the cottage as an animal rescue center. I think it's a lovely idea, so I'm going to let her have the cottage along with a generous donation to help her get her rescue operations started."

"That's awfully kind of you." And surprising. It'd been easy to suspect her of being the kind of woman who'd toss a death threat at me. It was harder to imagine that she might be the kind of woman who thought to do nice things for others. "Lidia will be grateful."

Luella Marie waved her hand in a dismissive manner. "It'll be good PR for me. People love sob stories about homeless animals. And if anyone thinks they can cash in with the gossip rags about having seen me in Camellia Beach, I can explain to the press that I was here to check out Lidia's dog shelter before writing her a check. It's the perfect cover story. I've even scheduled a photographer to take pictures with me holding cute puppies."

A cheer rose up from the crowd around the nest. I was anxious to get back to watch the turtles, but there was one more thing I needed to ask her. "A few days ago someone tied a note to a stuffed dog. Someone stood hidden in the woods across from the Chocolate Box and threw it at me. The note was a warning that I needed to stop asking about Cassidy's secrets. Was that you?"

She bit her lower lip and shook her head. When she spoke, her voice took on the lovely singsong accent of the island. "Honey, if I wanted to threaten you, I wouldn't stoop to skulking around in prickly bushes. I've spent a fortune to make my face look young again. I'm certainly not going to risk marring my surgeon's work by walking around in some thorny bushes. And the snakes. There's poisonous snakes hiding out in the underbrush just looking to kill someone. That's not somewhere you'd find me."

"It must have been someone else." Someone with a secret worth killing over?

Luella Marie leaned toward me and whispered, "If I were in your shoes I'd take that threat to heart. Tread with care, my dear Penn. Camellia Beach might look like a paradise, but there are secrets aplenty buried deep on these shores, secrets no one wants uncovered."

When I asked her what she meant by that, she told me again to "tread with care" before walking away from me and the crowd on the beach.

Feeling just a bit shaken by her warning, I returned to watch the baby turtles. Dozens had broken out of the nest and were pulling themselves on their tiny flippers toward the ocean. They were the future. The ones who survived into adulthood would return to this beach to make nests of their own. I hoped I would still be living here to witness it. I hoped I would still be running the Chocolate Box.

Like those tiny sea turtles having to battle through the waves in order to make it to calmer waters, every time I thought I'd resolved the shop's disputed ownership, something else happened to push me back. And now everything rested on the results of the court-ordered DNA test. Part of me wanted to give up. But if those tiny sea turtles could keep pushing and swimming after being knocked back to the shore over and over, I could do this. I could be just as determined as a sea turtle... I hoped.

THIRTY-NINE

THREE WEEKS. Three *long* weeks. The day I'd dreaded had finally arrived. Harley and I had an afternoon appointment to meet with the judge handling Mabel's contested will in his chambers. Mabel's children would be there as well.

I hadn't slept at all the night before. And if judging by the looks of my bloodshot, baggy eyes, you'd have thought I hadn't slept for over a month. No amount of makeup was going to fix that.

I put on a blue batik sundress that reminded me of the ocean and ate all of the chocolate I could find in the apartment before meeting up with Harley. He drove my car to the county courthouse in Charleston's historic downtown.

The judge's chamber smelled musty. It wasn't a large room. The clerk had to drag in extra chairs to accommodate everyone. She then had to push the chairs together until the seats were touching each other. The three Maybank children arrived as a unified group. They were dressed in what Bertie would have called their Sunday best. Both Florence and Peach were wearing gleaming white gloves and pearls. Peach's silky pink suit served as a lovely contrast to Florence's vintage teal with white polkadots A-line dress. Edward wore a dark gray suit with such a perfect cut and fit it screamed money. None of them greeted either Harley or me. They barely looked in my direction before taking their seats.

The judge entered from a door behind his desk. He was an older man with thinning hair. His robes were open. Underneath all the formality of his position he wore a causal polo shirt and Bermuda shorts. He was carrying a manila envelope. When I saw it, I sat a little straighter in my chair.

He greeted Edward warmly and asked about his golf game. They chatted amicably just long enough for me to lose any hope that I'd get a fair hearing. Finally, the judge settled down in his oversized leather chair and tapped the envelope on the desk. "I feel like a game show host," he said and laughed. No one joined in.

He cleared his throat and opened the envelope with a letter opener that looked like a tiny dagger. All the air seemed to leave the office as the judge took his time as he silently reviewed the report the lab had sent. My lungs struggled to get a smooth breath as I watched him, his expression grim and unchanging. A chair to the right of me creaked. Conversations of people passing by in the hallway sounded unnaturally loud and intrusive. Even the tick-tick-tick of the gunmetal gray institutional clock hanging on the wall hurt my ears.

Harley reached across the distance between our chairs and offered his hand. I grabbed onto it, probably squeezing the life out of his fingers. He didn't complain.

Finally the judge, who had to be the slowest reader in recorded history, lowered the report. He removed his reading glasses. He looked at me only briefly before turning toward Edward.

"You're the one who provided a sample to the lab?" the judge asked him.

"That's correct, John," Edward replied. I don't know if it was my imagination or not, but I thought he sounded smug.

"I see," the judge said before turning back to me.

"You've held us all in suspense long enough, your honor," Harley said. "What does the report say?"

"She's a Maybank." The judge dropped the words into the room so abruptly, I was certain I hadn't heard them correctly.

"Excuse me?" I asked, but no one was paying attention to me.

Edward had flown out of his chair. "You swore to me you had lied to her about being her mother!" he shouted at Florence.

Florence remained with her back straight and her head held high. But she'd bitten her bottom lip and had crinkled her brows in puzzlement. Carolina couldn't be my mother, since she'd died years before my birth. And Peach couldn't be my mother, since she was too young to have gotten involved with my father. So that left Florence. She had to be my mother. But something about that conclusion felt wrong. Florence looked about as dumbfounded as I felt.

Peach had turned toward me and was smiling as Edward continued to yell, cursing Florence to high heaven for putting them in such an embarrassing position. My thoughts stumbled as I considered what seemed like an impossible scenario. Peach must have been fourteen or fifteen when I was born. Had my father seduced a minor? No. That couldn't be true. But just in case it was, I leaned toward her and started ask her about it when the judge rapped on his desk with his ham-sized fist.

"I'm not interested in getting involved with family

squabbles," he said. "We've held this estate in probate long enough. Your mother chose to give her home and business to one of her grandchildren. I don't see how anyone could object to that. Unless you insist—though I don't see why you would—I'm not going to schedule a hearing date. Instead I'm going to dismiss your lawsuit and release the full inheritance to Ms. Charity Penn. Now get out of here. All of you. I have work to do."

Florence and Edward argued with each other as we filed out of the judge's chambers. They didn't even look in my direction, not even once. I stood in the middle of the courthouse hallway and watched as Florence left without even giving me a second thought. I wasn't sure how I felt about that or about her or about any member of the Maybank family. Did I even care that she'd left? Peach pulled me aside and gave me a quick hug before running after her older siblings.

And that's how it ended. Or perhaps that's how it all began.

By the time Harley and I returned to the Chocolate Box my thoughts had returned to chocolate. I was wondering aloud how a chocolate bonbon with a spicy pumpkin filling would taste. It would be coated in dark chocolate…with a swirl of white chocolate threading through the dark. And it'd have to be pumpkin shaped, of course.

Harley laughed and kissed me and told me, "I'm going to end up weighing a gazillion pounds. In all my born days, Penn, that sounds delicious."

* * * * *

Penn's Moon Benne Wafer Cookies

Penn? Yes, you read that right. Our local firecracker Penn, who can be a disaster in the kitchen, came up with this mouth-watering recipe. To be fair, Bertie Bays contributed the benne wafer recipe. The recipe makes a crispy thin wafer with a powerful sesame flavor that is sandwiched between white chocolate on the top and dark chocolate on the bottom. Is it a candy or a cookie? Perhaps it's both!

This recipe for these simple black and white chocolates is perfect for cookie swaps or a way to add a touch of elegance to your parties. Your friends will be begging you for your recipe while asking for more.

Ingredients

½ cup of sesame seeds
(important for the wafer's distinctive taste)
½ cup of all-purpose flour
(gluten free flours also work with the recipe)
½ tsp of baking powder
Pinch of salt

6 tbsp unsalted butter, softened
¾ cup brown sugar
1 egg
¼ tsp pure vanilla extract
1 bag of white chocolate chips
1 bag of fair trade dark chocolate chips

Preheat oven to 325 degrees Fahrenheit. Make sure the oven rack is in the center position for an even cooking.

Toast the sesame seeds by heating them in a dry pan over medium-low heat. You want the seeds to turn a light golden color, so they'll release their flavors. Keep a close eye on them, you don't want them to burn.

In a bowl, combine the dry ingredients: flour, baking powder, and salt.

In an electric mixer, beat the butter and brown sugar together until smooth and creamy. Add the egg and vanilla extract. Mix at a lower speed until combined. Add the flour mixture continue to mix at the lower speed until the batter is smooth. Add the toasted sesame seeds and fold in with a spoon.

Line the baking sheets with parchment paper or a baking liner. Using a teaspoon, drop the dough onto the baking sheet. You can use the back of the spoon to help form a round shape in order to make sure your cookies come out moon shaped. Leave about 2 inches between the dough. The cookies will spread. Yes, you want them to spread!

Bake 8 to 10 minutes or until the edges of the cookies turn a dark brown. (This is important, otherwise your wafers won't have that delightful snap.) Let cook on the baking sheet for 2 minutes. Transfer the cookies to a wire rack to cool completely.

Melt the white chocolate chips using either a double boiler or following the microwave directions on the bag. Using a tablespoon, coat the top of the cookies with the melted white chocolate. Place cookies in refrigerator for 30 minutes to 1 hour to cool.

Melt the dark chocolate chips using either a double boiler or following the microwave directions on the bag. Using a tablespoon, coat the bottom of the cookies with the melted dark chocolate. Place cookies in refrigerator for 30 minutes to 1 hour to cool.

Store in the refrigerator. Makes approximately 2 dozen.

Bubba's Spicy Cocoa Pork Tenderloin

Bubba says chocolate and romance is too cliché. What everyone loves is a good pork dinner. We're lucky he agreed to share with us his go-to meal when he's looking to impress that special someone in his life.

Ingredients

Pork:

1 tbsp cocoa powder
2 tsp allspice
2 tbsp dark brown sugar
1 tsp sea salt
1 tsp black pepper
2 1-lb pork tenderloins, trimmed
3 tbsp extra-virgin olive oil

Sauce:

4 tbsp extra-virgin olive oil
3 cloves of garlic, minced
1 onion, finely chopped
1 tsp sea salt
½ tsp black pepper
3 tbsp cocoa powder
½ cup vegetable broth
1 tsp red wine vinegar
1 can (14.75 oz) crushed tomatoes

Preheat oven to 400 degrees Fahrenheit. Make sure the oven rack is in the center position for an even cooking.

Whisk cocoa powder, allspice, brown sugar, salt, and pepper in small bowl. Place pork on foil-covered baking sheet. Rub cocoa mixture into pork. Drizzle with olive oil. Roast 25 to 30 minutes or until temperature at center of pork reaches 145 degrees Fahrenheit. Remove from oven. Let rest for 10 minutes.

While meat is cooking, make the sauce. Heat oil in medium saucepan over medium heat. Add garlic, onions, salt, and pepper. Cook until onions are transparent. Stir in cocoa powder, broth, vinegar, and tomatoes. Simmer covered for 10 minutes, stirring occasionally. Season with salt and pepper to taste.

Cut pork into ½ inch slices. Spoon sauce over the pork and serve.

Bertie's Cheer-Me-Up Chocolate Chip Pancakes

This editor has been told time and again that the secret ingredient in Bertie's light and flavorful pancakes is love. Love may help them taste this good, but it takes a few other ingredients to make these the best pancakes in the South. Perfect for a Sunday morning brunch, you'll be going back for seconds.

Ingredients

6 oz Greek yogurt
1 egg
½ cup flour (gluten free flours will work with this recipe)
½ tsp baking soda
6 oz of fair trade 70% or more dark chocolate, chopped

Combine yogurt and egg in mixing bowl. In a separate bowl, combine flour and baking soda. Combine yogurt and egg mixture with bowl with flour mixture. Stir in chopped chocolate. Yes, the batter is thick. Heat butter in nonstick pan over medium heat. Spoon batter into pan. Turn when begins to bubble. Cook until golden brown on both sides. Makes 4 large pancakes or 8 small. Serve with maple syrup, butter, and fresh fruit.

ACKNOWLEDGMENTS

EVERY BOOK IS special to me in its own way. I'll always remember this book as being the one where I got to use my wildlife biology background, feature sea turtles, and the natural environment as part of a bigger mystery. I'd like to thank author Mary Alice Monroe for her expertise on turtle patrol teams and how they work. And I need to give a big shout-out to the talented dog behavior expert, Susan Marett, for taking the time to answer my questions and provide insights into the mind of a dog trainer. Without her, Stella would still be running around like a wild beast. Also, Susan has been so patient while working with me and my pups over the years. I've learned so much from Susan…not just about dogs but also about myself. She's wonderful.

I must thank my agent, Jill Marsal, for believing in my series, and my talented editor Anne Brewer (and all the folks at Crooked Lane Books) for making this book possible. I've said it before, and I'll say it again: y'all make publishing a book fun.

I'd also like to thank the incredible authors in the Lowcountry Chapter of Romance Writers of America, Sisters In Crime, and Mystery Writers of America, especially Vicki Wilkerson Gibbins, Cynthia Cooke, Amanda Berry, Nina Bruhns, Dianne Miley, Nicole Seitz, and Judy Watts for patiently listening as I worked through the sometimes bumpy process of writing.

Finally, a million thanks to Jim and Avery. These books are for you and wouldn't happen without you. I love you.